Writer-politician Sir Joseph Mallalieu was born in 1908 and educated at Oxford, where he was President of the Union and a Rugby Blue, and also at the University of Chicago. After working for some ten years on various London newspapers, he joined the Royal Navy and served at sea from 1942–45, during which time he wrote *Very Ordinary Seaman*. He was a Labour MP for Huddersfield for many years and has occupied several government posts, including that of Navy Minister (1966–67) and Minister of Technology (1968–69). He was knighted in 1979. He lives near Aylesbury in Buckinghamshire and lists his recreations as 'walking, gardening and watching Huddersfield Town'.

By the same author

J P W MALLALIEU

Very Ordinary Seaman

GRANADA
London Toronto Sydney New York

Published by Granada Publishing Limited in 1956
Reprinted 1963, 1964, 1965, 1966, 1967, 1969, 1973 (twice),
1978, 1983

ISBN 0 583 12808 4

First published in Great Britain by
Victor Gollancz Ltd 1944

Granada Publishing Limited
Frogmore, St Albans, Herts AL2 2NF
and
36 Golden Square, London W1R 4AH
515 Madison Avenue, New York, NY 10022, USA
117 York Street, Sydney, NSW 2000, Australia
60 International Blvd, Rexdale, Ontario, R9W 6J2, Canada
61 Beach Road, Auckland, New Zealand

Printed and bound in Great Britain by
Cox & Wyman Ltd, Reading
Set in Times

To
James Conlon and J. A. Macintyre
Leading Seamen

Special Preface to this Edition

WHEN I wrote this book, I had just come in from sea. My memories, hot or cold, were vivid, the stuff came pouring out, I seldom paused for a fact or to marshal a thought. So *Very Ordinary Seaman* is no artistic masterpiece.

It was intended to be, and mainly is, a report of what happened in the long course of a few short months. Many people, even among those who did not serve in the Royal Navy, have found that the experience embodied here has tallied with their own; and so in 1963 they are continuing to buy a very ordinary book which was written in 1942. I am grateful.

Now that I have re-read it after so many years, I find that I get something more from it than a reminder of past facts, however exciting or however bleak they may have been. I hadn't much liked the Britain we lived in before the war; but I was myself comfortable in it, earning my living without consciously doing harm to anyone else. I didn't want to leave it when war came. I didn't anyway want to fight; but there it was. I had landed myself in the Royal Navy. Even the passing of years cannot soften the hatred I felt for some of the things which I then had to get through.

Yet out of it all one memory, or perhaps one feeling, still persists. I served with men who, like myself, would rather have been elsewhere, whose main thought, in the meantime, was to look after themselves. We were pitched together in dirt, cold, boredom and danger; yet after a time, without knowing it, we became a community. Without orders, and certainly without conscious virtue, we found that we had stopped working against each other or for ourselves and had begun to share whatever came of misery or of pleasure. I liked this and hoped that when the war was over we could carry some such feeling from service into civilian life.

I do not think that anyone, looking at our country in 1963, would say that this hope has been realised. But I still hope that anyone who reads this book will see in it the certainty that human nature is capable of neighbourliness; and will catch from it the belief that war, with its attendant vileness, is not the only circumstance which can bring the best out of mankind.

J. P. W. M.

WATERSTOCK, 1963

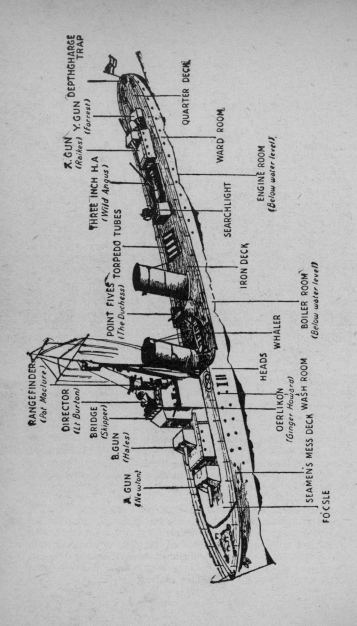

RANGEFINDER
(Pat Maclure)

DIRECTOR
(Lt Burton)

BRIDGE
(Skipper)

B. GUN
(Hales)

A. GUN
(Newton)

POINT FIVES
(The Duchess)

THREE INCH H.A
(Wild Angus)

X. GUN
(Raikes)

Y. GUN
(Forrest)

DEPTHCHARGE
TRAP

TORPEDO TUBES

QUARTER DECK

WARD ROOM

ENGINE ROOM
(Below water level)

SEARCHLIGHT

IRON DECK

BOILER ROOM
(Below water level)

WHALER

HEADS

OERLIKON
(Ginger Howard)

SEAMEN'S MESS DECK WASH ROOM

FO'CSLE

Chapter One

1

ONE morning in late February a man walked out of the Burnt Oak tube station, hesitated a moment, then turned left over the railway-bridge and down the hill. He had no hat; and, with his hair newly cut to Service shortness, his head felt cold in the morning air. He stopped, put down the suitcase he was carrying, turned up the collar of his overcoat, and went on again, his back and shoulders slightly bent from the weight of the case.

He reached the bottom of the hill and began to climb a long, curving road flanked with neat, red-brick, semi-detached houses. He looked at the houses apathetically and remembered how smug they had seemed when he had first seen them in the afternoon sunlight nearly two months ago. He'd been walking up that road then on his way to his Medical, realising that his time as a civilian was nearly over; and all the red-brick houses, basking in the sun, had seemed to say: " There's another of them. He's got to go. But we stay here, thank goodness! "

This morning the houses seemed cold, reserved, and silent.

The chilled, forlorn-looking figure stared at their little blue curtains, their polished door-knobs, the fancy ironwork round their gates, and began to think of his own warm flat in Central London, where, for seven years, through peace, war, and blitz, he had lived by himself until an hour ago.

" God alone knows when I'll live there again."

He saw once more the glow from his bedroom gas-stove, heard it plop as he turned it out for the last time, thought of his housekeeper, perhaps even now turning her key in the lock of the empty flat and going in to strip his bed or get ready the rest of the furniture for storage.

He shivered slightly and forced the picture from his mind.

It was no good looking back. He was in the Navy now. No more flats or gas-stoves or housekeepers until the war was over.

He tried to keep his mind out of the past, which made him sad, out of the present, which almost hurt, and in the future, which, though full of foreboding, was to be for him a new, possibly interesting, and probably exciting life.

"You can thank your lucky stars you're not going into the Army."

He hated the idea of the Army. It was fourteen years since he left his Public School, but he still remembered the two O.T.C. parades a week, the route marches, the blancoing, the polishing, and the doing-things-by-numbers. He remembered the stories about the Army in this war. Friends had repeated their Sergeants' puerile jokes: " Anyone here fond of music ? Well, move that flicking piano across the room "; or, " Anyone here know shorthand ? Well, get up to the cookhouse and peel spuds." It made you feel sick. It was so childish. Why the hell couldn't they treat you as human beings ?

He had heard the Navy was different. But now as he reached the Naval Recruiting Centre, and went through the swing-doors, he could not help feeling trapped. No escape now . . . no going back to the tube. This was the Navy, and he was in it.

He went through the hall, along a corridor, up one flight of stairs, and knocked at a door marked Master-at-Arms.

He remembered this door well.

Two months ago he had walked through it and found a little grey-haired man sitting behind a desk and had told him he wanted to volunteer for the Navy. The little man had said: " You know, we've got a long waiting list. Some boys are having to wait two months before we can even give them a Medical. However, sit down and I'll take your particulars. But remember, we can't guarantee to call you for months yet. And if the Army gets you in the meantime, that's your funeral. What's your name ? "

" Robert Williams."

" Any relatives in the Navy ? "

" No."

" Ever been in gaol ? "

" No."

" Ever been to sea before ? Ever been out of the country ? "

" Yes. Twice to the United States, once to South Africa, and many times to the Continent. As a passenger."

" Ever had any A.R.P. training or experience ? "

" Only roof-spotting."

" That's not much use."

" I thought it might come in handy for a crow's nest," said Williams, mentioning almost the only part of a ship he knew by name.

" Any objection to vaccination ? "

" No."

" What are you in civil life, Mr. Williams ? "

" I'm a journalist—on the *Daily Examiner*."

" Oh, that's my paper. A lousy rag."

That was the end of the questions. The Master handed the

questionnaire across the table. "Read that through and sign it," he said; and while Williams did so, the Master filled in another form. When Williams had read and signed, the Master smiled.

"Well, you're in luck, Mr. Williams. One of the party for a Medical this afternoon has dropped out and you can have his place. Be back here at three and show this chit at the table downstairs when you come."

Williams had come back at three, stripped, put his trousers and coat on again, and joined a dozen men of all ages from eighteen to forty who were sitting on chairs outside a large, screened enclosure. They waited twenty minutes. Then the first of six doctors looked each one over rapidly, asked them if they suffered from fits, made them walk along a line with their eyes shut, and listened to their hearts. Then they were told to wait until the next doctor was ready for them.

"Read the bottom line on that card," said the eyeman.

A long pause.

"Well, start from the top, then." The doctor held his hand over Williams's left eye.

He got as far as the fourth line down, then stuck.

"Try with the other eye."

When that was a little better the doctor said, "Try another card," and walked across the room to change the cards, turning for a moment to gossip with another doctor. In a flash Williams had taken his glasses out of his pocket and looked carefully at the lower lines. When the doctor came back, he read four lines correctly and got most of the way through the fifth.

"Let's try with the other eye again. No; perhaps that would be asking for trouble," said the doctor, and Williams had passed his Medical.

To-day, as he hesitated outside the door marked Master-at-Arms, he could have kicked himself. Why had he pulled out his glasses ? Why hadn't he let the doctor fail him ? He'd have got some nice soft office job instead of having to go to sea and be seasick.

He put down his case, knocked at the door, and poked his head in. The little man with the grey hair was still sitting behind his desk. He looked up. "Are you one of the party going away this morning ? Right. Wait next door, lad."

2

"Next door " was a large schoolroom, with desks and chairs round the walls. In it were twenty men, sitting on their suit-cases, listlessly reading newspapers, leaning awkwardly against the walls or lounging on the desks and chatting with a forced cheerfulness. Williams put his suitcase in a corner, sat on it, lit a cigarette, and stared at a newspaper. But he hardly read a line.

He kept glancing at the others in the room, catching sentences from their talk, wondering whether they felt as gloomy as he did.

One man looked so dejected that Williams began to feel almost cheerful by comparison. This man was also sitting on a suitcase, but was making no pretence of reading the *Daily Telegraph* which was folded in his lap. He just sat, and stared vacantly in front of him.

" Poor devil! " thought Williams. " He's probably the father of eight children. Instead of breakfast by a warm fire in Ealing, he's back at school in a cold classroom."

He glanced towards the window and recognised two figures standing there. He remembered them well from the Medical. He remembered saying to a neighbour, " Good heavens! those kids can't be more than fifteen."

In fact, one of them was sixteen, the other fifteen and a half. They had come to the Master-at-Arms and sworn that they were both eighteen. Their birthdays had been last week, they said. They wanted to join the Navy. The Master had looked at them sharply and sent them off for a Medical; and here they were in the classroom, with their bags packed, and their faces shining with excitement, ready to sail at once to the ends of the earth.

" I wish I could feel like that," thought Williams.

The Master-at-Arms put his head in at the door and called two names. Immediately the two bright-eyed kids left the window and followed the Master to his room. Two minutes later they were back, crestfallen.

The Master had looked at them with steely eyes. " You know, I ought to send you to prison. Wasting the King's money like that. Eighteen, indeed! We've checked on you. Don't you know what happens to little boys who tell lies ? If I wasn't a kind-hearted old man, I'd have the pair of you put in irons. As it is, I'm letting you go with a caution. Be off with you—and don't forget to come back again in two years' time."

The two boys picked up their bags and went, using language that would have surprised the Master-at-Arms.

Two minutes later the Master came back and began to call names.

" Grassington ? " The gloomy one jerked up his head, said " Here," and stood up.

" Holt ? " Something moved in the far corner of the room, a sleepy voice said " What ? Oh yes. Here," and a long, lanky figure uncoiled itself from a desk and lumbered into the centre of the room. Holt had been snoozing. His eyes were only half open. His flushed face seemed likely to stretch into a yawn at any minute. He now stood, towering above the Master, his head swaying slightly from side to side.

" Come on, Lofty," said the Master. " You're not tucked up in bed now."

" I wish I was."

" Fletcher ? " A boy of nineteen jumped up quickly, said " Here, Master," and stood beside Holt. Fletcher was tall, but Holt stood inches above him.

" Price ? "

" 'Ere oi am, roight 'ere," and a slightly built man in wide grey flannels and a sports-coat heaved his case from the floor and took his place on the other side of Holt.

" Is it cold up there, Lofty ? " he asked, looking up.

" Keep silence," said the Master. " Gray ? " One of two boys who had been sitting together on a suitcase went to the Master.

" Hart ? " His friend followed him. The pair of them stood there, smiling rather shyly at the others and occasionally whispering to one another.

" Oo, look at them two love-birds! " said Price.

" Keep silence. Low ? "

" Here, yer honner. I mean, sir. Here," and with a run and a jump Low landed beside the group, stuffing a paper bag into his pocket. He kept looking at his neighbours, nudging them when the Master looked down at his paper, pretending innocence when the Master looked up.

" Taylor ? "

" Here," said a voice in sepulchral tones, and another boy, shorter than Holt, but still tall, ambled forward. His mouth was slightly open, showing teeth whose whiteness stood out against the yellow of the skin. The expression on his face suggested a nasty taste. He joined the group and looked dolefully from side to side.

" Williams ? Well, that's all the *Frobisher* lot. You're to go by train to South Down. I think there's one from Waterloo about eleven-thirty. Williams, come into the other room and I'll give you the railway vouchers and your papers."

Williams followed the Master into his room and was handed a railway voucher for nine, and a bulky envelope addressed to the Commanding Officer, H.M.S. *Frobisher*, South Down.

" Don't lose 'em," said the Master. " Cheerio "; and that was that.

3

The party reached Waterloo with three-quarters of an hour to spare.

" Oi'm going to get some grub," said Price. " Meet you at the barrier in 'arf an hour's time. Anyone else coming ? "

" I'm sticking to Mother," said Low. " Want a liquorice allsorts, Mother ? What about some grub ? "

" I'll get the tickets first," said Williams.

He was just moving off to the booking office when a quiet

voice said in his ear: " Er, do you think it would be all right if Hart and I went to buy some handkerchiefs ? There's a shop just outside the station, and it seems a pity to waste our clothing coupons."

It was Gray, one of Price's " love-birds."

" Go ahead. But don't be late."

When eleven-fifteen came, there were only six of the *Frobisher*-bound party at the barrier.

" Who's missing ? " asked Williams. The six stared at each other and tried to remember faces they had seen for the first time two hours before. " What about those two love-birds ? " asked Price.

" Hell! " said Williams, remembering.

" What about that long stream of gnat's spit ? " said Taylor. " You know. Six foot five of flick-all. You know the feller."

Of course. Holt. Where the hell was he ?

" Oi reckon 'e's gone to sleep somewhere," said Price. " 'E'll make us miss the flicking train. Whoi can't 'e turn up on time loike the rest of us ? Oi dunno," he said, looking at the clock. It was 11.24.

" Well, it's no use *all* of us waiting," said Williams. " The rest of you get into the train and I'll wait at the barrier until the last minute."

The last minute came and Williams warned the inspector that three members of the *Frobisher* party were missing. He did not know their names, could only say that one was very tall indeed and that the two others were smallish and had been to buy handkerchiefs.

" I'll look out for them," said the inspector. " You take the tickets with you."

Just then a long, unhurried figure appeared through the crowd. Williams shouted at him and they both jumped on the train as it started.

" Huh! That was a near one. Didn't realise the time had gone so fast. I was at the bookstall," said Holt.

" Well, you caught it, which is more than two of them did," said Williams gloomily. He saw himself already standing before a fiery Admiral trying to explain how he had let his party get astray.

The train was full. Williams and Holt found room in the corridor for their cases and sat on them. But they could not get up the train to find the others.

" I'm not looking forward to this much, are you ? " asked Holt. " Do you know what sort of place *Frobisher* is ? "

Williams did not. He had received a curiously polite calling-up notice which said that " *Dear Sir, A vacancy has occurred in His Majesty's Royal Navy for an ordinary seaman. If you wish to accept it, will you notify the Naval Centre, Edgware, and report there on February* 23 *at* 9 *a.m.   From there you will be sent to* H.M.S. Frobisher, *South Down.*"

And that was all he knew about the *Frobisher* except " that it's one of the few ships in the Navy the Germans can never sink.   I believe it's a holiday camp or something."

" A fine sort of holiday we'll get."

Holt had been in a City bank since leaving school ten months before and had just got his routine really taped.   He knew, he said, to a fraction of a second when he must get up if he was to arrive at the bank without causing an uproar.   He didn't mind the raised eyebrows when he was a minute or two late.   He didn't mind, much, the sharp rebuke when he was ten minutes late.   But he thought it better to avoid the storm that had greeted him when, once, he turned up forty-five minutes late.

" I hate to disturb them," he said.

They changed to a branch line after an hour and joined the rest of the party, crowding themselves and their suitcases into one carriage.

The feeling of strangeness and uprootedness which had kept some of them silent and most of them ill-at-ease was already fading.   They talked, made jokes, laughed at the jokes whether they were good or not, and generally set themselves to be friendly.   Low offered his paper bag round.   It was three-quarters full of liquorice allsorts.

" Go on, I've plenty.   Never without them.   My missus's mother keeps a sweet-shop.   I've got thousands and thousands in my bag.   My missus packed 'em herself.   ' Don't forget the liquorice allsorts, Jackie,' she says.   ' Not bloody likely,' I sez; ' sooner forget my name.   Much sooner,' I sez."

" Wot ?   You married, Jackie ? " said Taylor.   " Flicking hell !   There ought to be a law.   They ought to put your missus in jug.   Cradle-snatching, I call it."

" Cradle-snatching nothing.   I'm twenty.   Quite a big fellow now.   I've been married two years.   Got a kid.   Like to see a picture ? "

Out came the photographs.   Jackie showed his " kid ".   Taylor showed himself on a motor-bike in plus fours.   " Natty suit that.   Sold it just before I joined up.   No flicking use to me now.   Got twenty-eight bob for it I did."

" Twenty-eight bob for a suit loike that ?   Chroist !   Oi wouldn't clean moi boike with it," said Price.

" You bet you wouldn't, not while I was around.   It was a nice piece of material," said Taylor, showing his teeth and imitating the mincing accent of the salesman.

" Say, I wonder what they'll do about your uniform when we get down ? " said the gloomy-looking Grassington, speaking almost for the first time and looking at Holt.   " They can't get many as tall as you."

13

"No," said Jackie Low. "When they 'ook one as long as 'im, they chucks 'im back again. No use to us, they sez. Can't fit 'im into a hammick. Make a good tent-pole in the Army."

Fletcher was an ex-Boy Scout and Sea Scout. He had been apprenticed in a printing firm and had had to break his apprenticeship when he was called up.

"But I'll get back after the war. How long do you think that will be ? " he asked.

"Years and flicking years," broke in Price. "With this flicking Government, anyhow. All the bungling that's going on! It makes you toired. *And* the profiteering."

This shocked Grassington out of his torpor.

"The Government's all right. The trouble is that people won't back it. There's too much of these damned party politics. And the Trade Unions always asking for more money. They ought to give everyone Service pay for the duration and put 'em in uniform. That would soon put an end to these strikes."

"Oi've been working for foive years and never been out of uniform once. Overalls," said Price. "And as for giving everyone Service pay, what about Lord Nuffield ? Oi've worked my guts out for him, and what does 'e do ? Gives another basstud hospital, 'e does, with *moi* money. Oi makes 'is basstud cars and 'e gives orspittles. Put '*im* on Service pay."

And so the time passed until the train reached South Down.

As soon as they saw the station's name, they lost their new-found cheerfulness and felt again the weight of apprehension and strangeness. They gathered their things, Taylor muttering, "Where's my flicking gas-mask ? One of you basstuds has pinched my gas-mask. Hey, has anyone got my gas-mask ? "

It was under a seat.

At the end of the platform, by the ticket-barrier, there was a portly sailor—the sort Will Owen used to draw. His cheeks were purple-rose and were puffed out as though their owner was ready to blow on his hands or cool a cup of tea. White hair showed beneath his cap, his legs bulged from khaki leggings, and, as he moved, his body strained at the buttons of his overcoat.

"You lads for *Frobisher*? Come on, boys, I'll put you on the road," he said.

"I'm afraid there are two missing. They missed the train at Waterloo. They'd gone to buy some handkerchiefs," said Williams hurriedly, expecting that deep voice to roar at any moment and the purple in the cheeks to burst in flame.

"Oh, went shopping, eh ? Well, they'll turn up later in the day," said the sailor.

4

Three years before, H.M.S. *Frobisher* had been a farm. But now the fields were surrounded by high barbed wire and, instead of crops and farm buildings, there were tarmac roads and long lines of huts.

Williams and his party had not been inside the main gates a minute before they found themselves formed into two ranks and marched off with their suitcases.

" It's started already! " said Price. " They moight 'ave let us walk for the last toime instead of dumping us straight into this ruddy marching."

But the marching was not strict; more of a slope, in fact, and the self-conscious column was led, not by some explosive petty officer, but by an ordinary sailor pushing a bicycle. They marched or walked one behind the other in the grey February light, three hundred yards along a straight tarmac road. At the top of the road the tarmac opened into a vast, flat square with drill-sheds and Navy-like appliances round the sides. There were boats that could be raised and lowered, masts, rigging, and other things the party could not name; and on the square itself were squads of sailors, standing at attention, marching, or doubling.

The party skirted the square, passing groups of sailors who were at work on the various appliances. The sailors stopped work to look at the new arrivals and shouted " Rookies! " or " Go home, you bloody fools, before it's too late! GO HOME."

The sailor with the bicycle now turned right, away from the square, and down a frozen road which ran between two lines of huts. The tail of the queue of civilians, all with suitcases and gas-masks, was hanging out of the back door of one of the huts. " That's the Divisional Office. Join up with that queue, lads," said their guide, and went off on his bicycle.

The queue moved slowly into the hut and towards a table. At the table there were two red-faced, elderly men in the uniform, it seemed, of the Great Western Railway Company—Chief Petty Officers, said Fletcher. There were half a dozen other Chief Petty Officers standing around. There was a pile of small brown attaché cases on another table and there were several ordinary sailors, either writing at more tables or sitting waiting, as messengers, for orders.

Williams and his party had nearly reached the head of the queue when one of the Chief Petty Officers at the table said: " Well, that's your lot, Tom. Now, Arthur, you're next."

" Have all real sailors got faces like that ? " said Williams to Fletcher, looking at " Arthur ".

" I expect it's the sea air."

" The rum, more loike," said Price.

The face they were looking at was a deeper purple even than the face of the sailor who had met them at the station. There were lines around the large mouth. The skin was rough from long exposure to sun, water, and wind in years gone by.

15

" Arthur " put on a pair of steel spectacles, took off his cap, showing a grey fringe round a bald crown, looked at the white papers on the table, and said: " All right, Harry, go ahead."

The queue moved forward again slowly until, at last, Williams reached the table, handed over the bulky envelope of papers, and was told: " All right. Go over there and take one of those attaché cases. A present from His Majesty. Then wait with that lot."

" That lot " was a group of six men who were standing behind the table. The rest of Williams's train party soon joined this group.

When they were thirty strong, " Arthur " put away his spectacles, said " Come on, lads; follow me," and stumped along a corridor marked " Officers Only " to the front entrance of the hut. In the roadway he formed his party into " threes ", said " Party, 'shun. Right turn. Quick march " all in one breath and guided them away.

They came to another frozen mud road lined with more huts and parallel to the one they had just left. At the first hut the Chief said " Halt! Break off, lads, and follow me."

The hut was made of wood with a corrugated-iron roof, but it seemed warm, particularly after the cold outside. Steam heat came from iron pipes which ran along the edge of the floor.

Immediately inside the door there was an open space, with a wooden table and two wooden benches on either side. Stretching from the open space to the far end of the hut were two rows of two-tiered iron bedsteads jutting out from the walls with a four-foot gangway between.

" Now," said the Chief, " we'll just get you settled in and then go over for a meal. I'll read your names out and you take one of those beds, starting with the top one this end on the right and working your way along. Redfern ? "

A pale-faced boy, with pleasant, even features and hair that was certainly longer than Navy pattern, picked up his belongings and heaved them on to the nearest upper bed. " That's right," said the Chief.

" Hardcastle ? "

Without a word, 'a thick-set boy lurched to the lower bed and dumped his things below Redfern's. They looked an odd pair.

Next came a boy who looked straight from the farm. He moved even more awkwardly than Hardcastle, rolling from side to side as he walked, and answered to the Chief's call of " Perry ? " with such a strong West Country accent that everyone smiled and Low began to mimic him.

Williams found himself with the lower tier of a bedstead at the far end of the hut with a moon-faced boy above him. Two of the party from the train, Holt and Fletcher, shared the bed on one side, and on the other were two strangers who were exchanging names.

"My name's Cole," said the shorter of the two in a hard nasal voice. "What's yours?"

"Oh, I'll have a bitter. I'm Harry Robertson. Where do you come from?"

"Good old London .Finest place in the world."

"Me too. Not much room here. I suppose these are our lockers," and he swung open the door of one of the two lockers which stood in the space between their bedsteads and the next one.

"That's right. You take this one, I'll have the other."

By now the Chief had finished calling the names and everyone had put their suitcases on their beds.

"Don't unpack your gear yet," called the Chief. "We'll go over to the mess deck for some grub and fix things up after."

He led them, without the formality of falling in and marching, to a huge hut, some distance away. In it were rows of long tables and benches, and half-way along one side was a hatchway through which a few cooks could be seen. This, then, was the mess deck. At the moment it was empty. and the Chief led the way to a table at one end and close to the wall.

"Now, lads, this will be your table as long as you are here. Sit down anywhere here. The food will be along in a moment."

When it came, in big dishes wheeled on a trolley by a cook, the Chief served it with the help of Holt. The food was good.

"Oi bet they don't give yer food loike this all the toime," said Price. "They gives yer one slap-up meal when yer arroives so's yer don't run away; and when they've got yer, they 'eaves basstud pig's swill at yer, Oi bet."

When they had finished, one or two began to smoke. But not Williams. He remembered what had happened to a friend of his who joined the R.A.F.

"Our first night some of the boys lit cigarettes after the meal," this friend had said, "and one of the sergeants bawled out, 'Put those bloody fags out. You're not in Lyons Corner House now. This is the R.A.F.' Well, dammit! We weren't in the R.A.F. We were still civvies, but this kid—he wouldn't be more than twenty—was shouting at us as though we'd been the kids and he a bloody colonel."

Williams did not want to be shouted at.

The Chief came back and saw the smoke. "By the way," he said, "it doesn't matter now, as this is your first day. But in the ordinary way, you mustn't smoke on the mess deck."

*　　*　　*

Back in the hut, the Chief pointed to a notice-board on the wall.

"Now, lads, you want to study that. There, at the top, is your address—your name with 'Ordinary Seaman' after it, your

17

official number, and your ship's book number. You'll get those to-morrow. Then Class 16S—that's this one. You're Class 16S. Then FX—that's fo'c'sle, the part of the ship you belong to; your watch—second part of port; and H.M.S. *Frobisher*, South Down. See your people get that address right.

"Then below that is Class Instructor C.P.O. Arthur Graves. C.P.O. is Chief Petty Officer. Arthur Graves is me. Then your Divisional Officer, Lieutenant-Commander Rankin, R.N. He's a very nice fellow. Your Sub-Divisional Officer, Lieutenant Hollis, R.N.V.R. H'm! Royal Naval Volunteer Reserve. Saturday-night sailor, 'e is. Still, there it is.

"Now, over there is the routine of the ship. You want to read that carefully. Save you from being adrift and getting in the rattle. It looks a bit complicated, but you'll soon get used to it."

He shifted the quid of tobacco he had been chewing and shot a stream of yellow liquid into a tin spitkid beneath the blackboard. This done, he looked at the group around him.

"Now, lads. There's supper at six. Anybody got a watch? Right! That's in just an hour's time. So you may as well get on with your unpacking. When you've done, stow your empty suitcases on this bed here. We seem to have got one to spare. And don't you worry. All us C.P.O.s 'ave got sons of our own in the Navy. We'll see you through all right."

5

Half an hour later he came back with two sheepish-looking figures behind him.

"Here's two more for the party. You'd better get your cases off those beds after all. Stow 'em in that corner for the time being. There you are, you two—those are your beds," and the class recognised the handkerchief buyers, Hart and Gray. They had caught the next train from Waterloo. They had expected to land in gaol, but found themselves, instead, gathered gently back to their group.

"Now," said the Chief, "there's a bit more routine. There's a system of class leaders here. One of you's made leader, and his job's to march the rest to meals and see the hut's kept clean, and so on. Redfern, you'll have that job, and Holt, you'll help him. I'll tell you the duties in a minute. Now, the rest of you, you help the leader and his deputy as much as you can. They've got a bloody job in some ways, and it's up to you to help them and do what they say.

"Each day, four of you will have to act as cooks. Nah, you don't have to cook the bloody stuff! You simply go over there five minutes early and dish the food out. Then you clean up afterwards. Redfern, you and Holt and you two late-comers there, what's-your-names—Hart and Gray? Well, you four go over now and get the stuff, just for to-night. I'll bring the class over."

The class marched over in threes, hatless and with their civilian gas-masks slung on their backs. As they came into the mess deck, they were greeted with more shouts and whistles and " Go home, you poor boobs " from the sailors already eating their supper there.

The newcomers all felt self-conscious, even if a few, like Price and Cole, put on an aggressive air. They began to long for the moment when they could get their uniforms and so become inconspicuous.

Redfern squeezed into the place next to Williams, after serving the meal.

" Well, the food's still good," he said. " Half a week's ration of butter for one meal."

Soon, Williams asked the inevitable question.

" I was in a bank," said Redfern.

" Good God! Another one? So was Holt."

" Did he hate it as much as I did?"

After supper, Williams and Redfern decided to have a cup of tea in the canteen. A sailor who left the mess deck at the same time set them in the right direction. But they missed their way and stopped another sailor.

" Sure," he said, " I'm going there myself. I'll show you. Just come in, have you? It's not a bad place. You soon get used to it. The Chiefs are grand. Most of the officers are all right, but watch out for Lewis. He's a sod. They say he lost his ship and is taking it out on us. He'll pick you up for anything. Got a light? Christ, don't use a match. Scarce round here. Give me one off your stub."

Redfern and Williams queued for tea and got it in ten minutes.

When they got back to the hut they found some of the class already writing letters home. Almost immediately one of the loudspeakers posted all over the camp piped " Darken ship— Darken ship," and the Chief came in.

" Come on, boys, darken ship. Pull the blinds down, do the blackout."

One of the letter-writers looked up. " What's the date to-day, somebody ? "

" Blimey ! " said the Chief, looking at him. " I'd remember the bloody day I joined, I would," and spat into the spitkid as he went out.

He had been gone two minutes when the door swung open again and in came half a dozen sailors shouting, " Anyone here from London ? Anyone here from Brummagem ? Anyone here from Manchester ? Any Yorkshire men here ? "

That was a revelation. These " sailors ", these men in their smart collars and their bellbottoms, who had seemed such

19

seven-sea salts on the parade-ground—why they were home-sick, too! They were just boys who, a week or two ago, were walking about in flannels. They were little more "sailors" than the newcomers. They were just "trainees" like them, after all.

Several of Class 16S called out, " Yes, I come from London," or " I'm from West Bromwich. I know Brummagem all right," or " I'm from Salford."

As soon as he had heard the call " Anyone here from Brummagem ? " Williams's moon-faced bedmate looked up from his packing and said, " Yes, I do." A trainee walked over quickly, firing eager questions. " What part do you come from ? Why, I don't live a mile away. You know the Town Hall ? You know that street that runs round the back of it ? You know the baker's shop on the corner ? Well, I'm next door to that. What's your name ? "

" Nevison."

" I know some Nevisons. One of 'em used to go with a sister of mine. Any relation ? Name was Jack."

" That'll be my brother. 'E used to go with a girl called Gladys from round that way."

" That's right. Our Glad. Well I'm flicked! Come all the way from Brummagem to this flicking place and run slap into a feller from your own doorstep. Flicking hell! Hey, lads, this lad comes from same place as I do."

" What's it like here ? " said Nevison, beginning to gain assurance from the notice he was receiving. " Bloody awful, I suppose."

" Oh, it's not too bad. The food's lousy. That fish we had yesterday. Lucky to miss it, you were. *And* they run you around. Who's yer divisional officer ? Oh, him, he's all right. We've got Lewis. He's a sod. A bastard, flicking sod. One of these days I'll catch up with him in the blackout. Oh, and you'll have innocerlations or whatever they're called. *And* vaccination. They're flicking awful. One feller in our hut nearly had his flicking arm off. Took off moaning in a stretcher to the sick bay, 'e was. My arm was sore for days; AND I 'ad to do P.T. with it."

By now the group had swollen into a crowd as other members of Class 16S came to listen to their fate; and, as the talk went on, many of them who, up to now, had used little or no bad language began to throw " flicks " and " runts " into their conversation. They also lost much of their stiffness, talked louder and more freely, seemed altogether more at home. They were in full cry when the far door swung open and a man came in.

There was silence at once and several men, sitting at the benches writing, hesitated, then stood up rather awkwardly.

" Please sit down," said the man, and " It's only the Padre," said one of the trainees.

The Padre looked along the hut and saw several figures in uniform. " Look, you boys. Clear out now, will you ? I want to talk to these boys for a minute. You'll have plenty of time to talk to them later on.

" The rest of you, just gather round here, will you ? I'm not going to preach a sermon at you, so don't be afraid. But there are so many of you here. I think there's six thousand of you in all—and you're only here for ten weeks or so. I find the only real chance I get of seeing many of you is the night you arrive.

" I always tell the men who come here to remember the three Ws. Three Ws—Welcome, Wanted, and Willing. Welcome. You're all welcome. If you don't know that already, you soon will. Wanted. Goodness me, you *are* wanted. Wanted more than ever before. The Navy's playing a greater part in this war than it ever did. Yes, you're really wanted. Willing. Everyone here is willing and anxious to help you—your Chief, all the officers here, your shipmates, your fellow-trainees if you prefer it, and the Chaplains. If ever you want any advice, go to your Chief. Or, if it's about personal matters, by all means come to me. My office is next door to the church—and you can't miss that; it's just opposite the canteen. And you can't miss me either. I'm the one with the beard.

" Now, boys, that's all the sermon. Here's a bit of advice. When you go ashore—you get leave every other evening and on either Saturday or Sunday each week—don't go trooping into South Down. There's nothing there at all except a couple of cinemas which are usually crowded. Most of the men go in once and say they'll never go again. I advise you to make for some of these Services' canteens. There's one at Beddingham, just about two miles from here. There's not much in the village there, but the canteen has got good food, billiards, magazines, and comfortable chairs. It's well worth going there.

" Well, I must get on. Six other new classes have come in to-day, and I've only seen two of them so far. Good-night."

" 'E's telling us not to go to South Down because 'e doesn't want us to get at the beer or knock off a couple of W.A.A.F.s. Them parsons make me toired," said Price.

Then the Chief came back, and Redfern showed him the list he had been preparing for the past hour. It was a list of the special duties for the next week for each member of the class. Some days a man would be cook, other days hut sweeper, passage sweeper, or C.P.O.s mess cleaner. The Chief pinned it on the notice-board.

" Now, lads. Here are the jobs you'll have to do in your own time. They don't take long if you all do your share. It's the leader's job to see you do them properly. So do as he says. And now it's getting near time to turn in. You've all found the washrooms and lavatories, I suppose ? "

They had. At the far end of the room a door opened on a passage which ran for about a hundred yards, linking a number of huts. Half-way along were the steps down to the washroom, where there were five large sinks, some twenty basins, with hot and cold water laid on, and six showers with wells underneath in which it was just possible to sit. Farther on were the lavatories. Everything looked clean.

Williams had had his wash and was putting on his pyjamas as the Chief came by.

The Chief paused and looked. Then he said in a low voice: "I've always wondered about those things. I could never see the sense myself of taking clothes off to go to bed and then putting more on to get into bed."

Inside two minutes Williams was asleep.

Chapter Two

1

THE whole camp was awakened at six the next morning by a strident bugle, broadcast through the loudspeakers. The notes of the call, jumping briskly up and down the scale, pierced through the soft, misty layers of sleep and struck the nerve-centres of six thousand unconscious men. The sleepers tried to fight the sound. But it was no use. The bugle insisted, and when, at length, it reached its climax and was still, it was followed by something even more shattering.

Class 16S swung their feet out of bed, and were sitting, more asleep than awake, on the edge, trying to realise where they were, when heavy feet came quickly along the corridor outside.

The main hut lights were switched on, and a fiery-faced figure burst in, letting out roars which would have sent the cattle flying for safety across the sands of Dee.

" Rise and shine. Show a leg, show a leg, show a leg. 'Eave-oh, 'eave-oh, lash up and stow. The sun's scorching your eyes out."

All thirty men were out of bed and on their feet when suddenly the voice changed. " That's right, boys. Get out and get washed

22

and then sweep the hut before breakfast." It was Chief Petty Officer Arthur Graves.

He stumped out of the hut, and in a few seconds his voice could be heard roaring next door.

But the sun was by no means shining. It was still dark. It was snowing; and gusts of bitter wind swirled the flakes through any door that opened.

Williams went down the passage to the washroom, shivering. He had to wait a minute or two before he could get to a basin. Then, as he began to wash, he was showered with lukewarm water by a fat boy next door who was sluicing himself vigorously and indiscriminately. A face that was round, chubby, and bucolic jerked itself from the basin, large saucer eyes looked at Williams and a fruity voice said, " Sorry, mate, Ah've been splashing you. Sorry, mate."

"They might give us some hot water on a morning like this," said Williams.

" Not in the Navy, mate. They keeps their 'ot water for the summer."

A dry, incisive voice behind them said: " Is the water cold?" and they saw an officer, with his coat collar turned up, eyeing them.

" Yes, sir, it *is* cold."

The officer looked at the fat boy, at the water, and at Williams, drew himself into his great-coat and moved away.

" The dirty bastard! " said a redhead from a basin farther along. " One of these days I'm going to knock his ruddy block off. Took my bleeding card yesterday, 'e did. I'll stuff it down 'is bleeding neck before I've done with 'im."

" What did 'e do that for, mate ? "

" I was coming down the Divvy Office steps, I was, and slipped on the flaming ice. I was all sprawled out on the ground when this bleeder Lewis comes by and says to me: ' Why the flicking hell don't you salute, my man ? ' and I sez, ' 'Ow the flicking hell *can* I salute when I'm flat out on the bleeding ground ? ', and 'e sez, ' Give us your flicking card.' "

The three left the washroom together. " How long have you been here ? " Williams asked the redhead.

" Came in a week to-day. What class are you in ? "

" Sixteen S."

" So am I," said the fat boy, chipping in. " I didn't see you yesterday."

The redhead turned through one of the doors of the corridor into his own hut and Williams and the fat boy rejoined their class in theirs. They all dressed hurriedly, no one knowing how long it would be before another bugle-blast blew down the loudspeaker and they'd have to fall in or something.

The Chief soon came back, telling them to make their beds.

"Look, you folds your blankets like this and your rug like this. Put the blankets at the top of the bed like this, put the pillow on top, then put the rug at the foot of the bed like this."

His hands worked amazingly fast, and in about fifteen seconds there was a bed all neat and tidy.

The class managed somehow. Then the Chief set them sweeping the hut and emptying the spitkid and then gave them the programme for the day.

"After breakfast, we'll go down and get your station cards and pay books. I expect that will take up most of the morning. This afternoon we'll start getting you your kits. Now, you've nothing to do for the next twenty minutes, but at seven-fifteen you gets fell in outside the hut and march over to breakfast."

"Can we wear our overcoats?" said the fat boy. "It's cold outside."

"Nah, it's not cold. Just fresh. And crikey, with all that fat on, you don't need no overcoat. What's your name?"

"Bellenger. And fat or not, Ah'm still cold."

"Get away. What will you do when you get to sea and there's ice all over the deck and you have to go on watch?"

"Put me coat on. And Ah *have* been to sea. In the Merchant Service. My dad was in the Navy and he sent me off for a trip two years ago when Ah was sixteen. Ah wore dozens of coats. Dozens of 'em."

"All right, Sinbad. Put your coat on if you like."

Sinbad! The perfect name. It was to stick.

At 8.15 groups of sailors, without their overcoats, began to pass the front of the huts in twos and threes, towards the parade-ground and, five minutes later, a bugle blared once more on the loudspeakers.

Class 16S looked at each other uneasily.

"That bugle will be for Divisions," said Sinbad with an authoritative air.

"What the 'ell are Divisions when they're at home?" asked Price; but before he could get an answer the Chief had come in.

"Come on, lads. We're going off to have a talk by the Divisional Officer. Fall in outside. Yes, put your coats on. We'll have to do a lot of standing about to-day. Now, get fell in, tallest on the right, shortest on the left. Here, Sinbad, you're the shortest, and you, there, knock off skylarking. What's your name?"

"Low, Chief."

"Well, don't fool about when Divisions are on. Fall in behind Sinbad, and you, you that's sucking something—what is it? A sweet? Put it out, man. Don't you let the Commodore find you sucking sweets during working hours. Get fell in behind those other two."

At this, a boy whose face was fleshy and pink like a young calf, spat out a sweet and strolled cheekily to his place.

" What's your name ? "

" Hall, Chief," said the calf, leering at the rest. The Chief looked as though he would say something more, but he went on with his sorting. Williams found himself in the last row with Holt and Taylor, who seemed to be losing some of his dolefulness. " Nice fellow, that Chief," said Taylor. " I'd have knocked that little sod's ears back, I would."

The Chief marched them, by back ways which avoided the parade-ground and the Divisions now taking place on it, to another wooden hut. Two new classes still in their civvies, were already sitting in the front rows.

Two more classes followed Class 16S. They sat and waited.

Suddenly there was a stir. Chairs were pushed back and men scrambled to their feet. Along the gangway came an officer in a top-coat. He said quietly, " Sit down, please," as he stepped on to the platform and removed his coat and gloves.

He had a remarkable face. A mouth that was exceptionally wide, cheekbones that stood out so prominently that the sallow cheeks seemed to be hollowed out of the face, a high forehead growing all the higher as baldness had forced the hair back. Somehow the face seemed streamlined yet firm, ugly but attractive; and his voice, when the officer began to speak, was decisive but pleasant. He leaned his elbows on a high writing-desk and began.

" I'm sure all of you are feeling very strange this morning. You're beginning a new life and I expect it's quite different from anything you have seen before. So I'm going to give you a few tips about it. I'm, by the way, your Divisional Officer. My name is Lieutenant-Commander Rankin. I'm the fellow you see if you want help. And I'm the fellow you get sent to if you get into trouble.

" You'll probably find a lot of things here seem irksome. To begin with, you'll have to do a lot of drilling on the parade-ground out there and you may say to yourself, ' Why do they make us do all this Army stuff ? I want to be a sailor.' Well, if you want to be a good sailor, you must first learn how to obey orders promptly. Many times at sea you find that the quick, almost automatic obedience to any order means all the difference between a life being saved and a life lost. And we find that the best and quickest way to teach you how to obey orders is this Army stuff on the parade-ground. So, in the next few weeks, when you are being shouted at out there and are tramping your feet off, try and remember what it's all about.

" There's one order that I want you to learn to obey right away. Every other night and every Saturday or Sunday you are given leave. That leave expires at 10 p.m. and not at ten-twenty or ten-fifteen or even at ten-one. If you are late, without a very good excuse, you are liable to get into serious trouble. You may say ' Good God, what does it matter in the middle of a war, if I'm half a minute late getting past the gates at *Frobisher?* ' Well, of course, it doesn't really matter to the outcome of the war if you are a minute late here or even an hour late. But when you go to sea you'll find that what are called liberty boats put off from your ship to take men ashore on leave—we call them libertymen. That boat will leave the jetty or the dockside or whatever it is at a definite time to take the libertymen aboard again when their leave is over. And if you are half a minute late you'll miss it. There won't be another liberty boat until next day, so by the time you reach your ship you won't be just half a minute adrift. You'll be twenty-four hours adrift. And it may easily happen that in the middle of the night your ship will get sudden sailing orders, and she'll put to sea without you. That means that someone who has already got enough work on his own to do will have to do yours as well, and the efficiency and safety of the ship will be impaired.

" So from the very beginning we try to get the habit into you of coming back from your leave to time. If by any chance, through no fault of your own, you see that you are going to be adrift, you must bring back reliable evidence that you were not to blame. If you are in a car smash, for example, you must get a statement signed by the nearest policeman. Otherwise, I'm afraid, we shall not believe you. We're very disbelieving people in the Navy."

He stopped to blow his nose and his audience rustled slightly. They had kept absolutely still, in spite of the cold, until then. After a moment he went on again.

" I want to say a word about Class Leaders. Your Chiefs will have told you something about them already. They're put in charge of you and you must do what they tell you. If they tell you to do the wrong things, you can bet your life we'll very soon change them. They haven't asked for the jobs. They've been chosen for them without any pushing on their part. Maybe some of them would much prefer not to be Class Leaders. Anyway, I want you to remember that they have the right to give you orders and that disobeying an order in the Navy is a very serious offence indeed.

" Always obey an order first, however stupid it may seem, and then argue about it afterwards if you want to. And there is plenty of scope for arguing. If you want to complain about something you can go to your Chief Petty Officer and he'll bring you to me. If you don't like my decision, I can take you to the Commodore. If you don't like the Commodore's decision, you can go to the Commander-in-Chief, Chatsport. And if you don't like his decision, you can appeal to the Lords of the

Admiralty. But *their* decision is final. If you don't like it, all I can say is that you'll have to find another war."

He got his laugh.

" Now," he said, " you all know what a sailor's uniform looks like. I think it's by far the smartest Service uniform in the world. I'll tell you a little about it.

" You've probably heard that the three stripes round a sailor's Blue Jean collar were put on to commemorate Nelson's three victories. This isn't so. They were put on by mistake. But go on telling your girl-friends about Nelson's victories. It won't do any harm. A collar of a sort had been worn for many years by sailors to keep the oil from their pigtails from running over their clothes.

" Then there's the silk which you'll wear round your neck and fasten at your chest. Long ago, sailors used to wear a piece of cloth round their foreheads to keep the sweat out of their eyes when they were firing their guns. On a long voyage the material would wear out and they'd get more from the Pusser's store. The Pusser didn't go in for fancy colours. He usually stuck to the one, black. So when Nelson was killed at Trafalgar, most of his men were wearing these black scarves round their heads. They took them off and bound them round their arms as a sign of mourning; and British sailors have worn them ever since.

" Your bellbottom trousers. Even in modern times, in peace-time, you'd find sailors scrubbing decks in bare feet, so it's convenient to have trousers that pull right up over their knees out of the wet."

He came to a sudden stop. " Well, now, are there any questions you want to ask ? " There was a silence for a moment.

" Any questions at all on anything I've been talking about ? "

At that Price stood up. " Yes, sir. 'Ow much money do you think is wasted each year in the Navy in giving sailors this 'ere out-of-date uniform ? "

Lieutenant-Commander Rankin looked shocked. " None," he said. " I don't think a penny is wasted. It's a great thing to remember your past, to feel a comradeship with the great sailors of bygone days who have made the Navy what it is. I wouldn't have the uniform changed for anything. I think you'll agree with me when you have worn it a little."

He then picked up his coat and hat, a Chief called " Attention " and everyone got up. But Lieutenant-Commander Rankin had forgotten something. " Oh, by the way, are there any actors here ? "

" Yes, sir," said a rather sugary voice from half-way down the room.

" Good. What acting have you done ? "

"I was in a repertory company when I was called up, and I've had quite a lot of West End experience."

"Good. What's your name? Denton? Well, give your name to the Entertainments Officer, will you? We try to run shows here from time to time, and anyone who can act is very welcome."

Class 16S spent the rest of the morning waiting in long queues for pay books and station cards. Their pay books would be their identity cards all the time they were in the Service. Their station cards they would give up whenever they went out of the *Frobisher* gates and would finally surrender at the end of their time there, ten weeks from now.

"I wish it was time to surrender them now," said someone as they all shivered outside an inevitable hut.

Also outside the hut, waiting to go in, was another class, temporarily without their Chief. They were lounging in the cold and stamping their feet to keep the circulation going. One of them was the actor, Denton.

He looked sleek, with well-polished hair, but his dark face was grubby. Apparently he was the Class Leader, for he suddenly looked at the rest with half an ingratiating smile on his face and said: "Well, I suppose we'd better fall in properly while we wait."

At once a loud voice from the group said "Why?" and Denton could find no immediate answer to this. A light flush showed itself beneath the olive of his cheeks, but he neither said nor did any more.

"That boy's going to have trouble with his class," said Williams to Holt.

"I bet ten to one on the class," said Holt to Williams.

2

Then they queued for part of their kit.

The Wren who was issuing great-coats looked quickly at each man, gauged his size and handed a coat across the counter, saying, "Try this on, Jack." Nearly always she got a reasonable fit first time. But when she came to Holt, she was stumped. Her eye went quickly to where his head might reasonably be and landed on his chest. It travelled upward with widening surprise, and then she stood back and said, "I don't believe it."

"Nor did my mother, but she was wrong, too."

The Wren shook her head thoughtfully. "It's no good. I'm sure I haven't one to fit."

"Goody! Can I go home?"

"What's up?" called Sinbad from the end of the queue. He was cold and wanted to get inside the hut. Low called back in a loud voice: "They can't get a coat to fit old Shortarse here. They say they're not used to giraffes."

Holt turned round, stretched out a long arm and threatened to break Low's neck.

"All right, Shortarse, I mean yer Honner; I'm neutral."

"Stop skylarking, boys," said the Wren in a firm voice and brought Holt behind the counter to be measured.

Eventually they got back to their hut with the gear they had collected. "Well, there's no more we can do to-day," said the Chief, "so if you want to write any letters or anything, you'd better get on with it. Smoke? Well, as it's the first day. But of course normally you can't smoke in working hours. You get a 'stand easy' in the morning and another in the afternoon, and you can smoke after breakfast and in the dinner hour. And don't go throwing your fag-ends all over the deck. It only makes it worse for the sweepers."

"Deck?" said Alf Taylor. "Deck? I thought this was a ruddy floor."

"Well, it's a deck. The road outside is a deck. The parade-ground is a deck. When you walk out of the gates, you probably think you are going into South Down. But you're not. You're going 'ashore'. You may think this place is a camp. Well, it's not. It's a 'ship'."

"Will you excuse me a moment, please, Chief? I feel seasick," said Low.

"You'll be sick enough in a few months' time without pretending."

"Have you been to sea in this war, Chief?"

"Nah! I'd been out of the Navy fifteen years when the war broke out. Got a nice little job looking after a warehouse. And then I gets called back. Another two months and I'd 'ave been fifty-five and over age. But they got me all right. Twenty-five years! It's time someone else did a bit;" and he spat into the spitkid.

By now, most of the boys were feeling themselves again. You could see that particularly at meal-times.

At the first meal, the day before, they had all walked in quietly and sat down with their best party manners. No one had complained about his share of the food, and no one had tried to grab.

But at dinner-time to-day it had been different. No doubt the cold air had brought out appetites, and though they had begun to file in quietly, those behind soon began pushing until the doorway into the mess deck was jammed. The plates were closely eyed as they were passed along the rows, and things started when Hall, the cheeky, calf-like boy, kept an extra large helping instead of passing it down. A square, tough-faced boy, who only needed a cauliflower ear, and the sullen Hardcastle,

29

did the same; and three men towards the end of the row were left without dinners. One hammered on the table, and Cole stood up and shouted with his rasping nasal voice: " 'Ere, you pass them dinners down. 'Ere, leader, these dinners aren't being served out fair. We've got nothing down 'ere and some of them in the middle 'ave got two 'elpings. Coo, look what the cooks 'ave 'elped themselves to! think yer at a bleeding banquet, don't yer ? "

Yes, the four cooks had kept enormous helpings.

Redfern tried to sort the mess as best he could. He found several spare plates, which had been picked at on the way along, and handed them to the disgrunted Cole and his two starving mates.

" Just you wait till I'm cook," said Cole to the class in general.

It was too late to do anything about the cooks' helpings this time. The cooks had dug into them at the first sign of trouble, and Price, who was one of them, told the assembled company to go and flick itself.

" Oi've done the work, 'aven't Oi ? " he said. " Oo fetched yer bleeding dinners ? Oi did. And Oi know well enough that when you basstuds get cooks, you'll swoipe all yer can. Oi'm going to look after myself while the going's good."

3

At six next morning there was the same, sleep-shattering bugle, but a different cry.

" Wakey, wakey," crackled a high, parched voice. " Rise and shine, the morning's fine. We're off the sunny coast of Spain, 'eave-oh, 'eave-oh, lash up and stow, there's not a sign of rain," and a wizened little man strode along the hut, darting fierce glances from side to side. His head was like a crescent moon, with the tip of the chin turned upwards to meet his forehead jutting down.

He came along, screeching, until a fierce glance contacted some object and sent him diving for the bed in which Holt lay asleep. " WHAR-AR-YOU ? " he yelled into the unconscious ear, and, the next second, Holt had jerked himself upright and hit his head a crack on the mattress above him. Two more seconds and he was diving into his clothes. The wizened man went through the far door to electrify another hut.

A quarter of an hour later he was back shouting: " Come on now, fall in. Get a move on there. If you don't hurry I'll make you fall in outside in the freezing cold."

" I thought we were off the sunny coast of Spain," said Low, but not loud enough for the Chief to hear. " Where do we fall in, Chief ? " he added louder.

" In the passage. Get a move on. You're all adrift."

So they lined up in the darkened passage with all the other classes.

"Two hands from each class to clean the C.P.O.s' mess." Everyone shrank into the shadows to dodge the eye of the class leader. But Redfern had already drawn up his list of duties and sent Hardcastle and the farmer's boy, Perry, off to the Chief.

"Four cooks from each class to the galley." Price, Nevison—Williams's bedmate—and two others went from Class 16S amid reminders about the size of helpings and general threats from the rest.

"Remainder get back to your huts, make your beds, and have a good sweep up."

Just before breakfast-time their own Chief, Graves, came into the hut, and was set on by Alf Taylor. "Who's that Chief that looks like a gnome? The man who woke us up this morning—the man who fell us in?"

The Chief scratched his head. "Looks like a gnome? Fell you in? Well, old Wacker Paine's duty chief this morning. Was he a chap with a screechy voice?"

"Yes, that's him," they all shouted together. "You should have seen him get Shortarse out of bed. Electric shock wasn't in it!"

The Chief smiled. "Old Wacker's all right. 'E 'ad a son through 'ere not so long ago. Doesn't give a damn for nobody."

"Why's he called Wacker?" asked Alf Taylor. "Does he hit people?"

"Nah. Every Paine's called Wacker in the Navy. Same as Fishers. They're called Jackie, after old Jack Fisher. Who's 'e? WHO's 'E? Blimey, when were you lads born? 'E was one of the big Admirals in the last war. Then, there's 'Rattler' Morgans, 'Dusty' Millers, and 'Pincher' Martins."

"We've got a Martin in the class," said Low. "He looks like a 'Pincher'," and pointed to a boy of eighteen who was sitting on his bed reading a paper-backed thriller. The boy looked up. He *did* look like a Pincher. He had the same curving chin as the fiery Chief "Wacker" Paine, but his forehead, instead of pointing down, bulged out as though it was badly swollen. His eyes were set deeply beneath this protuberance and became almost invisible whenever he smiled, which was rarely.

Off went the bugle again and, with a "Come on, time to fall in for breakfast," the Chief pushed them out of the hut.

They spent the whole of that morning in medical and dental inspections and having the first of the inoculations about which they had been warned on the first night. As usual they had to wait in long queues, under the eye of a man with three red stripes on his arm who kept shouting "Keep silence, you!"

"That flicking sergeant seems to think a lot of himself,"

said Alf Taylor, "bawling 'is flicking head off. Keep silence yourself. Stuff it up, you silly bastard." All this under his breath.

"Sergeant?" said Sinbad, almost choking. "Sergeant? There ain't no such things in the Navy. Them three stripes on 'is arm are good-conduct badges. 'E gets one after three years in the Service, another after eight, and another after thirteen. 'E gets threepence a day extra for each one."

"All right, Admiral, he's still a sergeant to me."

"And they can keep their threepence extra a day," said Price. "Oi'm not staying three years in this bleeding Service, not if Oi can help it."

And up came the three-badge man. "I've told you to shut your traps five times this morning already. I'm not going to bawl my guts out just to please you. All three of you, put on your gas-masks;" and thus effectively muzzled, Price, Taylor, and the indignant Sinbad waited for their turn.

By the time they had all been through their inoculation and inspections it was dinner-time.

After dinner, Williams and Redfern went to the canteen for some cigarettes and found a queue that stretched through the door.

"I had to queue twenty minutes for a haircut this morning," said Redfern.

"I had to queue five for the lavatory."

"Well, it's better than smash and grab."

A small trainee in front of them turned a cherubic face to look at them.

"Just come in?" he asked. "When are you being kitted up?"

"This afternoon, I hope."

"Well, watch out what boots you get. Don't let the Wrens chuck anything at you. Make sure they're large enough. Mine were too small and I've had absolute hell. You see some of the lads limping about like cripples after a week or two of square-bashing."

The queue now began to move forward and the cherubic sailor turned to move forward with it, humming, half under his breath and over and over again, the first line of a song which ran " *Blue champagne, purple shadows.*"

Williams and Redfern remembered his tip that afternoon. They tried on their boots over thick socks and rejected two pairs until they felt reasonably sure of a fit. Then eventually, after long, long waits, they staggered back to their hut with kitbags, suits, hats, Blue Jean collars, jerseys, lanyards, silks, and their two pairs of boots each, and began eagerly to try them on with the Chief as technical adviser.

The jersey and the bellbottoms, with their absence of fly buttons and the corset-like flaps overlapping at the top, were

32

easy, but God! the Blue Jean collar with its folds and fastenings round the waist, and that blue straight-jacket of a jumper which goes over jersey and collar! To make everything worse, their freshly inoculated arms were just beginning to ache.

" Oh, blast it! " said Alf Taylor. " I can't get into my flicking waistcoat."

" Waistcoat ? WAISTCOAT ? " said the Chief and Sinbad together, turning more purple than ever. " That's not a waistcoat. Jumper, if you like. Blouse, if you like. But don't call it a waistcoat."

" Jumper, blouse, or flicking camisole, I can't get into the bastard. Come and give a pull, somebody."

He was eased into it with a great deal of gasping, groaning, and bad language.

" And now, I suppose, I've got to get out of the flicker."

Getting out was even harder than getting in. One after another, they bent down while their bedmates pulled and tugged until eventually they were out again.

Then they had to fold their new clothes.

" You're making a hell of a mess with those things," said Taylor to Williams from across the gangway. " Here, I'll show you. I used to work in a cleaner's and presser's. See, you fold it in half like this, then you roll the bastard in a leetle, dinky ball like this. Hell, my arm's sore! "

Suddenly he screamed. Was it his arm ? No. " *Sierra Se-ue, I'm sad and lone-lee, Sierra Sue, I lurve yew on-lee,*" he bawled at the top of his voice and strolled back to his bed.

Their boots had to be studded that evening. The Chief brought in a last, a hammer, and a supply of studs. When the wretched Williams got to the last he began by hitting his thumb, then hit several studs so unevenly that they became hopelessly bent or fell out altogether.

The exasperated Hardcastle, who was behind him, said, " Let me do the thing myself," took last and hammer, and finished the job with a series of swift taps.

He was a shoemaker and could not bear to see his own job bungled. Williams thanked him humbly.

Next day their names were to be stamped on their kit, so they dressed once more, and for the last time, in civvies. It was Williams's turn for cooks, and after the 6.15 fall in he went to the galley with Fletcher, the ex-boy scout, printer's apprentice, " Pincher " Martin of the bulging forehead, and Miller, the square-faced basher without the cauliflower ear.

They got the plates, knives, forks, and spoons from the galley and laid them on their table. Then they had to wait three-quarters of an hour for the food.

" I wish we didn't have to waste so much time hanging about," said Williams.

" Yes, it's a badger," said Fletcher.

Williams was just about to ask him what he meant by " badger " when he realised that Fletcher was using the word as a substitute—no doubt the result of boy-scout influence.

Martin sat on a bench and stared at the floor. Miller pulled out an illustrated magazine on physical fitness and began to study pictures of wrestlers and express parochial contempt for their dorsal development.

" Call that a back? Why, there's a fellow in Newcastle, Wild Bill Riley they call him, who sent his photo up to *Health and Strength*. Arms as big as a bleeding 'orse. Neck like the backside of a bloody bull. *Health and Strength* wouldn't believe 'im. Sent a man down to look at 'im, thought the bloody photo was faked. The chap they sent soon found out 'e was wrong when a fellow the size of a flicking elephant opened the front door to 'im. Coo! 'Is blinking eyes nearly popped out of 'is bleeding 'ead."

" Coo! " said Pincher Martin, looking up and imitating Miller. " Coo! ' You too could have a body like mine.' You ought ter pose for one of them adverts."

At last the food was ready. Williams himself took the job of dishing it out.

But Pincher Martin was not having any of his methods. He said, " I'm going to take darn good care I get a big breakfast this morning. I'd nothing at supper last night."

" Look, lads, let's stop this. There's enough to go round if we share it out equally."

"Why the 'ell should we share the stuff out equally? Everyone else pinches as much as they can when they're cooks."

" Yes, and look what happened yesterday when they did. Three people nearly went without altogether."

" That's their funeral. I'm not going to go without. I know damn well that the others will look after themselves when they're cooks, and I'm bloody well going to, too."

" You bloody well are not. If one lot of cooks swipes the biggest share, of course all the rest will."

" What makes you think that the rest will stop swiping if one does ? "

" I don't know that they will. But we can try."

" Not bloody likely. I want to eat," and seizing a plate, Martin pulled out three large sausages, though there were only two on the other plates. He was just making for the mashed potatoes when Williams snatched the plate out of his hands, put one of the sausages back in the dish, and passed the plate to Fletcher, who put it in an empty place.

But it was no use. Martin put his hand into the dish of mash, grabbed a handful of it, and rushed off to another plate. Then he grabbed a third sausage and scuttled away to the far end. The inrush of bodies, which engulfed everyone at that moment, made immediate retribution impossible.

It was Redfern who got the plate with the one sausage. Everyone else had neatly avoided it. He went quickly to retrieve his share. But he was too late. Pincher Martin, true to his promise, had made a big, if hasty, breakfast.

"If I were you," said Williams to Redfern, " I'd threaten to report anyone who does this smash-and-grab stuff with the food."

" We'll have to do something about it, anyway."

4

At 8.15 they were fallen in, still in civvies, and marched to the edge of the parade-ground to watch Divisions.

All round the edge of the tarmac, some six thousand sailors stood, lounging, gossiping, or just staring. They blew on their hands, stamped their feet, and waited. Then a bugle sounded. At its last note the six thousand closely packed men bulged inward and began to race from all sides towards the centre of the parade. They crashed into each other, jostled each other, tripped each other, cursed each other. But in thirty seconds this jumbled mass had turned to stone, chaos had been changed into immaculate order, and the six thousand, three deep and at attention, were ready for inspection.

"You falls in by Classes," said the Chief, "and the Classes falls in by Watches, and the Watches falls in by Divisions. You can see the parade split in three. Those are the three divisions —Foretop, Maintop, and Fo'c'cle. You're fo'c'slemen. You'll fall in over there to-morrow. Each Division's divided into Port and Starboard Watch. You're Port Watch. Each Watch is divided into two parts, First and Second. You're the second part of Port Watch. Each part of the Watch is under a sub-Divisional Officer—that's Lieutenant Hollis, for you. Both watches of a division are under a Divisional Officer. That's Lieutenant-Commander Rankin for you. The feller who spoke to you yesterday. Behind these three divisions over there is the Gunnery section. You'll get into that when we've finished with you in Seamanship ; and on the left is the Signal School— bunting tossers, you know, semaphore and all that. They're being inspected now, and by-and-by old Baldhead will drive up."

" Who's Baldhead ?" asked Redfern. " Baldhead " was the Commodore.

The inspections proceeded.

" Roman Catholics, fall out!"

Immediately a number of sailors broke away from the ranks and scrambled over to a drill shed—except one, who stubbornly marched while the others ran. It was Chief Petty Officer " Wacker " Paine. Then two Padres, one of them with the black beard they had seen on the first night, walked on to the parade-ground, their white surplices fluttering in the slight wind. The bearded one stopped at the steps of the nearest dais, facing the lines of men. The second went on, past a centre dais, to a third. Then they both waited while officers finished giving their orders.

Suddenly, far off, by the main gate, a bugle sounded and half a minute later, a little car, with a pennant fluttering from its bonnet, came round the corner and stopped by the centre dais. The whole parade was now at attention, the officers saluting facing the centre dais, while a sailor jumped from the front of the car and opened the rear door. Out stepped Baldhead, a red-faced man with a thick, gold-topped cane. He returned the salutes and mounted his dais.

" Off caps."

At once right hands were swung up to heads, caps whisked off, and hands, with caps, brought down again to the side. One man in that six thousand let his cap fall to the ground. He did not move.

" That's right," said the Chief. " Don't you forget that if you ever let your cap drop on the deck during Divisions, you must stand still. Don't try to pick it up until you're stood easy."

The parade was now " stood easy ", the sailor picked up his cap, the chaplains mounted their nearest dias and the morning prayers began.

The wind blew the words away. Then both chaplains got down and went off the way they had come.

The officers remounted their dais, ordered " On caps," and stood their Divisions at ease while the Roman Catholics came clattering back from their service in the drill shed. Long after the others had fallen in, Wacker Paine was still marching back to his place, his chin jutting out defiantly, while the Commodore, some thirty officers, and some six thousand men waited his convenience.

From behind a drill shed came the sound of a band, and then the band itself came marching on to the parade-ground, leading a guard with fixed bayonets. The guard stopped opposite the flagstaff at one end of the parade, but the band kept on until it was opposite the Commodore. There it turned about and stopped. A drum rolled and finished with a sudden tap. At the tap the whole parade turned left to face the flagpost and the band began to play the National Anthem as a signalman ran up the White Ensign.

The band played a few bars of the Marseillaise.

" H'mm! " thought Williams. " National Anthems of the Allies, eh ? I wonder when they'll play the Internationale."

Another roll of the drums, another tap, and the parade turned again, to face its front. A moment later it had turned left again, and again at the command of the drums, the stationary men had begun to march and the band burst into " Blaze Away ". The band headed the guard down the parade-ground and, turning, brought it past the Commodore's dais. The rest of the marching Divisions formed a long line heading for the edge of the parade-ground, where they split into classes and went to their morning's work.

" Well, that's Divisions," said the Chief. " You get that every morning except Saturday and get a Commodore's in-spection thrown in. Come on now, we must get back to the hut. and have your gear marked."

* * *

At 12.15 they fell in for the first time in their uniforms. None of them felt self-conscious now they were like everyone else in the camp. They fell in quite smartly beside the other classes of the second part of port watch, and waited. Then the Chief said to Redfern: " Here's Hollis, the sub-Divisional Officer. Call your class to attention, turn and salute him, then report your class. Say ' Sixteen Class correct, sir. Four cooks away.' "

Redfern turned to find an uncomfortable little man standing in front of the rows of classes, saluted as best he could, and stumbled out his report.

When all the classes had reported correct, Lieutenant Hollis called out, " Second Part of Port Watch, 'shun! " and, as he did so, rose on his toes and almost lost his balance. But he recovered and called " Move to the right in threes, right turn," followed by " Carry on, Class Instructors."

" Quick-march-left-wheel-get-out-of-the-bloody-way-there," said Chief Petty Officer Graves, all in one breath, the last part of the order being addressed to two men in overalls who were pushing a cart towards the mess deck.

It was then that Redfern remembered that he had not yet done anything about the cook question. How had Williams been getting on with his cannibals ? He halted the class outside.

Williams was not getting on well. He had strong and active support from Fletcher, but Miller backed up Martin. Martin had waited his chance and picked the juicier pieces of meat from the dish with his fingers. Williams caught the fingers a rap with a ladle, but Martin still got an extra helping of vegetables, took the plate to the far end of the table, and threw the food into his mouth as fast as he could.

The mess deck was already filling up. It was bitterly cold outside. Redfern could not keep the class waiting any longer. He went to Martin and said: " If you ever do anything like this again, I'll report you to the Chief, you greedy little pig."

" You can go and flick yourself," said Martin between mouthfuls.

37

The class fell upon their dinners, not, however, before they had seen the size of what remained of Martin's helping. Those who seemed to have got smaller shares than the rest blamed it on Martin and were ready to tear him to bits.

When they returned to the hut, Redfern said: " Look, boys. You saw what happened at dinner just now. One bloody little pig pinched twice his share and some of you had to go short. It's not fair. If there is any more of it, I warn you I shall report it to the Chief. There's no reason at all why the cooks shouldn't serve the meals out fairly. I suggest we pick four cooks and let them do the job all the time without having any other duties. They won't have to sweep the hut or do C.P.O.s' mess and they won't have to fall in to march to meals. What do you say ? "

" It depends who you pick for cooks," said Low. " You're not going to let Martin be one, are you ? "

" I said we'd *pick* the cooks."

" Oi don't want to be the bloody cook," said Price. " Oi want some flicking time to myself, Oi do."

" No one *has* to be cook. I just thought four of you might prefer the job if it meant getting out of the other things."

" I wouldn't mind doing it," said Fletcher. " I'll be one," said Nevison. " I'll do it so long as I don't have to do the flicking sweeping," said Taylor. " Come on, Perry, you be the fourth. You're a good hand at feeding pigs."

Because of his country accent and his lurching gait, the whole class thought Perry was a farmhand. But he was really a carpenter in a small Worcestershire village. He grinned amiably and said " Ah!". This was taken for consent and the matter was settled.

That afternoon they marched to the parade-ground and with something of a swing for the first time, feeling like real sailors, remembering the others at Divisions in the morning. They marched with a swing, that is, all except one. That one was Perry.

Normally, when a man marches, his right arm goes forward with his left foot while his left arm swings behind. Then, as the right foot comes forward, the left arm comes forward with it and the right arm swings back. But not when Perry marched. His arms swung forward together and swung back together. As they swung forward, his stomach bulged out and his head went back. As they swung to his side again, his head came forward and his stomach went back. It was like a farmhand shoo-ing home his cows.

The Chief soon found that the class was not keeping good step. Looking along the lines, he saw Perry's lumbering gait. He stopped the class dead in the middle of the parade-ground.

" Crickey!" he said. " What the 'ell's the matter with you ? 'Ere don't shove both arms out together like that. First one, then the other. 'Ere, come out of the class. Now look, left arm, right foot, right arm, left foot. No. Not left arm, left foot. Left arm, right foot. Blimey!"

He pushed Perry back into the ranks and set the class off again. Up went Perry's arms together as before. The Chief kept shouting " Left arm, right arm, left arm, right arm " at him, but this only confused him and put the rest of the class out of step, so the Chief gave it up for the time being and steered for a drill shed. There he handed them to a Leading Seaman with his Leading Seaman's anchor or " hook " on his arm, and left them, still muttering to himself.

The Leading Seaman had to teach them how to salute, how to " Off caps ", and how to turn right and left. Near " Stand easy " the Leading Seaman began to march them off the parade. They had hardly taken ten steps before he shouted " Halt " and came walking to Perry with the light of zeal and discovery in his eyes.

" You can't march properly, can you ? " he said, and began to demonstrate Perry's faults. " Look, it's quite easy. Left arm, right leg. Right arm, left leg. Try it."

Perry did. Up went both arms together, exactly as before.

Just then the loudspeakers piped " Stand easy ", and the Leading Seaman, quickly giving up the struggle, marched them off the parade-ground to their hut.

The opening round in that struggle between Perry's marching and the Navy had ended strongly in favour of the former.

5

Next day was Saturday. There were no Divisions, no parades. Instead, the whole class put on overalls and began to clean the hut immediately after breakfast. They manoeuvred the tables through the narrow windows on to the roadway and brought the benches through the door. There, four of them scrubbed the woodwork with soap and hot water until it was white. Inside, the others pulled the iron bedsteads to one side, swept the floor, washed it with hot water, soap, and soda, and polished it. Then they pulled the bedsteads to the other side and did the other half. Then they put everything back and marched to the heavy-gun battery to clean the guns.

Saturday was the day when the Captain made his rounds. If he found any of the huts dirty, he blamed the Divisional Officer, the Divisional Officer blamed the sub-Divisional Officer, and the sub-Divisional Officer blamed the Chief. Worse than that, it was said, he stopped the leave of the whole class and made them scrub the hut over again instead of going " ashore ".

Class 16S polished guns in the battery while the Captain inspected their hut. They wondered if all had gone well. They all wanted to get ashore that afternoon for the first time.

All *had* gone well. The Captain made no complaint and the class quickly got out of their overalls and began to get ready to go ashore. The process was elaborate. First a wash. Then they had to get out their best, their " Number One ", suits and stow away their working or " Number Three " suits. They polished their boots, put all kinds of cream on their hair, and fixed white lanyards.

Number 16 Hut was like a boudoir, with men instead of girls queueing for the mirror and saying to each other, " Will you square my collar off behind ? " or " Fix this lanyard for me, mate," or " Look out, you silly sod, you'll spill that hair oil all over my flicking cap." And when they were ready and were marched to dinner, their table manners came back lest a spot of gravy or a piece of potato might fall on their clean suits.

It was just as well they had cleaned and preened and polished, for when they had fallen in, in three long lines in front of the Divisional Office, it was Lieutenant Lewis who inspected them. He stood by while three Chiefs, each with a waste-paper basket, went down the lines collecting station cards. He watched while the men were called to attention and given the command " Open order, march." Then he began:

He stopped in front of the first man and looked at his feet. Then he looked at his knees. Then he looked at his stomach, then at his chest, then at his face, then at his hat. He paused a moment while the wretched man held his breath, expecting at any moment to hear Lieutenant Lewis say to the Chief, " Take this man away and shoot him, please." Eventually, Lieutenant Lewis opened his thin lips and said, " Put your cap on straight." Then he passed to the next man and went through the motions all over again.

He found something wrong with nearly every man. It was either " Put your cap on straight" or " Square off your lanyard " with most of them. With one or two it was " Is that your Number One suit ? Well, it's in a disgusting state. Clean it over the week-end and show it to me in the Divisional Office at twelve-thirty on Monday." One man was put off the liberty boat altogether because he had dirty boots.

None of Class 16S got past without some correction given in just the tone of voice to take away much of their pleasure in looking smart. But, anyway, they would be ashore in five minutes.

Or would they?

A Chief Petty Officer saluted Lieutenant Lewis and then turned to the libertymen. He began. " All leave expires INSIDE the gates . . . inside, not outside . . . at twenty-two hundred to-night . . . at ten p.m. Libertymen must not take out more than twenty duty-free cigarettes or one ounce of duty-free tobacco. They must not go outside a ten-mile radius of

the ship. They must not visit the London Road Coffee House."
(" *What the devil is that?* " said every newcomer on the boat to
himself.) " They must not make water in private air-raid
shelters. They must be properly dressed at all times. Lanyards
are to be worn and gas-masks are to be slung in the proper
manner over the left shoulder. Pay proper respects to all officers.
On their return to the ship, libertymen must proceed to their
Divisional Office to collect their cards. They must on no account
loiter in Slop Alley." (" *Hallo, what goes on down there?* " said
every newcomer.) " Should an air-raid warning occur, they
are to obey promptly all orders by Air Raid Wardens."

When he had finished, he again saluted Lieutenant Lewis
and again turned to the libertymen. " Now, you'll march smartly
down to the gates. If you don't, I'll have no hesitation in turning
you round and marching you back," he said. " Libertymen, in
threes, right turn. Quick march."

6

It was a bright, sunny day, though the air was still sharp.
Williams, Redfern, and Holt had decided to take the black-
bearded parson's advice and walk to the W.V.S. canteen at
Beddingham.

Now that they were out of the camp, they began to feel strange
in their uniforms; and the farther away they got from the
sound of bugles and the sight of sailors, the greater became the
pull of civilian ways. The sense of strain, of watching their
step, of wondering whether they were doing something wrong,
passed off. They walked through the sunlight, gloating over
the countryside, the civilians, and the silence, that had come
from another world. They buried themselves in it gratefully.
By the time they reached the canteen they were hungry.

" Another week of this and I'll be as bad as Pincher Martin,"
said Redfern. " I pretend I'm watching him because I'm class
leader and have to get a fair share for everybody. But really
I'm watching to see that he doesn't pinch any helping of mine."

" I'm glad you're watching Pincher," said Holt. " It lets me
get double helpings without being seen."

Inside the canteen there were a number of settees, plenty of
small tables with hard chairs, two ping-pong tables, a billiard
table, and masses of magazines. The three took one look at
all these and turned to more important matters. They saw a
long counter. On the counter were many plates. These plates
were filled with all kinds of cakes. Williams bought six, because
he had not the face to ask for more, but Holt and Redfern had
ten each. They bought some bread and butter, the one bar of
chocolate each they were allowed, and a cup of tea. Then they
started in.

41

" Now," said Holt when they had all finished, " what about supper ? "

They could get supper in the canteen any time after five. There were scrambled eggs on toast, price 6*d*. And there would still be cakes unless some of the soldiers, sailors, and airmen who were now filtering into the canteen swiped the lot.

" What about a walk ? " said Redfern.

" Walk ? " said Holt. " Not bloody likely. Call me at five; " and he eased himself into a corner of a settee and went to sleep.

" I'm going to read a bit," said Williams, and sat down on the settee next to Holt. He was asleep in five minutes.

Redfern went out by himself.

They ate again, heavily, at five, looked through some of the illustrated magazines for a while, and then had a couple in the local. It was a quarter to eight and dark when they came out. They had not to be back at *Frobisher* for another two hours yet, but they were beginning to feel the weight of the place descending on their shoulders.

They were not the first back to the hut. Grassington was there. He'd been in to Chatsport and found a marvellous restaurant where you could get a huge meal for 2*s*. 6*d*. He described the menu in detail. Hart and Gray were there. They'd found the same restaurant. " You tried the roast beef, did you ? We had the chicken," said Gray. " And that sweet was good, wasn't it ? "

Fletcher and Robertson came in soon after with a small suitcase full of chocolate.

" Coo, where did you get that ? How the hell did you manage it ? What's the name of the shop ? "

They had found a shop which allowed you to buy 7*s*. 6*d*. worth of chocolate at a time, and by going round the queue several times they had managed to spend more than £2. They doled out bars of chocolate all round.

The next one back was the calf-like Hall. He was in a bad humour. His mother and father had come down, bringing a big cake. But when he tried to get the cake through the gates, he had been stopped by a fat Master-at-Arms and told that no one was allowed to bring food on board. Luckily his mother was still outside the gates, so he handed the cake back and she was going to send it in by post. Still, he would have to wait a day for it. He might even have to wait two days.

Then a whole bunch came in—Low, Taylor, Sinbad, " Farmer" Perry, and several more—all obviously merry. They had their hats well back on their heads, enough to curl the thin lips of Lieutenant Lewis. Low skipped around the hut, offering liquorice allsorts to anyone he could find; Taylor, a light shining in his normally dull grey eyes, came up to Williams and said, "Well, Mr. Williams, did you have a good time? We did. South Down is a bit of a hole. That old bearded pirate was right. Still, the beer's not too bad, and we found a canteen with some good cakes in it."

"So did we, Mr. Taylor," said Williams. "I ate ten."

"Beat you," said Alf. "Had sixteen myself. All right it was. And you should have seen Farmer Perry in the pub, swilling the beer down and chucking the girls under their chins. Proper snake in the grass, that feller."

It was getting on for ten and there was still no sign of Price, Hardcastle, Nevison, Miller, and Martin. It looked as though they were going to be adrift. Apparently they had gone to see a football match in Chatsport and had later run into Robertson and Fletcher in some café. They were last seen eating their heads off.

The rest turned in slowly, still exchanging their eating reminiscences but keeping one ear open for rounds. Rounds took place every night about ten. A Chief Petty Officer put his head into the hut door, calling "Attention for rounds," and everyone who was not yet in bed had to stand to attention while the Chief followed by the officer on duty and a Master-at-Arms, went quickly through the hut.

As soon as they were passed, the lights went out and the Duty Chief came through again shouting, "Pipe down; get turned in there. Come on now, keep silence." But the whisperings and occasional gigglings went on.

It was not until past eleven that the five missing men turned up, very subdued and apprehensive. They were greeted with a whispered "Where the hell did you get to?" from an interested class who were comfortably conscious that they were not in any trouble themselves.

Price had known of a really good pub, not far away, where three of the barmaids were blonde and didn't need much encouragement. He could find the way all right in the blackout, and there was plenty of time before the bus. The rest had trailed after him and in no time were lost. They had come on another café, and finding that it was not far from the bus station, they had given up the thought of easy blondes and got down to the serious business of eating again. They left in good time to catch the last bus and arrived to find a queue three hundred yards long.

"Three hundred yards long?" said Alf Taylor incredulously.

"Well, thirty yards long at least," said Price.

They had missed that bus, the last that would get them back on time. But they had got a policeman to sign a chit saying that they were at the bus stop in good time, and the policeman had given his name and number and had said that they knew him at *Frobisher*. When they had finally got back, the fat Master-at-Arms had listened to their story, looked at their chit, and told them to report at their Divisional Office at Stand Easy on Monday morning.

The general impression was that they would get ninety days' cells. But they got off with a caution. Lieutenant-Commander Rankin listened to their story, looked at the chit from the policeman, told them never again to rely on the last available bus, and dismissed them, greatly relieved.

Chapter Three

1

CHIEF PETTY OFFICER GRAVES was nurse to the class from early morning until late in the evening. He brought them an iron to press their clothes. He taught them how to wash or " dhoby " their socks and underwear in the big sinks of the washroom. He brought his own needles and thread and taught them how to mend. And he taught them how a sailor " uses his loaf ".

He said, " If you are ever late for parade, sneak out the back way without being seen and then march across to wherever your class is as though you were carrying a vital signal from the Commodore."

If the class paid attention when he was trying to tell them something, acted smartly on state occasions like Divisions, and behaved themselves when officers were near, the Chief let them have a good deal of head. He would pass Low's jokes and sweet-sucking with no more than a " knock off skylarking " or " spit that bloody sweet out ", when there was no one near. But one day Low was sucking his liquorice allsorts when the Training Commander came up. Low did not see the Training Commander, but the Chief *did* and called out in a loud voice: " Class 16S, sir. Instruction in Lowering the Whaler." This reporting of the class was unnecessary, but it served to warn Low and the rest that something unusual was happening. Low promptly swallowed his sweet.

When the Training Commander had passed, the Chief got out of the boat where he had been demonstrating something to three of the class, and came up to Low.

"Look 'ere. I've told you twenty times a day, ever since you came, to behave yourself when officers are about. Why don't you use your bloody loaf? If the Training Commander had seen you sucking your bloody sweets, we'd both 'ave been in the rattle. You'd 'ave lost your bloody card and I might 'ave 'ad my pay stopped. You're a fine lot," he went on, turning to the class. "If I were to run you in, you'd say, 'The dirty old bastard'; but if I don't run you in and then get into trouble myself, you'd only say, 'The silly old runt.'"

"'E was quoite roite," Price said. "That's just what you would say, Low. We've got a bloody good Chief, but some of you are going to spoil 'im and make 'im turn nasty on us."

He might well have turned nasty when he caught the gambling school in session, with little piles of coppers and sixpences on the table. "'Ave you boys read that notice on the wall? Well, then, you know you could get cells for this. Don't keep your bloody money on the table like that for everyone to see. What would happen if Lieutenant Lewis came in? Use your ruddy loaf, and don't any of you go losing your fortnight's pay overnight. That always leads to trouble."

And it *did* lead to trouble, for a few days later Hall, almost in tears, reported to Redfern that his cigarette lighter had been stolen from his locker and Redfern reported the theft to the Chief. The Chief had to report it to the Divisional Officer, who ordered a search of the lockers and cases of everyone in the hut. But there was on lighter.

When the search was over, the Chief sat the class down and lectured everyone.

"You see what 'appens. You get gambling schools going and lads begin to lose money, just as some of you 'ave lost it this last week, I know. Now, I'm not saying that any of you pontoon players 'ave pinched 'All's lighter. But it's gone. Everyone in the 'ut is suspect and the most suspect are naturally those 'oo 'ad most reason to pinch things. Well, I'm not going to 'ave it. I've never 'ad things pinched before in none of my classes and I'm not going to let it start with you. Pinching's one of the worst things you can 'ave on a ship and I'm not going to let any of you go to sea with bad 'abits if I can 'elp it. Give us those cards. There's to be no more card playing, with or without money, while you're in this class. If I catch anybody doing it, I'll put 'im straight in the rattle. Now don't say you 'aven't been warned."

He was angry. But after he had stuffed the cards into his pocket, put on his spectacles, and opened his Seamanship Manual at Nautical Terms, his thoughts wandered.

"I remember once when I was on the old *Vindictive* on the China station," he said. "There was a ship with us that 'ad a thief on board. They caught 'im three times running, 'is

45

messmates did, and warned 'im each time. I don't know what was wrong with the chap, but 'e couldn't keep 'is 'ands off other people's property; and in a small mess deck, where everybody's living on top of everyone else, that won't do. The fellows got so they didn't like to put anything down for a minute.

"Then they caught 'im stealing a fourth time. It was a watch. They found it in 'is locker. 'E swore blind that someone 'ad put it there, but as it 'appened two of 'is messmates 'ad seen 'im pick it off a table and put it away 'imself.

"No one said anything to 'im. But that night, when 'e was asleep in 'is 'ammock, one of them 'it 'im under the jaw to make sure 'e was senseless and then 'e and three others carried 'im up on deck and put 'im a wash-deck locker. Wash-deck locker? It's a great iron chest for keeping brushes and buckets in which you use when you're scrubbing the deck. Its sides and lid are solid iron, but its bottom is a thick iron grating so that the water can run out. They put this chap into the locker, locked the lid, unscrewed the locker from the deck, and chucked the whole lot overboard."

"Did the chap drown?" asked Sinbad.

"No. This two hundredweight locker with an open grid for a bottom floated to Australia and the chap was washed ashore there twenty-five years later none the worse."

*　　*　　*

The Chief was a practical teacher. He hated formal instruction from the Seamanship Manual. He would take out his glasses, open the book, and begin to read in a hesitating way: "*A hammock is slung by clews which are made of three-strand white hemp, and ¾ of an inch in circumference; the nettles are secured to metal rings through which the lanyards are spliced. In slinging a hammock, care must be taken to give the centre nettles 1½ inches more scope than the side ones, length of nettles being gradually diminished towards the sides.*"

But that was enough for everyone, and Jackie Low would break in with "What's a hammock like at sea, Chief? Is it comfortable?", and the Chief would put down the book, take off his spectacles, and say sharply: "Of course it's comfortable. It takes the motion of the ship, though it can be awkward at times. I remember on the old *Vindictive*, we rolled so much one night that I was tipped right out of my hammock into the one alongside.

"Very useful they can be, too. If you lash yours properly, it will keep you afloat for twenty-four hours if you drop in the oggin. Oggin? Why, the drink, the sea, man. Don't you understand plain English? I remember last war, in the Battle of Jutland, we used ours to stop shell-holes in the ship's side. No, we did, no skylark. Saved our bacon, I can tell you."

"What's it like at sea, Chief?"

"Well, it depends what sort of a ship you get. In some of these big ships nowadays you 'ave to take a twopenny bus ride before you can *see* the sea. But they're putting most of you chaps in destroyers, and its a pretty rough life. I've 'ad good times in destroyers, even in the last war. On quiet days you sit up on your gun on watch and read or smoke in the sun. But you don't get so many quiet days. Either the sea's so rough you can't stand, or you're out on some job or other and have to keep your eyes skinned. No, you'll find it hard, all right."

"Do you get much time off, Chief ? "

"Well, that depends where you are. If you're in harbour, you'll work the same sort of hours as we do 'ere. Knock off at four and then the non-duty watch'll go ashore until next day. What sort of work ? Oh, scrubbing the decks, painting ship, lashing things up ready for sea. All sorts of jobs. You've got to be ready for anything.

"When you're at sea, it'll depend a good deal on where you are, whether you are in danger areas or not. In safe waters, you'll work what they call Cruising Stations. That means that only one part of a watch is on duty. You're the Second Part of Port Watch. You may have the Middle Watch—that's from midnight until four a.m., and you stay up on your gun or on lookouts or wherever your cruising station is while the rest get their heads down in their hammocks. Then at four a.m. you gets relieved by the next duty part of the watch, that'll be the First Part of Starboard Watch, and they'll stay on duty right through the Morning Watch until eight a.m. Then the First Part of Port Watch will come on for the Forenoon until twelve-thirty p.m., and they'll be relieved by the Second Part of Starboard, who'll stay through the Afternoon Watch until four p.m. Then you come on again for the First Dog for two hours and you're relieved at six p.m. by the First Starboard, which keeps the Last Dog until eight. Then it's First of Port for the First Watch until midnight.

"That's what they call being in four watches. It's all right, that is. Only one watch in four. If you're lucky, you gets the Last Dog and then you don't 'ave to turn out again until the Forenoon. Last Dog and all night in. Sailor's paradise, that is.

"But in dangerous waters you'll work in two watches. That means that the 'ole of one watch is on duty at a time. Port Watch takes the Middle, perhaps. Then Starboard Watch is up for the Morning and up comes Port Watch again at eight a.m. for the Forenoon. And so it goes on right round the clock. You don't get much sleep on that. Six or seven days of that, with Action Stations thrown in, and you're not fit for much."

"How do you find out where you've got to be on watch ? "

"Well, first thing that 'appens when you join your ship,

you'll be given a card. It'll 'ave the number of your mess on it, say Number Three. It'll 'ave the number of your locker in the mess and the number of your gas-mask locker nowadays. Then, on the card you'll find your Part of Ship—that's the part of the ship where you do your work. It may be the Fo'c'sle, or the Iron Deck—that's in the centre of the ship—or maybe it's the Quarter Deck, right aft. You'll find the Watch you're in—Port or Starboard—and the Part of the Watch—First or Second. You'll find your Action Station—it may be the same for Day and Night or it may be different—your Cruising Station, and your Defence Station. Sometimes you get the same station for Action, Cruising, or Defence. Sometimes you get a different place for each.

" Jesus Chroist," said Price. " 'Ow big is this card ? "

" Oh, they write on both sides. You can stick it in your pocket. But you'd better get to know where your stations are pretty quick. If you are adrift on watch, you get in the rattle before you know where you are. Oh, and you'll find your Abandon Ship station on the card. You'll not forget that, I don't suppose."

2

The Chief was not always good at explaining. He went over a model Fo'c'sle with them.

" That thing there, that's a Fair Lead. Why's it called a Fair Lead ? Why, because it gives you a fair lead, of course," he said, and the class came away with a jumbled mass of bollards, fair leads, deck bolts, Blake screw slips, and Blake screw stoppers tumbling about in their heads.

But always he gave them a sense of the life at sea.

There was a model wheel and compass where the class practised steering a ship.

" Hey, don't heel that ship over like that. You'll have every pot on the mess deck smashed," shouted the Chief, as Alf Taylor swung the helm over 30 degrees to starboard and then suddenly swooped it back to 35 degrees to port.

Then there were knots.

" What's a bowline for, Chief ? " asked Nevison.

" Why, if you're in the drink and one of your messmates throws you a rope, you ties it round your waist with a bowline. Or when you're coming alongside another ship you throw 'eaving lines over. 'Eaving lines ? They're ropes—you'll get some practice with them later—and they've got a 'eavy knot on one end. You takes about a quarter of this coil in your left hand and throws the rest, with the 'eavy knot, with the other. The 'eaving line lands on the deck of the other ship, if you're a good shot, and the lads there tie it to a 'awser. 'Awser ? That's a strong rope or wire. Then you pulls your end of the

48

'eaving line and drags the 'awser from one ship to the other and makes fast. You'll find that the chaps on the other ship 'ave tied your 'eaving line to their 'awser with a bowline—unless they're like you and 'ave just joined the Navy. God knows what sort of a knot you'd find then. Probably none at all and the bloody 'awser's dropped in the drink."

He made them practise climbing from the whaler to the lower boom. They went up a long narrow wire ladder on to a pole fixed horizontally some twenty feet from the ground. Then, grasping a wire, they walked along the pole and down another ladder. It was not easy. Half-way along, Alf Taylor's foot slipped.

"This ruddy pole," he gasped. "I'm trying to be a sailor, not a flicking tight-rope walker. Help me down, Shortarse."

"You wait till you get to sea and you come off shore leave one night with a heavy sea running, and a ruddy gale and you with a load of beer inside you," said the Chief. "Try climbing the Jacob's ladder from the whaler then and see how far you get. It'll be tinkle, tinkle, splash, and they'll be signalling the Depot for your relief."

They were given all sorts of lectures—on discipline, naval customs, politics.

The Chief loathed them.

"Bah! Much better get a Wren to give you an hour's instruction in darning. You'd find that a ruddy sight more useful." And when volunteers were wanted for submarines, or Asdics, the anti-submarine detector listening device, he said: "Don't you volunteer for anything in the Navy until you knows what it's all about. If you volunteer for a thing and don't like it, you can't get out of it, and there you are, stuck for the duration in something you 'ates, with nothing to show for it but a ruddy badge on your arm without pay."

3

Some of the class scarcely needed a warning against volunteering. They shirked everything they could, particularly work in the hut, which had to be done in their own time. They had to be driven. Hall, for example, had to be told after breakfast that it was his turn to sweep the hut. He had to be told again after tea. He had to be told a third time just before Rounds. Price usually had to be told, too, and always complained bitterly. "Oi swept the busstud up yesterday. Oi gets the flicking sweeping every day. Whoi do you always pick on me?" Low did the work cheerfully, but badly. He whisked the broom about, raised the dust, and made everyone cough. One or two just shirked.

It was an agreement that one man should fetch newspapers

for the whole hut every morning from the canteen. All went well until a Saturday when no papers arrived. Low, who was an ardent fan of the *Daily Mirror* comic strips, found it was Hardcastle's turn. Hardcastle said that he had been to the canteen and the papers were sold out.

Low, seriously alarmed at missing one instalment of Reilly-Ffoul, hared off to the canteen and returned with the *Daily Mirror* and the news that the canteen still had plenty of papers.

The whole class turned on Hardcastle. " You ruddy liar. No papers, indeed! You're too bloody lazy. You *read* the papers all right when someone else brings them—and PAYS for them."

Hardcastle said he didn't want the flicking papers and was backed up by Miller and Martin. " We don't *have* to get them. If you want a flicking paper, get it yourself."

The next day, being Sunday, there was a rush for papers. Robertson only managed to get one for the whole hut, and Hardcastle, who was bursting to see if he had come up on the Unity Pool and had gone to get a paper for himself, got none. The class were delighted. They taunted Hardcastle. They asked him which teams he was interested in and how he had marked his coupon. They read bogus results to him, first extremely favourable to his coupon and then the opposite.

When at last he tried to snatch the paper, Price tore out the football page and set fire to it.

* * *

Next morning, Grassington, Holt, Robertson, and Dusty Miller were detailed to sweep the hut.

Dusty was saying he'd be flicked if he'd sweep up and the others were saying he'd be flicked if he didn't when the Chief came in with " There's too much bad language in this hut. Some of you fellows want to wash your mouths out. What's going on ? "

Dusty said: " I've swept this floor once, Chief, and some basstud has dropped cigarettes over it. Make *'im* sweep up. I don't see why I should."

The Chief knew his Miller by now. " Look here. Some of you lads act like a lot of kids. You want a blinking nurse watching over you all the time, telling you to do this and do that. Crickey, can't you get on with a simple job like sweeping without somebody standing over you ? You know, it won't do you any bloody good trying to shirk when you get to sea. You may get away with it once or twice, but your Petty Officer'll soon get wise to you and when 'e's got some particularly dirty job for someone 'e'll send for *you*. You'll find yourself being shoved around and shoved around hard, not just gently as you are 'ere. You work together a little more and shout the bloody odds a little less and you'll get the ruddy work done a sight sooner. Crickey! I wouldn't like to be on your ship. You'd let the ruddy thing sink rather than lift your little finger to do something you thought somebody else should do."

* * * *

Under the Chief, Redfern, as Class Leader, had the thankless job of driving the shirkers and stopping their outbursts. A mixed group of all ages, environments, and temperaments, alike only in being totally unused to the discipline of living together, was dynamite. The first thing to do was to know the technical details of the job, what instructions the class was to have that day or the next, and exactly when they should be out of the hut to fall in; so that the class was always coming to Redfern to ask what the programme was or whether they had time to write a letter or have a shave, relying both on his knowledge and on his watch.

He gave as few orders as possible. There were some rules which had to be kept. It was difficult, at first, to stop the boys from talking after " Pipe Down " at 10 p.m. They called it being treated as kids. But Redfern pointed out that if he did not stop them talking, the Duty Chief would take their cards and put Redfern himself in the rattle for not keeping order, most of the class were reconciled to the curfew.

But one Saturday night Hardcastle and Pincher Martin came on board tipsy. Pincher was giggling and Hardcastle singing. Redfern told him to stop. Hardcastle threatened to knock his block off and Martin went on giggling.

" You can knock my block off if you like, but you're going to stop singing and get into bed. If you don't I shall send for the Duty Chief and get him to take your card."

" Oh, go home to mother."

" Are you going to get into bed ? "

" Like flick I am."

" Very well," said Redfern, and went for his clothes. Hardcastle watched him for a few moments as he dressed. Then with a stream of invective against Redfern, the Navy, and life in general, he heaved himself fully dressed into his blankets and went to sleep, and Redfern got back into his own bed.

* * *

Holt, his deputy, absorbed himself into the hut life from the beginning. He was a regular member of the pontoon school, he was always nearly late for everything, he regularly went to sleep in the cinema lectures, where it was dark, he went ashore to the pictures whenever he could, he argued, quarrelled, swore, swopped magazines and dirty jokes, complained and laughed like anyone in the class.

His height delighted everyone. He could clean the rafters of the hut without standing on a chair. He could reach out of his bed, across the intervening bed, and cuff Sinbad's head

51

when that old salt became obstreperous. The class loved to see Holt and Sinbad having an argument. Holt seemed to grow taller and calmer, Sinbad shorter and redder, as the argument went on. Finally, Sinbad would shout, " You just bend down forty-five degrees and I'll knock your ruddy ears back," and the class would say, " Go on, Sinbad. Get ten others and fight 'im."

Everyone in the class liked Holt. He possessed and made no attempt to conceal the impressive names of Richard James de Courcy Holt, but he was affectionately known as Shortarse.

The incident which sealed his popularity occurred after a pillow fight which had raged along the passage and through three huts. The fight was fierce but friendly until someone thought of putting his tin hat in his pillow and hit some tough youth with it. The youth was temporarily stunned, and before he could recover the Duty Chief had arrived and the combatants scurried back to their huts and got into bed.

They were just settling down for the night, with rounds over and only the emergency lamp burning, when the door of Class 16s was burst open and a huge figure plunged in and stood in the gangway between the beds, panting. He had only two teeth, sticking out like fangs, and a nasty-looking black bulge on his forehead as though he had just been hit by a tin helmet.

" Who done it ? " he gasped. " Which of you flickers done it ? I'm going to smash the faces of every one of you flickers unless I find the basstud who done it."

No answer.

" You dirty, sodding basstuds. I'll get the lot of you. I'll smash your bloody bones to pulp, I will. I'll make you sorry that you ever was born."

" Flick off," said a voice.

" 'Oo said that ? 'Oo said that ? Which of you flickers said that ? "

The blankets on one of the beds moved as Shortarse eased his head out. His head was followed by his neck, his neck by his shoulders, and his shoulders by the upper part of his body.

The gorilla stared. There was enough showing from the bed to make two men already, yet more was coming. The voice from the bed added two more words. It said, " I did."

The gorilla's mouth opened and shut several times. He was having some trouble with his breath. At last he said, " I'll get you for this, you bastards," and heaved himself out of the hut. Class 16S saw him no more.

* * *

Williams was treated gently. He was an older man, they thought, and therefore entitled to consideration. One or two were even anxious about the effect of rigorous P.T. on his health and strength.

52

" Could 'e stand it ? Why didn't 'e ask to be excused ? That chap in the next 'ut 'ad done, 'im wot 'ad the gout. 'E went down to the orrifice and said, ' Look 'ere. That flicking P.T. of yours 'as brought on me flicking gout. I'm not doing any more of the flicker,' and the orrificer 'ad said to 'im, ' I should flicking well think not. You'd better not do any more flicking square-bashing either,' and the chap had said, ' Oh, I can manage the flicking square-bashing. I want some flicking exercise. It's just the flicking P.T. that brings on my flicking gout.' Why didn't Williams try it on ? "

They took pity on someone who was so obviously helpless. Real work, putting studs in boots, folding clothes, using an iron, mending socks—an office worker could not be expected to know about these things.

And they asked him things—how to spell words or translate French tags which were always cropping up in letters from girl-friends; and several times Hardcastle consulted him about phrases he wanted to put in a letter to a girl on Tyneside who was asking for explanations.

Fletcher, who had talked about printing that day in the train, tickled the others immensely by his refusal to use the bad language which flew so generally about the hut. " Well, I'm snookered," or " Oh, you badger," he would say, and they were delighted. The phrases had quite a vogue. Pincher Martin would turn on Hardcastle with a sudden " You besom, you. You've snookered my collar." But after a while they grew slightly contemptuous. " Why don't you say what you mean ? " asked Pincher. " What's the sense of saying basket when you mean bastard ? "

" If I used a word like that in my house, my old man would wallop me."

" So would mine, but I'm not in my house. And my old man's not here."

Harry Robertson was quiet as a rule, but could be stirred by some particularly glaring generalisation of Price's in the arguments on politics, religion, sport, and women, which rolled up and down the hut in the evenings.

He took his new job seriously and spent quite a lot of his spare time reading his Seamanship Manual, but he could not forget Civvy Street.

" What are you going to do after the war, Harry ? " they would ask him.

" Oh, same as I did before, I expect. Fell-mongering. I'd a good job."

" What did you have to do ? "

" When I first went in, after I left school, I was handling the skins in the warehouse, learning to sort them. My dad was in the business, you see, and got me in, too. He was foreman in

53

the warehouse and taught me how to tell one skin from another and how to sort them. It's a hell of a job. There are so many kinds. My dad's been in it for forty-one years and says he can't see the end of it yet. There's always something new to learn. After three years, when I was seventeen, the boss took me out of the warehouse and sent me as assistant to one of the travellers. We went all over the shop. It was grand!"

"Why did you join up, then? Weren't you reserved?"—

"Well, yes. We were handling a lot of Service stuff—fur-lined gloves and that sort of thing that they use on ships. But you see, whenever I got back to London I'd find that another of my mates had gone and it got to be lonely in the end. So I said to my dad, 'Well, I suppose I'd better be going too,' and he said, 'Very well, if you think so, Harry,' and here I am. But I'll be glad, all the same, when I can get back to my job."

As for Alf Taylor, Alf of the doleful face, sudden ear-splitting song, and the cry of anguish, his cry was often raised. A lull in the hut would be shattered. "Oh, flick me! Some bastard's stolen my Jean," and there would be Alf, with his hands hanging disconsolately at his sides, his mouth slightly open, and his figure motionless in exasperation. The Jean would, of course, be under Alf's "waistcoat" as he would call his jumper, or in his locker. But five minutes later he would again be accusing all and sundry of pinching his "flicking trousis". Such anguish went into these frequent cries that the hut gave him the name of Calamity.

He had no respect for authority and was always being pulled up for failing to salute. "'Ow the flicking hell did I know 'e was an officer? Yesterday I saluted six cooks, ten sick-berth attendants, and a ruddy Naffi canteen manager, to say nothing of petty officers, chief petty officers, and the like. I can't tell one peaked cap from another. Stuff my buckets!"

But he was interested in learning new things and particularly wanted to get over to the Gunnery Section and have a go at the guns.

He had been working in an aircraft factory when the war broke out, and as soon as he was eighteen he made himself such a nuisance that the firm were glad to give him his cards and let him join up.

"Bloody fool I was, I suppose. Could've stayed there all through the war. But I wanted to get into something."

*   *   *

This group was not exactly a clique. But if one of them thought of going to the pictures or the canteen he would find out whether another was thinking of going too. In the same way, Price, Cole, Hardcastle, Miller, and Martin hung together.

Price talked incessantly in a whining voice about the cold, falling in, about everything they had to do. Like Calamity

Taylor, he was always losing things. The class would go to sleep to the sound of " Oi put me basstud gloves on me bed not two minutes ago and now one of you basstuds 'as swoiped 'em," and would wake next morning to hear Price saying " Yes. One minute they was there, the next minute they was swoiped. Oi dunno. Can't leave anything 'ere for a basstud second."

The gloves were in his greatcoat-pocket all the time.

" Oi'm a Communist," he would say. " Oi don't think Jerry's so bad. There's a lot over 'ere who are as bad, anyway. Look at this blasted Government. They just represent vested interests. They're not put there by the people—not by us blokes 'oo 'ave to fight their basstud war, anyway. We were too young to vote when the last General Election was on. But we're not too young to foight, not bleeding loikely."

" What constituency do you live in ? "

Price did not know.

" Well, who's your M.P. ? "

He did not know.

" Well, if you don't take enough interest in politics even to know your M.P., how the hell do you expect to get a decent Government ? "

" Oh, shut your flicking mouth."

" Is that the way they teach you to argue in the Communist party ? "

* * *

Cole had a lot to say, too. He " explained " things to the class while the Chief was demonstrating them and talked so learnedly about the contraption for releasing the whaler when it had been lowered to the water that it became known to the class as " Cole's Disengaging Gear " and Cole himself became " Professor ".

He really was a quick learner. One day they were receiving a lesson in boxing the compass and after a few minutes Professor Cole went fast asleep. The Chief did not notice him for a moment, then he bellowed. The Professor woke up and was told to recite the compass points backwards from east to north. Cole did so, then put his head against the wall and again went off to sleep. He finished that period running round the parade-ground.

It was a wonder how anyone got a word in when Cole and Price were around. But Dusty Miller could talk the others down. He had a loud voice, used mainly to denounce anyone who suggested that there was a better wrestler than his particular favourite or to assert that So-and-so had bigger biceps in his championship days than someone else, and that there was no town in the world like Newcastle.

Dusty wanted to be taken for a real sailor. He saw how the dye ran out of Blue Jeans when they had been washed a few

55

times, so that the collars of " old hands " among the trainees were light instead of dark blue. He washed his collars over and over again and even put them on the deck and scrubbed them with a stiff broom until the last trace of dye had been removed. He brought extra long ribbons from a shop in South Down, sewed them to his jumper, and, instead of tying them in a bow, he left them flowing free and said it was " tiddly ". With the help of Calamity Taylor he cut open his bellbottoms and put gussets in, so that instead of being the regulation thirty inches round the bottom, his were thirty-eight.

So dressed, he marched into a lecture by Chief Petty Officer Wacker Paine. Wacker took one look at the bellbottoms and an expression of disgust curled over his face.

" Call yourself a sailor. You look more like a flicking cowboy."

Dusty did not mind. He was put off the liberty boat by Lieutenant Hollis for being improperly dressed, but he went on wearing his non-regulation suit, seemingly afraid of no one and nothing—except water.

They had been issued with lifebelts and were taken by the Chief to test them in a tank. The idea was that they should go into the tank with their belts on, so that even non-swimmers would get confidence when they found they floated.

Dusty stood on the edge of the tank, his magnificently built body quite naked except for his lifebelt, and looked at the water. " Go on," said the Chief, " we haven't got all day "; then, realising what was the matter, he began to coax. At last Miller lowered himself into the tank, but wouldn't leave go of the side. The Chief became more insistent and lifted the hands from the side and pushed him into the middle of the tank. Miller began to scream and struggle. He reached the side and clung to it.

" Let me get out, Chief, let me get out! I can't stand it! "

So the Chief pulled him out.

He was soon the complete sailor again and went into Chatsport to get himself tattooed.

" Coo! " he said. " It's a grand place, that tattoo shop. You can get all kinds. You can 'ave a picture of your ship, or 'e'll do a girl's face on your chest. Or you can 'ave a Chinaman with a knife through 'is forehead and blood dripping out. Buckets of it. Then there's a snake. And there's one of those long-necked bastards. That's right. A gee-raffe. *And* elephants. All sorts of animals. Oo-oo! and a lovely thing to remind you of your mother—a flicking great tombstone. Covers the whole of your back, it does. Coo! Flicking smashing, it was, I can tell you."

The rest of the class took his word for it.

Grassington still kept to himself. He had cheered up, but he seldom went out with any of the others. His wife often managed to come down to stay at the Blue Boar, and there he was with his wife and two children strolling through the streets, pater-familias once again and, for a few hours at least, no longer the uprooted civilian in fancy dress.

Then he volunteered for a special course because it looked like a sedentary occupation, and left the class and *Frobisher*, before the end of his time.

*   *   *

Low and Sinbad were just the reverse of Grassington. They mixed with everybody. Low went in for the boxing competition and came out with a black eye. He played soccer for the hut side, and though he had never played or even seen rugger in his life he volunteered to play in an inter-Division match when someone dropped out at the last minute. At the end, he came back to the hut gasping, with blood on his right leg. " Now that it's all over can anyone tell me who won ? " And always he sucked his liquorice allsorts.

Sinbad was always full of wide-eyed interest. He read his Seamanship Manual, he asked the Chief endless questions, he joined in any argument that was going. And he laughed. That laugh of his made his podgy body quiver like a jelly. It turned his face more and more scarlet. The longer the laugh lasted the fruitier it became, until those who wanted to sleep either stuffed pillows over Sinbad's head or began laughing themselves. He talked about the Navy with an air of pontifical wisdom, quoting " my tart's father ", who had served thrity years in the Navy, as his authority. Sinbad was determined that once he had got himself into the Navy, nothing but death should get him out.

Low and Sinbad were one of the first bonds to link the class together. Other bonds grew out of their common experiences, like that pillow fight, and Dusty Miller in the tank ; and the scrubbing of Hall. Hall did not wash. He began to smell, and a man who smells in cramped living-quarters, where everyone is on top of his neighbour, becomes a public nuisance. One evening some half-dozen of the class carried the struggling Hall to the washroom and bathed him forcibly. He wept bitterly, but was none the worse afterwards.

Above all, there was Perry's ploughboy marching. Every day the class had to be halted, and Perry would be pulled out of the ranks to be shown how to swing his right arm as his left foot went forward. Then the class would move forward again.

But Perry was still lumbering in the same old way. The in-structor would bring him out again and put someone on either side of him, holding his arms and swinging them at the right moments. Perry would grin rather sheepishly, but would lapse into his old habits as soon as his arms were released.

Then he was set to walking round the parade-ground, swinging his arms properly, while the class got on with their instruction, and as his fame spread he would be watched by every instructor on the parade and receive advice, usually unhelpful, from their delighted classes.

Things went on like this for three weeks and then, one day, the class marched off and were not halted. Soon the front ranks sneaked glances to the rear to find out why. And then they saw. Perry was marching right, swinging his arms in proper time and looking straight to this front.

The Navy had won.

*   *   *

Several weeks later they were to go over to the Gunnery; but, first, there was a seamanship examination. They heard terrible stories of men in other classes being kept back a week because they had failed their examination, and that, to boys who wanted to get at the guns and who, moreover, wanted to get home on leave, was a fate worse than death.

They need not have worried. The Chief himself was examiner. At the end he said the whole lot had failed and marked down Very Good or Very Good Indeed on all their papers.

The next day they transferred to Gunnery.

Chapter Four

1

" You're in the Gunnery Section now. It's very different from the Seamanship Division. You've got to stand on your own feet, and you'll be watched every moment of the day. So take care you don't slip up.

" You must call your instructors ' sir '. That may go against the grain, but you've got to do it, all the same. And you've got to pay careful attention to what they tell you. You're coming to one of the most important aspects of war-time Navy life. You can't afford to have people making mistakes on guns. So take care you learn what your instructors have to tell you.

" If you don't, you'll be killing one of your own pals when you get to sea, if I don't kill you before you leave here."

A strange man, this Gunner's Mate. He preached murder that morning, and in the evening asked Williams what political party he belonged to.

" The Labour Party, sir."

" You know, that's not going to do you any good. I used to belong to the Labour Party once. But I gave it up. I found it wasn't any good. You find these things out pretty soon in the Service."

" What do you belong to now ? "

" The Communist Party," said the Gunner's Mate, winking broadly. " Come over here and have a talk."

The Gunnery Section was full of strange men like this.

On their first day the class idly played at throwing their hats on to pegs in a lecture-room. Suddenly there was a roar, and a lion-like, red-headed man yelled " 'Shun," and the class petrified itself. The Lion-man stared at the class.

" Perhaps I had better tell you that the parade-ground is 357 yards long and 173 yards wide," he said. " If it comes to a choice between standing on my feet in a stuffy lecture-room bawling my guts out at a crowd of ill-mannered hooligans, and sitting in the sun while these same hooligans work off their surplus energy running round the parade-ground, I shan't hesitate to choose the sun for myself, and the parade-ground for the hooligans. Do you get the idea ?

" Class, off caps. Hang your caps on the hooks. Don't leave any holidays. Sit down on the benches. And shut your ruddy mouths. Didn't I tell you not to leave any holidays ? Who's hat is that ? "

Calamity turned yellow, moved his hat to a peg alongside the others, and came back muttering, " ' Holidays ' indeed. If he means ' gaps ', why the flicking hell doesn't he *say* ' gaps ' ? " he grumbled.

The Lion-man began instruction. The contraption in one corner of the room, he said, was a practice loader. As an introduction to gunnery the class was to practise picking up dummy shells and charges, placing them on a tray fixed to a breech, and ramming them forward so that they slid up the open tray on the other side. He formed them in teams of seven and set them one against another to see how many shells and charges they could ram into the breech in a minute.

Each team threw itself into the job, while the Lion-man stood by with his watch in his hand and roared abuse and encouragement until the minute was up.

When every team had had its turn, the Lion-man said: " That's not bad. Not bad at all. You're one of the best classes I've had for some time. Do it ten times as fast as that and they *may* consider putting one or two of you into gun crews when you get to sea—if one of a real gun's crew falls ill."

He paused. Then: " Being in a gun's crew's all right. But it's not like the old days. A gun's all very well—but give me a cutlass."

" Did you really use to have cutlasses in the Navy, sir ? "

" Of course we used to have cutlasses. We still do. If you get on a small ship you'll find 'em there all right. Use 'em if someone tries to board you."

" How do you use them ? "

" Like this: cut, thrust; cut, thrust "; and the Lion-man began to prance round the room beheading imaginary enemies. " But this doesn't get us very far with loading. Now, number three team, you did best. Come again and see if you can break your record."

From the Lion-man they marched off to the Bull-frog. The Bull-frog was a tubby little man with bulging eyes and baggy cheeks. Did he come from a whisky marsh ? Or was he Charles Laughton ? He certainly looked evil-tempered and sinister.

" Left, right; left, right. Mark time. Pick your feet up. PICK YOUR FEET UP. You. YOU, you bloody great clodhopper, I'm talking to YOU! " and he pointed a menacing hand at Perry. " Class, halt. Right turn. You there, that clodhopper. Give me your card."

It was a serious thing in *Frobisher* to have your card taken. It meant no shore leave; it meant explanations before your Divisional Officer, and, probably, seven days' " Number Eleven ", or worse.

The Bull-frog looked at the card, screwing up his eyes until they were nearly covered by pouches of skin. " Perry, eh ? And where might you come from ? Oh, you do, do you ? Do you know Church Street ? And do you know a fellow who lives there called George Perry ? "

" That's my dad," said Perry.

" And that's my brother," said the Bull-frog, at which there was a great deal of ee-ing and ah-ing and shaking of heads.

Then the Bull-frog tucked Perry's card into his own pocket with a slow, underhand smile and turned to the gun.

" This gun is worked by a crew of seven," he said. " The class will number off into gun crews. The first seven will number off one to seven. The eighth in the front rank will begin again at number one, the ninth will be number two, and so on, until you've all numbered. Gun crews, NUMBER."

" One," said Redfern. " Two," said Low. " Three," said Martin. " Four," said Fletcher. " Five," said Nevison. " Six," said Grassington. " Seven," said Williams. " Eight," said Holt, who had been looking at the gun instead of listening to the Bull-frog.

" As you were," yelled the Bull-frog, and walked slowly to where Holt stood. He looked at Holt's feet; he looked at his knees; he looked at his chest, which was about level with his eyes. Then he forced back the rolls of fat at the back of his neck and looked at Holt's shoulders. He stepped back a pace and peered at Holt's face. He turned slightly sideways and looked again, letting his eye run slowly down the full length of Holt's body.

"H'm," he said. "Fifty fathoms, and no flicking bottom. Let me see your card. H'm! name of Holt. Where do you come from, Holt ? Oh, you do, do you ? Do you know Station Square ? Do you know the Rose and Crown there ? Ever been in for a drink ? No, of course you haven't. Too young! " And he tucked Shortarse's card into his pocket.

The class were numbered off in gun crews. Number one crew stood at ease behind the gun, and Bull-frog began. " Number one gun's crew, 'SHUN. NUMBER. STAND-AT-EASE. Now then. Hat the order ' One ', number one, and number one only, springing to attention and moving at the double, will take up 'is position hat the left of the gun, in rear of the handwheel, facing the muzzle. ' ONE '."

At this Redfern leaped out of the ranks and doubled to the position.

" Hat the order ' Two ', number two, and number two only, springing to attention and moving hat the double, will place 'imself hon the right of the gun facing the breech. ' Two '," and Low shot forward to his place.

" Now," said the Bull-frog, when No. 7 was in place, " hat the order ' change rounds ' you will hall move up one. Number one will take the place of number two, number two will take the place of number three, and so on. Number seven will take the place of number one. CHANGE ROUNDS."

They got into a hopeless muddle, and there were seven more station cards in the Bull-frog's pocket.

" Now we'll try that again," he said, grinning at them fiendishly. They got it right at last, were allowed to rest, and the next gun's crew was put through it.

By the end of the period not one of the class still had his station card. But as they marched away, the Bull-frog handed the cards to Redfern. " 'Ere. You'd better not leave these behind. They come in useful sometimes."

The class went on to Cheerful Charlie, who was doing a spell of instructing to recover from eight days in an open boat. He taught them about ammunition. He showed them the various kinds of projectiles—star shells, semi-armour piercing, and high explosive—and the charges which propelled these projectiles. He showed how S.A.P. shells were intended to explode, not on impact, but when they had bored their way into the ship's side. The impact with the ship's side set a fuse going which exploded the shell after an interval.

In the middle of explaining about the fuse on a high-explosive shell, he was reminded of a story.

" Talking of these H.E.s being fused to go off at a certain

time reminds me of a night I spent in Portsmouth last winter. We'd just come in from sea, and I goes into a pub and sees a nice-looking girl sitting in a corner and she gives me the old glad eye, and, by and by, I goes over to her. It all finishes up with me going home with her, and the first thing I says when we gets to her house is, ' Have you got an alarm clock ? I've got to get back to the ship by eight a.m.,' and she says, ' Don't you worry about an alarm clock. I know something that will sight setter sits behind the gun with a small key which fits into the fuse. Using the key, he can turn the fuse to any setting, so that it will go off at, say, eighteen thousand feet or twenty-four thousand feet or whatever he wants. Yes, Chief ? "

The story did not make sense, because a tall, formidable-looking man, with stone-grey hair and a severe face, was standing in the doorway. It was Dartmoor Dan, the Gunnery Instructor, or Gunner's Mate, who had a habit of creeping silently into lecture-rooms, to inspect the instructors as much as the trainees.

The G.I. went out again, and Cheerful Charlie blew out his cheeks, winked, and finished his story.

2

The class spent some weeks going from Cheerful Charlie to the Bull-frog and from the Bull-frog to the Lion-man, but not always for instruction in the same part of gunnery. One day they marched into a new lecture-room which had charts on the wall and instruments on a long table. It was only when they heard the familiar " Let me see your card " that they realised they were going to have an hour with the Bull-frog.

The Bull-frog and the class were now firm friends. He was always on A.R.P. duty when they were on duty and he slept in the trailer pump-house with four of them. Every night he used to " win " cocoa and cake from the Chief Petty Officers' Mess and give them to the trailer-pump party. It was because Fletcher, on seeing him come into the lecture-room, had greeted him with " Any cake to-night, Chief ? " that the Bull-frog had asked to see his card.

That day he told them about the methods by which the guns were all aimed and fired at once, how three men, perched in the director, laid and trained all the main guns of a ship on to the target.

" If hevery gunlayer on the ship is laying just 'is hown gun, you'll get a different hangle on hevery gun, so that, hinstead of hall 'itting the target, you're spattering hall round it. But hin the director, you put your best gunlayer. 'E lays 'is sights and passes on what 'e thinks is the correct hangle to hevery gunlayer by means of these 'ere receivers." He pointed to the brass-enclosed dials on the table before him. " The gunlayer on the gun watches the pointer in 'is dials and when it moves 'e moves 'is gun. That means that hevery gun on the ship 'as got the same hangle of helevation. And it's the same with the trainers. They follow their receivers. Well, the director layer may 'ave made a mistake. The shells fall short, see? All 'e does is to raise the hangle a bit, all the gunlayers follow suit, and Bob's you huncle."

Another day Cheerful Charlie taught them lookouts. At one end of the room he had a table on which were a number of model ships. At the other end was a rail. Four of the class stood at the rail with a pair of glasses each. The main lights were switched off; in a few minutes the table was faintly illuminated.

"Now, that's the sort of light you'll get at night at sea. Look through the glasses and tell me how many ships you can see."

The four at the rail looked hard for about a minute. "How many do you see, number one?"

Number one was Fletcher. He said there were eight. Cole said there were ten. Nevison could see thirteen, and Price said he had counted twenty for sure and thought there was another one on the extreme right.

There were only six.

When the lights came on, Shortarse was fast asleep. Cheerful Charlie went straight across and shook him. "Look here, my lad, I know that it's turned warm to-day and that you've had a lot of work. But you'd better not get into the habit of going to sleep when there's any lookout work to be done. So just pick up this shell, will you? It weighs about sixty pounds. Carry it round to the next lecture-room, and ask the Instructor what he would like you to do with it. I want to see if he has got the same idea as me," he added with a leer.

Bull-frog was in the next lecture-room. "Oh," said the Bull-frog, "it's old six foot five of flick-all, is it? Well, I think the Instructor next door would like to see you. Just take your projectile round and show it to 'im, will you?"

And so it went on, for Shortarse, until stand easy.

Most of their instruction was on the 4.7 quick-firer. They were drilled in the details of the job to be done by each member of a crew: number one, the gunlayer; number two, the breech worker and captain of the gun; number three, loading number or rammer, and so on to number seven, sight setter and communication number. They were given exercises on the gun, each taking different position for each exercise until they could repeat the formulae in their sleep. They were given loading practice, not on the loading machine any more, but on the gun itself with real shells and charges filled with rubbish to the right weight. It was hard work.

A week before they had expected to go on leave the course

was extended for another two weeks to include training in land warfare.

The course was new. "I don't know much about this thing," said a Chief with a tommy-gun in his hand. "But once you are used to handling weapons of any sort the others usually come easy. This 'ere is the magazine," he said, holding up a circular object and then fixing it with some difficulty to the gun. "Now, this will be the cocking handle. It ought to work like this," and he pulled and pushed at it, pointing the gun at the class, up in the air, or anywhere.

Suddenly, rat-a-tat-tat, and the gun fired. Three small holes appeared in the corrugated-iron roof.

"Now, boys, I'm sorry about that. Must 'ave touched the trigger when I was jerking the cocking handle. That's the worst of these American things. They're not made as safe as our own stuff. Now, don't say anything about this or you'll get me in the rattle, proper. I'll just mention it to the office, but don't you say a word, will you?"

Next day they again marched to this drill shed and again were faced by an Instructor with a tommy-gun in his hand. But it was a different Instructor. So the other old boy *had* got in the rattle after all. Poor old boy! Still, it *was* his fault.

They settled themselves and the Instructor began.

"This," said the new Instructor, "is a tommy-gun. It's an American weapon. You'll 'ave seen it used on the films, I dare say. I don't know much about it myself, but I'll soon learn," at which the class, as one man, threw themselves on the deck.

The last two weeks passed pleasantly if rather slowly. Grassington left *Frobisher* to begin his course, and the two love-birds, Gray and Hart, deciding to take a course in Asdics, left also. The remainder washed and ironed, and argued.

The class had not yet had their gunnery tests and everyone wanted to pass and get a recommend. The recommend might mean a course at the famous naval gunnery school near Chatsport. Anyway, everyone was genuinely interested in gunnery, tests or no tests. So they argued regularly with each other about deflection, trajectory, angle of sights, and what to do if the gun misfired three times in succession—"Chuck the ruddy thing away," said Low—and many other things to do with guns.

The first week in May came and went and the second dragged slowly through the Monday, Tuesday, and Wednesday. On Thursday the class was to leave *Frobisher* and march into a week's leave.

They held themselves back and tried to concentrate on other things—saying good-bye to their old Chief, stocking up with the right number of cigarettes, putting in an extra bit of soap for the old lady, and, above all, ironing. The hut iron was in constant use every spare moment of the day. The class ironed their

Number One suits. They ironed clean handkerchiefs. They polished their boots, brushed their best caps, washed their lanyards, and put all kinds of concoctions on their hair. Then, at last, they went to bed.

Low was out again at 4 a.m. Williams was last out and yet was fully dressed when the bugle blew its piercing blast at six. How the class turned on that bugle! " Go on, you silly flicker. Blow your bastard guts out," shouted Calamity Taylor.

" Wakey, wakey. Roise and flicking shine," yelled Price.

" This time to-morrow I'll be fast asleep in bed and my missus will bring me up a cup of tea about eleven," said Low.

" This time to-morrow I'll just about be getting into bed. And not by myself, either," said Dusty Miller.

They carried their gear to the waiting lorries and marched to breakfast.

Then there was tragedy. Somebody upset a cup of tea over Calamity's Blue Jean.

Calamity leaped up. He grabbed his handkerchief and began to mop. The stumbling offender, after a moment of panic, mopped too. But it was no use. The Jean would not look the same until it had been washed. Then Calamity remembered that his only other Jean was packed deep in his kitbag which was already loaded on the lorry. He rushed out; but the lorry had gone.

Williams and Price followed Calamity out. They found him standing speechless, but calm, where the lorry should have been.

" Oh, well," he said at last. " It _would_ have to happen to me! Oh, flick it, flick it, flick it! "

Williams and Price seized him by the arm and bundled him into the hut. They undid his collar and dragged it from under his " waistcoat." They rushed it to the washroom and soaked it. Then they rushed back to the drying-room and, putting a sheet of newspaper over the hottest pipe, they held the Jean against it for a few minutes. Then they rushed for the iron and steamed out the creases and the remainder of the damp. Then Redfern seized the iron and ran with it as a parting present to the Chief for his next class; and all of them arrived breathless on the parade-ground just as the three classes who were leaving that morning received the order to fall in behind the band.

As they were falling in, Cheerful Charlie came by. He waved a hand.

" Lads, you're leaving home."

They jeered.

They were _going_ home. As they stepped out behind the band, they held their suitcases with one hand and swung their disengaged arms shoulder high in the best parade-ground manner, backs straight, heads up, swinging away home for a week.

They were going home. No need to think of anything but that.

Chapter Five

1

"LADS, you're leaving home."

The hot May sunshine beat down on pig-swill piled in the colonnade outside the windows of H mess. Fumes from the pig-swill passed heavily through the windows and mingled with the smell of food and sweat within.

Four hundred men, in space designed to house two hundred and fifty, struggled to stow their hammocks or to wash in basins which had no plugs. Four hundred men, exhausted by the heat before their day's work had begun, jostling stickily for breakfast round a trestle table, gasping for air—these were would-be officers of the Royal Naval Volunteer Reserve; and among them were Redfern, Holt, and Williams.

The three had been picked from the class at *Frobisher* as potential officers—C.W.s for short. If, after at least three months at sea, they were recommended by their Captain, they would appear before an Admiralty Selection Board. If they were recommended by the Board, they would begin a three months' Officers' Training Course. If they lasted the course and were recommended by another Board at the end of it, they would become Acting Temporary Probationary Sub-Lieutenants.

In the meantime they were housed in the Royal Naval Barracks Chatsport, awaiting draft.

Within five minutes they wished they were back at *Frobisher*. Within two days they wished to God they were at sea. One man alone made the place bearable.

This was Chief Petty Officer Crump, who was in charge of the C.W.s. He had a lively tongue and his sayings had long ago become barrack legends handed down from one group of C.W.s to another. A C.W. called Blunt, who was generally reputed to be mad, arrived late for parade one morning and began to put on his equipment in his usual lackadaisical manner.

"What the bloody hell do you think you are doing, Blunt?" roared Crump.

"I'm meditating on the Gospel according to St. John."

"The Gospel according to St. John? St. John? 'Oo the bloody 'ell is 'e? Another of you flicking C.W. candidates, I suppose."

On their first morning Crump addressed the C.W. Company. As he talked, he took six quick little steps to the right, then turned sharply about and took six quick little steps to the left, doing this over and over again until he had finished talking. And as he talked, his pale eyes stared over the heads of the men he was addressing at the red brick wall behind.

" You are the Duty Company. You will be on duty from now until o-eight-three-o to-morrow morning. It is your duty at all times to defend the barracks against invasion.

" You are responsible at all times for your equipment. DON'T leave it lying about in the rain. 'Ang it on an 'ook in the armoury And not on hany 'ook. 'Ang it hon your hown 'ook, so you'll know where it is. You falls in next, 'ERE, at sixteen-fifty this evening. You falls in after that at twenty-one-thirty. 'ERE. And if you gets the double red through or you hears it on the broadcaster during the day or if at night you gets the single red and they pipes you to fall in on the Quarter Deck, you falls in 'ERE . . . FIRST. DON'T go wandering off into the night . . . bleating like sheep . . . and getting lost. But fall in 'ERE . . . HAT THE DOUBLE.

" And any times you falls in, DON'T come dribbling along in twos and threes, chattering yer bloody 'eads off. You gets fell in at the rush as quick as Christ'll let you, when you 'ears the pipe. AND," said Chief Petty Officer Crump in conclusion, " them as is keen gets fell in previous."

He was about to march the company to the parade-ground for Divisions when a fat stoker strolled by between him and the squad. His mouth opened to blast the stoker, but he thought better of it, took a pace back, put his head on one side, looked at the stoker, then at the company, and said, " Huh! The man with the child-bearing 'ips! Company, 'shun. Right turn. Sling arms. Quick march."

Half-way across the parade-ground he shouted, " Halt."

" Lads, I've some good news for you. My first roses 'ave burst in bloom. I'm a lover of the soil, I am. A lover of the soil. I'm like Beverley Nichols. When I sees a daffodil, I swoons. Company, quick march." -

The hardest work was easy and pleasant under C.P.O. Crump, but even he could not keep the attention of Redfern, Holt, and Williams from the draft notice-board.

At last, three weeks after they had first come into barracks, a list went up with five names on it—Denton, Hamilton, Holt, Redfern, and Williams. They had to report to the office immediately. At the office they were told they were being drafted to the *Marsden*, a six-year-old destroyer which was in dock for a refit. She would be recommissioning in a few days' time. They were to have a medical examination that morning and were to leave next day to begin a week's Gunnery course at the Naval School near by.

" What sort of ship is she ? "

The man in the Divisional Office opened his *Jane's Fighting*

Ships and showed a picture of a destroyer of the same class as the *Marsden.* She looked all right. She was 1,200 tons, and that was bigger than some.

" What run is she on ? "

" Well, I believe she's been to Russia. She'll probably do that again, but, of course, I don't know."

" I hope to Chwist it's not Wussia," said Hamilton, who had some difficulty with his Rs.

" Why not ? " asked Williams. " Is it a very bad run ? "

" I don't know anything about that. I just don't want to help Wussia in any way. I hope the Wussians and the Germans wipe each other out. I'm a Conservative. Do you think there is any chance of changing my draft ? "

The man in the office looked at him. " You'll have to see the Commander. Now you'd better be getting over to the medical. If you're late, old Surgeon-Commander Planter will chew you into small pieces and you won't need to change your draft."

Off they went, Denton and Hamilton walking a little ahead of the others.

Denton, the *Frobisher* ex-actor, was the last man on earth that the three would have chosen for a shipmate. And now there was to be his poisonous friend Patrick as well. The future looked black. But there was no time to fuss about it. They reached the sick-bay and were directed into a small room in which were two desks, three chairs, and a washbowl. The only person in the room was a sick-berth attendant.

" Get undressed as quickly as you can, you fellows; the Commander will be here any minute and if you're not ready when he comes, God help you. Get undressed and then form single-file here." He pointed to the side of the second desk, where a chair was already in position.

" By the way, listen very carefully to anything the Commander says to you. And don't forget to say ' sir.' He's very touchy."

They had just finished undressing when a wild, white-haired little man rushed into the room, throwing angry glances all over it like an irritated ferret looking for rabbits. He rushed to the desk, plonked down a suitcase and cap, bawling at the same time: " Come on. Get undressed. What the devil are you hanging about for ? Get into line. You, there "—this to Hamilton, who was first in the line—" step up to the chair. GET . . . A . . . MOVE . . . ON. Now then," switching the tone of his voice to one of polite but scarcely audible inquiry, " any knocks or bruises on your head ? "

" No, sir."

" What did I say to you ? "

" You said: ' Any knocks, blows, or bwuises on my head,' sir."

" What did I say to you ? "

Silence.

" WHAT DID I SAY TO YOU ? "

Silence.

" I said nothing about blows. I said, ' Any knocks or bruises ?'
Why can't you listen ? Breathe in. Don't make such a damned
row. Breathe in quietly. Breathe deeply. Turn round, bend
down, fold your arms, breathe in. Relax, man, RELAX. Turn
about. Fold your arms above your head. Squat down. Stand
up. Touch your chin with your left knee . . . left . . . LEFT,
you dud. You C.W.s are one big bunch of duds. Do you hear
me ? DUDS. Now touch your chin with your right. Hold your
hands out like that. Clench your fists. Look at my hands, man.
Don't gaze at my face. WATCH WHAT'S BEING DONE. My
goodness! I'm not allowed to swear at you. If I were, you'd
learn a thing or two, you dunderhead. Watch me, man. Now,
put your feet together. Shut your eyes. Touch the tip of your
nose. Sit down on that chair and cross your knees. Step up, next
man. BUCK UP "—this to Holt, next man in the line, who had
failed to move a pace forward quickly enough to satisfy him.
" I'll make the whole lot of you dress and send you out of the
room if you aren't very much smarter than this." Then he
turned again to the now quivering Hamilton.

" Cross your knees. Now kneel on the chair. No, the OTHER
WAY. You *are* a lot of duds. Stand up. Dress."

He switched his attention to Holt. When he came to his
chest he listened carefully. " What's the matter with your
heart ? "

" Nothing, sir, except that I'm a bit nervous."

The Surgeon-Commander shouted with laughter and passed
Holt through the remainder of his examination with little fuss.

Williams was next. He had watched carefully everything that
was said or done to the other two. He had taken the step forward before the Commander could bellow at him, gave the right
answers to his questions, and did as he was told exactly.

" What job had you in civil life ? "

" I was a journalist, sir."

" Journalist, eh ? Now tell me. Why do newspapers always
print such lies ? "

" Well, sir, they're not allowed to print what they like. The
Government gives them lies to print. So do the advertisers."

" Advertisers, eh ? " Turning to the sick-berth attendant and
pointing to Williams, the Surgeon-Commander said, "He'll stay."

Redfern went through without being torn to shreds, but the
unhappy Denton caught the full blast. He began badly by
being a second late in stepping to the chair.

" Why the devil don't you watch what the others did ? "

" I'm sorry. I thought I *had* watched. But I must have been
thinking of something else just for the moment."

"Say ' SIR ' when you talk to me! Don't you dare forget the sir or I'll send you out of the room."

The examination proceeded. "What exactly was your job in civil life ? "

" I'm a Civil Servant, sir."

" What sort of Civil Servant ? How much were you paid ? "

" Three pounds ten a week, sir."

" In other words, you were an office boy. That would have been the right answer to my question, wouldn't it ? "

" Yes, sir, I suppose it would."

" What branch of the Civil Service were you an office boy in ? "

" The Forestry Commission, sir."

" How many trees does the Commission plant a year ? "

" I'm not quite sure of the exact figure. I mean, it sort of varies, you know, from year to year."

" Well, it doesn't matter about the exact figure. Give me a rough idea. How many trees, roughly, does the Commission plant in a year ? "

" I don't know, sir."

" You don't know! Why the devil didn't you say so in the first place ? "

When the rest had dressed hurriedly and left the room, the Surgeon-Commander beckoned Williams and said: " Now, come and sit down. Make yourself comfortable. Tell me about this advertising business in newspapers."

He talked to Williams for thirty-five minutes about advertisers, politics, Jews—especially Jews—foreigners and other subjects, while queues of men waiting examination piled up outside his door. His views were violent, but his manner was always friendly. His performance, repeated six or seven times daily, at medical examinations, was an act put on to test the temperaments of the men who came before him. Or perhaps Surgeon-Commander Planter wanted to make himself a barrack legend like C.P.O. Crump.

2

They were told to muster on the edge of the parade-ground at 8.15 next morning, and, praise the Lord, there was Calamity Taylor staring gloomily at two bright red, single-decker buses.

" Well, if it isn't my old pal Calamity," said Williams.

Calamity's eyes brightened, which was the only way his face seemed to show pleasure, and putting on what he called his " C.W. voice " he took Williams's hand and said, " Well, well, well! Isn't this just topping! I say, old man, are you going on this ripping gunnery course ? " Then, in his natural tones: " Have you got a draft to the *Marsden* too ? *And* old Sawn-off ? Good old Shortarse! Wonder they can find room for you on a destroyer. Submarine's more your mark. Use you for a flicking torpedo."

" What's happened to the rest of the boys ? "

Professor Cole, Jackie Price, Nevison, Harry Robertson, Jackie Low, they were all coming on the same draft. They would be around somewhere. They'd gone off to see if they could get any chocolate in the canteen. They ought to be back any moment.

" What about the rest ? "

Fletcher had applied to get on his brother's minesweeper. An elder brother already at sea could claim his younger brother. But there were no vacancies in that particular ship at the moment and so he had been drafted to some shore base—as a fire-watcher, he said. He was fed up. Perry had gone to train as a shipwright. Hall was still in a camp near by.

Miller and Martin had been drafted to a cruiser. Martin had gone and was thought to be on the other side of the Atlantic already. But Miller had wangled out of it. He had come back from leave with some hard-luck story about his mother, how she was nearly blind and half dead and without support except from him. He had gone to the Welfare Section in barracks and they had managed to get his draft cancelled while enquiries were made.

Just then one of Calamity's " sergeants " arrived, a Petty Officer with three red stripes on his arm. He looked about forty-five and had seen a good deal of service, judging by the ribbons on his chest. He had a pleasant face.

" *Marsden* draft," he called. " Keep silence and answer your names."

He read a list of twenty names. There was the cherubic-faced Lovelace, who had spoken to Williams and Redfern once in the canteen and warned them to get good-fitting boots. He was still humming *Blue Champagne*. And there was Rhoades, the red-haired boy who had been in the washroom their first morning at *Frobisher* and had threatened a sticky finish for Lieutenant Lewis if ever he caught him in the blackout.

There was the draft from Class 16S. The rest were strangers. They piled into the bus and drove away to the Gunnery School, H.M.S. *Royal Ark*.

This school had a reputation throughout the Navy for its efficiency and its discipline. The routine and square-bashing were said to bring 18-stone men down to about 12 stone in a few weeks. They really went through it on the parade-ground, so old hands said. If one man was a fraction out of time in sloping arms, the whole squad, with heavy equipment and rifles at the slope, were made to double across the parade, up a steep bank and back again in the boiling sun. If they were not quick enough, they were sent up the bank a second time. When they got back, the instructor would say: " That's much better. You can do it

71

again just because you didn't do it like that the first time."

But that was square-bashing.

The gunnery was grand.

The *Marsden* draft was not going to live on the *Royal Ark*. They were only going to rub up their knowledge of the minor jobs in the gun's crew and were to be driven back to barracks each evening. The key positions on the gun, like layer, trainer and captain, were to be filled by men who were already at *Royal Ark* and had just finished one of the courses.

The *Royal Ark* did not look by any means forbidding. It was an island, not a ship, and was reached by a long bridge, guarded by polished-looking sentries. Its buildings were of soft-coloured red brick and looked neat. There were trees and green grass plots everywhere. In the brilliant sunshine it was more like a holiday resort than a gunnery school.

The party unloaded themselves from the buses and were formed into a squad and marched to one of the gun batteries in a long building at the far end of the island, overlooking the sea.

"Watch your marching, lads," said the three-stripe Petty Officer who had come with them. "If you get picked up here for being slack, you'll know all about it. This isn't barracks, you know."

They marched into the battery, which was already becoming warm in the morning sun, and were formed into two lines. After a minute a youngish officer came out of an office with papers in his hand and said to the Petty Officer: "This is the *Marsden* draft, I suppose. You are Petty Officer Blair?"

"Yes, sir."

"Where is the G.I.?"

There was a movement in the shadows on the other side of the room and a little white-faced man with big ears pattered over briskly and gave the officer a salute which came straight from the drill book.

"Oh, G.I. This is your party. We had better get them sorted into crews for a start. You've got your lists?"

"Yes, sir," said the G.I. in a low, scarcely audible voice. He sounded as though he was looking into the open grave of his mother.

"Well, carry on then. You can try them out on number two and number three guns."

"Aye, aye, sir," said the G.I., and another Petty Officer, also with three badges on his arm, stepped up to the officer, saluted less formally than the G.I., and said, "Petty Officer Morgan. Reporting the *Royal Ark* party for Marsden correct, sir."

He was short and pale. But he was not tense. He moved almost casually.

"Very good. Fall them in alongside the remainder, leading hands in front."

About ten men, all wearing some kind of badge on their arms, filed in.

The G.I. began to call names. "Newton."

Newton was a three-badge seaman who might be about thirty-seven, but ages in the Navy are deceptive. Boys of twenty-three look thirty-five after some time at sea.

"Come out here, Able Seaman Newton," said the G.I., and Newton strode out, completely self-possessed and a little bored, among all these rookies. He looked like a man who knew his job and was going to make sure that everyone knew he knew it.

Four other names were called, and then came Price.

He looked uncomfortable. "This flicking 'eat. Whoi don't they put some fans in this basstud place? Oi dunno."

Another name completed the first gun's crew. "You'll be A gun's crew," said the G.I. "Next lot are B gun's crew. Able Seaman Hales?"

A tallish, thin man, with side-whiskers, looking about the same age as Newton, came out of the ranks. He had a long, piercing nose, but his eyes were quiet and humorous.

"He'd never have got those whiskers past Lieutenant Lewis, the old sod," said Low.

Two more were called and then came Able Seaman Carter, a lumbering man, whose big body was yet too small for his mouth.

Lovelace stepped up beside Carter, who split his face into a welcoming leer and passed a remark to Hales out of the corner of his mouth about Lovelace's cherub face. Robertson fell in beside Lovelace.

"Petty Officer Blair," said the G.I., "you can take A and B crews to number two gun. Get started right away."

Then the G.I. came to X gun's crew. "Able Seaman Raikes?"

Raikes rolled out of the ranks, like an obedient bull, but there was something in his eye which said that obedience was not the first of his virtues, nor the last of his vices. His mouth seemed to smile, but not his eyes. He was a man to be distrusted, with his deceptive smile, his slightly bald head showing beneath black frizzy hair, and his assumed manner of compliance.

"Able Seaman Forster?"

A tubby man of anything between eighteen and twenty-five came out. But he must be more than eighteen with one stripe on his arm. That meant at least three years in the Service. He nodded to Raikes and Raikes nodded slowly back.

Redfern, Williams's ex-bedmate Nevison, and three others completed the crew.

"Now Y gun's crew," said the G.I. "Leading Seaman Forrest?"

A man who had been standing in front of the squad jerked himself to attention and took a position behind X gun's crew. Forrest had black curly hair and a sallow complexion, due either to exposure in the sun or to a bad liver. He had steady, penetrating brown eyes and, like Raikes, lips that seemed framed into a smile when his eyes were not smiling. He looked bitter and contemptuous.

Others followed him. " Barber " was a round-faced Yorkshireman. At least his " aye " had sounded Yorkshire. " Wright" was thick-set and waddled. He was older than Barber, but goodness knows whether he was older than Forrest. Forrest looked a good thirty, but might have been more. Wright was certainly well into the thirties.

Then Calamity. His slightly glazed eyes had been watching the procession of men leaving the ranks and the sound of his name did not register at first. The G.I. called it again and Calamity jerked himself into motion.

" Rhoades ? " The red-haired, flush-faced Rhoades, ambled to the group.

" March smartly to your place," said the G.I. sharply, spitting out his words like a cat who has just seen an inquisitive puppy.

" Low ? " and a second later " Williams ? "

" Petty Officer Morgan ? That's X and Y guns complete. Take them off to number three gun," said the G.I.

Petty Officer Morgan marched X and Y crews along a passage which led off the hall in which they had been standing and halted them in another room which was three parts filled with a gun, standing in its shield. He stood them at ease, and let them take off their hats and jumpers.

" Don't let's have any lolling about while you're here," he said. " They're very particular. I know it's bloody hot, but you'll have to stand properly at ease all the time, whether you're working on the gun or not. *I've* a stiff collar. So you can manage it. Now we'd better sort the crews out."

He took X gun's crew first. Raikes was already detailed as captain and breech worker. Forster was his layer.

" Well, we want a sightsetter," said Petty Officer Morgan, " Better have someone from the south. We had a Geordie on the job on my last ship, and nobody in the T.S. could understand a word he said. Any one of you four come from the south ? "

All four remaining members of the crew raised their hands. Petty Officer Morgan looked at them undecidedly for a moment and then pointed to the nearest one.

" Where do you come from ? "

" Surrey."

" We'll try you. You sound clear enough."

The others were given their jobs. Redfern was rammer and Nevison projectile supply.

Then Petty Officer Morgan turned to Y gun's crew. Leading Seaman Forrest was the captain—it was going to be no fun and games on the gun with that surly-looking know-all. The Yorkshireman, Barber, was his layer and Wright his trainer. Williams was determined to get the job as sightsetter. He had often done it in the drills at *Frobisher* and would perjure himself to get it now.

" Any one of you lot from the south ? " said Petty Officer Morgan, and Yorkshireman Williams had said " Yes " before the other three could draw breath.

" Well, you'll do." Calamity was rammer. Low projectile supply, and Rhoades charge supply.

Then X gun began drills, much the same as at *Frobisher*, while Y gun's crew stood at ease behind the gun and tried to keep awake. Each man watched his opposite number, noted his mistakes, and looked to see if this was different from the guns at *Frobisher*.

The only difference was that the gun was housed in its shield, which was made of thin steel, and at the front, on either side, had two shutters known as ports. There was little room between the wall of the shield and the gun itself, particularly with the brass training and laying handles which jutted from the gun, and the training and laying receivers in their brass containers.

Otherwise, the gun was the same, and so was the drill. P.O. Morgan pretended to be the T.S., or Transmitting Station. He called the orders to the sightsetters, who repeated them to the gun's crew. " Y gun well. Y gun closed up, cleared away, bore clear. All positions line up. Check receivers."

The morning passed rather slowly.

But they had an hour and a quarter for dinner. They had a quick meal, went to the water's edge and lay in the sun. Williams found himself next to Denton.

" By the way," he said, " didn't you tell the Surgeon-Commander you were a Civil Servant ? I thought you were on the stage."

" Oh well, you see, I'm sort of on the stage in my spare time. I used to take parts in a repertory company whenever I could sort of spare the time. I shall go on the stage properly after the war. Jolly good fun."

Calamity Taylor looked Denton over with his mouth slightly open, as always, but he said nothing at first. But when Denton had begun to talk to someone else, Calamity leaned over to Williams: " I say, old chap, who is that sort of twirp ? Jolly good fun, what ? "

" Oh, he's a C.W. from *Frobisher*."

" Stuff my flicking buckets. These flicking W.C.s get me down. Oh, you're all right. So's Shortarse and old Redfern. But flick me. ' Jolly good fun '. Flick me."

Denton went on talking for the remaining hour while the others slept in the sun. He seemed to be telling his life-story to another man, who, presumably, had come in to take the anti-Russian Hamilton's place. Denton was telling him how, at *Frobisher*, he had been detailed to take the class at gunnery because they were short of instructors, when Williams went to sleep.

Then they had more gun drill. Some of it was interesting because it was new. They saw for the first time how a damaged striker was changed and saw the sharp-pointed needle that plunged into the fuse that fired the charge that blew the shell into the house that Jack built. The syrupy Denton kept up the interest. He had not been detailed for a gun's crew, but had been sent with the other spare hands to brush up their gunnery that afternoon. Spare hands might be wanted on a gun in action.

He stood scornfully by, criticising X gun's crew, who were again at work on the gun. " Good God, that's wrong. Isn't it extraordinary ? That fellow's a three-badge A.B. and he doesn't know the simplest thing."

Then the spare hands were called to make an improvised gun's crew. Denton was captain. Within the first minute he had made three elementary mistakes. " You see, sir, at *Frobisher*, all the fittings were not on the gun. We just went through the motions. I've never seen a real interceptor before."

The interceptor was the contact which linked the gun to one or other of the two director circuits and set the gun-ready lamp burning in the director. If the interceptor was closed, the director could fire the gun. If the interceptor was opened, it could not. The interceptor was obviously important and, equally obviously, instructor-of-gunnery Denton did not know much about it. Calamity was delighted, and leaned over to say in a penetrating whisper, " Bad show, eh ? What ? Sort of lets the side down."

" Keep silence," said Petty Officer Morgan.

Everyone made mistakes except Leading Seaman Forrest, the captain of Y gun. He had looked as though he knew his job, and he *did*. He gave his orders in a dry, Scots voice, clearly, exactly, and acidly, seeming all the time to have some secret joke with himself which turned that mouth of his into a derisive smirk. He handled his crew as though he had been doing it all his life.

Next day the drill was the same, but the G.I. himself took Petty Officer Morgan's place and issued orders in a toneless, weary voice, dabbing at the sweat on his pallid face. Y gun's crew, which had had the least practice on the previous day, was given first go, and for a time all went well. But when they came to test circuits, there was trouble. The director electric circuits are tested by inserting a miniature cartridge into an opening in the breech, and pulling the master trigger in the director. If the main circuit is correct, the electric current released by the trigger will fire the cartridge or " tube." Then a new " tube " is inserted and the process is repeated with the auxiliary director circuit.

But in case both these director circuits break down, the gun can be fired independently by the gunlayer. He presses his pedal, which sends the striker plunging forward, into the tube. When this is done in drills it is the rammer's job to extract the tube and show it to the instructor with the words: " Tube fired by percussion. Good and central blow." But Calamity got the words muddled: " Tube fired by concussion. Good and central cut."

" Good and central cut ? Good and central cut ? What do you think you are ? A flicking butcher ? "

Then Williams, repeating what he thought were the G.I.'s words, told Forrest to " close your breeches."

" Breeches ? Who said anything about breeches ? I said breech, man. Tell the captain to close his breeches at Navy Week when all your young women are watching and some will blush and some will widdle."

Then when they came to practise loading ten rounds into the gun, Rhoades, in his hurry to bring a charge from the rack, crashed into the G.I. and dropped the dummy charge on his toe.

" You bloody great ape! . . . I'm sorry I called you a ' bloody great ape '. But I meant it just the same."

By the end of the day they were exhausted. But they knew the drill by heart.

Next day they were to have a test under action conditions in the Battle Teacher. This was a small room containing the complete breech of a gun. But instead of a barrel there was a long tray, like the one they had used on their first day in gunnery at *Frobisher*. A spring had to be pulled back and then released to shoot the dummy charge and projectile out of the breech along the tray. Each gun's crew had to load and fire twenty rounds, and while they were doing it, men from above threw water over them, dropped smoke-bombs and fire-crackers, and crashed all kinds of implements, from drums to sheets of metal.

They were given sea-boots, oilskin trousers, coats and sou'-westers, and anti-flash fabric gloves with long sleeves and white helmets rather like balaclavas but with a long, loose-fitting neck which fell over the shoulders. Then X gun's crew were marshalled inside. They were one man short and Williams was detailed to work the spring.

They were given a few rounds of practice with the lights on and without effects, and then the test began. The lights went out and it was a while before their eyes became accustomed to the dark. Then an officer, as though from the bridge, began to talk through a loudspeaker. He gave them the range for the night and then they heard him discussing the weather conditions with another officer. Suddenly they heard him say: " Hallo, what's that on the horizon there ? There. Red seven-o. It looks a bit suspicious to me. All guns with S.A.P. and full charge, load, Load, LOAD."

Williams repeated the order and the voice through the loud-speaker went on: " Yes, I'm sure it's something. It's a ship all right. Looks like a Jerry. Yes, by God! I believe it's the *Prinz Eugen.* Enemy in sight Red seven-o, a cruiser. Range one-o-o. Open fire. Buck up, number one gun. For Christ's sake get a move on."

Raikes pressed a switch, the spring went forward and forced charge and projectile up the tray. As he did so there was a crash of drums and metal from above and a smoke-bomb exploded in the room, nearly choking them. Williams bent forward to force back the spring and a cascade of water shot over him from above. Redfern rammed home new charges and projectiles and Raikes again pressed the switch. Again the crash from above, again the smoke-bomb exploding; and this time there was a new horror. A fire-cracker was thrown down and detonated with an ear-splitting crack. " What the devil was that ? " said the loudspeaker. " Have we been hit ? Jackson, find out where we've been hit."

More cascades of water, more smoke, another fire-cracker, and the crash of metal on metal and boom of drums. Round after round went through the breech and up the tray until the crew were sweating and gasping and soaking. At last the twentieth round was fired, the row stopped, and the crew were released into the corridor outside. One or two of them looked shaken, especially Nevison, but in a few seconds they were grinning at each other and getting their soaking clothes off.

Williams had to keep his on, and go back with his own gun's crew in a moment. During the first few rounds he had been too intent on pulling the spring correctly to worry. Then he had been startled by the fire-cracker and choked by the smoke. The water was not so bad. At least it cooled him off. And after a while he was well enough used to it all to look about him in the gloom and see where the crackers, the water, and the bombs were coming from. He felt confident about the second test.

When Y gun's crew test began, he watched until one of the watermen on his right hand was about to hurl a bathful into the room, and moved a step to the left to avoid it. But he did not notice a fire-cracker thrown from the other side. It hit him on the shoulder and fell at his feet. As it went off, he leaped back several feet and received a second cascade of water right over his head. He arrived in the corridor when it was all over, gasping and shaken.

That was the last of their instruction at *Royal Ark.* Next day they joined their ship.

Chapter Six

1

THE *Marsden* lay alongside a jetty at Oldhaven. She had been lying there for three months, ever since the beginning of March, with only a skeleton crew on board. Her engines had been giving trouble and the Oldhaven dockers had taken them out. They were back in the engine-room now, but the dockers were still on board finishing minor repairs.

Her new crew saw her as the buses bringing them and their gear from Oldhaven station came round the corner of a shed and stopped near the edge of a jetty. There she was, looking long, narrow, and top-heavy, her white-and-blue camouflage half-hidden in dirt, her two funnels blackened and marked with rust, and her decks heaped with junk.

She was not impressive, but her crew could hardly take their eyes off her. About half of them were new to the Navy and had never seen a warship at close quarters. Some had never been on the sea in any sort of boat or ship. They were interested, excited, and anxious by turns. The other half of the ship's company were old hands, by wartime standards. Some were regular Navy men who had done anything from four to twenty years in the Service. Others were Hostilities Only who had joined since the outbreak of war and had now anything from one to three years' service behind them. All these old hands had just come off leave and a good spell ashore after leaving their previous ships. They stared at the *Marsden* with distaste but with the critical interest that any man will show for what is to be his home for many months.

The ship's company left the buses and fell in on the jetty in groups—the seamen in one, the stokers in another, the torpedo men in a third. They shuffled into place, holding their small suitcases, and waited. Williams found himself next to Sinbad and, near at hand, were several men from *Frobisher* or *Royal Ark*.

In front of the seamen and facing them were the Leading Seamen called "hookies" or "killicks" from the anchor or "hook" which was their badge of rank. Forrest was there, still sneering to himself as he stared at the head of the seaman immediately opposite him.

Behind the Leading Seamen were a group of Petty Officers—little Morgan, the middle-aged Blair, and the white-faced G.I. among them. The G.I.'s face was the same, tense, pallid, and sweating. But in place of his stiff collar and carefully creased coat and trousers he was now in overalls, open at the neck, and tennis shoes. He was holding a stack of white cards and, turning, he said something about them to a huge Chief Petty Officer just behind him. This Chief had a huge head, with sandy hair showing beneath his cap. He had huge shoulders which slumped like heavy weights towards his chest. He had huge, long legs and kept shifting the weight of his body from one to the other. When the G.I. spoke to him, he gathered himself together and trundled a few steps to the gangway which led down to the ship, looked over, and came back.

" Yes, carry on with the cards. No sign of him yet," he said, staring high over the G.I.'s dwarf figure into the middle distance and swaying his head from side to side.

" I expect that's the Chief Bosun's Mate. Call 'im the Buffer because you run up against him so often," said Sinbad.

Buffers had been mentioned at *Frobisher*. They were like works managers in a factory. They gave the orders and saw that they were carried out. But the orders really came from the managing director, who, on a ship, was the First Lieutenant, Jimmie the One, or simply Jimmie. The first lesson learned by any seaman was to avoid the Buffer. The second was to avoid the Jimmie.

The G.I. now carried on with the cards. When Williams got his, he found that he was in One Mess, that he was to work on the Quarter Deck, that he belonged to the Second Part of Port Watch, that his action station was Y gun, and so on. Sinbad was also in One Mess, but his action station was simply marked " After Supply ", whatever that might mean.

" Ship's company, 'shun," and the Buffer lumbered to the head of the gangway, where he heaved his right arm into a salute.

" Ship's company correct, sir," he said to a tall young man with two straight Royal Navy rings on his arm, and a short black beard jutting from his chin. This was the First Lieutenant, or Jimmie.

" Very good. Stand at ease."

Jimmie sidled forward and addressed the crew, his right hand gently stroking the outside of his right leg in a slow automatic movement.

" Right," he said. " Now you've all got your cards, get aboard and stow your kit. The ship's company will muster here on the jetty in three-quarters of an hour's time. Ship's company, turn right, dismiss."

They filed down the gangway with an assortment of gear, small suitcases, larger suitcases which they had brought back from leave, and kitbags and hammocks. A few carried buckets.

At the foot of the gangway they turned right towards the fo'c'sle, along the narrow deck past guns and torpedo tubes, and dived into a narrow passage. Williams followed the crowd towards the light of a doorway at the end of the passage. There he was stopped by a man in overalls, who sent him right for'ard for One Mess.

The mess deck curved round a wide pillar which was A gun's support. Against the sides of the mess deck were wooden lockers covered with long cushions and, above them, iron racks for suitcases. There were four tables on either side of the mess deck with wooden benches beside them, and " right for'ard " past A gun support were two more tables, one on each side of the deck. This was One Mess, right in the bows of the ship where her sides curved in to form her stem.

At the extreme end, a square was railed off to take all the hammocks of the mess decks, leaving a yard-wide gangway at either side.

At most, the mess deck was 70 feet long—the length of the ship was only 300 feet. The widest place in the ship was only 27 feet.

The mess deck was not at the widest place and One Mess was not at the widest part of the mess deck. Yet twenty-five men were going to live in each of the three messes, making seventy-five men in all on the mess deck. It would be the only place where they could eat, sleep, read, and write, and stow their gear. It would not be comfortable.

Still, it did not look too bad at the moment. The sun, glinting on the water outside, was reflected through the open portholes and danced on the ceiling—or deckhead. The mess deck was clean; there seemed room to move although the deckhead was not more than 10 feet high and from it projected a large number of hooks, girders, iron bars, electric lamps, and electric wiring. It was true that the deck space, already restricted by the gun support, the hammock netting, and the tables, was restricted still further by one open hatchway in the centre of One Mess and one each in the other two messes leading to the watchkeepers' and stokers' messes and the for'ard magazine below. But the rest of the space was clear. You could walk around without banging your feet. That was something.

Redfern was in another mess. But Calamity, Shortarse, and Jackie Low were all in One Mess. So were Rhoades, Nevison, Lovelace and Price. So was the saturnine Scotsman, Jock Forrest.

Someone came past the gun support carrying an urn of tea and put it on the deck. He went to a shelf fastened to the gun support and took out a tin of condensed milk. Then he went with a cup to a chest also fastened to the support and dug the cup into some sugar. He poured milk and sugar into the urn, and stirred the mixture with a sharpening steel. " Tea's wet, One Mess," he said.

He was a killick, like Forrest, but was fair, with a pleasant, though careworn, look on his face. He looked about thirty and resembled Jack Hulbert. At least he had the chin, though there was no sign of the Hulbert smile. He poured himself a cup of tea and walked wearily towards the lockers and sank down. His name was Dowson. That week he had lost his mother and father in an air raid on the Lancashire town where he lived.

Before tea was finished there was a shrill whistling. "Clear lower deck. Hands muster on the jetty," and round the corner of the gun support there appeared a man whose skin was yellow like a Chinaman. But his eyes were large and round and open, and his face was almost breaking into a leer. He put a curious-shaped whistle to his lips, blowing some more shrill notes and repeating the pipe down the open hatchway to the watchkeepers' mess below. He was a Bosun's Mate.

On the jetty the seamen, at a bellow from the Buffer, sorted themselves into two groups, the fo'c'sle men and the quarter-deck men. But they were no sooner lined up than the First Lieut-enant came up the gangway and ordered the Buffer to re-form them into three sides of a square.

"Marsdens, 'shun. Ship's company correct, sir."

"Very good," said a gentle, casual voice, and there was another beard. It was the Skipper's.

"Stand them at ease, please, First Lieutenant," said the Skipper, climbing on a wooden box.

"I haven't very much to say to you just now, but it is going to be my policy to tell you as much as I possibly can at all times about our programme," said the Skipper. "As you probably know, the *Marsden* has been in here now for about three months. I expect that she will be in for about another week. Then we should be ready for sea. I can't tell you where she will go when she is ready because I don't know myself. But as soon as I'm told and am allowed to tell you, I will do.

"In the meantime, there's a good deal of work to be done. We're a new ship's company, new to the ship and new to each other. The gun's crews, and all the rest of us for that matter, have got to spend a good deal of time making sure of our jobs. And as you can see, there's a good deal of clearing up to be done. We'll probably have to paint her. We'll certainly have to clean her. To-morrow, or the day after, we'll have to ammunition ship. All these things will give us time to settle down and begin to weld ourselves into an efficient and happy ship's company."

He got off his box and went back on board.

"Fall out the officers;" and five men disappeared down the gangway.

"Marsdens, turn right, dismiss."

2

So there would be a week's grace before they put to sea. The crew would have time to get used to the ship, to find their way about, to get over the smell of hot engine air and slightly simmering paint.

The ship would be in four watches in harbour. That meant that everyone, except the duty part of the watch, could go ashore until 0730 the next morning. The duty part was the First of Port, and Williams, being in the Second of Port, was free.

But he stayed aboard. He wanted to get his kit crammed away in his narrow locker.

The man with the locker next to his had the same idea. He was busy emptying his kitbag and putting everything away neatly folded. He was very dark, this man, and was, officially, clean-shaven. That is, he had shaved that morning. Williams asked him what was the best thing to do with kitbags when they were emptied.

" Best shove it at the bottom of your locker, man. You'll not be wanting it again for some time. "

" How the hell does one get everything into the locker ? It looks too damn small." William's locker was already three-quarters full, although he had not half emptied his kitbag.

" You'll have to fold your things tighter than that, man. You'll get issued with any amount of stuff before we sail—warm clothing and the like. All that's got to go in too."

Williams emptied his locker and began again, with the black man watching critically as he refolded his clothes.

" Where do you come from ? " Williams asked.

" Ireland."

" The real Ireland, or Ulster ? "

" Belfast. It's real enough to me, man. By the way, my name's Maclure. What's yours ? "

Maclure had been in the Navy for two years and nine months. He had joined up the day after the outbreak of war and had spent most of his time on a merchant ship converted into a minelayer. He had volunteered for submarines. But instead of submarines, he got the *Marsden*. He said he was " chokka ".

" Chokka ? What's that ? "

" Fed up, man. Fed to the ruddy teeth. I don't want to serve on a destroyer. You get all the discomfort of a small ship and the pusser routine of a big one thrown in. Pusser ? That means ' as per Seamanship Manual '. Rig of the day Number Threes and all that. On a submarine you can wear anything you like. It's not a bad life."

While they were talking, the two Leading Seamen of the mess were sitting at a table making out a list. Dowson fixed the list to the mess shelf on the gun support. It was a list of cooks. There were four cooks for each day and six sets of cooks.

" Good God, do I have to cook ? "

" No, man; the cooks don't cook. They'll have a regular P.O. cook on board and an O.D. chef."

"P.O." of course was "Petty Officer" and "O.D." was "Ordinary".

"The cooks just get the food ready. They cut the meat and put it with the spuds on a dish, and take it up the galley. One of them will usually make a duff and take that up too."

A "duff" was any kind of pastry or heavy pudding.

"You'll soon learn to make duffs. Then the cooks get the plates out for meals and do the dishing up afterwards. Or at least, they're supposed to. You find a lot of them who don't."

"Who decides what we're going to have to eat?"

"Well, every mess has its own caterer. Ours is that round, sleepy-faced, ginger-haired bastard over there. He's called Howard, I think. He has to draw the milk, tea, sugar, jam, and corned dog. One of the cooks has to draw the meat, spuds, bread, butter, and vegetables from Tanky. That's the slang name for Captain of the Hold, who acts as butcher in a destroyer. I'm Tanky. God knows why. I don't know anything about meat—not until it's cooked, anyway."

There was a cold supper that night with some more tea, "wet" this time by Maclure. A good half of the mess had gone ashore and there was plenty of food and plenty of room to eat it.

There were Williams and the tubby Forster from the gunnery course at *Royal Ark*, Maclure and the two Leading Seamen, Dowson and Forrest.

Forster did most of the talking. He seemed to have been on every ship in the Navy and in most of the actions. Maclure kept looking at him out of the corner of his eye. Forster talked harder and louder. It was his opinion that the *Marsden* was a badly built ship.

"She was always having trouble when she was with us. That was before we got into the Med. She was always tied up to a wall whenever there was a dirty job to do; and we got browned off for it."

"You must have had a terrible time, man. What was it like at Jutland?"

"When was you in the Med.?" Forrest asked Forster in his slow, Scotch voice.

"Oh, I was about there for four months at the end of last year and the beginning of this. Got back in February. I was in that smash-up when the *Arthur* was sunk."

"Do you remember that air attack when they hit the *Arthur*? Just after daybreak when they comes over in swarms and drops three slap on her stern?"

"Yes," said Forster. "I was pulled out of my hammock by 'Action Stations'. I hadn't been on the gun two minutes before the *Arthur* sank. Then the bastards turned on us. We were closed up for two hours. I was thankful when they buzzed off and we were able to get some breakfast. I'll say I remember it!"

" So do I. Very well," said Forrest. " The *Arthur* was hit at three in the afternoon. She floated for three-quarters of an hour. I know because we went in to pick up survivors.

" Well, lads, all of us dish up to-night. We'll get the cooks going in the morning. Here, you get us some hot water in this kettle, he said to Williams, handing him a large rectangular container with a handle on it like a bucket. " You'll find a hot-water tap outside the galley on the port side. Right-hand side as you go towards the blunt end."

Forrest himself washed the dirty plates in the hot water and everyone helped to dry them and put them back in the mess shelf. The whole business took less than five minutes.

Williams went over to Redfern in Two Mess when he had finished. Redfern was in the duty part that night and had to stay on board. He had already mustered once—for a fire-party practice—would have to muster again to clear up the mess deck for rounds at 2100, and had to get up in the middle of the night to act as jetty sentry from 0200 a.m. until 0400 a.m.

The two of them went out by the starboard passage, called a " flat "—through which they had first come in. It was about 4 feet wide and along one side were a number of doors marked Petty Officers' Washroom, Canteen, and Store. On the other side was a large printed notice warning the ship's company against seditious propaganda.

Next to that was another notice in large red letters:

ACTION STATIONS

Following are the signals which will be sounded on the alarm bells:

Long rings	.	.	. Submarine warning
Short and long rings .		.	Aircraft warning
Short rings	.	.	. Surface craft warning

It is the duty of all ratings to memorise these warnings.

Past these two notices there was a sliding door with the words, " Transmitting Station " on it.

" So that's the famous T.S." It was a small cabinet filled with instruments, voice-pipes, and telephones. It looked complicated.

" Where does one get a wash in this place ? "

The washroom was in the " flat " on the other side of the ship, behind a sliding door. It was 10 feet long and 5 feet broad. It had a tiled floor. It had nine tip-up basins round the sides and at one end there was one tap and a shower. The shower did not work. This was the only washing-place provided on the ship for 120 seamen, torpedo men, and stokers. Farther along were five closed closets for Petty Officers, and farther along still were seven open water-closets for the 170 lower-deck ratings.

2030. The Bosun's Mate with the whistle came round again.

He walked on to the fo'c'sle, leering at the seamen lying in evening sunshine, blew some shrill notes, and called " Clear up mess decks and flats for rounds. Duty part of the watch muster in the canteen flat. Come on, you lazy bastards. Get going."

Half an hour later there came again the shrill piping in the distance. The men on the mess deck put down their books, stubbed out their cigarettes, or quickly finished slinging their hammocks from the iron bars screwed to the deckhead.

" Bloody rounds," said Leading Seaman Dowson, standing up. " *Attention for rounds.*"

A procession came on the mess deck, led by a man of about twenty-five wearing the badge of a Coxswain. On a destroyer, a Coxswain does the duties of a Master-at-Arms, policeman of the ship. The First Lieutenant followed him. Last came the yellow-faced Bosun's Mate, Buck.

The procession went quickly through the mess deck, ducking now and again to avoid the few hammocks that were slung over the gangway, and the First Lieutenant, preceded by the Coxswain, climbed through the hatchway in One Mess to the watchkeepers' mess deck below. Buck stayed above, leering with one eye at the seamen, who had by now slightly relaxed, and keeping the other on the hatchway. He stiffened himself as Jimmie and the Coxswain reappeared through the hatchway and went along the other side of the mess deck and out into the canteen flat. " *Carry on, the mess deck.*"

Williams soon turned in. He felt too lazy to sling his hammock. He kept his underclothes on, and using his oilskin and sweater for a pillow, lay down on the locker and put his overcoat over his legs and feet. He was almost too warm.

" *All the hands, heave-oh, heave-oh. Rig of the day, Number Threes.*"

Morning again and 0630.

Williams stirred himself, but no one else moved, so he lay back again.

Half an hour later there was another disturbance. A voice. Not a particularly loud voice, but penetrating, continuous, worrying. It rose and fell. It was a pleasant voice, it was friendly, it was humorous. But it made sleep impossible.

" Come on, my lads, lash up and stow. The sun is shining fit to burn your eyeballs. Heave-ho, my hearties. Come on, my sons—AND you know the sort of sons I mean. Out of it, you lucky lads. Get out of it. Undarken ship. Draw the blinds and put up the blackout. Come on, my hearties. Muster on the jetty at eight a.m. Rig of the day, sailor suits, buckets and spades. Get out of it. Here, you, do you want a sentry-box ? " and he turned to unlash one end of a hammock and bring its owner's feet with a thud to the floor. But the owner was too quick. He was out of his hammock before the man with the voice could touch it.

The voice belonged to Petty Officer Morgan, who had taken Y gun's crew at *Royal Ark* and was Captain of the Quarter Deck, in charge of the quarter-deck men.

They implored him to stop shouting . . . in vain, and one by one they tumbled out. It was the only way to stop that row.

Williams washed in cold water and was wondering about breakfast when he saw Maclure pick up the tea-urn and walk towards the galley.

" Here, you got the tea last night. If you'll tell me what to do, I'll get it this time."

" Come on; I'll show you," said Maclure.

He had already put rather more than a handful of tea into the strainer inside the urn. In the galley he picked a key off a rack, fitted it to a tap, and turned. Boiling water poured into the strainer and thence into the urn.

" That's all it is." And that's all there was for breakfast except for one slice of bread and butter. On a destroyer there was a big meal at noon and another for supper at six. In between times there was bread and butter, perhaps, and tea.

They mustered on the jetty at eight. The Buffer reported the ship's company correct to the First Lieutenant, and the First Lieutenant, looking anywhere but at the Buffer, whispered, " Two cooks from each mess." The Buffer, looking anywhere but at the crew, bawled, " Two cooks from each mess," and two cooks from each mess duly presented themselves in single line in front of the Buffer.

" Leading Seaman Barker; " and Leading Seaman Barker left the killicks' line and stood in front of the cooks. He had a sallow face, like so many sailors, and a small mouth. He wore a pencil which jutted from his cap along his cheek at an angle of 75 degrees. He called the cooks to attention and saluted the First Lieutenant, letting his hand crawl slowly up his side until it reached his hips and then whipping it suddenly to his forehead.

" Carry on with the mess deck." Leading Seaman Barker saluted again. " Cooks, right turn, double march," and away they went over the gangway.

" Gun sweepers amidships," whispered Jimmie to the Buffer.

" Gun sweepers amidships," bawled the Buffer, and out fell several men who had had " gun sweepers "marked on their card.

There was Wright, who was the Y gun trainer, Forster, who, the night before, had bragged about his experiences, Able Seaman Carter, the man from *Royal Ark* with the lumbering gait and the big mouth, and about seven others. The G.I. took charge of them. He gave the First Lieutenant an immaculate salute and then said in his low, tense tones: " Gun sweepers, right turn, double march," and away *they* went over the gangway.

" Flat sweepers," whispered Jimmie, rubbing his right leg. " Flat sweepers amidships," roared the Buffer, and several men came forward, Shortarse among them. He was office flat sweeper.

" Two hands from each part for side party," roared the Buffer. No one moved. It fell to Williams and Redfern, who were standing at the end of the rank, to be the quarter-deck men on the side party. Price and Robertson had been detailed from fo'c'sle. " Leading Seaman Dowson ? " said the Buffer. Dowson left the killick line, called the side party to attention, and saluted the First Lieutenant.

" There's a lot of oil on the side, particularly near the water-line. Get some stages over and start cleaning it off."

" Aye, aye, sir," said Dowson, and the side party doubled over the gangway just as the Buffer roared " Remainder of hands, part of ship."

Dowson led his party towards the mess deck. But before he reached the galley he turned left underneath a platform on which were some guns like machine guns. These were point-fives, used mostly for anti-aircraft work, and under their plat-form was the lumber rack, holding a number of planks, with ropes attached to each end.

" Get two of those out, will you ? " said Dowson. " They're your stages. We'll have to put them over the side in a minute. While you're getting them out I'll see if I can find some shale oil."

He came back with some black, oily-looking stuff in a tin and led the side party to the port side and showed them how to handle their stages.

" Now all we want is a couple of buckets and some cloths. Williams, you go and look for some buckets. There ought to be some in that wash-deck locker on the Iron Deck."

Williams knew what a wash-deck locker looked like. He remembered the Chief's story about the thief who had been thrown overboard in one. But all the decks looked to be iron.

" That's the Iron Deck over there, running from where you go into the washroom or the canteen flat all the way to that mark there," and Dowson pointed to a brass mark on the deck just aft of the torpedo tubes. " From that line aft is the quarter deck."

Williams found the locker and, surprisingly enough, two buckets in it.

" Ah've caught you ! Right in the act, you robber. Pinching ma bloody buckets from under ma nose." Williams turned. It was Leading Seaman Forrest, looking ominous. Williams said, hurriedly, that Leading Seaman Dowson had sent him for the buckets.

" Well, tell that robber to put 'em back when 'e's done with 'em."

Leading Seaman Forrest was in charge of the Iron Deck.

Williams was next sent to fill the buckets with hot water, and Dowson came with him to get what he called " softers and strongers ". " Softers " was soft soap, " strongers " was soda. They were both stowed in a cubicle in the lavatories. " There are no lavatories in the Navy," said Dowson—" only heads. Why the hell they're called heads I don't know. Something to do with Nelson, I suppose."

The side party went over the side two on each stage, with a bucket and a small tinful of shale oil. Dowson passed down a handful of woolly mixture which he called waste and a couple of cloths for each bucket.

The side had small stains of oil running down to the water-line, and at the waterline the oil was thick and widespread. They put on shale oil to wipe off the oil stains and wiped off the shale oil with hot soapy water. This worked well until they got near the waterline. There they discovered that the water itself was thick with oil. Every time they washed the oil off, the water put it on again.

" Just look at this, hookey," shouted Redfern. " The water's so full of oil we'll never get the side clean."

Leading Seaman Dowson looked gravely at the water, then at the side, then at Redfern.

" There's only one course open to you. Chuck your hand in! You shouldn't have joined the Service if you can't take a joke. Go on. Wipe the bloody side. I know it'll be dirty again as soon as you've done it, but Nelson wouldn't like it if you didn't try."

So they went on trying until the Bosun's Mate piped " Stand Easy."

At that Dowson helped them on deck and they went off for some tea on the mess deck. The mess deck was already crowded with tea drinkers, who, obviously, had knocked off work long before " stand easy ". Dowson went to the One Mess tea-urn, lifted it, then dropped it in disgust. " Sandy bottom," he said.

" Not a bloody drop left. We've been ! "

So taking a couple of dirty cups, he went to another mess and came back with the cups filled with tea and handed one to Williams.

They sat together on the lockers, but before they could begin to drink, the Bosun's Mate came through the mess deck calling, " Out pipes. Hands carry on with your work."

Williams looked at Dowson. Dowson looked at Williams.

" Well. You heard the pipe. Carry on with your work, the gentleman said." He took a sip of tea. " Nothing like work for bringing out the character." Leading Seaman Dowson lit a cigarette.

"Or bringing out warts," said Ordinary Seaman Williams, also lighting a cigarette.

They sipped and smoked in silence for a minute. The rest of the men on the mess deck, who had already had their tea, just sat and smoked.

Their contentment was suddenly shattered. A raucous voice broke into the mess deck, followed by the sallow face of Leading Seaman Barker, pencil jutting from his cap. "Away you go, then," bawled the voice. "Come on now. You 'ad yer time. Gerrout of it. Get a move on. Get a move on. Don't linger ... WANDER. Thin out, now. Gerroutofit."

Leading Seaman Barker was the killick of the mess deck.

"Come on, Williams," said Dowson. "We'd better get back to work before old Bolton-flicking-Wanderers breaks a blood-vessel."

They spent the rest of the morning washing oil and dirt off the side while the water and their shipmates put it back again.

Williams and Redfern moved their stage farther for'ard and were just getting the new patch clean when a shower of dirt came over the side.

"I say, I AM sorry, chaps," said Calamity in his C.W. voice. "Actually I didn't know you were there."

"You silly bastard. You've mucked up all the part we've just cleaned. Not that the water won't muck it up again even more than you have."

Calamity leaned on his broom and looked at them. "Not a bad job you've got down there. Out of the way, anyhow. You don't get the Buffer putting his ruddy nose in."

"What job have you got, Calamity?"

"Sweeping the flicking Iron Deck. I no sooner sweep the flicker than some dockyard matey drops a pile of muck all over it and I have to do it again. If I've swept the Iron Deck once, I've swept the flicking Iron Deck a hundred times this morning."

"I should chuck your hand in," said Dowson. "But don't go shooting your muck all over my side party. Here, Jock, can't you keep your Iron Deck party under control?"

Jock Forrest looked over the side. "Ye ain't seen nothing yet," he said to Williams and Redfern. "Just ye wait till I starts washing down with the hose."

Price and Robertson finished their section and set to work still farther for'ard. There was a sudden shout from Price.

"What the flicking 'ell is 'appening up there? Oi'm soaked through. Chroist! I'll catch the flicker 'oo's using that 'ose. Just let me get at 'im." Water was swirling across the Iron Deck and cascading over the side on to the occupants of the for'ard stage.

Jock Forrest switched off the hose and both he and Dowson ran to the side. " Ah'm sorry. Ah didn't know ye'd got up that far," said Jock.

" You shouldn't have joined if you can't take a joke," said Dowson. " Come up and get dry." Price climbed on to the deck and disappeared to get into overalls.

" You all ought to be in overalls for work like this," said Dowson. " Rig of the day, Number Threes! This flicking Jimmie must have come off a battleship. I'll see the Buffer about it. Never once wore Number Threes in the old *Duchess*."

The " old *Duchess* " was Dowson's last ship. He had been in her for two years and only left her because one of her paddles fell off and she had to go into dock for a refit. She had sailed up and down the east coast, shooting down aircraft—English or German, it didn't seem to matter—and had wound her paddles into Dowson's heart. He became known as the " Duchess " or the " Old Paddler " before the *Marsden's* commission was a week old.

At noon, Williams drew his first neat tot. In the Navy anyone over twenty is entitled to a tot of rum each day. If he does not want to draw his rum, he can have 3d. a day extra on his pay and go down on the books as " T " or Temperance. Williams was " G " or Grog. Redfern was still " U.A." or " Under age ".

The barracks tot had been mixed two parts water to one of rum, which is strict naval regulation. But on small ships " the water is very strong ".

The rum was served in careful measures, under the eye of the Officer of the Day, to the Leading Seaman of each mess, who carefully measured a tot to each member of his mess who " drew ".

For his service in measuring the rum the Leading Hand of the mess was entitled to " sippers " from every man, a " sipper " being a taste of each tot. Tots were the principal currency of the lower deck. If you did a man a small favour he might offer you " lighters ", which was the barest wetting of your lips in his rum. If you did him a slightly larger favour he might offer you " sippers ". A larger favour still would bring you " gulpers ", and a very big favour might, if you were lucky, bring you " grounders ", which was the whole tot. There was a regular table—" two lighters, one sipper; two sippers, one gulper; two gulpers, one grounder." Nothing short of saving a man's life in the most desperate conditions would bring you " grounders ".

Ask for anything and a reward in rum was expected. Williams had been sent to the T.I., or Torpedo Instructor, for more shale oil. The T.I. looked at Williams with a twinkle. " Does

Leading Seaman Dowson draw? This will cost him sippers. I'll be round to-morrow."

"Oh, he'll be round, will he?" said Dowson. "That's fine. The walk will do him good."

Williams took his first neat tot in a cup from Forrest and handed it back for " sippers ". He gave another " sippers " to Dowson, who was formally ticking off the names of the G.s as they drew. Then he put the cup to his own lips.

The rum smelt sickly and had an unpleasant taste. He let a small sip hang on his tongue for some seconds and then swallowed it. He felt it go down his throat and trickle slowly towards his heart. He took a larger sip, swallowed, and waited. The morning's tiredness began to fade. He sat on one of the lockers, looking at the brown liquid, swilling it round in the bottom of the cup and occasionally smelling it. He took another sip and looked round the mess. How attractive it seemed with the bright shafts where the sun came through the portholes, set off by deep shadows! It wasn't going to be so bad. He took another sip.

Old Dowson was talking away at a table. What a grand man he was! Like a younger edition of Chief Petty Officer Graves. He knew the technicalities of his job thoroughly and could explain them. But there was no show about him. Just a nice, quiet, cynical detachment from the Navy. And Jock Forrest, there—he was going to be all right after all. That curled, jeering, inward smile of his wasn't really a jeer. Just a mental reservation. He knew his job too, that was certain. One Mess were lucky to have two killicks like that.

Williams gulped down the last of the rum and seemed to rise on cushions of air. It was ten to one he would not be seasick, not at this time of the year. You couldn't pick a better time than early June to go to sea for the first time. Bright sunshine and blue, calm seas! People actually paid for that sort of thing, and here was he being paid 2s. 6d. a day for it, with food thrown in. And rum! He looked into his cup and found that a few drops which had clung to the side had now fallen to make a tiny pool at the bottom. He drained it, and went to fetch his dinner.

The dinner had been served on to plates by the four cooks who were supposed to know how many plates to put on. No one was allowed to touch a plate until the cooks were ready. Then there was a shout of " Dig in, boys; fill your boots," and the rush was on. When Williams got to the table, there was no plate left for him.

" Hey! What's happened to my dinner ? " and one of the cooks said, " There were twenty-five put out. How many are there in the mess, caterer ? "

" Twenty-five," said Ginger Howard.

" Well, we put twenty-five dinners out."

" What's the matter ? " asked Forrest.

He was told.

" How do you know you put twenty-five plates out ? "

" I counted them twice."

" And I counted them once," said Jackie Low, who was another of the cooks.

" Stop eating, every one of ye. One of ye's taken two dinners. One of ye's taken a dinner that doesna belong to him and there's a man here wi' nothing to eat."

He went quickly round the tables and in the middle of one was an empty but dirty plate. The food had been swiped.

" Look at this, every one of ye. That's Williams's dinner. One or some of you bastards has wooffed the lot. Ah get tired. Ye're grown men. Ah don't want to treat ye like children. But Ah *will* do if there's any more of this, and ye won't like it. When Ah was a boy, Ah was brought up proper, and when Ah got to a training ship and was *marched* in to meals, Ah didn't like it. We was not allowed to touch our food until we was told by a Chief. Ah didn't like that sort of thing and Ah don't want to do that to ye. But because Ah'm decent and lets you eat in a decent manner, there's some of you taking advantage.

" Now, this is the last time. If such a thing as this ever happens again, it's pusser's routine for the lot of ye. Ye'll fall in on the Iron Deck. No one'll be allowed in the mess except the cooks. Then ye'll be marched in and the other messes will laugh at ye.

" Now, let's look at your dinners. Here, you give us a bit of that meat. And Ah'll have some of your spuds. Give us a bit of your greens." Picking here and there from the largest helpings and piling his pickings on to the empty plate, he produced a good-sized dinner for Williams.

" Now Ah've warned ye."

They were at work again at 1315. Some of them were clearing the decks of rubbish or " gash ", putting useless junk over the side, carrying anything that might be useful for salvage on to the jetty. Some had been set to wash the paintwork on the upper deck with " softers " and hot water. The gun-sweepers, under the eye of the G.I., were cleaning and greasing the guns. A few old hands were sorting out the tackle in the fo'c'sle locker behind A gun or in the tiller flat, the large space below decks right aft where all the quarter-deck wires, ropes, and other equipment were stored. The side party went on cleaning the side and the sea went on making it oily again.

There was Stand Easy at 1430, officially for ten minutes, but it was nearer fifteen before " Bolton Wanderers " had got the mess deck cleared. At 1530 Dowson leaned over the side and told the side party to get in their stages, stow them away, and get cleaned up. The first liberty boat left at 1600 and the side party wanted to go ashore.

They were very dirty. They had put on Number Threes in the morning, but Dowson had sent them in to change into overalls after Price had got his wetting. This had saved their clothes, but their hands, hair, and faces were thick with grime.

The washroom was crushed out with men scraping and lathering to get the oil and dirt off themselves. Some of the basins could be detached and the procedure was to take one of these along the washroom flat to the hot-water tap outside the galley, which was the only source of hot water.

Williams got hold of a basin at last and soaked off the first few layers of dirt. He decided to soak off the remainder in a bath at a near-by sailors' hostel. He spent the night there and was back on board by 0730, when all night leave expired.

Next day was Saturday. Work went on as usual all morning, but the afternoon was a " make and mend ". Make and mends were originally designed to give seamen a chance to make new clothes or mend old ones, but nowadays, they are an excuse for " getting your head down ", " crashing your flicking great swede ", or any other nautical term for going to sleep. Most of the starboard watch and the first part of port watch went ashore after dinner.

Everyone on board slept until 1600, when Jackie Low wet some tea. The sound of clinking cups disturbed the sleepers and faces, bleared with sleep, appeared over the edge of hammocks. One of these faces looked like Stan Laurel's of Laurel and Hardy. But it was Dowson's. The man was a chameleon. One moment like Jack Hulbert, and next like Stan Laurel. Dowson looked at the table and then at Williams, who was just getting off the lockers below him.

" Who's going to bring me a cup of tea ? " he said.

" Get up, you lazy sod," said Pat Maclure from his hammock. " Get it yourself. And get me one, too."

Williams brought them both a cup. " Thank you. You're a real gentleman. You won't lose anything by this, I can tell you. You won't gain flick all by it, either."

The rest of the evening was spent in reading, writing, gossiping, and playing cards. Dowson had gone ashore, but Forrest remained sorting out his kit. He had a bright red mackintosh which was certainly not Service pattern. " Wherever did you get that, hookey ? " Williams asked.

" That ? Oh, there's a long story attached to that. A long story. Ah wouldna part with that coat for twenty tots. Not for two hundred tots." He sat down opposite Williams and lit a cigarette.

" It all began out in Gib. Ah'd been out there and in the Med. for nearly two years when the war broke out and Ah wanted to

94

get home. But they wouldna let me. Ah tried to get a draft, Ah tried everything I knew; but it was no good. The Drafting Master-at-Arms no speaka da English, so Ah hangs on and hangs on until it gets Christmas-time. Then Ah gets a draft chit to a new ship and Ah hears this ship is going to England. But the Drafting Master-at-Arms won't tell me where she's going. He just says, ' Get your kit packed and report to this ship in three-quarters of an hour.'

" Three-quarters of an hour, when Ah'd been there more than two years!

" Ah races back to ma mess and begins to throw ma kit into ma kitbag, and ma messmates, they throw stuff in too, and give me sippers—it was just tot time—until Ah don't know whether Ah'm standing on ma head or ma heels.

" At the last minute Ah says to maself, 'Whur's ma oilskin ? ' and at last somebody finds it underneath a pile of kitbags. It's too late to stuff it in ma kitbag. There was no room anyhow. So Ah puts it over ma arm, heaves up ma kitbag, and one of ma mates carries ma hammock for me.

" We runs down to the dock and there is the ruddy ship Ah'm supposed to be joining slipping away from the dockside. Ah jumps on to an Admiralty launch, and ma mate with me, and we says to the coxswain, ' Can you catch that ship ? ' and he says, ' Sure.'

" We starts off, and by and by he signals the ship that he's got one of her killicks on board and the ship says she'll heave-to out-side the boom.

" Well, we eventually gets alongside, they throws down a jumping ladder, and Ah heaves myself up, kitbag and all, and ma mate throws me hammock up after me and Ah waves good-bye to him. All of a sudden Ah sees me oilskin lying on the deck of the launch. Ah shouts to me mate, he picks the oilskin up and tries to throw it to me. But it falls in the oggin and that's the last Ah sees of it.

" Well, we gets to Liverpool and it's mid-winter, terribly cold and spitting rain and me out in the Med. for the last two years. Ah'd got no overcoat. Ah'd lost that months ago in Gib. Some robber swiped it. The only money Ah'd got was two-and-six and a Gibraltar ten-bob note, and Ah'd got to get to Pompey.

" Well, Ah gets a travel warrant all right and Ah changes ma ten-bob note at a bank—they gives me nine and twopence—and Ah gets on the train to London with some sandwiches and a bottle of beer. Ah travels down with another matelot and we reaches London at ten o'clock in the blackout.

" This matelot says he 'as a sister-in-law living at Ealing and we'd better stay there instead of going down to Pompey that night. Well, we gets to Ealing and we finds the sister-in-law's address, but she doesn't live there any more. It turns out that the matelot hasn't written to her for more than three years.

"Well, there we are in the freezing cold, with no money left, or not much, and nowhere to stay and me with no coat. We finds an air-raid warden's post and they lets us stop the night in there. Next morning we gets down to Waterloo more dead than alive with only one overcoat between us and the rain spitting down. We're standing shivering in the station when an old lady comes up to us and says, ' You poor boys. You're wet through. Haven't you got no overcoat ? ' She says this to the other chap. Ah'm wearing his overcoat at the time. Well, Ah sez to her, ' Lady, Ah've just come home from the Mediterranean and ma mate's lent me his overcoat.'

" ' Come with me. Come with me at once,' she sez, and she hauls us outside the station and into the first clothing shop she can find. ' Ah wants an overcoat for this gentleman,' she says. Well, it seems the shop hasn't any overcoats. ' We've got some oilskins,' says the salesman, ' but they aren't navy colour ah'm afraid.'

" ' Flick the colour,' says the old lady, or words to that effect, and she snatches up a red one and puts it on me. It fits. She pays the bill and pushes us on to our train with five shillings each for food-money before we have time to thank her. Ah'll never forget that old lady," said Jock, " and Ah'll never lose this mackintosh. If any bastard puts it on Ah knows it right away. You can't hide this colour. There's not another like it in the Service, Ah'll bet."

At *Royal Ark* and on the ship, Jock had always seemed so sure of himself, so stern, so acid. He knew what they were doing and did it without cackling.

But some strange old woman had seen him as a shivering boy. " Ah knows you boys thought I was an acid sort of devil at *Royal Ark*, didn't you ? Well, Ah *was* acid there. You've got to be. That's the way they wants it and Ah always believes in playing the Navy's game. It doesn't pay not to.

" But you can't go on being acid on a ship like this when you've got to live together. Ah'm not afraid of nobody. When they do things really wrong in the mess, like that business at dinner time to-day, Ah'll knock hell out of them. But there'd be no peace nor comfort in the mess if Ah made ye all stick to every rule and Ah'm not going to."

" How old are you, Jock ? "

" Ah'm twenty-four."

" I'm thirty-five. But you are old enough to be my grand-father."

On Monday, they ammunitioned ship.

" This is our first operation as a ship's company," said Jimmie. " Let's see if we can't get the job finished to-day. I know it's hot, but if you all put your backs into it we'll be finished by tea-time. If we're not, we'll just have to go on until we are."

Two deep drifters came alongside, their holds stocked with wooden boxes, and the ship's company set to work. Some got into the drifters and handed the heavy boxes to men above, who passed them along to others, who carried the boxes along the deck under the direction of the G.I. Other boxes and tins were unscrewed in the hold and their contents passed up singly— hundreds of shells and hundreds of charges. These were carried to the magazines and shell-rooms and there stored in racks.

The whole ship's company worked all day long and hard, sweat pouring off them and their muscles bulging, until by 1530 the job was done. The Jimmie had spent the day exhorting, cursing, screaming, encouraging by turns. Now he beamed on the sweating crew. " You've done a really good job, lads," he said and went below for a bath. The crew sank down in the mess deck and drank tea.

Williams decided to get a bath ashore and just washed his top half in the washroom with the aid of a bucket borrowed from Forster.

" When you've had your bath," said Forrest, " come along to the Shipwright's, if you feel like it. Ah'll be having a drop of beer in there about six-thirty. Ah'll have ma bath on the ship and catch the second boat."

Williams had his bath and took a tram for the Shipwright's. The conductress came to the top of the tram, refused his 2d.— " I don't take fares from sailors "—and flopped down beside him. " Phew! When the war's over I'm going to buy a tram and spend my time running up and down the stairs."

" I'll go half shares with you," said Williams, " if you'll let me run up and down, too, carrying heavy weights."

They laughed and sat in silence, resting while the tram rumbled on.

He got off the tram at the Shipwright's and waved good-bye to the conductress. Jock was already there with Forster, Maclure, and Dowson. Jock bought Williams a pint of bitter and the evening began.

It ended just after midnight, when the five of them gravely saluted Price, who was sentry on the gangway, and stumbled along the deck in the blackout to the mess. Forster was noisy and still had a long story to tell about " Our Albert ", although, of course, the real hero of the story was not " Our Albert ", but Forster himself. The story was punctuated by expressions of admiration for Gladys, the barmaid at the Shipwright's, at whom Forster had been making watery eyes all evening.

"Look here, Our Albert. You're drunk."

"I'm not drunk. I've only had ten pints." He had only had five, what with talking and making eyes. "When I was in Gib., I once had fifteen pints straight off and then brought the Skipper aboard in the motor-boat. Never so much as scratched the paint when we came alongside. 'Forster,' said the Skipper as he climbed the ladder, 'you're a flicking fine coxswain. Flicked if you're not.' Those were his very words."

"Our Albert," said Maclure, "you're a flicking fine liar."

The rest turned in quickly, but Jock was in no hurry. First, he took off his silk, stroked out the creases, folded it carefully and put it in his hat. Next he took off his collar, holding it unsteadily in the light, then folding it and putting it with his silk. Then he began to take off his jumper. He eased it a little this way, then eased it a little that way, then pulled; his tousled head appeared out of the bottom of it. Then he held the empty jumper to the light, looked at it first on one side and then on the other, then began to fold it, slowly and carefully. This done, he sat on the lockers and looked at his bellbottoms. He got up after a minute or two, satisfied, took off his bellbottoms and folded *them*. He took off his shoes and again sat down on the lockers, this time to inspect his socks. After a good deal of thought, he suddenly came to a decision and climbed into his hammock with his socks on.

First thing next morning there was a wail. "Whaur's ma sock? Whur's ma bastard sock? Ye robbers. One of ye's taken one of ma socks. AND he's taken one of ma boots. But Ah'll catch you, you rogue. You take one sock. You take one boot. There's a man on this ship with only one leg. I'll catch the bastard."

The missing sock was on the deck where Jock had dropped it in the early hours when his feet had begun to feel too warm in his hammock. The shoe was by its side.

That day they began to paint ship. Every stage in the ship was put over the side, manned by ratings with long paint brushes, with short paint brushes, with brushes that were thick and bushy, with brushes that were thin and straggly. Pots of paint were hung over the side above the stages, and then the stages, ratings, and paint were raised or lowered by leading seamen on deck whenever a patch was finished. They talked and sang as they worked.

Calamity and Professor Cole were scraping and repainting the funnel. They were perched at the top and rasped away with iron scrapers, sending a shower of old paint on to the deck below.

Jimmie watched them for a time, keeping clear of the shower of paint. He was in a good mood that morning, cheerfully allow-ing the men over the side to smoke; but as he stood looking at the funnel party a slow procession came aft from the fo'c'sle. It was the four 4.7 gun sweepers. They were the only men who had been excused painting ship. The first carried a ramrod. the second a small pot of oil, the third a handful of oakum. The fourth could find nothing better to carry than a piece of waste. They intended to take their time about cleaning their guns and so avoid the painting.

Everyone expected an explosion. But Jimmie just pointed a finger. " Ah, the four gun sweepers! Let me see: Wright, the Y gun sweeper, Forster, isn't it, the X gun sweeper, Carter, the B gun sweeper. Yes, and Newton, the A gun sweeper. That's right. Don't overstrain yourselves! Stick together, my boys."

At that moment there was a crash and something heavy smashed against the deck less than a yard from the First Lieutenant's feet. Calamity had dropped his iron scraper.

Jimmie yelled. He seized his peaked cap in both hands and looked as though he would throw it over the side. With a tremendous effort he got himself under control and demanded to know who had dropped the scraper. Calamity was brought down from the funnel and cursed, first by Jimmie, then by the Buffer, for being careless. Later he was cursed by his messmates for being a bad shot.

Professor Cole tipped a pot of paint over the Iron Deck and Rhoades lost two paint brushes over the side. Several men saw their hats float away on the tide. Everyone's overalls were spattered in paint and their hands were caked in it. It took them two days to put the paint on the side and another day to get it off the deck.

On Wednesday they had their first tests on the guns. The *Marsden* had four 4.7 quick-firing guns, a 3-inch high-angle anti-aircraft gun, and as additional weapons against aircraft, two Point-Fives, which were Dowson's pride and joy, and two Oerlikons, which fired small shells with great rapidity. Ginger Howard, the One Mess caterer, was said to be an expert Oerlikon gunner and had brought down at least three planes since the war and damaged many more.

The only difference in Y gun from the gun at *Royal Ark* was that for the first time the sightsetter really had earphones. The G.I. gave them a preliminary run through the drill in the old way, standing behind the gun and giving orders by word of mouth. Then he went down to the T.S., and all four guns began to go through their drills at once in obedience to orders sent from the Director and passed to the guns by the Transmitting Station.

That afternoon they had more gun drills, and this time the sightsetters, instead of standing in front of their range dials in the gunshields, sat on little seats attached to the rear of the gunshields with small trays in front of them. Jackie Low dumped the H.E. anti-aircraft shells on Y gun's tray and Williams turned the fuses on the shells to the figure he received from the T.S. with a key which fitted into grooves round the nose cap of the shell. That seemed easy, too, and the gun's crew felt confident.

There was no definite news yet about going to sea, although they had now been on the ship longer than the Skipper's week. There were, or course, all sorts of rumours, known as buzzes. Somebody had heard one of the stokers saying that one of the boilers was not ready yet, and by the time this story had reached the mess deck they were telling each other definitely that all three boilers would have to be taken out and that the ship would not sail for two months. But Price had heard one of the officers' servants saying in the heads that the wardroom expected the *Marsden* to be off the coast of Africa inside a week. And so there was soon a buzz that they were sailing the following day for Australia.

Few if any of the crew wanted to sail. It was a reasonably comfortable life in Oldhaven, in spite of the painting, the weight-lifting, and the gunnery drills. They got ashore three nights out of four and the weather was fine. The men who had been to sea before knew plenty of conrasts to this and did not like them. Those who had not been to sea and had looked forward to it now thought of it more cautiously.

Saturday and Sunday came and went without any news of sailing orders. The dockers were still on board, doing things to the steering and working in the boiler- and engine-rooms. Saturday was remarkable only for the Skipper's Rounds, which were preceded by terrific scrubbing in the mess decks. The Skipper found only one fault with One Mess, although he flashed his torch under the hammock netting and other places where rubbish might be hurriedly stowed. There was a brown rim round the strainer in the tea-urn.

He pointed this out to Jock.

" Ah never has that cleaned now, sir. They used to clean it on ma first ship and the tea was never drinkable for three days after the Captain's Rounds. All the body had gone from it."

On Monday they had a number of practice evolutions, and one of these meant getting out the collision mats, which had been rolled up for the past three months. As they unrolled one of the mats a rat jumped out and most of the sailors dropped what they were doing and tried to kick it over the side. The rat side-stepped and slid this way and that for a few seconds, but at last Price caught it amidships with his boot and over it went.

George Barber, the Yorkshire gunlayer of Y gun, yelled, " That'll bring us bad luck, Ah'll bet thi','"and ran to the side to see if nothing could be done to rescue the rat. He had to be stopped from lowering a bucket to bring it on board again.

He shook his head seriously. " Ah bet thi' summat'll 'appen to t' ship before t' week's art. Tha should nivver chuck a rat overboard."

Perhaps he was right. The following morning the order was piped to " Clear lower deck ", and when all hands were mustered on the jetty, the Skipper told them that they would put to sea for trials the next day, and that if the trials were successful they would drop some dockers at a south-western port and proceed immediately to join the Fleet. The ship was now under sailing orders and no one was to go ashore.

There was tension on the mess deck and a good deal of letter writing that afternoon after the Bosun's Mate had piped " Hands to make and mend clothes," and a good deal of cursing by those who had made dates ashore.

The loudest cursin' came from Raikes, the captain of X gun, who had arranged for a girl-friend to come from London that day. By the end of the afternoon the mess deck knew that Raikes was going to break ship to see this girl. He *did* break ship, by walking over the for'ard gangway at seven o'clock that evening while the sentry was marching on his beat towards the after gangway. He was seen, not by the sentry, but by little Lieutenant Seeley, who was on the bridge. Lieutenant Seeley immediately reported to Lieutenant Burton, the officer of the watch, that someone, whom he did not recognise, had gone ashore.

It was then too late to catch Raikes, but Lieutenant Burton made plans to catch him if or when he returned. He had the for'ard gangway removed and posted the Quartermaster and a Bosun's Mate at the aft gangway with orders to remain there. Then he posted the sentry on the jetty opposite the fo'c'sle, blocking the only way by which Raikes could return. The sentry was to stop him from jumping the jetty on to the fo'c'sle. These orders were carefully repeated to Redfern when he relieved the old sentry at 2200.

At 2315, when it was now nearly dark, Raikes returned. He went straight to the sentry: " Turn your back a minute, old cock, or go on your beat up the jetty for a bit while I jump aboard."

Redfern was in a difficult position.

He had been told to stay where he was. If he turned his back and let Raikes get aboard, it was possible that nothing would be said. But it was by no means certain. More important, Redfern had a strong sense of duty when it came to questions of sentries and lookouts. " I can't do that, Raikes," he said.

Raikes gave him one look and jumped aboard. Redfern immediately shouted to the Quartermaster, who had come running for'ard just as Raikes was climbing down the ladder from the fo'c'sle to the Iron Deck. Raikes was placed under open arrest, which meant that he was on bail awaiting trial.

Redfern's action in giving away a messmate caused a great
stir on the mess deck. None of the old hands and very few of
the new ones thought that he had done right. One old hand, a
fierce-faced Scotsman who looked like a dead-end kid and was
already known as " Wild " Angus, told everyone that he would
" fill that flicking C.W. sentry in " as soon as he came off watch,
and had to be stopped from doing so by Raikes himself; and
though the storm subsided that night and was temporarily forgotten next morning in the excitement of putting to sea, it was
to revive.

Chapter Seven

1

" CLOSE all X doors and scuttles."
The sunshine was driven from the mess deck as, one after
another, the portholes were closed and the heavy iron scuttles or
" deadlights " were clamped over them. Below the waterline,
watertight doors were fastened.
" *Special sea duty men to your stations.*"
Men who had to transmit the Captain's orders down the voice-
pipe or telephones on the bridge went hurriedly to their posts.
The June morning was bright and sunny on the upper deck,
but that did not help the mess deck. It was gloomy and ill-lit,
like a room that is always blacked out. The seamen there were
anxious, like a football team waiting before a game. Of course
they would be back again by nightfall for another ten days of
repairs. Still, they might *not* be back.
They lolled on the lockers, smoking, pulling on sea-boots,
waiting.
It came to eleven o'clock.
" *Fo'c'sle men on the fo'c'sle. Quarter-deck men on the quarter
deck. Stand by for leaving harbour.*"
Wasn't there less of a leer than usual on Buck's face ? The
men jumped off the lockers and went to their part of ship.
Tugs began to pull and the *Marsden* to slide backwards from

her berth. As they watched the narrow harbour entrance coming nearer they half-hoped that the *Marsden* would catch her screws or graze herself. Nothing serious, of course, not enough to hurt anyone. But just enough to allow them another few days on land, watching the Civil Defence teams playing cricket in the sun, drinking beer in the pubs, and having room to stretch. But they passed through without mishap into the wide, twinkling water beyond, let go the hawsers which bound them to the tugs, pulled their fenders inboard, and began to stow their heaving lines in the tiller flat. All at once a slight tremor ran through the ship and set up a faint jingling in Y gun shield. The propellers were churning the water and the blue sea was turning to white as a wake formed and fanned out behind the ship. The tremor was soon a shaking and the jingling a rattling. The dead ship was coming to life as her screws turned for the first time in more than three months.

" *Afternoon watchmen to dinner.*"

It was Buck again, blowing his little pipe. As they would be still in safe waters even when they reached the open sea, the crew were to work in four watches during the daytime. That meant that only the " part of the watch " would be on duty and the others could get their heads down, read, or lie about in the sun on deck. The second part of port had the Afternoon. They went to the mess deck.

It looked sombre and cheerless in the yellow electric light. The pots on the mess shelf and the kettles and fannies which swung from the deckhead rattled as the ship slowly gathered speed. Worse, there was a high-pitched, incessant hum, boring like a gimlet through ears and into heads. It came from an anti-mine dynamo.

" Christ, what a noise! Does it go on like that all the time ? "

" Yes," said Forster. " We had it once for fifteen days when we were fooling about round the coast. But you get used to it. Hey, Jeffries, get down in your cabinet! You're not paid sixpence a day extra for hanging about up here."

" No, old cock," said Jeffries. " We get threepence a day extra for sticking it down there. And threepence a day extra for going mad while we're at it."

Jeffries was a Leading Seaman in charge of the Asdic cabinet. He had to spend his watches in a little room in the watch-keepers' mess, listening through earphones and watching dials. It was stuffy in the cabinet. That would not matter if the ship went to Russia, but it was uncomfortable in midsummer off the south coast. Much worse than the heat was the noise which came through the earphones, the steady " ping " at frequent intervals as sound-waves were sent out from the ship and the answering " pings " when the sound-waves hit some object below the surface and sent echoes back to the earphones. Jeffries had to stick it for hours at a time. He was now snatching a quick dinner before going on watch.

"*Second part of port watch to cruising stations.*"

Williams went through the wash-room flat to the Iron Deck and there turned to climb a steep iron ladder to the fo'c'sle. A few yards along the fo'c'sle was another and steeper ladder which led to B-gun deck. B gun was his cruising station.

There was not much to do on watch. Once the crew had put an S.A.P. shell and a charge on the tray, their only duty was to provide lookouts on the bridge, two at a time for half-hour spells. Williams and Calamity Taylor got the first half-hour. There were two little chairs behind the bridge, one on each side. The chairs could swing round as the lookouts turned the stand to which the lookout glasses were fixed. Each was responsible for an arc of 90 degrss.

Williams sat down on the starboard chair and an officer with a bright red beard came up. This was Sub-Lieutenant Carr. He was not more than twenty-one. He had a boyish cheerfulness about his face and seemed quite indifferent to the conventions of the Navy, talking to everyone with the same carefree disrespect.

He was Officer of the Quarters in charge of X and Y guns, as well as being in charge of the Quarter Deck.

"Do you know anything about these things ?" asked Carr, waving his hand towards the glasses on their swivelling stand. "Well, get the glasses focussed first. Try on that house over there. Got it ? Now you sweep from ninety degrees to a hundred and eighty degrees. This pointer here moves round as you move your glasses and tells you what bearing you're on. And don't just stick to the horizon. Start at an elevation of twenty degrees—this other pointer gives you the angle of sight—and sweep round the full ninety degrees at that angle. Then come down to fifteen degrees and sweep again, and so on till you come to zero on the horizon. They tell you to report anything you see, but that's really all tripe. When you're near land anyway. The wretched Officer of the Watch would never have his glasses away from his eyes if the lookouts reported all the things they saw. Watch particularly for aircraft and for any other ships coming up astern. You can leave anything ahead to the other fellow."

The other fellow was not Calamity, but Professor Cole. For there were two other lookouts sent from other parts of ship. Cole and Williams took ninety degrees each on the starboard side, while Calamity and another took ninety degrees each on the port side.

A small sailing ship came from behind a little promontory. Williams thought out his words carefully for a few seconds and then called " Red one-one-o, a small sailing ship, sir." A quiet voice, this time from the bridge proper, said, " Bearing ? "

Williams repeated "Red one-one-o," and then realised that he was the starboard lookout. "GREEN one-one-o, sir," he flustered, and the Skipper said, "Very good."

Calamity had not done much better. He too had begun by mixing red and green. Then he had failed to report a ship—"Why, the flicking Skipper could see the bastard as well as I could"—and had ended by reporting everything he saw from seagulls to seaweed, and that had not been well received either.

The rest of their gun's crew was lying on the gun deck, reading, smoking, and listening to the wireless. The breeze fanned their faces. The sun was hot and the war seemed far away. If this is going to sea, they thought, why did we ever stay on land ?

After some hours of speed and steering tests, the Bosun's Mate came round the mess deck just as the men were getting the supper ready. "Fo'c'sle men on the fo'c'sle," he piped. "Stand by for letting go anchor. The ship will anchor for the night."

A minute later there was a roar and a crashing just over the mess deck like a thousand tons of coal being emptied on the fo'c'sle. It seemed that any moment the deckhead would cave in and the coal come pouring into the mess.

"That flicking anchor," said Forster. It was only the anchor cable rumbling up from the cable locker, along the deck and down the hawse pipe into the sea.

As the anchor settled in the sea, a stillness spread over the ship. The whining of the dynamo had stopped, there was no shaking from the engines. There was just peacefulness, at first rather sinister, as though something had gone wrong, and then soothing.

The tests had been satisfactory as far as they had gone. But there would be more tests to-morrow. Pat Maclure, who, as Tanky, seemed to have access to all sorts of information, said that they would proceed to Plymouth first thing to-morrow morning, carrying out tests on the way. If the tests were still all right, they would drop the dockyard mateys and be off by 6 p.m.

The ship was under weigh early next morning, and while she went through the remainder of her tests, heading Plymouthwards all the time, the gun crews were given their first shoots.

They appeared in an assortment of clothing. Buck went round in khaki battledress. He had been a commando and had come back to the quiet life of the Navy after being severely burned by an explosion in Libya. After a week on the ship, he wished he was back in Libya. Explosions, he said, were nothing compared with Jimmie's temper. Jock Forrest wore his bright red raincoat. Hales, the captain of B gun, wore a deer-stalker's hat and, with his long side-whiskers, he looked like a Sherlock Holmes on tour with a second-class Shakespearean company. All the men wore sea-boots with white sea-boot stockings folded over the top, and some wore home-made jerseys over their jumpers.

The shoots went without a hitch and so, to the general dismay, did the rest of the tests. By 1600 on a grey afternoon they hove-to, well in sight of Plymouth, and a picket boat " manned " by Wrens came alongside to take off the dockyard mateys, happy at the thought of a night out in Plymouth before going back to Oldhaven. The *Marsden's* crew looked glum. Jock Forrest said, " Well, lads, ye can say good-bye to your nights ashore from now on," but no one else said a word.

The Pilgrim Fathers, leaving hundreds of years before from this very port, could not have felt worse than *they* did.

2

That night the ship went into two watches. First, starboard watch had four hours on and then went below for four hours' sleep while the port watch was on duty. The ship, in other words, was at Defence and no longer at Cruising Stations. Williams's defence station at night was on X gun, perched on the quarter deck overlooking Y gun. Here he had to stay crammed into the gunshield to avoid the rain which now poured down, with his headphones on to catch any sudden order from the T.S. Only routine orders came through, but later in the night, when the sea turned rough, he could hear Professor Cole being sick into a bucket in the T.S.

There was little room in the gunshield, but seven men had to cram themselves in; and no sooner had they found something like a comfortable position than one or other of them, usually wedged right at the front, had to climb out to go on lookout. No sooner had the others settled again than the old lookout came along with dripping oilskins and forced his way over protesting bodies. They lay or sat, wet, cold, and, most of them, struggling to keep their stomachs down while the ship heaved and the gunshields rattled. They thanked God when the starboard watch relieved them. They went unsteadily down the ladder from X-gun deck, seized hold of a rope which ran the length of the Iron Deck, and, keeping a tight hold, reached the mess deck, luckily none the worse for being heaved from side to side in the canteen flat.

Williams plumped on the deck near his locker, put down one of the locker cushions for a pillow, pulled a coat over his legs, and went to sleep.

He was woken by a crash. He thought the ship had been hit and that a shower of shrapnel was falling about his head. But it was tins of milk and food. A sudden violent roll of the ship had burst open one of the tinned-food cupboards and thrown its contents on the deck. He was too tired and too near being sick to do anything. All he noticed was that the ship's kitten, also on her first trip, was lying in a space between the lockers with her head on her paws, mewing as though the end of the cat world had come.

" A-L-L *the port watch.*"

Williams sat up, half asleep, and said in an angry voice, " All the port watch what ? " and then realised that, being in two watches, he would have to go on duty again after barely three hours' rest. He could not face a cup of tea. But he found a piece of dry bread and made his breakfast on that.

At dinner-time he took his rum and was sick. He was sick five more times that afternoon, but took a little comfort from the fact that half the ship's company were sick too. They were sick into buckets on the mess deck. They got up from locker or deck, rushed along the washroom flat and were sick in the Heads. Some stayed more or less permanently on the Iron Deck, where they were conveniently near the side. Williams found it preferable, in spite of the smell of sick, wet clothing, and food, to lie in the mess wedged between the lockers and the hammock netting, trying to breathe in when the ship went up and out when the ship went down.

This might have worked if the ship had done either at all regularly. But she seemed to rise slowly, then stay poised in the air for a while and then, without warning, drop to the bottom again with a crash. From time to time a wave would smack against her with a heavy thud and Forster would shout, " We're hit a milestone." From time to time a wave would catch her head-on and the water would come swishing over the fo'c'sle and Forster would shout, " We're in the submarine service, boys! " When it came to supper-time, and only a few wanted to eat, Forster would shout, " Big eats! Dig in. Fill your boots! " Forster was always shouting.

Then he was sick, too.

3

They reached harbour as a yellow dawn was breaking. Port watch had gone below at midnight and plumped down, foodless, exhausted, and wet, on the deck. They seemed barely to have dropped off to sleep when the Bosun's pipe woke them: " All hands, heave-ho, heave-ho. Both watches of the hands will be required in fifteen minutes' time for entering harbour."

The ship had ceased to roll and pitch and crash. They would soon be able to eat again and to wash again. But at the moment they only wanted to sleep. The port watch cursed the Bosun's Mate. One by one they struggled out of hammocks, off lockers, off the deck, reached for what clothing they had removed, and were ready for " *Forepart for'ard, after part aft. Stand by wires and fenders for going alongside oiler*," when it came.

But there was no sign of any oiler. They were running between two desolate-looking islands which stood up blackly against the yellow-streaked sky. There were occasional flashes from light-houses, but there was no other sign of life. The Quarter-deck men, huddled between Y gunshield and the entrance to the ward-room, wanted to know why the hell they had been called out so early. It was a good three-quarters of an hour before they slipped through the boom. It was twenty minutes more before they saw their oiler. During that time they passed ship after ship, lying ghost-like and silent in the half light.

When they neared the oiler, the order was passed down " Port side to," meaning that the port side of the *Marsden* would be alongside the oiler. They hurriedly got their wires and fenders ready on the port side and had just finished when the order came through, " Starboard side to." They had switched the wires, hawsers, and fenders to the other side when " Port side to " came down again.

" Don't worry, lads," said Sub-Lieutenant Carr; " they'll change their minds three more times at least before we get tied up."

They were tied to the oiler for about an hour. Then they moved to a buoy. It was half-past seven before they were piped to breakfast with the precautionary " Hands will be required at 0900."

They were all really hungry by now. There was only tea and a slice of toast, cooked against the electric fire in the mess. They would not have had even that if Pat Maclure had not brought out an extra loaf of bread. The other loaves had fallen on the deck and someone had been sick over them.

Williams asked Jock what sort of work they would have to do that day, whether they would get their heads down; but before Jock could answer, Calamity Taylor broke in with his most doleful voice: " I know exactly what will happen. We'll go out there at nine a.m. and Jock here will salute Jimmie and say ' Iron-deck party correct, sir ', and Jimmie will rub his right hand on his trousers leg and say, ' Out flicking brooms. Give the Iron Deck a good sweep up '. I know it all before it happens. Crystal gazer I am."

He was right. They spent the morning sweeping the decks and cursing the bare moorlands which ran down to the sea on either side of them. " I suppose there will be a time when we'll actually be glad to see this dump," said Williams, leaning on his broom and looking shorewards.

" Now I calls that a nice cheerful thought," said Calamity, also leaning on his broom. " Do you really think it's going to be as bad as all that, Bob ? "

But out of the corner of his eye Williams saw the Buffer come lumbering up, and nudging Calamity he began to sweep hard. But Calamity was still staring over the side and caught the full blast.

The Buffer had a sarcastic way of talking. He did not storm. He let Calamity have some acid tongue for a minute or so, and finished up with, " And I'm supposed to make you into a sailor. What the hell were you before you joined ? "

" Happy."

The Buffer looked at Calamity for the first time. His mouth opened and shut several times, but nothing came out so he moved away, " waddling like a flicking great duck," said Calamity.

* * *

That afternoon Buck piped " Clear lower deck. All hands muster aft." Someone said that the Skipper was going to address the ship's company, but Jock said, " No. It's a warrant. Raikes you know. They're going to sentence him."

The ship's company were lined up into three sides of a square. The fourth side was made up by Raikes, who was marched aft by the Coxswain and two escorts with web equipment. One of the escorts was Leading Seaman Dowson, who looked miserable enough to be the criminal himself. Raikes looked no different from usual with that half-smile on his face.

The First Lieutenant read a long indictment with a number of " wherefores " in it until he came to the name of the prisoner. Then the Coxswain shouted, " Off caps. One pace forward, march," and Raikes stood out to receive sentence. He got fourteen days' cells, to be served on a depot ship in the anchorage.

Raikes's sentence revived the violent arguments which had been aroused by Redfern's part in the capture. The *Marsden* was to be in harbour all night, and that evening was spent in heated denunciations and timid defence of a sentry who would give his messmate away.

Williams was one of the few defenders. He said to Raikes: " It's all very well for *you* to talk big about taking risks. But you were asking *Redfern* to take the risk . . . you just took the flicking night out. You'd no right to do that. Break ship if you want to, but do it without dragging any of your messmates into it."

" I wasn't dragging one of my messmates into it. All he'd got to do was turn his back. You can't expect a sentry to have his eye on a certain spot for the whole of two blasted hours. No one had recognised me. If he'd turned his back, I could have got on board without anyone else knowing, and he could just have said that he had seen no one. They'd just have thought that old Seeley was seeing things."

" Redfern would be afraid of losing his flicking commission," said Price. " 'E wouldn't take no risks."

" Yes, these flicking W.C.s. They don't give a damn about anyone except themselves," said Calamity.

" If anyone was thinking of himself that night," said Williams, " it was Raikes. He didn't worry about the sentry. He didn't worry about the ship for that matter. It might have had to go to sea suddenly and gone without one of its key men, the captain of the bloody gun. But old Raikes *had* to go ashore, so flick the ship and flick the sentry. He didn't give a damn for anybody but himself, and *he's* no flicking W.C."

" I wish I could talk like you," said Raikes. " Comes pouring out of you like a flushed lavatory. But whenever I gets up in front of the Skipper, he uses a couple of long words at me, and I'm sunk, I can't say a word, and they give me seven days number eleven or fourteen days' cells. Talkers can flannel out of anything in the Navy. But the only way people like me can get out of trouble is by sticking with my messmates and having them stick by me."

" That's right," said Able Seaman Newton, the captain of A gun. He was one of the oldest men on the ship and had been in the Navy for sixteen years. He intended to stay in it as long as he could, partly because he had made himself comfortable in it, and partly because he felt it would be difficult to get a job outside at his age. " People with a bit of education and pull can get by with all sorts of things in this regiment. But lads who haven't the gift of the gab are up against it. Do you wonder that we stick together ? "

" I see that all right, Stripey," said Williams. " You've got one set of ideas and you stick to it. But doesn't it occur to you that other people may have another set and want to stick to that ? Redfern may feel that when he's given a job it's his duty to do it properly. I bet you wouldn't let men from your gun go to sleep when they'd been all specially warned to watch out."

" No, I wouldn't. But I wouldn't go running to the Officer of the Watch about them. I'd soon see that they kept awake all right. Give them the dirty jobs if they didn't. But I shouldn't go crawling aft with complaints. Here, let me tell you what happened the first time we were out from Oldhaven. We were on watch on B gun just before we dropped the hook and one of your fellows a C.W., that long one, what's his name . . . ? "

" Shortarse."

" Well, he comes strolling to the gun a good half-hour late, smoking a cigarette as casually as you like, and says he hasn't heard the pipe. Well, it's a crime in the Navy to be late on watch, and if an officer had been looking over the bridge, as he might well have been, and had seen Shortarse strolling up late and me not reporting him for it, I'd have been in the rattle as well as Shortarse. More so. But I didn't report him. I thought that, well, maybe, it's his first day at sea. He's green. He doesn't know his way about. I just gave him a good bottle. But if I'd done my duty, as you call it, I'd have had him with his cap off in front of the Officer of the Watch and got him Number Eleven at least.

" But you can't always be doing that. It's not only that one of *us* does not get the same chance of flannelling himself out of

110

trouble. What really matters is that you've got to live and work together for months on end cooped up in a four-by-two mess that gets more like a pig-sty the longer you stay at sea; and if you feel that your messmates are going to report you for this and that or they think that you're going to do the same for them, life wouldn't be worth living. You've got to stick together."

Newton was no firebrand. He said he always voted Conservative because the Labour Government had cut the Navy pay. In civvy life, before the war, he would have been classed as a "steady decent working man " by the vicar and the squire. Yet here he was preaching and practising a form of class struggle and showing how even in the Navy the structure of society outside can set one group against another. Officers and men were literally in the same ship, but you were not all, by any means, in the same boat.

It was strange that three-badge A.B.s, like Newton, Carter, or Charlie Wright, who so obviously knew their jobs, and who were in the Navy as a career and not merely out of war-time necessity, should be content to remain A.B.s instead of " going through the hook " or even for petty officer.

But these men had all the privileges of Leading Seamen and most of the privileges of Petty Officers. They were never chivvied. Usually they were given some regular job, such as gunsweeper, which let them out of scrubbing decks, washing the paint work, or any other of the labouring jobs which were the constant lot of ordinary seamen. They could arrive on the mess deck long before " stand easy " and loiter there long after " out pipes."

And while they had these privileges they had no official responsibilities. They were elder statesmen who gave advice but were under no obligation to see that it was followed. They knew their way around. They knew to a fraction of a second when they must move unobtrusively to the port side of the ship to avoid some dirty job that was looming on the starboard side. They did, thoroughly, what jobs they were given on their cards, but avoided with equal thoroughness any of the stray jobs which were always cropping up for any seaman unwise enough to be on the spot. They made sure that they were as comfortable as possible and left it at that.

But they would come exactly on time, or a little before, to relieve you on watch. " If you are five minutes late coming up, you may find your relief coming ten minutes late to relieve you," said Carter one day. When the last five minutes of a watch seemed a year and one minute more an eternity, it was a great comfort to know that you would be relieved by a three-badge man and not by Harry Rhoades, who persistently overslept and came up twenty minutes late, saying that the Bosun's Mate had not piped the watch.

A Stripey would always do his whack in the mess. When he

was cook he always did his share of peeling potatoes, taking the food to the galley, fetching it back again, and dishing up the plates afterwards. When a three-badge man was cook, he didn't get his head down, like Price. But if he was not cook, nothing would induce him to lend a hand—" It just encourages the real cooks to shirk," said Charlie Wright—whereas Price had been known to do all the dishing up by himself, just because he felt like it.

Yes, you knew where you were with men like Newton, Carter, and Charlie Wright. They did their own particular job well and would never endanger the ship through casualness—" We want to go on living, same as you do "—and though they might, and frequently did, let one of their messmates in for some casual dirty job, they would never let a messmate down in the sense of giving him away to an officer.

It was not that they or any other rating disliked officers as such. On the contrary, they were prepared to admire and respect any officer who showed that he knew his job, and they realised fully what skill and endurance were necessary, if, say, the Skipper or the Pilot was to know and do his job properly. At sea, at all times, there was much less consciousness of distinction between officers and ratings than there is between manager and workers in a factory. There was often real friendliness and, off duty, at sea or in harbour, officers and ratings treated each other with courtesy and pleasantness.

But in matters of duty the three-badge A.B.s and the great majority of other ratings looked on officers just as schoolboys look on schoolmasters. They respected them professionally; they liked them personally; but they would not sneak to them. They were on the other side of the fence.

4

Raikes was removed first thing next morning by a picket boat from the depot ship.

At 11, the lower deck was cleared and the Skipper told the crew the ship's programme as far as he knew it. They would not be leaving for about a fortnight, he said. After that he didn't know what they would be doing. They would have two or three days for working up exercises, night shoots, torpedo runs, and the rest of it. Then they would take their place with the Fleet. He expected they would have to do a certain amount of screening for the Big Ships, which Sinbad explained as " going with a battle wagon and watching for subs. while she had firing practice."

" The poor little dears! They're not allowed out by themselves."

They sailed at 2.30 that afternoon for their own practice shoots. There was all the usual formality about leaving harbour—rig of the day Number Threes, standing at attention as they passed other ships on the way out, and the rest of it. But once they were through the boom, formality was discarded and all those who were not on watch got their heads down. They came up from the mess deck at 4 to prepare for the first shoot they had had with real charges and shells.

The guns' crews looked like hooded men. They had long white gloves and long white helmets to protect their skin against burns from the flash of the guns. It was cold in the wind as the ship tore through the water, and most of the men wore their duffel coats with hoods which came over the back of the head and covered the forehead, except Jock, who wore his red mackintosh—but he had several thick sweaters underneath it.

Williams was nervous about this shoot. He had heard how the flash of a gun would streak through the doors and hatchways, even reaching the for'ard mess deck. And as his position was in the very front of the gunshield, facing an open port, he thought he would be in line for the first bite of anything that came.

There was another complication. The ship was going so fast and making the gunshield rattle so much that he could hardly hear the orders that were passed through the earphones by the T.S. He had to guess at most of them and thanked heaven that the continual drills had taught him what orders to expect.

The guns were soon fully loaded and the crews stood by waiting for the fire gong which would sound in each shield just before the layer pulled his master trigger in the director. Williams gripped his range-dial handles, and when the fire gong sounded he shut his eyes. Two seconds later there was a crack which pierced through his duffel hood, through his anti-flash helmet, through his bala-clava, and through the earphones, leaving his ears dazed. He opened his eyes to find smoke swirling away from the gunshields and to see Calamity, quite undisturbed, ramming a new shell and charge up the breech. A few moments later came the fire gong again, followed by another crack which shook his hands off the handles and left his nose stuffed with sulphur fumes. He re-gripped the handles and cocked his eye at the range receiver in front of him, which gave him the range from the T.S. The figures in the receiver were clattering round, like the trip mileage indica-tor on a speedometer as you turn it back to zero. He put his range up 400 yards in answer to the turning figures, and as he did so the fire gong went again and the gun fired. He saw a streak of orange flash and then his eyes were clouded for a second or two by smoke. He set his teeth, gripped his handles, and made his whole body taut in readiness for the next crack. By the time the guns had fired ten rounds and the practice shoot was over he felt tired. So did the newcomers in the other crews.

Back on the mess deck they swapped experiences. Calamity, said Jock, had never turned a hair. He had kept shouting to Rhoades and Low for fresh charges, had rammed them home and then stood by impatiently for the gun to fire so he could ram home

113

another lot. Jackie Low, in his anxiety to keep up with Calamity's requirements, had dumped one shell hard on the tray but had forgotten to take his fingers from underneath it. He had hopped about for some seconds and thereafter had wrung his injured hand whenever he had a moment to spare.

On the other guns, all had gone well except that Nevison on X gun had been a bit jumpy. He had not liked the crack of the gun nor the flash that accompanied it, and, after the first one, he had begun to dump his shells on the tray and then make off for whatever cover he could find behind a locker on X-gun deck. This had delayed the loading of the gun once or twice and produced some choice language from Our Albert Forster, who was acting as captain during Raikes's absence in cells.

That night, in the darkness about 2330, they had an anti-aircraft shoot. For Williams this meant that instead of being in the front of the gunshield, he sat on a little stool attached to the rear of the shields and set the correct fuses on shells which Low placed on a tray in front of him. He had to keep his eyes open, first to watch for any changes on the fuse indicator from the T.S. and then to set the right fuses on the shells with his key. But at least he had his back to the muzzle and did not get the flash in his face.

The chief trouble was in fixing the key into slots in the fuse. Unless the key fitted, it slipped round without turning the fuse, and this nearly caused a disaster. The shells which Low placed on Williams's tray were well greased—too well greased. The key slipped badly, and after struggling with it for some seconds Williams had only moved the fuse a couple of notches, which meant that the shell would burst only a few hundred yards from the ship. But Calamity, in his impatience, snatched the improperly fused shell off the tray, rammed it into the gun, and next moment the fire gong sounded and the gun fired. The shells from the other three guns exploded far away in the air. But there was one black blotch well away from the others. Y gun's shell was showering its shrapnel almost over the ship.

When the shoot was over, Jock Forrest came over to Williams. " What happened to that shell, Bob ? "

Williams told him that the key had slipped and that he had let Calamity snatch it away before it was properly fused.

" Look here, you two, never do that again. If you snatch up a shell that's set zero, Calamity, you'll have the bloody thing exploding inside the gun and that'll be the end of the lot of us. You're to hang on to the bloody thing, Bob, until it's properly fused, and if the key keeps slipping, you're to call out for a new shell."

Williams had occasion to remember that later on.

By the Grace of God, the second part of port watch had the Last Dog from 1800 to 2000; and as they were in safe waters and were now going to patrol outside the boom until morning, they were in four watches, which meant that the second part of port were not on duty again until 8 a.m. They had all night in.

But the watch was up again long before 0800 to the pipe of " All the hands. Fore part for'ard, after part aft. Stand by wires and fenders for going alongside oiler."

At three that afternoon they were out again to do a torpedo run, which meant firing two dummy torpedoes at a target and then chasing them to pick them up when they stopped. There was a sharp escape of compressed air as the torpedo was fired and the tin fish streaked out of the tube and splashed into the water to begin its run. The torpedoes had a special gadget attached which burst into a fizzy flame when the torpedoes stopped and marked their position. When the *Marsden* came alongside she lowered her whaler and the whaler's crew towed the torpedoes into the side, where they were raised to the deck with a torpedo davit.

For once, said the seamen, the torpedomen had to work.

The torpedomen had always seemed a happy, easy-going lot. They kept to themselves and seemed to be on the best of terms with the Gunner (T.) in charge of them, and with the T.I., whose cheerfulness contrasted with the tense severity of the G.I.

The only work they seemed to have in the normal way was putting grease and oil on the Iron Deck, which Calamity would later have to sweep up, and occasionally painting their torpedo tubes or polishing the heads of their torpedoes. Because of this polishing and because the torpedoes were very seldom used in action, the whole outfit—tubes, tin fish, and men—were called the *Marsden's* " main ornament."

By six o'clock they were moored to a buoy once more, and all night in.

5

There were various ways of spending time if the ship was in harbour, and the crew were not allowed ashore. Some men wrote letters. Harry Rhoades had met a girl outside the pictures in Oldhaven and had fallen for her. He used to write whenever he could, and would look up at the end with a satisfied smile and say, " I've written fifteen pages to my Judy to-night." Judy was not the girl's name, but was a generic term used in Liverpool, and in New York for that matter, to describe all attractive girls.

Harry had got it really badly. One night he said, " You know, I was really happy in the Navy until I met that girl. I'd always wanted to go abroad and see places. But now it would suit me fine if the flicking war ended to-morrow and I could go home. Well, not home, perhaps, but anyway to Oldhaven. She's a smashing girl."

There were one or two other " gooey " men on the ship who used to spend a good deal of their spare time writing to their

" party " or best girl. Leading Seaman Jeffries was one. He had
seen as much action in this war as anyone on the ship, but he used
to say, quite frankly, " If my girl told me to stay home, I'd desert
to-morrow," and he used to bring out pictures of his girl whenever he could get anyone to look at them. Everyone, of course,
used to write letters from time to time. Jock Forrest used to
write to his " old lady," and her replies came in spidery, old-
fashioned handwriting. Leslie Dowson used to write to his wife,
threatening to enclose brown paper to wrap up the presents she
had not sent. But no one wrote as assiduously as the " gooey "
boys, who ignored the blare of the wireless with its indistinct
dance-band music or records played from the torpedomen's mess
deck, of George Formby singing " Oi'm going down thi 'ole to
get thi coal." They even ignored Tombola.

Tombola is the only legal form of gambling in the Navy. There
is plenty of gambling on the quiet, but the money is swept under
cover if there is any danger of an officer coming on the mess deck.
Tombola, however, is officially recognised. It is part of Navy life,
like rum and duty-free tobacco. Children play it and call it lotto,
people play it in pubs and call it housey-housey. In Tombola
everyone bought a card with three lines of numbers on it. Then
one man drew numbers from a sack and called them out. If a
number called was on your card, you crossed it off. The first
to cross off one line of numbers won a prize and the first to cross
off a whole card of numbers won a bigger prize.

Both the winner of the " line " and the winner of the " house "
had to check his card with the man who had drawn the numbers
from the sack and who had placed each number as he called it
on a board in front of him. When his card was proved, the
winner of a line drew, say, 10 per cent. of all the money that had
been paid for cards, the winner of a house drew 40 per cent., and
the remainder went into the canteen fund for buying gramophone
records and other things for the ship.

When the whole ship's company, except the officers, was playing, and better still when the *Marsden* was alongside another ship
and her crew came in to play too, it was not unusual to win eight
or nine pounds for a house. The prize had been known to go as
high as £20. So it was a tense moment when three or four men
had only one more number to cross off.

Newton, as befitted his established position in the ship, was
the man who drew the numbers from the bag, and something like
150 men, some of them Petty Officers and all of them grown up,
hung on the sound of his voice.

He did not merely *call* a number. Every number had a tradit-
ional name or a traditional way in which it had to be announced.
And the players had little jokes which became a tradition on the
Marsden.

When it seemed that everyone had bought his card, Newton

would say, " Any more for cards ? " and Jackie Low would call back, " Yes, no more." Then Newton would call, " Eyes down for the line," dig into his bag and call, " First number, All the sevens, seventy-seven; by itself, number two; bed and breakfast, two and six; five and nine, the Brighton line; two little ducks, twenty-two; seven and six, she was worth it; Jimmie's chum, number eleven; two, o, twenty; four and three, forty-three; spot below, number six," and so on until somebody had crossed off a line.

And the lucky man would shout, " Here you are! " Newton in his sing-song voice would say, " . . . and a line called," and Jackie Low, whoever had won, even if it was himself, would cry out, " Same old faces! You'll never live to spend it! "

When the line had been checked, Newton would begin again with " Eyes down for the House. Royal salute, twenty-one; five, o, change hands; all the eights, garden gates; one and two, one doz.; doctor's chum, number nine," and so on.

The players watched their cards in stern silence, broken now and then by come exclamation. Pat Maclure sat over his card while number after number was called, but never one that was on his. At last a number on his card came up. He crossed it off in disgust: " Blood! It's a pity to spoil the bastard. It would have been as good as new."

But as fewer and fewer spaces remained to be filled up on the cards, not a word was spoken and all concentrated tensely on the paper before them.

On and on went Newton's voice: " Kelly's Eye, number one; all the sixes, clickety click; Downing Street, number ten; top of the grot, nine, o; unlucky for some, thirteen."

But thirteen was not unlucky for one. As soon as it was called, Price jumped up with a great shout of " Here you are." Newton finished his sentence with " . . . and a house called," and Price went up to check his card. He came back dancing with £3 10s. in his hand, while the rest of the players broke into a babble of conversation.

6

They went to sea first thing next day. They were to carry out evolutions with one of the big battle wagons which had just come into commission. The battle wagon first tried her guns, letting out orange flashes and clouds of smoke, followed, a good ten seconds later, by the crack of the gun; and though the battle wagon was a good distance away and the *Marsden*, with other destroyers, was merely screening her from submarine attack, the concussion of those heavy guns rattled the ship.

Late that afternoon the *Marsden* went alongside the battle wagon. The sight put all thought of work out of their minds. The upper deck of the battleship did not seem much higher above the water than the iron deck of the *Marsden*, but her superstructure towered far above. She was very long. She could have used the *Marsden* for a motor-boat. And she was so clean.

Not that the *Marsden* was dirty. She could hardly be that. She'd put in very little sea-time so far and she had been thoroughly scrubbed, swept, and painted whenever she was in harbour. But the battle wagon shone. The Marsdens said it was the gold braid that glinted in the sun on her quarter deck. They had never seen so many naval officers together before. There were Captains, Surgeon Captains, Paymaster Captains, all sorts of Captains.

" Oi suppose they use their Lieutenant Commanders for ditching the gash," said Price.

They were both back in the anchorage by 1700, " Our Albert " Forster wondering how the big-ship sailors had enjoyed their trip, whether any of them had failed to be sick, and whether they would leave their buoy again before Christmas.

The *Marsden* did not even reach *her* buoy. She had hardly got through the boom when she swung round and went out again. She was being sent to pick up the Commander-in-Chief, who was paying a visit. The run was only an hour and a half there and back. The sea was calm. The shore itself looked lovely and peaceful from the sea. But the *Marsden's* ship's company were not pleased. They would have preferred to have a wash in one of the buckets and play tombola. But there it was.

Jimmie said that the C.-in-C. might want to see the *Marsden's* crew perform some evolutions. But the C.-in-C. asked for a cup of tea instead, which was brought him in the wardroom by Arthur Denney, the Skipper's steward.

Denney was a baldish man of thirty-five, with impish grey eyes. He had been a waiter in civil life and wanted to get back to his hotel.

" How long have you been in the Navy ? " the C.-in-C. asked.

" Two years, sir."

" What do you think of it ? "

" Oh, it's all right for people like you who've been in it since you were boys," said Denney.

The C.-in-C. laughed and Denney went up to the bridge with a cup of tea for the Skipper.

Denney took a good deal of licence in his dealings with the Skipper and nagged him for not wearing enough clothes in cold weather or for staying too long without sleep on the bridge when the *Marsden* was at sea. He would struggle from the quarter deck to the bridge, with the ship rolling and the sea coming over, carrying a plate of sandwiches in one hand and a cup of coffee in the other, and would tell the Skipper that he intended to stay on the bridge until the sandwiches and coffee were finished. He was always coming into the mess deck in a disgruntled mood, complaining that the " Old Man won't eat," or that the " Old Man's been up there for thirty-six hours. He'll wear himself out."

The *Marsden's* crew soon began to feel that they were wearing *themselves* out. They were at sea almost every day and many nights. While at sea they were always having dummy runs on the guns until they were sick of it. But even these drills could be enlivened. Williams with his earphones could hear everything that passed between the T.S. and the other guns or between the director and the rangefinder and the T.S. The talk had been strictly technical, but as the crews began to find themselves and to be sure of their jobs, they dropped formality.

Jack Price was communication number in the rangefinder at cruising stations, with Pat Maclure, and sometimes sang to the T.S.—to keep them warm, he said.

" You poor basstuds, you need something to cheer you. You've only got an electric stove to keep you warm. We're at the top of the flicking mast, with no flicking roof to our flicking heads and the flicking rain pouring in and the flicking wind whistling round us loike a basstud, but we can't shiver. There isn't room. 'Ere's a song for you," and he began " Sea Fever " with variations to the words. " *And all I want is a tall ship, and a flicking star to take me flicking well home by.*"

Lieutenant Burton broke in to tell the T.S. that he was proposing to test communications.

" One, two, three, four," counted Lieutenant Burton.

" Four, three, two, one," echoed Price in the rangefinder, mimicking Burton's voice.

" Who's there ? "

" Rangefinder 'ere, sir," replied Price in his normal voice. " Are you calling us ? " as though Burton's " Who's there ? " had been the first words he had heard.

Lieutenant Burton began his counting again. " Was that clear ? There seems to be a good deal of crackling on the line."

" I don't know about crackling," said Price, mimicking, " but there's a hell of a lot of cackling. I can't get to sleep."

" Who *is* that ? "

" Rangefinder 'ere, sir. Are you calling us ? "

Once the communication testing was done, the songbirds were at it again. " This is Bing Crosby calling " was followed by an appalling noise which was Leading Seaman Dowson crooning. He had strolled into the T.S. on his way to make ki (cocoa to civilians) in the galley and offered to cheer the gun's crew with a snatch of song. He was begged to get on with his ki.

In the pitch darkness of the gunshields the crew on watch sang too. Harry Rhoades of Y gun had a lovely voice and used to sing songs he had learned from his Irish mother while the others hummed in accompaniment. Usually they sang popular songs and other favourites which reminded them of home. Sometimes they startled the T.S. with *Abide with me* and *Hark, the herald Angels sing*—" Christ, is that what you call yourselves ? " asked Professor Cole from the T.S.

It all helped to pass the time and to keep the crew warm through the long cold hours of the middle watch. But the best thing of all was ki. Jock Forrest never once left the gun himself. But he would allow one or other of his crew to go to the mess and prepare a fannyful of hot cocoa for the crew. It got rid of sea-sickness and made the watch seem shorter. Ki was as good as rum. Better in fact. You could drink buckets of it without affecting either your head or your stomach.

There was always ki after the first two hours of a watch at night, there was ki again when the crews came off watch and got down to the warmth of the mess deck. It was remarkable how spirits rose when the time for ki came near. Men who had shivered into silence about 0300 stirred again when, at 0330, the T.S. came through with the order, " Time to change lookouts. Only half an hour to go." At 0345 the Bosun's Mate piped " A-L-L the starboard watch " and the port watch began to sing again and make jokes. Then came the pipe, clear in the earphones, " Starboard watch to defence stations," and the port watch began to gather themselves and their coats from the deck of the shield in readiness to nip down to the mess deck as soon as their reliefs appeared.

It was glorious to get into the warmth, to suck down a cup of hot ki, and then climb, more or less fully clothed, into a hammock or to plump down on the lockers, until, it seemed, only a few minutes later the Bosun's Mate was round again piping " A-L-L the port watch " and then " Port watch to defence stations " and the weary round of cold wakefulness would begin again.

In the fortnight they had five nights and two days in harbour.

The first day in harbour they worked hard, painting the ship, scrubbing the Iron Deck, and setting up traditional life-lines to hang on to when walking along the deck in heavy seas.

The new life-lines started all sorts of buzzes. They were going to Russia right away. They were being switched to Gibraltar and were preparing for the Bay of Biscay. They were going to Brazil. But they went on as before for several more days. Then one dinner-time, on their second day in harbour, when they had been scrubbing and painting all morning, there was an unusual pipe. " Hands to make and mend clothes. Leave to the starboard watch from thirteen hundred to eighteen hundred." There was a shout from the starboard watch, who would have five hours ashore, and sighs of relief from the port watch, who, though on board, would at least have a chance of getting their heads down.

Unhappily, this chance soon faded. A few minutes after the libertymen had been taken ashore in one drifter, another came alongside and the duty watch were piped to muster on the Iron Deck. They were told to unload stores from the drifter and among the stores were more than a hundred sheepskin coats. At once the temperature in the ship dropped until sheepskin coats became a necessity. They could mean only one thing. The ship was really going North and the buzzes had her on her way to Murmansk that evening. The cheeriness, which had flooded the mess deck an hour before, froze.

Everyone on the ship, even those who had not been to sea, had some idea of what this Russian run was like. You were about three weeks there and back, unless you stayed in one of the Russian ports for a time. During those three weeks you were attacked by aircraft for anything up to ten days on end, and by submarines for about sixteen days. You might not be hit, but the stories you heard suggested that you probably would be. And if you *were*, and landed in the oggin, God help you. You might be killed outright by the sudden shock of the icy-cold water, or you might live on for as many as ten gasping, biting, body-destroying seconds. It was not a nice prospect.

" Someone's got to do it," said Dowson. " But why the hell should it be us ? "

When the drifter was unloaded, Buck came round, without his leer, piping " Away motor-boat's crew," and within a minute it was known throughout the mess deck that the *Marsden* had received orders to sail at 1800 that night and that all libertymen were being recalled from shore immediately.

A squad of pickets went ashore under Petty Officer " Rattler " Morgan to round up the men from the cinema, the canteen, or wherever they might be. Within an hour the first boatload of dazed libertymen was being unloaded on to the *Marsden*.

" What the hell's the matter ? Where are we going ? "

" Russia."

But they were not going to Russia. At 1730 lower deck was cleared and the Skipper gave them the news. They were sailing in half an hour for Iceland to screen an American cruiser which was going to take up her station there. They would stay in Iceland for at least three weeks, screening one of the big ships. After that, said the Skipper, he did not know. The crew did. Russia, they said to each other.

Yet the Skipper's news had eased the tension. Iceland was not too good. It was a nasty crossing. It was a long way from home. But still, it was not Russia. Thank God for small mercies. Even the Skipper's final " Remember, we've only been practising up to now. From now on it's the real thing. We may get shot at at any time. So keep your eyes wide open," did not worry them. They were not going on that bloody run just yet after all. Thank God for that.

" Close X doors and scuttles "; " Special sea-duty men to your

121

stations "; " Fo'c'sle men on the fo'c'sle, quarter-deck men on the quarter deck. Stand by for leaving harbour "—none of these brought that sinking feeling in the stomach which many had felt when they first heard them piped at Oldhaven in the sunshine . . . was it only two weeks ago ? It was bloody to be going to sea, really going to sea across waters that could pick a small ship up and crash it down, which were swarming, so they said, with U-boats, which got steadily colder the farther north you went. It was bloody, but nothing more. They were not going on that Russian run . . . yet. Not for three weeks at least. And in three weeks anything might happen . . . the *Marsden's* steering might break down . . . they might have boiler trouble—one of the stokers had said that number one boiler could do with a clean already and they'd only been out for two weeks . . . Yes, anything might happen.

So they set sail for Iceland at six in the evening at the end of June.

Chapter Eight

1

THERE had been nothing June-like about their last station.

As the *Marsden* went north the weather became drier. But it was even colder and, before going on watch, the crew put on at least three jerseys, and pulled their thick sea-boot stockings well up their thighs.

It was more pleasant than ever, at the end of a night watch, to get below. When the ship was in two watches, as it was on the way to Iceland, hammocks could be left slung instead of being stowed in the netting; and though this meant that it was almost impossible to walk upright through the mess deck, this was nothing compared with the joy of coming off watch, slipping off sea-boots and climbing straight in to snatch some sleep.

The only discomfort on the way up was when the American cruiser the *Marsden* was escorting signalled that she was proposing to do a speed trial.

This was a chance for the *Marsden* to test herself, though a destroyer ought to be able to outpace a cruiser easily enough. But it would be useful practice to work up to top speed and would, moreover, show the Yankees what the Royal Navy was like.

The trial began. The *Marsden's* rattle increased, her white wake fanned out still wider, her stem pitched into the water and heaved showers of spray over the fo'c'sle. Most of the crew, even those off duty, came to watch and grinned to each other as they pulled steadily away. The Engineer went on the bridge and announced that they were now going full speed at 33 knots and asked permission to have a special pennant hoisted, which meant, apparently, that they had got the measure of their rival.

The American cruiser acknowledged this pennant, and put on speed. Effortlessly, with her stem barely heaving, she drew quietly alongside and, within a few minutes, was showing her stern.

" You had better haul that flag down," said the Skipper to the crimson Engineer.

" Good old *Marsden*," said Price. " She couldn't keep pace with the old *Duchess*, could she, Les ? "

" Ah, the *Duchess*. I remember her going so fast her paddles scarcely touched the water."

They stayed off Iceland a month, but the crew never had a chance to land. If their only job had been to screen the battle wagon which was lying there, the crew would have been well satisfied; for the battle wagon only went out twice and then for less than twenty-four hours each time. But the *Marsden* was never idle and was seldom tied to her buoy. She always seemed to be duty boat, parading up and down, up and down, outside the entrance to the fjord, watching for submarines. Or else she was sent to chase a sub. which some plane thought it had seen. She would be away two nights without seeing anything and return to find that a cruiser wanted a practice shoot and she was to be screened.

But one morning drifters came alongside and the ship's company, instead of scrubbing the side, had to haul sacks of potatoes and greens on board, with cartons of tinned milk, butter, and sugar, and crates of frozen meat.

Immediately the buzzes started. They were going to Russia. They were going to screen a minelaying expedition off the coast of Norway. They were going to Halifax, Nova Scotia, to bring back an aircraft carrier. Price spread these buzzes in the mess deck, one after the other.

When the Skipper cleared lower deck after dinner he announced that they *were* going on a minelaying expedition. They would be away about seven days. There would be minelayers escorted by a cruiser and a number of destroyers. They must expect trouble. They must keep their eyes open.

They sailed in miniature convey at 1800 with the destroyers fanned out round the minelayers and the cruiser. They went at once into two watches, but for three days nothing happened. Even the sea was calm. The crew kept their watches, swept up during the Forenoon, drilled on the guns, ate, read, and slept.

Some were able to doze even on watch. As there was not much room in the gunshields, one or two of the gun's crew used to crawl into lockers near the gun. Shortarse had been known to sleep standing. He sometimes slept coiled like a snake round the Kelvin Sounding Machine near the warm funnel. But usually he slept in the B-gun breech bag, with his head under cover and his feet taking the air.

On the fourth day port watch was in the mess deck drinking tea for the morning stand-easy when an explosion shook the *Marsden*. It shook her crew even more. The old hands said it was a depth charge and began to get ready for action stations. But Pat Maclure said that the minelayers had begun to drop their mines; it was a normal thing for an occasional mine to go off when it was being laid and nobody on a minelayer thought much about it.

They turned for home about six and the buzz went round the ship that they were to take the minelayers all the way back to Scotland. For once this buzz seemed to be true, for by the end of the seventh day, when they should have been in sight of Iceland, they were still at sea with no land near. However, early next morning, they were summoned back to their fjord by an urgent signal and, flashing a good-bye, swung round at top speed and left the convoy.

They raced back and entered the boom just as darkness was beginning to fall. The first things they saw were two cruisers entering the boom ahead of them.

" What the hell are they doing here ? " asked the Duchess. " There must be something up."

" Hey, look at that battle wagon," said Our Albert Forster. " She's got steam up; and her boats are in. *And* her lower boom is in. God's teeth! She must be going out. What the hell's up ? "

They soon found out. The *Von Scheer* had left her Norwegian harbour and was heading for the Denmark Straits between Iceland and Greenland. If she could slip through there, she would be at large in the Atlantic. Every available ship in Iceland was being held with steam up, ready to intercept her.

The Marsdens were tired. Even though they had seen no action, they had been at sea. Seven days at sea with only broken sleep. They were unwashed. They wanted a night in. Instead they were being rushed into action. They hardly spoke to one another, but flopped down on lockers while an oiler poured oil into the *Marsden's* tanks.

But as soon as they had tied up to the oiler, the motor-boat was called away. As Charlie Wright went with it and Charlie Wright had wangled himself the job of postman, the thoughts of the crew were suddenly diverted from the *Von Scheer*. They had had no letters for more than three weeks, and now that there was a chance of getting some within the hour, they became like children on Christmas Eve.

The motor-boat came chugging back, loaded with sacks. The mail was sorted into messes in the ship's office, and the leading hand of each mess went to fetch it when it was ready and re-sorted it into individual piles. Some of the piles were big and their owners leaped on them, counted—" I've got fourteen "; " Well, I've got twelve "—tore open every envelope, reading bits of one letter, then switching to the next, and when they had glanced at the last, beginning all over again and reading each one through thoroughly.

One or two men had no letters at all and cussed. One man had no letters, and just looked blank as though life had left his face. This was Harrison, Dowson's mate on the point-fives. He went to his locker, brought out a magazine, and tried to read while all around him his messmates were absorbed in their letters.

Some were reading out little bits. Jackie Low had been sent a copy of his local weekly paper. " Ha! " he shouted. " Good old East Ham! They're still at it. ' *Girl's body found in garage.*' ' *Two slain with axe.*' That's the stuff to give 'em."

" Hey, Bob," shouted Calamity. " What does ' *a votre bonne sante, mon ami,*' mean ? Where the hell does this girl get that sort of stuff from ? Seems kind of suspicious to me. Looks like one of those Free Frenchmen is being a bloody sight too free."

" Christ Almighty ! " said Carter, lumbering over from his mess to speak to Jock. " I gets no letter for three bleeding weeks and then the missus thinks it enough to send ten lousy lines. I'll show her. I'll go aft this bloody minute and stop her allotment."

" How many times have you written her ? " said Jock.

" I haven't written. Been too busy. Can't write letters when you're at sea."

" There's the bloody matelot all over. Writes no flicking letter himself, but when his wife, who's probably sweating her guts out in some munitions factory to keep her home going, only sends ten lines, he wants to stop her allotment. Ye're all the same. Ye go out boozing whenever ye're ashore and ye picks up the first girls ye can find and spends money on them, and then ye gets a letter from the wife saying ' *Kitty and me went to a dance last Tuesday just for something to do,*' and ye starts raving. ' The slut,' ye says. ' The flicking bitch. Gallivanting around when Ah'm risking ma life at sea. Ah'll stop her flicking allotment.' "

" How do you know my wife went to a dance last Tuesday ? "

"Hey, just listen to this," said Barber. "My girl says, 'I must close as I have joined the N.F.S. and have to go fire-watching.' Firewatching indeed! I know the sort of watch she'll be keeping. Last Dog and all night in with a flicking fire-man."

"Well, Oi will say this," said Price, "they 'aven't forgotten me. At least me mother still loves me. She's sent me a dirty book. Price fourpence."

The whole mess deck was alive with smiles and banter; the *Von Scheer*, the *Marsden*, even the sea itself were forgotten for fifteen minutes; and when the letters were all read, and the crew were sitting back, digesting, Low said: "Well, they can bring on their *Von Scheer* or any other bastard ship they like now. I'm ready to tackle the old *Tirpitz* in a flicking rowing-boat."

They did not have to tackle the *Tirpitz* or anything else that night. By the time they left the oiler, the "panic" had sub-sided. The *Von Scheer* had turned back as soon as she had been spotted by scouting planes.

"I'll bet those German bastards are as glad as we are," said Pat Maclure.

2

By now the *Marsden's* crew had become so absorbed into the life of the ship that they no longer found it strange or unnatural. They managed to live with little friction. Yet they lived on top of each other and by any civilian standards they were most uncomfortable at sea or in harbour.

Within three weeks of leaving Oldhaven, One Mess was left with only fifteen plates and saucers, ten cups, and about as many knives and forks for twenty-five men. Even in daytime in har-bour, when the hammocks were piled high in the hammock net-ting, there barely seemed room to move. There were always kettles or fannies hanging from the deckhead, and boxes of onions or potatoes on the deck itself. Lockers overflowed and sweaters, watchcoats, oilskins, duffel coats, and sheepskin coats piled on the deck.

These piles got wet even in harbour, because the steam-pipe, from No. 1 boiler-room to the capstan engine, leaked and buckets placed to catch the drips of boiling water were usually upset.

The crew found it hard to keep themselves clean in this mess. At sea, when they were not supposed to undress, it was not much use trying. But when the ship came in, a packed mass of dirty seamen would try to bathe themselves in buckets, shouting "Shut that bloody door" at every newcomer who wedged his way into the washroom. They would swing up their buckets and pour the contents over themselves—and everyone else. Any towels which managed to escape the douche from a bucket became soaked in the condensed stream which streamed down the walls.

No wonder that some of the men gave up the struggle to be clean, and that the mess stank of feet.

Jock did his best to keep the mess " decent." He never allowed a man to eat with his hat on. Even at the worst of the knife shortage he never allowed anyone to use his jack-knife at table. For all meals, at any time of the day or night, he insisted on having the oilskin cloth laid properly on the table.

" Ye tired bastards ! " he shouted at some men who had put cups of ki on the bare boards. " The cloth's right beside ye and ye dinna put it down. Well, ye'll pu' it down now because that's the way Ah likes it."

He saw that the food was equally shared and that sufficient was kept hot for men who were still on watch when meal-times arrived. Both he and Dowson spent a lot of time making duffs for the mess and teaching others to make them. Both did more than their share in scrubbing the mess out and trying to keep it clean. The motto of both was " Do as I do," not merely " Do as I say," and, on the whole, their example was followed.

There were, of course, exceptions. Rhoades was one. He ate more and worked less in the mess than anyone else. When it was his turn to fetch the supper from the galley he went fishing from the Iron Deck. When it was his turn to dish up, he would be found with his head down, on top of a pile of hammocks in the netting. If he was detailed to sweep the mess, he spent his time leaning against the gas-mask locker reading a scrap of paper. And when his messmates cussed him, he just grinned sheepishly and said, " Sorry. I didn't know I was cooks," and tumbled over to do his job.

Yet Harry could work.

Williams was once caught for a casual job of work during the First Dog when the rest were off duty. He had to wind the handle of a winch to lift one of the torpedoes. It was hard work for one man and he was soon exhausted. Harry Rhoades, who, as usual in harbour, was fishing over the side, suddenly left his line and said, " Here, Bob, let me take the other handle. It'll be easier with two of us," and spent the next half-hour swinging at the handles.

He was a strange man. He swore more than anyone on the ship. Almost every third word was unprintable and yet he never meant anything by it. He would say, " Yes, I know it's silly. I never do it at home. It's just a habit on the ship," and go on swearing.

His casualness was always getting him into trouble with the Buffer and he was always threatening, in the safety of the mess, to break the Buffer's neck for him and cursing the day he joined the Navy. Yet he could do most jobs well and took great delight in giving directions whenever he happened to be working in a group. He certainly *was* lazy, but he was also good-hearted, and would not deliberately have shoved his share on to another of his messmates if he had thought about it. The real trouble was that he seldom thought about anything except his " Judy " in Oldhaven.

He *had* got it badly. He wrote fifteen-page letters. He set about saving money so earnestly that he would not even buy a box of matches and was always pestering his messmates with a " Give us a light, please," until Jackie Low, in a burst of impatience, gave him a box and told him never to ask for a light again. Harry grinned, but next day it was " Give us a light, please," as before.

Another man who shirked mess work was Price. Price was a bad sailor and at sea spent most of his spare time lying on a locker or in his hammock. That meant no hardship for the others, since at sea, those who ate dished up and Price ate little. But in harbour he made up for it, yet was still disinclined to do mess work. His fellow-cooks were always nagging him. One supper-time, in harbour, when Jock, Price, Harry Rhoades, and Williams were cooks, Price was in his hammock and did not begin to climb out until the supper table was half laid.

Williams called to him: " Come on, Jack; you're cooks."

" Oi know, Oi know. What do you think Oi'm getting out of my hammock for ? "

" I should say you were getting out just slow enough to miss all the work and just fast enough to swipe the biggest helping."

" Oo's speaking ? Oi bet you not done more work than me."

" I couldn't have done less."

" You don't know what hard work is."

" Possibly not. But I can recognise shirking when I see it."

" Shut you flicking mouth. You 'aven't got the hook yet."

" No. All I've got so far is your share of the work."

In Two Mess, Denton brought shirking to a fine art. He would be lolling on the lockers after dinner smoking a cigarette, when one of his messmates would shout, " Here, Denton, you're a cook. Come and give a hand with the dishing up," and Denton would say, " Oh, so I am. I mean to say, I'd sort of forgotten. Thank you for reminding me," and go on lolling.

Rather than do a job and be done with it, he would argue for half an hour, or else he would slink off so that he could not be found when there was work to do. At first he got away with it, but Wild Angus, the killick of his mess, though no talker, had considerable experience with shirkers. After getting a series of dirty jobs, Denton became less conspicuously absent from his mess duties.

*   *   *

For the most part the lower deck, after five weeks or so at sea, had settled down together reasonably well. Just as in the hut at *Frobisher*, they had developed their own conventions and worked up their own jokes which bound them together, whether they liked it ot not, inside their iron world.

One of the conventions was that it was " bad form " to speak well of the Navy. Not that you often wanted to when you were wet through or jerked out of your hammock in the middle of every night or kept hanging about on the quarter deck in the chilly Icelandic wind. But anyone who *did* praise the Navy was damned as " All for it."

Nearly everyone " dripped " bitterly, called himself a fool for having joined, and swore that he would get outside at the earliest possible moment. Their normal greeting was " Hallo! Are you happy in the Service ? " a question which expected the answer " You bet. I'm all for it."

At least once a day Leading Seaman Dowson would announce that he was chokka, that he was going to chuck his hand in, only to be told, " Go on. You're all for it. You'll sign for another ten," or else, " You shouldn't have joined if you can't take a joke."

When Buck came round with his daily pipe of " Men under punishment to muster," even little Sinbad would get up quickly and shout, " Come on, boys, that means the lot of us."

Another convention was that you must not brag about your past experience at sea. Whenever Forster or anyone else did this, those nearest him would hum the first line of *Pop Goes the Weasel* and " Listen to old Jack Strop. Come on, Stripey, tell us about Trafalgar."

It was almost a convention, too, to be violent and uncivil. Instead of " Please pass the butter," you shouted, " Pass that flicking slide or I'll very probably slash you." Instead of " Excuse me, please," you shouted, " Gangway before I *make* a bastard." If you were dropping something from the quarter deck into the tiller flat where men were working, you did not say, " Look out, boys, I want to drop this down." You simply threw it down, shouting as you did so, " Under below. Too flicking late."

None of these meant anything except, perhaps, that you were among friends and had no need to be polite.

The " family " jokes were of the same kind as the conventions. If you asked Dowson if he had a bit of spun-yarn he would invariably reply, " No; but I've got a bag that's had cakes in it." Shortarse would say, " No; but I've got a sister in the Wrens," or " No; but I've got an aunt in Australia "—in a helpful tone of voice. If Low saw anyone pull what looked like a lot of money from his belt he would say, " Cool! He ought to be made tell where he got it."

129

But the man who made the most jokes was Buck. In the first week of the commission his pipes had been according to the book. They always remained according to the book—on the quarter deck, but by the time they reached the mess deck they became more and more garbled as the weeks passed. He would blow a few notes and pipe ; " When ' Hands fall in ' is piped, hands will muster amidships with their tin helmets, anti-flash gear, gas-masks, and identity discs. Don't say you haven't been told. Don't say you didn't hear the pipe. Just say it wasn't on your flicking card."

Coming back into the harbour one night, instead of the formal " Fore part for'ard, after part aft, stand by wires and fenders," he produced, " Fore part solid, after part daft, stand by Marks and Spencers "; and once, after an American destroyer had been alongside for a night in the fjord, he piped, " Liberty guys will muster by the after smoke stack," and instead of " Away motor-boat," he cried " Away gasoline gig."

He would never make a joke when there was a serious job on, as when they were putting to sea for some possibly dangerous work, but in harbour he let himself go. He used to stop just inside the mess deck, blow on his pipe, call out the order, and then move through to One Mess, where the procedure would be repeated before he sank down the hatchway into the watch-keepers' mess below. Sometimes when he was almost at the bottom of the ladder he would think of something else to say to the seamen. Then his head would pop up through the hatchway, the leer would spread over his face, he would blow his pipe and add some ribald comment. " Men under punishment and stoppage of leave to muster "—here he would descend to the mess below—" Men under punishment and stoppage of leave to muster. Leave "—here his head would pop up through the hatchway again—" Leave—and this doesn't touch you, you ugly bastards—to watchkeepers only from thirteen hundred to eighteen hundred."

Commando Buck was not afraid of anyone, not even the First Lieutenant. Once when Jimmie was in a particularly aggressive mood and was spitting orders all over the bridge, he saw a smile flitting over Buck's face.

" What are you grinning at, Bosun's Mate ? " he asked sharply.

" Oh, nothing, sir, except I like the way you do your Big Chief stuff." Jimmie glared at him and then grinned too.

3

After the minelaying expedition and the *Von Scheer* "panic," the *Marsden* was in harbour for two days—a record since they left Oldhaven. But they were not idle. First they washed the Iron Deck with a hose and scrubbed it with stiff brooms. Then the torpedomen, fiddling as usual with the main ornaments, spilled pools of oil over the deck. The oil had to be wiped off and the deck washed again. Then they put black-leading on the Iron Deck and left it to dry. Specks of dirt stuck to the black-leading, so they washed the deck down again with the hose. That left stains of salt. So they washed the deck down again with ordinary water to remove the salt. By the end of the day they wished they had gone to sea.

The next day was worse. Rhoades, Redfern, Williams, and three others were put over the side in the whaler and told to paint patches which the sea had laid bare. They began at the stem and were hauled slowly aft by Leading Seaman Dowson.

When they began, the sea was calm in the fjord and they stood in the whaler and painted what patches they could reach. But after ten minutes one of those Icelandic winds sprang up.

" It blows up here as quick as Jimmie," said Calamity Taylor.

At first, hundred of little ripples hurried over the surface, but in no time the ripples had turned into waves and the whaler heaved, upsetting paint and painters. Dowson tried to keep the whaler into the side, but she kept swinging, so that the painters either could not reach the ship at all or trapped their fingers between the gunwale and the side. At best they could only sit with poised paint brushes and make quick dabs whenever they were in reach.

Then one of the heaving lines broke and the stem of the whaler swung broadside to the sea. Immediately the waves bounded into the boat, soaking the painters.

They all shouted at once. Dowson also shouted, but the wind was so strong that no one in the boat could hear what he said. They could only see his mouth opening and shutting.

The stem of the whaler swung right round to face aft. Dowson threw down a new heaving line, and Redfern, after a struggle with his chilled fingers and a lot of advice from Rhoades, secured it. Dowson then pulled the whaler farther aft, where, he said, there would be some protection from the wind. There was. The waves no longer came over the gunwale. But other things did. Someone threw an empty bottle out of a porthole. Then, while Dowson was down in the watchkeepers' mess telling them not to throw any more bottles if they wanted to keep their ears in anything like a normal position, the fo'c'sle men started washing down the fo'c'sle. They washed the water into the whaler. Dowson, hurrying back, had a violent argument with Petty Officer Blair and, getting the worst of it, dragged the whaler still farther aft, out of the way of the hose.

Then came the climax. The six men in the whaler stared at what had happened. They swore. They shouted to Dowson. Then Redfern began to laugh.

" My God! " he said. " I should never have been able to imagine that. If you were in civvy life and someone asked you

131

what snags you'd find when you were painting the side of a ship from a whaler, you'd never think of THAT. You might imagine trapping your fingers or people throwing bottles out of portholes or sweeping water off the fo'c'sle or waves washing over. But you'd never imagine that just as you were passing the Heads somebody would flush the bloody things and all the muck would come into the boat."

But that was what *had* happened. The boat was nearly a quarter full of sea-water, mixed with paint, and on the surface, floating gently from side to side, was the muck from the Heads.

The only man who did not seem disturbed was Rhoades. He had long ago abandoned painting and was staring at the sea.

" Look at those waves," he shouted, grabbing Williams's arm. " Isn't it funny how they come rolling at you ? "

" Flick the waves," said Williams, watching the muck.

The six of them were wet and chilled when they climbed inboard. But at dinner-time there was a tot, and after dinner there was some good news. Jimmie announced that to-morrow the *Marsden* would ferry libertymen from other ships to Reykjavik and the non-duty watch would be allowed ashore for six hours. The port watch were non-duty. They had not set foot on land for thirty-seven days.

4

Jock Forrest would not go ashore. He had sailed the world for five years and lost any desire to see new places. He was curiously unexcited by many things. Redfern had one night pulled him off the mess deck to look at the Northern Lights. He had looked blankly at the sky and said, " Yes, we get those at home. And do you know, folk come out in their cars all the way from Edinburgh to look at them! " He had shaken his head slowly at such folly and gone back to the warmth.

As he was not going ashore he offered to " do a sub." for Dowson, who was not enthusiastic about going but was browbeaten into it by Maclure. Redfern also managed to get a sub., by offering two bars of " nutty " or chocolate to anyone in port watch who would agree to do his duty for him.

The *Marsden* overflowed during the run. Libertymen from other ships were jammed into the mess deck, stood three deep along the canteen and washroom flats, and even braved the wind and spray on the Iron Deck.

When they reached Reykjavik, Williams left the others and went to a stone church on the hillside which he had noticed from the sea.

The church was empty. There was no sound in it and no sound came into it from the outside. It was not big, but the roof was high. Williams sat in a back-row seat and took in the reviving silence, the emptiness, and the height. For thirty-eight days he had been aboard without a second's silence or privacy. He had been bounded by low deckheads, by the ship's curving sides. But now, in this church, he could stare upwards at a roof that was far above him and stretch his arms without danger of hitting anyone or anything. He could sit on the back seat without anyone climbing over him, without water dripping on him, without anyone asking him to move. He could sit, and sit in silence. Eventually he went to sleep, still sitting.

It was raining when he came back to the long main street, which was crowded with Icelanders of both sexes, American soldiers, and British sailors.

The finest looking were the Icelandic girls. They were fair-haired, finely built, and carried themselves with dignity. It was obvious that the sailors were getting nowhere with these girls. Smiles, leers, and passing whistles or hallos were entirely ignored. The girls sailed past, leaving the sailors looking silly.

Williams walked through the crowds until he saw a familiar figure standing dejectedly on the kerb and staring at his feet. The collar of his oilskin was turned up, his cap was tilted down, and the rain ran down his hat, along his nose and dripped into the gutter. It was Dowson " enjoying " his run ashore.

" My word, Duchess, you look chokka."

The Duchess lifted his eyes from his feet. He pushed a hand beneath his oilskin and brought out a bunch of notes. " Here, take these, Bob. Flick me if I go ashore again as long as I'm in the Navy. Go on, take the flickers. They're no use to me. Does *anyone* want some kroners ? "

The kroners were snatched from his hand by Pat Maclure, who with Jackie Low, Rhoades, and Calamity, had been into a shop asking for fish-hooks. They had been in about twenty shops already without finding the hooks. Instead, Jackie had bought a mouth-organ for himself and some silk stockings for his wife. They cursed the high prices, but thought the shop-keepers were grand.

" They all speak English," said Jackie, " and they smile at you when you go in. If I were a shopkeeper and some bastard foreigners dumped themselves in my town, I'd throw the flicking till at them."

" Come on, boys," said Pat, " the Duchess is going to buy us all some tea. Big eats. Dig in. Fill your boots."

They went to a teashop and ate fresh fried eggs and chips, coffee made with fresh milk, with unlimited sugar, and fresh bread with fresh butter. Even the Duchess began to feel better and looked at the loose change in his pocket. Calamity was puzzled by the small five-aura pieces with holes through the middle. " What the hell are those bloody little washers for ? "

After tea they met Redfern coming out of a tea-shop. He

had found the best cream cakes he had ever tasted. They all went back for some more, and stayed more than an hour, eating and gossiping.

" It will be nice to be sick from overeating instead of just sea-sick," said Redfern.

When they got back to the ship they found that the others had been bored with Reykjavik. The beer was as poor as spit, said Harrison, who had drunk twenty-five bottles during the afternoon. Others said the girls were " bloody snobs."

Harry Rhoades protested.

" You think you can pick up any flicking girl you flicking well like. You've only got to whistle at them and they'll come. Well, these girls are different. They're not sluts. They're dignified. That's what they are. Dignified."

" Like flick, they are. Carrot fashion," said Our Albert Forster. " They just think that sailors have no money."

" Well, they're flicking well right," said Duchess Dowson. " That black-faced Satan, Maclure, pinched all mine."

" You don't get these girls here going into pubs like the girls at home. They're dignified."

" What tarts go into pubs ? " asked Our Albert. " If I ever caught my sister in a boozer I'd thrash her."

" I don't see why girls shouldn't go into boozers. Not if they stick to beer. But I wouldn't let my girl start swilling gin and lime. Beer's all right," said Nevison.

" No; they shouldn't go into boozers at all. If I caught my sister in one, I wouldn't thrash right away. I wouldn't shame her in front of a crowd. I'd wait for her to go home and do my thrashing then."

" What about Gladys ? " asked Williams, remembering the barmaid at the Shipwright's in Oldhaven.

" Oh, Gladys was different. She worked there. But you shouldn't have women on the wrong side of the bar. I remember one tart in Londonderry nudging my arm just as I was about to drink. I knocked her right over a table."

" I hope her brother came in and thrashed you," said Rhoades. " AND did it before the crowd instead of waiting till you got home."

" Oh, you're gooey," said Our Albert, abashed. " Go on and write another thirty pages to your Judy."

This was one of the few times when a mess argument was about women. Some people think that when men are cooped together for long periods without even a sight of a woman, their minds become obsessed with women and at the first chance they leap ashore like rampant bulls. But when the Marsdens touched civilisation and they began to think again in terms of normal life, women were not the first objectives. A pint of beer, several pints of beer, cream cakes, and a bath came much higher up the list. At sea, where there was nothing to remind them of women, they forgot them, all except the gooey boys, and lived the ordinary life of the ship without suffering any discomfort from their natural instincts.

5

Next morning a drifter came alongside and the quarter-deck men, brooms in hand, strolled over to see what was happening. Suddenly George Barber put his hands on his hips, put his head back, and said, " Well, flick me. Just look what's coom oop," and there, standing in the drifter, with his eyeless grin, was Raikes, back from cells. He had been brought on another destroyer.

Sub-Lieutenant Carr, who was Officer of the Day, was standing by the gangway when Raikes climbed up. " Hallo, Raikes," he said. " Go back to your old billet in Number Two Mess, and then report to the Coxwain, will you ? "

Raikes's first question when he reached the mess deck was: " Why haven't you sods gone to Russia ? If a fellow can't miss a Russian convoy by doing fourteen days cells, the Navy's not what it used to be."

But there was still no sign of a Russian trip. The *Marsden* kept putting out on patrol, but nothing happened on these trips and the ship's company began to be bored. Even the First Lieutenant had some difficulty in thinking up work for them.

They all cursed the time-passing jobs they were given in the Forenoon.

" We fall in at eight a.m.," said Calamity one dinner-time as he flopped exhausted on the lockers, " and Jimmie says, ' Sweep the Iron Deck.' We fall in again at nine-thirty. ' Iron-deck party correct, sir,' says Hookey, and salutes. Jimmie rubs his leg, hums and haws a bit, then he says, ' Give the Iron Deck a good sweep up.' At eleven a.m. we falls in again. Hookey clicks his heels, salutes, and, says Jimmie, ' SWEEP UP THE FLICK- ING IRON DECK.' "

The quarter-deck men, however, were under the direct charge of Petty Officer Rattler Morgan, who had strong views about time-wasting. As soon as they had given the quarter deck its necessary sweeping and scrubbing, they were told to put their brooms down the tiller flat and muster on the three-inch gun platform. There, Rattler taught them how to do knots and splices or anything else they wanted to learn.

And they *did* want to learn. However much they dripped— and they all dripped all day long—everyone wanted to learn his job; and Rattler taught them clearly and patiently. It did not matter how " solid " a man was. If he was willing to learn, Rattler was willing to teach.

When he could not teach himself, Rattler would send two or

135

three of his men to " help " one of the old hands. One day Williams found himself detailed to " help " Wild Angus with a job of wire splicing.

Wild Angus was a particularly tough sailor. He was not more than twenty-eight, but he had been around, and though, unlike Forster, he did not talk much about his experiences, he had been on some of the worst of the Malta runs. He was also a tough civilian. He had been a member of one of the Glasgow razor gangs. As a boxer he could match anyone on the ship, even the Buffer.

Williams expected that Wild Angus before long would give up the struggle of explaining things, but he did not. He explained the job as clearly and as patiently as Rattler.

The fo'c'sle men sometimes had lessons from Petty Officer Blair, but he was less patient than Rattler. He was moody, sunshine one minute and thunderstorm the next. He formed strong likes and dislikes. He would take a great deal of trouble with the men he liked. But if he once disliked a man, as he disliked Professor Cole, he gave him no peace. Cole was always being sent off on dirty jobs. His trouble still was that he knew everything much better than anyone else. When they were letting go the anchor, it was the Professor who tried to give the orders. Naturally Blair sat on him. Lovelace was one of the favourites. He was never sent to make up a gap in the iron-deck party or to scrape the funnel. This favouritism irritated the rest of the fo'c'sle men, but neither Cole or Lovelace seemed the worse for it.

When Blair was Duty P.O., and had to shake the hands, he did so malevolently. There was none of Rattler Morgan's good humour about his " Wakey, wakey," and he was always threatening to take sluggards " aft with their caps off," which meant taking them before the Officer of the Day and landing them in Number Eleven punishment. When he was supervising the lowering or hoisting of the whaler of the motor-boat, he bawled. He grudged lending things from his fo'c'sle locker. Yet he could be friendly.

One dinner-time Williams went to the canteen to buy cigarettes—6d. for a packet of twenty—from Ray Forbes, the bespectacled canteen manager's assistant. There were several petty officers leaning over the little counter, gossiping with Ray, Blair among them. When he saw Williams waiting behind he called out, " Come on now. Make way there. There's a gentleman behind waiting to be served."

Williams looked at Blair. " Good God, Chief ! That's the first time I've been called a gentleman by a petty officer. It's usually ' You flicking bastard.' "

" Ah! that's when you're on duty. You're all flicking bastards when you're on duty. But the canteen's nothing to do with the Service. So you're a ' gentleman ' here."

The Buffer, in some ways, was like Blair. He could be friendly and helpful off duty. But on duty he could be a pig. He had never forgiven Calamity for his cheeky tongue and never let him rest for a minute. If Calamity, bending over the Iron Deck with a scrubber, stretched his back, the Buffer would be on him like a dive-bomber. Calamity usually gave back as good as he got, but the Buffer had the whip hand. Calamity refused to check his tongue and took both sarcasm and dirty jobs with resignation.

"I'm not going to let that old bastard get me down. I'm going to learn my job in spite of him, but I'm not going to be a flicking yes-man to anyone."

The Buffer, to do him justice, was not selective in his targets. When he felt like it, he lashed out at anyone, officers included. Williams of course caught many blasts.

"Where do you think you are ? " asked the Buffer one day. "Take your flicking cap off in the petty officers' mess. Now, what do you want ? "

"I want a bundle of waste, Chief."

"A bundle ? Do you know how much a bundle is ? It's fifty-six pounds. Do you know how much waste costs ? It's one-and-tenpence a pound. Do you think I'm going to let you take fifty-six one-and-tenpences ? If you do, you're bloody well wrong."

"I meant a handful."

"Well, why the flicking hell didn't you say so ? "

This was too much for Williams. "If we are going to be literal, Chief, don't you ever call me a bastard again. My mother and father were married to each other years before I was born."

"Huh, a literary gent, eh ? Here, take the bloody key and don't forget—only a handful. And bring the key back."

When Williams returned the key of the waste store, the Buffer was sitting on a locker mending a pair of boots and singing in a voice like the drone of a million bees.

Just now, as the stay in Iceland dragged on for no apparently good reason, tempers on the ship were inclined to be on edge. The *Marsden* kept putting out on patrol for twenty-four hours, then putting back again for a scrub and paint. The crew were neither at sea nor in harbour nor ashore. They were becoming restless.

One morning the Buffer came down to the Iron Deck where Leading Seaman Jeffries and several ratings were cleaning the whaler.

"Here," he said, "don't shove all your muck on the Iron Deck. Put it over the side. Call yourself a leading seaman, do you ? Blind leading the blind, I call it."

Leading Seaman Jeffries said something to the other ratings

as the Buffer turned his back. Immediately the Buffer swung round. " What's that you say ? Using obscene language, are you ? Obscene language to a superior officer in front of junior ratings ? "

Jeffries said he had used no obscene language. He had merely told the ratings to watch where they threw the muck from the whaler. But the Buffer was now in full flood.

" Get out of that boat, Jeffries. I'll teach you to swear at a superior officer. Come on. I'm taking you aft," and solemnly the pair of them went aft to see the Officer of the Day.

The Officer of the Day, that morning, was Lieutenant Seeley, a little R.N.V.R. officer who was earnest but not quite on top of his job. He was nervous of the Buffer, nervous of leading seamen, nervous of ratings, and terrified of the First Lieutenant.

He heard the Buffer's story and turned to Jeffries. Jeffries denied the charge, but, after looking at him intently for a moment to give himself time to think, Seeley said, " First Lieutenant's report," which meant that a prima-facie case had been made out and Jeffries must " go for trial " before the First Lieutenant. If the First Lieutenant could not make up his mind about the case, he would say " Captain's report," and Jeffries would be dealt with by the Skipper personally.

The charge was serious. If proved, Jeffries would lose his hook, which meant loss of pay and de-rating to A.B. By the time " First Lieutenant's requestmen and defaulters " was piped, the whole crew knew the story and were wild with the Buffer.

The First Lieutenant stood on the quarter deck with the Officer of the Day beside him and a green baize-covered card-table in front. To the side of the table stood the Coxswain, with a sheaf of requests and charges with which the First Lieutenant would have to deal that morning—requests from ordinary seamen to be rated A.B.'s, requests from A.B.s to be drafted ashore for a gunnery course, requests from either to be transferred to the torpedo-men's section; charges that So-and-so had lost his pay book, that someone else had been adrift at early-morning muster, and that a third man had dropped a wire scrubber overboard.

Jeffries, as the senior hand of defaulters, was called first. He doubled out of the line of waiting men. " Off Caps." He stood to attention while the Coxswain read the charge. Then Lieutenant Seeley reported the earlier proceedings and the Buffer repeated virtually what the Coxswain had read. The First Lieutenant then turned to Jeffries.

Whatever he might be like in monents of excitement when lowering the motor-boat or the whaler, the Jimmie already had a reputation among the crew for the fairness with which he dealt with requestmen or defaulters. Every man on the lower deck believed that he would get a square deal from the Jimmie whenever he was behind that green baize table.

" What have you got to say ? "

" I say I never used any obscene language, sir. I say it was a deliberate lie, sir, and I'm quite prepared to tell the Captain so."

" Any witnesses ? " said Jimmie to the Coxswain.

Two ratings who had been in the whaler were brought forward. Neither of them had heard anything. Jeffries had spoken in a low voice, the wind was blowing, and there was some shouting from the painters on the fo'c'sle.

It was a difficult problem. Jeffries had said *something*. He had said it in a low voice. If he kept his voice low he was probably saying something he did not want the Buffer to hear; and the Buffer surely wouldn't invent a serious charge like this. Yet, just because Jeffries's voice was low, the Buffer might have misheard.

Jimmie decided on a compromise. " Look here, Jeffries, I know we're all getting a bit nervy with not having much to do just now. We're all browned off. . . ." But he got no further.

" Excuse me, sir. If I had said anything like what the Chief Bosun's Mate says I did, I'd be quite prepared to take my punishment. I'm not afraid of punishment, sir. But this is a deliberate lie."

Jimmie's jaw snapped. " Case dismissed."

Next afternoon their spell of apparently pointless activity ended. The Skipper cleared lower deck and announced that they were sailing south that evening with a troopship which was taking soldiers home on leave from Iceland. They would take her to a Scottish port and report back to their base. After that he did not know.

The crew were tired, not of doing nothing—they had been made to do a great deal, what with going out on patrol and painting the ship—but of doing things which seemed to have no point. Now they were going to have a real job and a job which took them south again, nearer home and into warmer water. It would also take them off the Russian route.

They closed X doors and scuttles without a qualm at six o'clock that evening.

Chapter Nine

1

AT 0430 next morning, just after port watch had finished a Middle and climbed into their hammocks, there was a sudden sharp ringing like an insistent telephone bell. The watch tumbled out of their hammocks, cursing freely.

" Bloody subs.," said Pat Maclure.

The ringing tone was in steady, long burrs.

Williams stumbled to the Iron Deck, where dawn light was breaking through thick clouds, and clumped to his action station at Y gun, forced his way into the gunshield past George Barber, put on his phones and reported " Y gun well," and then, at a word from Jock, " Y gun closed up, cleared away, bore clear."

There was great activity in the front of the gun, on the stern of the ship where the depth-charge trap was fixed. Torpedomen were already setting fuses to a depth ordered by the bridge and were manoeuvring the heavy, barrel-shaped charges from their storage places to the trap.

This was a tray which tipped at the touch of a lever and rolled the charge into the sea, where it exploded, seconds later, at the depth for which it was fused. One charge was always kept ready in the tray, fastened with iron stays. This charge was now freed and, at a word from the bridge, would slip into the sea.

The *Marsden* had veered to port from the troopship and the two other destroyers which accompanied it. Leading Seaman Jeffries, in his Asdic cabinet, had pinged a submarine at Red 45 and the *Marsden* was chasing it. There was no sign of a periscope and the bridge was relying entirely on the reports from Jeffries. He sat at his table in the cabinet off the watchkeepers' mess with earphones on his head and his eyes on the indicators before him. Every few seconds he reported the growing strength of the echo as the *Marsden* approached the hidden submarine or any sudden weakening as the submarine slid away. The moment a weakening was reported, the Skipper changed course slightly until Jeffries could report that the echo was strong again.

All at once, the T.I., standing by the telephones which connected with the bridge, shouted " Stand by " and followed quickly with " Let go one charge ", a torpedoman pressed a lever, and a barrel rolled off the trap into the sea. Seconds later, Y gunshield seemed to heave into the air and the whole ship shook violently. The sea threw up a black mushroom of water and smoke, which hung in the air before showering down on the surface. Immediately the torpedomen rolled another barrel into the trap and waited while the *Marsden* heeled over to make a figure eight. Four charges were dropped.

There was no sign of the submarine. After crusing for a few minutes to see if oil or debris reached the surface, the *Marsden* turned back on her course and the Bosun's Mate piped " Starboard watch to defence stations."

" Fetched out of bed for a lot of bleeding mackerel," said Price as port watch returned to their hammocks.

Twice more that trip the Asdics got a ping which they took to be submarines and once they got a ping which Jimmie on the bridge thought was a sub., but which Jeffries was certain was a school of porpoises. Each time " action stations " was sounded, but no more depth charges were dropped.

On the morning of the third day, when the buzz was that the steering was faulty and the ship would be putting into Glasgow for repairs, Harrison, who was Sub-Lieutenant Carr's servant, came into the mess deck and hinted that if his lips were not sealed he could tell everyone a thing or two. He was pounced on by Jock.

" If you've heard a buzz and want to tell it—good," said Jock. " But if you come round here, say you know something and then won't tell it, Ah'll fill you in, you great loafing flunkey." By threats and persuasion the seamen induced Harrison to say that he had heard Carr forecasting that within a week the ship would be at Gibraltar.

But within the day the ship was back at her base.

2

They stayed ten days. They were sent on patrol. They were sent chasing submarines. They were sent screening a big ship which was having one of its periodic shoots and which, through some error, dropped fifteen-inch shells into a bay, causing alarm and despondency among the residents.

One day they went with two big ships, several cruisers, and a host of destroyers and were attacked by the R.A.F. Torpedo bombers swooped on them, dropping smoke trailers instead of torpedoes, Spitfires raced about the sky, occasionally diving to mast level and just pulling their noses up before they hit one of the ships. Half-way through, a lumbering aircraft towed a sleeve target across the sky and Oerlikon gunners on the ships fired at it. The first run failed because the target detached itself, but the second run was more successful and the sky flashed with red tracer shells tearing at the target, but not often coming near. Much the best shooting—or so it appeared to the Marsdens—was done by the One Mess caterer, Ginger Howard, who winged the target once and had several near misses.

Through all these trips to sea, the *Marsden's* crew went on learning their jobs. They were never allowed to slacken. Carr and the Skipper continually watched the lookouts, asking them suddenly what make of aircraft was approaching from Green seven-o or what class of cruiser they had reported on the horizon at Red four-five. They insisted that reports should be made in the proper form, and that the lookout should make sure the Officer of the Watch had heard by continuing to make the report until the officer gave them the " very good ".

One time, Redfern reported an object to Jimmie. Jimmie ordered him to repeat the report. Redfern, keeping his eyes on the object, did so. He felt a dig in his ribs. " Look here," said Jimmie. " Speak up, can't you ? This isn't the Secret Service. There's a hell of a wind up here and I can't catch a bloody word." So Redfern bellowed his reports.

Practice for the guns' crews seemed unending. The first thing they did whenever they put to sea was to test circuits by firing tubes. Dummy runs, more practice shoots, practices in local control with the director out of action, took place every day. Several times they had practices in gas-masks. Once they had casualty practice. In this Jimmie crept behind some member of the gun's crew, told him that he was injured, and waited to see how long the rest of the crew took to fill his place.

When this particular practice was about to begin, Jimmie seemed to be in an aggressive mood. During the gas practice immediately before he had been caught in a cloud of tear gas without his mask and, to the great delight of everyone, including the doctor, had staggered about the fo'c'sle with tears streaming down his cheeks.

He came along the quarter deck and asked Jock sharply why his interceptor was not closed. Jock turned to look at his interceptor, with that secret half-smile round his mouth.

" What the hell are you grinning at, Forrest ? Do you think this is funny ? "

Jock climbed slowly out of the gunshield and faced Jimmie. " Ah can assure you, sir, that Ah don't think anything about a gun is funny."

" All right, then. Get on with it," and Jimmie tapped Jock on the shoulder to show that he was a casualty. Jock lay down where he was and Charlie Wright, the trainer, took over his duties as captain of the gun. Two members of the supply party then carried Jock to the front of the gun.

" What the hell are you doing that for ? " yelled Jimmie. " Have you no heart ? Fancy pulling a wounded man in front of the bloody gun where he'll catch all the blast. Take him into the wardroom flat, you fatheads, and here, give him a cigarette."

Lieutenant Seeley, the Officer of the Quarters for A and B guns, ran up and down fussily supervising the disposal of the casualties and maintenance of the crews until Newton became exasperated. He left his shield and stood in front of Seeley.

" You know, sir, on the last ship I was in I had the Officer of the Quarters removed because he was too panicky."

" Well, I hope that I shan't be as bad as that," stuttered Seeley, and fussed off to worry Hales on B gun.

While they were in port each watch was given an afternoon ashore. Williams, Jock, and Pat Maclure went to the free-of-charge pictures in a giant corrugated-iron hut and then walked in what passed for sunshine to achieve a thirst for beer.

The beer was sold in another giant hut with a bar at one end, a stage at another end, and in between, chairs and tables. Round the walls were mural paintings showing Jack ashore, dancing in hot climates with half-naked hot mommas.

When the three of them arrived every chair was taken, the air was thick with smoke, and someone was pounding on a piano, but could barely make himself heard above the din of talk and singing. They bought beer tickets, found three empty pint glasses, all badly chipped, and handed them with three 9d. tickets across the counter.

They had been looking forward to a pint of beer. They held their glasses in the air and looked at the dark brown liquid. They took a gulp. Instantly disgust spread across their faces. It was not the chipped edges of the glasses that threatened to cut their lips, it was not the thick smoke that made their eyes run. But that liquid, which the Naafi canteen notice said was made by a particularly famous brewer, tasted as though it had come from a pig-trough. They had to force it down.

But the effect was not unlike the effect of real beer and, any-way, they still had three beer tickets. So they drank another pint each. Then they strolled out of the canteen to the jetty and waited in the cold for the ship's motor-boat.

They found that most of the other libertymen had managed to force down more than two pints. Harrison had obviously had many more and was in a state of dissatisfied drunkenness. He stood in the middle of the mess deck and surveyed his mess-mates.

" I'm chokka with this ship. Everyone in it's a bastard. You're all right," he said, suddenly catching sight of Dowson and swaying at him. " And you're all right," he said, lunging at Pat. " And you're all right. And *you're* all right."

" I know," said Jack Price. " We're all all right, but we're all a lot of bastards."

" That's right," said Harrison in a tone of great surprise, suddenly seeing his way clear.

Sinbad came off shore more purple than ever and with some-one else's hat. " Ah was in the motor-boat coming back," he said in a voice that rose higher and higher until it almost vanished into a squeak, " and someone picks my hat off my head and throws it into the air expecting it to land on my head again.

143

But what *does* land on my head is a cap size eight. Which was no bloody good to me, mate."

He flopped on a locker and began to laugh. He laughed on and on in a croaking chuckle, like an elderly goose clucking, until someone stuffed a duffel coat over his head.

Another man lurched in, sat down on one of the benches in front of the mess table, put his elbows on the table and his head in his hands. He was sick over the table. Another made water over a pile of coats, which, as usual, were on the deck. Jock stormed at the pair, but they were both too far gone to take much notice. It was the old Duchess, Dowson, who, by milder methods, made them clean the mess.

Next day an Admiral came aboard. He was a Big Shot around those parts, but did not like formality. So the crew were mustered aft in their working clothes and stood to attention as a smart-looking launch drew alongside.

The first thing they noticed about the Admiral was his gold braid, rings of which seemed to spiral all the way up his arm. The second thing was that the Admiral was clean. That made him unique in the *Marsden*. Even the Skipper and Jimmie looked shop-soiled beside him, and the rest of the crew looked filthy.

The Admiral was short and fat and perky. He strode forward with a smile on his fresh-coloured face and mounted a little stool in the centre of the square which the crew had formed. The Skipper, who had always seemed like a distant and rather unapproachable god to his crew, looked like an uneasy schoolboy as he stood beside him.

The Admiral was worried that he had not been able to come aboard to welcome them when they were last in. But he was very glad to see them now. They were badly needed. They had already had a good deal of work and would shortly be getting a good deal more. " All you sailors on small ships have to work hard. The only people who are allowed easy times are admirals. I *have* to stay here. I'm not allowed to go to sea. I wish I was. (" The bloody liar," said the ship's company.)

" All I can do is to get to know you as well as an admiral can get to know all the men under his command. You won't be here long, I don't suppose. You'll be off again to sea. But never forget that it's the little ships which make the Navy and which eventually will win this war. However uncomfortable you may be, never forget that.

" And now," he said, turning to the Skipper and climbing off his stool, " may I come and smoke a cigarette in the wardroom ? And by the way, if you've any old shipmates of mine on board I would like to have a word with them."

He waddled off, and next day the *Marsden*, to the dismay of her crew, sailed again for Iceland.

They had a bad time. When they cleared the islands, they ran into heavy seas which swept the fo'c'sle and tore over the Iron Deck. The *Marsden* pitched, and, every time she pitched, showers of spray poured over the bridge, drenching the officers and lookouts. Worse, water forced its way into the fo'c'sle locker and through the ammunition hatchway into the mess deck.

One man who had slung his hammock beneath this hatchway was soaked by a cascade of water. He sat up gasping curses on whoever stopped destroyer men from getting the " hard layers' money " which was usually given to sailors in particularly uncomfortable ships. Then he took his hammock and himself in front of one of the electric stoves. The water kept pouring in, and the steam-pipe to the capstan engine continued to drip.

A particularly violent wave smashed the breakwater on the fo'c'sle and sprung a leak in the deck. Through this more water passed to the mess deck until there was a good inch and a half swishing from side to side below.

Besides pitching, the *Marsden* also rolled. Every time she rolled, every movable thing about her rolled too.

The seamen rolled. Harrison had his hammock slung just above one of the mess-deck tables. At breakfast-time he was standing on the table pulling something out of his hammock when Ginger Howard asked him to move. Then the ship rolled and Harrison was thrown over an open hatchway, across the deck, and under the far table.

" Thanks," said Ginger, clutching a tea-urn, " but you needn't have moved *that* far."

The mess crockery also rolled. At meal-times, the few who were able to eat stood beside the table clutching their plates and trying to keep themselves upright. At dinner, Jock was carving the meat, when meat and dish slid off the table across the deck with Jock sliding after them, trying to spear the meat as he went. Tea-urns upset, adding to the liquid on the deck. Suitcases crashed down off racks; coats, hammocks, and magazines became lumped together in one sodden mass. Spew swished from side to side in the flood. The stink was horrible, and made the sick men sicker than ever.

Besides pitching and rolling, the *Marsden* had a trick which is peculiar to small ships. She would lie for a moment poised on the top of a wave and then suddenly crash into the trough. It seemed that the crash would break her back. Kettles and fannies, swinging from the deckhead, jumped off their hooks and landed with a clatter or a splash below. One man was thrown out of his hammock. All felt concussed. The smack of the waves against the side—Forster's " milestones "—were nothing compared with this back-breaking thud.

Those who had to go on deck got soaked. However carefully

they waited their chance at the entrance to the washroom flat and, seizing a lifeline, raced aft when they thought the way was clear, they were caught by an icy wave and had to spend four hours in a gunshield soaking wet. The Petty Officer wireman tried to make his way aft with a bag of light-bulbs. He was caught by a wave before he had gone five yards and hurled against a winch. His shoulder was broken against the winch, his bag was swept overboard, and he would have gone too if, with his legs out-board, he had not managed to clutch the guard-rail with his undamaged arm. Another man was caught by a wave when he had fallen in for part ship work in the Forenoon. He was crashed against a rail and broke his leg.

After that, everyone who had not a duty on the bridge was kept below. The Buffer came round personally to pipe " No one, repeat NO ONE, is allowed on the upper deck. Those aft are to remain aft. Those for'ard are to remain for'ard." That meant there was no more working part-of-ship during the Forenoon. The guns' crews had to keep their watches in the canteen flat, which was warmer than in the gunshields. Only the lookouts were allowed in the open air and they could climb to the bridge without going on deck at all.

They welcomed the chance to go on the bridge. They were soaked and sick, but felt sicker every minute they stayed in the stench of the mess deck, and at least on the bridge the air was fresh. But how that ship rolled! It was nothing for her to go over to 45 degrees. At one time she reached 51 degrees. Every few minutes, waves of spray came over. They seemed to hang in the air, poised, for several seconds, and a lookout would say: " This one is going to hit us." He was always right. But always he was too tired and too sick to duck.

Their main job was to watch, not for submarines or aircraft—they would not be out in this weather—but for things being cut adrift or carried away by the sea. The guard-rails on the port side had been smashed, the scrambling-net on the starboard side was dragging in the sea, held only by a few cords. The wash-deck locker on the Iron Deck, with all Jock's precious brooms and buckets in it, had been stove in. That was just too bad. The sea was washing over all the time and no one could have worked for long on the Iron Deck or the quarter deck without being swept over.

But when the whaler swung loose and seemed likely to go overboard at any moment, the Officer of the Watch had to risk sending twelve men, under the Buffer, to secure it, while Jimmie shouted orders above the howl of the wind.

The whaler was three parts full of water. Jimmie told a seaman to pull out the plug. When the seaman had climbed up and done it, a shoot of water came from the plughole and hit the Buffer.

146

"Who pulled that bloody plug out? Put the flicking thing back at once."

Not that the shoot of water made any difference to the Buffer. He was soaked already, like everyone else.

When the whaler was secured, the unhappy party went below to see if they could find any means of drying themselves. But it was no use. Their spare clothes were wet, and even if they had managed to find dry ones, they could not have remained dry long. If they lay in their hammocks, water might pour on them through the leaky deckhead. Or else there would be drips from the condensation. The air in the mess deck was fetid, but the deckhead plates were cold. Drops of water formed on them and fell into the hammocks under the vibration of the ship. If the men tried to sleep on the lockers, there was still the drips. Worse, they might be hurled, whenever the ship lurched, on to the sticky mass which covered the deck itself. When they tried to walk, their rubber sea-boots slid from under them and either they fell flat in the stickiness or they crashed against tables, gun support, or iron stanchions, and were bruised.

No one ate much during four long days—they should have reached Iceland in two at the most. Most of the crew were too sick for anything except dry bread and biscuits. But even the real sailors, like Jock and the Duchess, went short because the P.O. cook said it was too rough to cook. On the first day out, a fanny full of custard had upset over him. On the second day he was hurled across the galley and tried to steady himself by putting his hand on the red-hot stove. After that, he said, he would cook no more until they reached the Serpentine.

So Jock and the Duchess and a few others existed on bully beef, washed down by spare tots which never before had been offered so profusely or so cheaply.

It was only when they came under the lee of Iceland that the ship began to steady herself and Williams, climbing to the bridge for a lookout duty, came face to face with a dishevelled-looking Carr.

"Have you been sick?" asked Carr.

"Have I ever been well?"

"Well, never mind. It will soon be over now," and Carr added "Thank Christ!" with an ardour which nearly made the ship roll again.

When the *Marsden* reached her buoy, the motor-boat had lost its screw, snatched clean off by a wave; the guard-rails along the Iron Deck were smashed and the iron stanchions which held them were bent in halves; the paint on the ship's sides had been battered off—"O Christ!" said Calamity, as he looked at the bare patches and realised what *that* meant. On the fo'c'sle only about a foot of the breakwater remained. The rest was at the bottom of the sea—"Send us to look for it, Oi shouldn't wonder.

147

Rig of the day Number Ones," said Price. The splinter cushions round the wardroom flat were rent. The Carley floats along the Iron Deck were dislodged.

In the mess deck itself, a thin scum of sick lay on the surface of an inch of dirty water from which protruded mounds of peas, spilled from their containers, potatoes, broken plates, coats, a variety of papers, and all manner of clothing. There was about an inch of assorted slime below the water. The stench of wet, dirty socks, of wet, dirty clothes of all sorts, of wet, decaying vegetables, and of sick, was nauseating.

Jock and the Duchess set all available hands to clear it up almost before the ship had tied to her buoy. Even the sickest men lent a hand. They mopped, they shovelled, they scrubbed, they dried, and they polished. They threw open the portholes, they tied up the gas-mask locker which had sagged on its legs, they " ditched " the broken pottery, and they sorted the sodden socks and clothes. They took coats, mufflers, jerseys, and sea-boot stockings and wrung them over the side. They opened the hatchway leading to No. 1 boiler-room, climbed down the little ladder, pressed the heavy handle of the door, and, laden with their damp burdens, staggered across the iron platform and thence down the long iron ladder. There they manoeuvred themselves between asbestos-covered pipes, steam gauges, and more ladders until they could find an empty place to hang their clothes. Then they forced themselves into the washroom and tried to get clean.

At once there was a general drip. Everyone had lost clothes in the morass. Price, his nose blue with a permanent cold, cried, " Someone's knocked moi flicking coat off its bleeding peg. Of course, no one thinks of picking it up again. They just let it loi in the muck. Oi dunno," he added, like one who had tried to teach his children manners, but was now giving up in despair.

" Stuff my buckets! Where's my flicking hammock ? " Calamity was rummaging in the bottom of the hammock netting and heaving out one hammock after another. He found that his hammock had been on the top after all.

" Ye robbers," wailed Jock. " Somebody's took ma shaving brush. Somebody's took ma soap. Come round, ye flickers, and Ah'll give ye the razor. Then ye'll have a complete set."

It was a long time before they could sit down to eat. But how they *did* eat! There were two eggs each, fetched by Pat from the oiler. There were three rashers of bacon. There were cupfuls of chips. There was figgy duff (a mixture of cake and pudding with figs in it) and " cus "—custard to civilians. As soon as they had finished, all of them looked round for spare helpings. Jock had eaten fairly well throughout the trip and did not like " afters " anyway, but when a too-eager hand seized his figgy duff and cus he held it with a grip of iron.

" Just because Ah very seldom eats duff, it doesn't mean that anyone can go Woof! Woof! wi' ma share. Ah gives ma share to the man Ah chooses. To-day, Ah chooses maself."

The next day was Sunday. They swept the decks, then changed into Number Ones for Divisions, which meant a quick inspection of the ship's company by the Skipper and a short service on the mess deck. A flag was draped over the munition winch and the Skipper read a few prayers. Then a Bosun's Mate piped " Unrig church ", the flag was taken off the winch, and the Skipper addressed the ship's company.

" We're up here to relieve a destroyer which is due for a boiler clean. I expect most of you think that we are about due for a boiler clean ourselves. Well, we are. We're also due for some repairs. But we'll have to stay here for about two weeks, doing the usual jobs and anything else that crops up, and then we'll probably go south. I don't know where. Maybe Greenock or Rosyth, in which case I can promise at least one night ashore in the bright lights—if you can find any. But, as I say, I don't know. So all you can do for the moment is Watch and Pray. Pray hard! "

4

They only put to sea four times in the next two weeks—three times on routine patrol, once to chase a submarine reported by aircraft. The rest of the time it was too rough for the Big Ship they were supposed to be escorting to leave her buoy and the *Marsden* gratefully stayed moored to hers.

Some of the time was spent by the petty officers in drawing up lists of repairs.

One morning, when he should have been sweeping the quarter deck, Williams was inside the shield of X gun, having a smoke. The G.I. came upon him there and, instead of asking what the hell he was doing, began to talk.

" Got to look over these guns to see if there's anything wants doing."

" What about A gun ? It looked rusted up."

" Oh, A gun's all right, or will be after a good clean. Anyway, I'm not going to report it. Not until we're safely down south."

" Why not ? "

" Everybody will be reporting things. Those guard-rails can't be straightened out. That deckhead will have to be riveted. There's something wrong with one of the fuel tanks. And the steering's a bit wonky. Then the boilers want cleaning. If we shove much more down, they'll say, ' Hell, you're not fit to stay at sea longer than's necessary. You go to the base and have your jobs done there.' Then we don't get no leave. Of course, if we don't put in enough they'll say, ' H'm! that's not much. Better get it fixed up in Iceland,' and we don't get no leave *that*

149

way. You've got to strike a balance. Enough to get us away from Iceland, but not so much that they'll dump us at the base."

Everyone on the ship began to think of getting home. The Skipper had made no promises. There might be no leave at all. At best it might only be a night ashore, which would be no use to most of those who wanted to get home. But wishful thinking was strong.

" I wish I was home," said Jackie Low one night. " I wish I was home sitting in the armchair, by the fire, with my carpet slippers on and the missus handing me a cup of tea and the nipper squitting all over the floor just to make it home-like; and the *News of the flicking World* and the *Daily Mirror*, every day, up-to-date, and not six bastard weeks late as it is up here. Coo!"

" Home!" said Jock. "Ah knows what home is like for you married men. Ye comes home on a Friday night with your pay packets and your wife sweeps the kids off the easy-chair and says, ' Sit down, *dear*,' and brings you a cup of tea. But when it's Monday it's ' Get out of that chair,' she says; ' Ah wants to sit down.' "

" We don't all have to live in Scotland. I'm talking about a real home, in London."

" Sooner live in a flicking pig-sty."

" Call my home a pig-sty, would you ? Don't insult the flicking pigs. What 'ave the poor little bastards ever done to you ? You may be big, but I've got a punch. I'll knock you right through that bastard hammock netting. I'll knock you so hard they'll 'ave to get the bastard radiolocation set out to find you."

" If you so much as lays a finger on me Ah'll tell ma grannie."

" I want to go home and I want to stay home. Not for twenty-four bleeding hours. For twenty-four bleeding days, more like."

" Man, you'd soon be chokka if you stayed home for twenty-four days," said Pat Maclure.

" Chokka after twenty-four days at home! Not bleeding likely."

" You ought to be a Conscientious Objector, man. Didn't you join up to fight and get the bloody war over ? Well, hanging about on leave's no way to do it."

" Just listen to the man," said Jock. " He's all for it. Chokka when he gets some leave, is he ? You're writing to your girl now. Just you tell her that you're not going home on leave because you're chokka. Just tell her that!"

" I'll do no such thing. I want to go on leave as much as you do. But I want to get home for good. I *would* get chokka if I was hanging around home for more than ten days."

" Listen, you black-faced Satan. Ah went home early in the war for forty-two days. Ah wasna' recalled. Ah had every minute of ma leave. And Ah wasna' chokka. *And* Ah had ma penniless pongo brother with me for nine days with his seven and sixpence Army pay which he spent on Friday night and then left me to carry him into the pubs all the other nights, *with* all his penniless pongo friends. People kept saying to me, ' You still here ? ' and Ah sez, ' Yes, Ah'm still here. And Ah'm staying here until ma leave is up.' Anyone who says he's chokka with more than a week's leave ought to be locked up."

" If we only get twenty-four hours' leave, they won't get me back on time, I can tell you. I'll be adrift." That was Rhoades.

" Don't blather, man. You knows you don't mean it."

" I *do* mean it."

" Well, if you do mean it—which you don't—you're a bigger fool than you look."

" Why ? I want to see my folks."

" Do you think that no one else does, fathead ? "

" No; we all want to get home."

" Well, don't you realise, you red-headed lump of gash, that if you overstays your leave, the others won't be allowed to go at all. Or the next leave will be stopped and we'll spend our boiler-cleaning time painting ship."

" No, I don't."

" Harry, your head's like our front room. Flick all in it," said Leading Seaman Dowson.

" I'm going to tell my folks I'll be home on leave, anyhow."

" Don't be a fool, 'Arry," said Price. " Don't say you're expecting any leave at all when it may be only twenty-four hours. Your mum will imagine you're coming 'ome, and she's not going to get a very big disappointment, is she ? "

But in spite of Price's warning, nearly everyone on the ship began to think of leave and home as a certainty. It made them all much chirpier than they had been since they left Oldhaven. One morning, when a group was painting on the fo'c'sle, the First Lieutenant arrived in one of his aggressive moods. He saw paint spattered about the deck and exploded. Everyone within reach received a basinful of his invective, but just as he turned away, Price said in a not very soft whisper, " 'E shouldn't 'ave joined if 'e can't take a joke," and Sinbad burst into giggles. The First Lieutenant swung round. " I don't come on the fo'c'sle to be laughed at," he shouted, and then, suddenly cooling down, walked away. That night, when Jimmie came through the mess deck for rounds and began to climb down the hatchway to the watchkeepers' mess, Price said, more softly this time, " 'E's going down the 'ole to get the coal," and Shortarse put his hand over Sinbad's mouth before he could giggle again. Sinbad went purple, but the situation was saved.

Everyone did their work in the mess without having to be told and a wide variety of duffs were served up by various amateur cooks. Calamity Taylor took to slipping in from

151

sweeping the Iron Deck to make some extra special duff and was caught by Leading Seaman Barker.

" What are you doing, Taylor ? "

" Scrubbing my flicking hammock." He went on rolling his duff.

" Funny, eh ? You'll find I can be funny too." But he did not take Calamity aft, as he would certainly have done a few weeks before.

" Hey, what shall I do with this fanny of spuds ? " said Calamity a few minutes later.

" I'm a gentleman, so I can't really tell you," said Low. " But for Christ's sake hang on to the handle. You can get the fanny down again quick enough, but the handle hurts." Then seizing the handle himself, he took the fanny to the galley where the P.O. cook dripped at him for not having had it there twenty minutes earlier. But the P.O. cook only dripped. He did not refuse to cook the spuds, which merely showed how lively the whole ship felt.

Lovelace perpetually sang *Blue Champagne*, Calamity his *Seera, See-ew, I'm sad and lonelee,* and Nevison kept repeating " Never before " and " Square Four ", parts of two jokes which he had picked up from Jack Price. But such things no longer irritated anyone.

Williams even abetted some crooning. Dowson had boasted one night that he knew and could sing both words and music of every popular song in the last twenty years. Pat Maclure and Williams tested him with *Sahara*.

" I know *Sahara*. Of course I do. It goes like this."

" That's *Onward Christian soldiers*."

" It flicking ain't, you know. That was flicking *Sahara*. You don't know your own tunes. Try again."

Pat gave him *Whispering*. Again there was a hoarse rumbling in Dowson's throat.

" That's not *Whispering*. That's *Hark, the Herald Angels*."

Mention of hymn tunes brought Ginger Howard across. He had been a choirboy in his time and still had a good voice. He and Williams had a private joke that they were wrestling for the souls of the seamen on the lower deck and particularly for that of Wild Angus. That was all right until Wild Angus began to take the wrestling seriously.

" I'm afraid we shall have a hard and bitter struggle with this erring soul, brother Williams," Ginger said, looking at the Duchess. Then, changing his tone: " There's only one way to deal with sods like you; and that's to have a swear-box. Penny a swear and the proceeds for the Great Ormond Street Children's Hospital."

" Not bloody likely. We had a swear-box once in the Med., and the first time we touched Alex. the flicking treasurer pinched the bastard, went ashore, and came off tight as a drum."

But the idea caught on. Every swear-word—damn not counting as anything—was to cost one penny.

"For flick's sake don't have it during meals or we'll *own* the bastard hospital," pleaded Calamity, but it was decided that it should apply in the mess at all times, but at no time outside it.

"Ah dursn't ask for anything," moaned Jock at supper-time. "Ah have to fetch it maself." When Rhoades, reaching for the bread, jogged Dowson's arm and spilled his ki, Dowson said, "You come out of the mess and I'll tell you something that will be to your advantage, you blundering great bastard."

He put a penny in the box.

Next morning Calamity could not find his sea-boots. He stood in the middle of the mess deck, white and strained, his lips tight shut. All at once he pulled out a sixpenny bit, shoved it into the swear-box, and shouted: "Which of you flicking bastards has pinched my flicking sea-boots. All right, all right, that's only threepennorth so far. Come on, you flickers, or I'll knock the bloody ears back on your bastard heads. Six-pence. Okay?" Then putting on his C.W. accent, he went on: "I should be most grateful if one of you gentlemen, perchance, peradventure, could inform me where-the-flicking-hell-my-bloody-bastard-sea-boots-are."

There was more than £2 in the box by the end of the week.

Liveliness from the lower deck spread aft, and one day, instead of the eternal painting and scrubbing, the crew were told to weigh anchor by hand as a practice in case the capstan engine broke down.

"Now that's what Oi calls a sensible evolution," said Price. "The way that flicking steam-pipe leaks in our mess, the basstud engine will give out any day now."

All the seamen mustered on the fo'c'sle. They put long spars into the capstan, lined themselves along the spars, and waited for the word "Go". The Buffer stood on a bollard to call the time, Jimmie and Rattler Morgan stood by to shout encouragement, and Carr brought a squeeze-box accordion to provide rhythm for pushing.

The deck was slippery after a light fall of rain, but Jimmie, with a precautionary "Those who fall will get trampled on," called out "One, two, six, Go," Carr squeezed his accordion and the seamen began to push. There was a loud snap. One of the spars had broken. The capstan brake was still on.

"Damn," said Jimmie.

They began again. The seven remaining spars were now overcrowded and the seamen got in each other's way. Wild Angus kicked against a water hydrant and turned it on, making the deck more slippery than ever and drenching those who came near it.

"Go on, push," yelled Jimmie. "Are you afraid of a little salt water?"

"Yes, sir," said Wild Angus. "We're fresh-water sailors."

The Buffer, standing on the bollards and waving his huge hands, shouted, "Only another five turns, you bloody liar," Jimmie shouted, "Come on, keep her running, lads," and Rattler shouted, "Come on, lads, the last hundred yards."

By the time they had weighed anchor everyone was breathless and warm.

Next day they were duty boat. They were to go round the fjord picking up libertymen from the various merchant ships which were ominously accumulating there. But it was too rough, even in the fjord. The *Marsden* had to go round the ships, signalling them that the trip was off, and then turned into driving snow and wind back to her own buoy.

It was Sunday and only the duty part of the watch were on the upper deck to drop the two anchors. Sub-Lieutenant Carr, as Officer of the Day, was in charge of the fo'c'sle and the second part of port watch were there to carry out his orders. The orders really came from the bridge and, as the wind was so strong and the snow falling so thick that neither shouts nor signals from the bridge could be properly understood, the Navigator bellowed down a voice-pipe to a communication number who passed the order to a runner who passed it to Sub-Lieutenant Carr.

Some of the orders puzzled the communication number and puzzled the messenger. They also puzzled Sub-Lieutenant Carr. "Veer starboard anchor to six and then let go port when we next yaw," yelled the Navigator, who was Dartmouth and R.N. The communication number, who was Selfridge's, passed the order to the runner, who was Fleet Street, who passed it to Sub-Lieutenant Carr, who was R.N.V.R.

"I don't know what it means . . . but 'Very Good,'" said Sub-Lieutenant Carr, and asked Jock Forrest to interpret.

Later the Navigator spoke again. "Tell the fo'c'sle officer to let the anchor go himself," meaning that he was not to wait for further orders from the bridge.

"Hell's bells! Do they mean all you boys can just flick off and leave me to do the dirty work myself?"

That evening, because the sea had quietened, the Big Ship sent part of her marine band to play on the *Marsden's* mess deck. The mess deck was small. But the band played softly and a nice clean sailor sang the *Anniversary Waltz* without once attempting to imitate Bing Crosby.

"Now, why don't *you* sing like that?" said Williams to Harry Rhoades. But Harry was lost in the music and remained so, long after the band had gone. At last he said, "That's the best evening I've ever spent, except once when I heard Jeannette

Macdonald singing *Ave Maria* on the wireless. Flicking smashing that was. The most beautiful song you ever heard."

5

But it was not all singing for the *Marsden's* crew, not even in harbour. The wind got up so quickly and so fiercely that there was always a danger the ship would drag her anchors. Anchor watches had to be set, which meant that four men had to be on continuous patrol of the fo'c'sle through the night, keeping their eyes open for the slightest sign that the *Marsden* was shifting her position.

Somehow, having to get up in the Middle Watch was more irritating in harbour, where it was exceptional, than at sea, where it was a matter of course. That and the icy wind which cut into them when they were working part of ship during the day helped to wipe out their cheeriness.

Then, the promised two weeks had gone and there was still no sign of a relieving destroyer; and almost every day merchantmen were trickling into the anchorage, some Yankees which had crossed the Atlantic, some British, and some flying the hammer and sickle of Soviet Russia. A convoy to Russia was very much in the wind.

Perhaps the most aggravating thing of all was something that was intended to be soothing.

One evening the non-duty watch were invited to the pictures on the Big Ship. The starboard watch went off in the Big Ship's launch, climbed the gangway, and were met by a petty officer who asked them if they knew the way to the cinema.

Forster at once said, " Yes, I know the way all right. I was on the K.G. Five for four months. These Big Ships are all the same." He landed the party in the wardroom, where the officers were finishing their dinner. The destroyer men gaped for a moment and then hurried out.

" Coo! " said Price, when they got back. " You should 'ave seen the basstud. Sick-bay that's better than Guy's, she 'as, and corridors twice as long as this ship and wide, too. No ' Get-out-of-the-flicking-way ' there! You march past five abreast. And on the mess deck you can walk foive minutes between each rating. Makes this ship look a bit of a pig-sty."

Harry Robertson sat with his head cupped in his hands.

" That wardroom! There they were. The waiters, all clean with white jackets and blue cuffs and the officers listening to the Marine band and eating oranges. Eating *oranges*! " He had been given a quick vision of the promised land and woken to find himself on the *Marsden*.

The contrast depressed the whole ship's company. It was no good listening to other stories, of how the Big Ship's crew had to do P.T. every morning and run twice round the deck, how one man had been given five days' number eleven for being improperly dressed at rounds during the evening—he was wearing a pair of plimsolls instead of boots—of how another had got five days' cells for leaving his hammock slung until 0700. The oranges, the cleanliness, and the space overshadowed all the inconvenience of pusser routine. Discontent increased.

Ill-feeling on the mess deck came to a head two nights later. They had been at sea all the previous night, being tossed around on patrol, and they had worked part of ship during the Forenoon. They were weary and irritable. After the inevitable Tombola, several men began to play pontoon in One Mess, among them Raikes and Shortarse. After about ten minutes Chris Boothroyd came to the table. He, like Raikes, belonged to Two Mess and was on X gun, and saw too much of him. He looked at Shortarse. " I wouldn't play cards for money with people like him," pointing to Raikes. " He'll only fleece you."

At first Raikes thought this was a joke, and took no notice, but Chris persisted.

" Seriously, Shortarse, I warn you about Raikes. He's got a bad reputation all over the ship; and all over the Navy from what I hear."

Raikes stood up. " Are you calling me a cheat ? " That death's-head smile of his was playing about his mouth.

" You've got ears, haven't you ? You heard what I said."

Raikes jumped over the table and hit Boothroyd a smack under the chin which sent him across the mess deck and sprawling over the far table. Cups upset and one fell to the deck and broke. Boothroyd snatched it and, as Raikes rushed at him, struck with it at Raikes's face and cut it. Raikes hurled himself through Boothroyd's guard, seized him by the shoulders and butted him between the eyes with his baldish head. Blood spurted from Boothroyd's nose.

It was then that Williams looked out of his hammock. He did not know how the fight had started. He only saw that two men from another mess were breaking One Mess crockery and he was tired of having to drink his tea out of saucers or old tins. He also saw that Raikes was butting fiercely at the face of a much smaller man. He jumped out of his hammock and forced himself between Raikes and Boothroyd.

For the moment the fighters were content to shout at each other.

" I'll get you one of these days, you bloody swine," yelled Boothroyd, near to tears.

" Come on, then. Now's your chance."

" I mean I'll get you in action. You just wait," and suddenly Boothroyd dived behind Williams, picked up another cup, smashed it and lashed out at Raikes. Raikes was ready for murder.

But Wild Angus arrived. He seized Boothroyd's wrist and twisted it until he dropped the cup and fell in a sobbing, bleeding heap. Raikes, beside himself with anger, went on yelling threats. Wild Angus said nothing. He was a head shorter than Raikes and no broader, but he faced him squarely, pushed out his chest and bumped him with it. Raikes took a step backwards, still shouting. Wild Angus took two steps forward and bumped again. Raikes took another step back. Wild Angus bumped him into his own mess and the fight was over.

Next morning Williams was sweeping X-gun deck when Raikes came to look at his gun.

" Good morning, Mr. Williams."

" Good morning, Mr. Raikes."

" Nice and peaceful to-day."

" Yes. No crockery being smashed."

Raikes grinned, this time with his eyes as well as with his mouth. " I ought to have knocked your flicking head off."

"If you're going to knock flicking heads off, I wish you'd do it in your own mess."

" I'll mention that to my manager, Mr. Williams. Good morning," said Raikes, grinning all over his face.

" Good morning, Mr. Raikes," said Williams, grinning back. The fight cleared the air.

August ended. Sunday was the third anniversary of the outbreak of war. They had a special service on the quarter deck to mark the National Day of Prayer. That night, when they were lying in their hammocks before " pipe down ", Price began to talk.

" Oi never 'eard a word of that service this morning," he said. " Oi shut moi moind to it. All the toime the Skipper was spouting 'is prayers, Oi was spitting into the sick-berth attendant's 'at."

" Spitting in his hat," said Calamity in his C.W. voice. " I call that simply beastly."

" Oh, they weren't gobs. They were nice clean, watery ones. The S.B.A. was 'olding 'is 'at be'oind 'is back loike a sarspan and Oi 'it it plumb in the middle six toimes out of seven. The leading stoker next to me split hisself laughing."

" You ought to have listened to the prayers instead of spitting. Might have done you some good."

" Some good, indeed. It's all troipe. Oi know. Oi used to go to church. Oi was in the flicking choir. Know all those prayers by 'eart before 'e says 'em. ' *We 'ave erred and strayed from Thy flicking ways like lost basstud sheep.*' Troipe. All religion is troipe."

" It flicking ain't, you know."

" Well, if there's a God, whoi doesn't E' stop this war ? Whoi does 'E let little kids in both countries that 'ad nothing to do

157

with making this war get bombed to death ? If 'E's up there, whoi doesn't 'E send the bombs on the 'eads of fin-anc-eers and big business men of both ruddy countries ? It's the poor little basstuds who'd nothing to do with it that cop it. Foine sort of God!"

" Do you want to know my opinion of the cause of this war, mate ? " said Sinbad.

"It's loike a picture Oi saw once where the chap is standing up before 'is congregation preaching, and all of a sudden 'e pulls a six-shooter out of 'is trousis and says, ' Dearly beloved bretheren, this is a stick-up.' Religion and big business! That's what causes war."

" Jack, do you want . . .? "

" How do you know that there ever was such a person as Jesus Chroist ? All they've done is to foind a few bits of stone with carvings on them and some professor-loike looks at 'em and says, ' There's a word. Jesus. That looks religious loike,' and then all you silly basstuds start going to church and hearing troipe."

" Jack, do you . . .? "

" Look at that story in the Bible where Chroist feeds all those six thousand flickers on the sea-shore. Feeds the lot on six basstud kippers and then, when they've finished, they gathered up twice as many kippers as they started with. Do you believe that ? "

" Jack ? "

" SHUT UP, you. And if you believe in God, tell me 'oo put 'Im there ? God made the world, did 'E ? Well, 'oo made God ? Answer me that."

" I can't answer that. I wasn't there. Nobody can answer it," said Harry Robertson, " but I know of cases where prayers have done a lot of good. Look at the National Day of Prayer. We had one. Then we had Dunkirk and all those men taken off safely. It shows you."

" Troipe. We 'ad a National Day of Prayer to-day. And what did we get ? Scrubbing the flicking Iron Deck."

" Jack, do you want to know my opinion of the cause of war ? " said Sinbad, rushing out his words before Jack could stop him. " It's to thin out the population. That's what it is."

" Thin out the population ? Troipe. Before the war the population of every country was falling. Every country except China. The women in China 'ave 'em in litters and a woman's no sooner 'ad one lot than 'er old man's at it again."

Harry Robertson got out of his hammock and rummaged in his locker. At last he emerged with a Bible, hoping to find some quotation in it which would squash Price. Calamity saw the Bible. " Let's have a look at that, Harry. Some time since I saw one."

Calamity began to turn the pages. He came to the 23rd Psalm, paused, and began to read.

"*The Lord is my shepherd.*"

"That's right. We're just a flock of flicking sheep. Wouldn't 'ave joined if we weren't."

"*I shall not want.*"

"Not want ? Not want ? I want to go home."

"*He maketh me to lie down in green pastures.*"

"Wet hammocks more like."

"*He leadeth me beside the still waters.*"

"STILL waters ? Oh, flicking yeah!"

"*Yea, though I walk through the valley of the shadow of death, I will fear no evil: for thou art with me; thy rod and thy staff they comfort me.*"

"Valley of the shadow of death ? " A pause. No comment, then:

"*Thou preparest a table before me in the presence of mine enemies.*"

"You're darn right there. ' *In the presence of mine enemies.*' That's you, you flicking gannets, dive-bombing the food."

"*Thou anointest my head with oil; my cup runneth over.*"

"Not in this mess, it doesn't. Lucky if you can get half a flicking cupful. And it's not oil, cock. It's flicking great drips of bleeding water."

"*Surely goodness and mercy shall follow me all the days of my life.*"

"'E means the Buffer. I don't think."

"*And I will dwell in the house of the Lord for ever.*"

"If the roof doesn't leak, roll on my flicking twelve."

Calamity then went on reading to himself until the lights were switched off for " pipe down ".

6

Next day the relieving destroyer arrived with mail. Better even than the mail, Jimmie mustered all hands in the fore mess deck out of the rain and told them they would sail that afternoon, that they would go straight to Rosyth for a boiler clean and repairs, and that there would be seventy-two hours' leave for each watch.

"Well, that's one piece of good news, isn't it ? "

At this there was a sudden swell of sound, made by no distinguishable words but unmistakable in meaning. It was like the sound that sometimes comes from a political meeting when the speaker puts into words what his hearers are feeling in their hearts.

The trip down to Rosyth was rough. Water again swished about the mess deck and poured into hammocks. Many of the crew were sick. But because the stem of the ship was pointing in the right direction none of these hardships seemed to matter. They arrived in Rosyth early one morning, passed under the Forth Bridge, and tied up in a dock alongside an immaculate-looking destroyer which was just finishing her repairs. Again they cleaned the mess thoroughly, and then the starboard watch began to clean themselves and search for the Number One suits, ready to go home first thing in the morning. Most of them had already left before port watch woke up.

The routine for the port watch who were left on the ship was easy. They did not have to fall in at all, but were expected to give the decks a cursory sweep in the morning. At 1300 the non-duty part was allowed ashore and need not return until 0730 next morning. The duty part got their heads down, but had to remain on the ship.

Williams, naked to the waist, went into the washroom about 0830 in the morning, picked up a loose bowl, and strolled casually to the hot tap outside the galley. There he saw a girl, dressed in overalls, talking to one of the dockyard mateys.

It had not occurred to him that a girl would ever set foot on the *Marsden*. It was a shock to find himself standing, more than half naked, on the Iron Deck with a girl not more than two feet away. However, she took no notice and he filled his bowl. Other men came out of the washroom even more naked than he and ran back, giggling like schoolboys.

There were a good many other girls in various parts of the ship doing all kinds of men's jobs—taking the bricks out of the boilers, acting as carpenters' mates, even doing some riveting. The whole ship was alive with dockyard workers of both sexes getting down to the repairs.

Williams slept on a coil of rope until dinner-time. That afternoon he went into Edinburgh with Jock and Pat Maclure. They arrived at a hotel, booked a room which happened to have three beds in it, and was therefore still vacant, spent an hour in one or other of the luxurious baths, and then went out to drink real beer.

They had dinner in the hotel, beautifully served, but in very small portions. They swallowed the meal and washed it down with beer.

" When do we eat ? " asked Jock.

Back they went to the pub where they had had their first beers, and got down to sausages, bacon, a small chop, and some chips, followed by large helpings of apple tart.

Not all the libertymen got as far as Edinburgh. Harrison, Carter, Charlie Wright, and Hales went ashore together at 1300, in Number Ones with gold badges shining on their arms. At 1500 a taxi drew alongside the *Marsden's* gangway and three men staggered out at considerable intervals, one after the other. The duty part looked up from their hammocks or letter-writing.

First into the mess deck was Harrison. His jaw was fixed, his teeth were set, and his eyes were glazed. He staggered in, caught hold of a table and clung there. After a few minutes he steadied himself and looked towards his hammock. The mere thought of climbing into it seemed to upset him. He shook his head violently and, losing his grip on the table, almost overbalanced. Several messmates went to help him, but he brushed them aside with sweeping gestures which again all but toppled him over. When he was steady, his eyes slowly travelled to the lockers and fixed on an empty space wide enough for a man to lie on. He began to edge himself towards it; there was a bench in his way. He fell over it, his head landing on a kitbag, and his feet waving in the air. His feet waved for a few seconds and then were still. Harrison had gone fast asleep where he was.

At this point in came Charlie Wright, the Y-gun trainer. His face was ashen. He, too, saw the empty space that had attracted Tom, and began to manoeuvre himself towards it like a ship carefully coming alongside the jetty. When he judged that he was in the right position, he flopped towards it. But he missed and fell in a heap on the deck. Immediately loud snores showed that *he* was fast asleep.

The next man in was Carter, his huge mouth wide open and gasping like a fish that has just been dragged from water. He saw the empty space, made straight for it as though he was crossing Niagara on a tight-rope, hit it, and flopped down there. Seconds later he, too, was snoring his head off.

No more came in. Hales had gone off by himself, in a manner of speaking. He had been separated from the others by two policemen, who put him in a cell. He spent the night there and arrived back at the ship under escort next morning. As he had committed no misdemeanour on the ship, no charge was made against him.

The three days passed quickly. After the one night Williams spent aboard with the duty part he was woken at 0815 by Shortarse, who brought him a cup of tea and two buttered rolls which had been brought aboard by men returning from night leave. Life seemed luxurious. The luxury was not spoiled by the sight of the immaculate destroyer alongside putting to sea, its repairs completed. Not a man on that ship could raise a smile. They had come back from leave and now were off for God alone knew how long. They stood, dully holding their fenders or mechanically letting go their wires, staring into a future which stretched, bleak and forbidding.

Pat Maclure watched them.

" Go on. Go to sea, you bastards."

He did not forget that in four short days the *Marsden*, too, would be slipping backwards out of the dock on her way to destinations unknown.

Chapter Ten

1

THEY went straight back to Iceland.

Williams arrived at the ship from his three days' leave simultaneously with Sub-Lieutenant Carr.

" Had a good leave ? " said Carr.

" Fine, thank you, sir. Did you ? "

" Yes; but I've come back with a hell of an overdraft and a hangover."

" Any idea where we're going ? "

" Iceland, I'm afraid, but I don't know."

Leave expired at mid-day, and at four that evening hands fell in amidships and were addressed by Jimmie. " Well, I'm afraid we're going back to the old stand. I'm sorry about it, but there's nothing we can do about it. We sail at 1800, so, in the meantime secure for sea." And that was that.

They arrived in their old fjord three days later, and two hours after they had dropped the hook they were pulling it up again to go on patrol. Luckily the sea was much calmer and the leak in the deckhead—though not the one in the steam-pipe—had been patched. But it seemed colder. White clouds always threatened to drop snow, and frequently did.

They had one day in harbour and had leisure to notice some ominous signs. The anchorage had filled considerably. There were several more merchant ships flying the hammer and sickle, and one of these spent the morning practising with an Oerlikon gun which she had just fitted. The Russians seemed to fire in a carefree manner. Red tracers flew mast high over the *Marsden* and over an oil tanker that was lying close by. Another remarkable thing about this ship was that she had women on board. But most remarkable of all to the eyes of the *Marsden's* crew was that she was loaded with tanks. They were clearly visible, lashed on the upper deck. They had faintly hoped that she was on some outward journey, but now knew for certain that she was on her way home.

Later in the day a battleship, two cruisers, and several destroyers arrived with an aircraft carrier.

The lower deck was jittery. The Bosun's Mates were even instructed to listen down the wardroom fanshaft, but the only news they brought back was a piece of dialogue between Jimmie and Sub-Lieutenant Carr.

" I'm fighting for King and country," Jimmie had said.

" *I'm* fighting for my wife and kids. *And* for good old Joe Stalin."

This got no one anywhere. Then the Navigator's Yeoman reported that the Skipper had called that morning for special charts of the trip to Russia. That seemed to settle it. But later the Navigator's Yeoman reported that more special charts, this time written in Norwegian, had just come aboard. The crew believed in their hearts that they were going to Russia. But there were other possibilities and hope dies hard. They became irritable again.

Our Albert Forster was unusually trying. His stories about past exploits had been told to everyone on the ship, and as his audience dwindled his volubility mercifully decreased. But when they rejoined the ship at Rosyth there were two new members of the crew to replace the P.O. wireman and the seaman who had been hurt on the way to Iceland.

Forster seized on the unhappy new seaman and began all over again. Whenever anyone passed them, they would hear " and all the rest flicked off and left me alone on the bridge," or some other unlikely tale.

Price dripped more than ever, complaining all day long that he had lost his balaclava or that some " basstud ' had pinched his sea-boots. The Buffer strode around balefully and Jimmie shouted whenever he got the chance.

The only people who seemed little disturbed were the three-badge A.B.s. To them, leaving home was no great hardship. In a much more real sense than to any of the others, the ship was their second home. After all, they *had* chosen the Navy as their life's work, and they had found out how to be as comfortable as possible in it.

The crew passed their time as best they could. They played Tombola half-heartedly—at the end Jock tore up his cards and wailed in disgust, " Ah've wasted ma time. And Ah could have done ma dhobying." They quarrelled. They half-listened to well-worn gramophone records broadcast through the wireless loudspeaker.

They commented acidly upon the news which crackled on the wireless itself. " Large numbers of our fighters crossed the Channel to-day and shot up goods yards, harbour installations, and goods trains in enemy-occupied France."

" From all these operations," said Dowson, " one of our trains is missing."

Alvar Lidell came to the award of a Victoria Cross and quoted the recipient. " I merely did my job," the hero had said.

" Christ! " said Jock. " One of these days a man who's won the V.C. will say ' Ah thoroughly deserved it. It was the least they could give me! '

163

" Ah'll spend ma next leave looking for that chap to shake his hand."

At the end of the news there was a personal " appearance " by a merchant seaman who had spent eighteen days in an open boat and lost a leg. He told of the hardships he had suffered and finished: " But as soon as I'm fit again, my one ambition is to go back to sea."

This was too much for Dowson. He jumped to his feet. " The bloody liar," he said. Then, seizing his razor, he swung round on the wireless. " The lying bastard," he said with all the emphasis he could command, and strode from the mess deck to have a shave.

Next day there were what Jock called " more buzzes than that." Conferences of commanding officers were being held on board one of the battle-wagons. At first the *Marsden*'s Skipper was not called and the ship's company told each other that it was all right, they were not going after all.

Then the Skipper *was* called and their fate seemed sealed. In the early afternoon, when they fell in to work part of ship, Jimmie announced that they would sail that afternoon for another fjord farther north, and after that " they might see some fun." At four they did sail, looking forward to the fun as mice look forward to the arrival of a cat.

2

The new fjord was much narrower than the others in which they had dropped anchor. Steep rocks towered above them on either side, shutting out the sun for the greater part of the day. It was bitterly cold when they arrived early on Sunday morning and went as usual to the oiler, passing a dozen other destroyers, a cruiser, and a small aircraft carrier on the way.

They had a short service on the mess deck, this time with two hymns. But as neither of the hymns was on the hymn-cards, the singing was not a success. Most of them were wondering whether the Skipper would have any news for them when the service was over.

He had. When the last hymn was sung, the Bosun's Mate piped " Unrig church," the flag was taken off the ammunition winch, the Skipper pulled out a large chart, fixed it to a blackboard, and began:

" As you have probably all guessed by now, a convoy is going to Russia and we are going with it. We sail to-morrow evening. It will be the biggest convoy, by far the biggest, that we have ever sent to Russia."

The escort was even bigger than the convoy itself.

" In addition to all those destroyers and corvettes, there will be the cruiser and aircraft carrier which you'll have seen lying in the fjord. There'll be a couple of trawlers to pick up survivors, and there'll be a couple of submarines to deal with any big surface craft we may meet. In addition, just in case the *Tirpitz* or some other German ship should think of coming out, there will be a battle fleet. We shan't see that. They'll be away over the horizon behind us "—(" bloody long way behind us ", whispered the Duchess)—" but they'll be there all the same. Our course will be roughly this," and he pointed with a cane along the chart. " We should have it fairly quiet for the first two days, but from *here* on we'll be escorted all the way by U-boats. And we are certain to have heavy air attacks about *here*, where we're within range of German airfields in Norway. We shall pick up a home-bound convoy. If all goes well, we shall be at sea for about seventeen days.

" Now before you start and after, I want you all to get as much sleep as you possibly can. After the first day we'll be in two watches, and you know what that means. Now, are there any questions ? "

The mess deck had been almost silent while the Skipper was speaking, but now there was a rustle as each man turned to his neighbour with some comment about the news. After a moment the P.O cook asked: " Who owns that island there ? " and pointed to an island on the chart which the Skipper had described as a lurking-place for U-boats. " I don't know," said the Skipper, looking round at Jimmie. But Jimmie shook his head. None of the other officers could help. " Well," said the Skipper, turning back to the P.O. cook, " *you* can have it."

As soon as the Skipper and the officers left, the whole atmosphere on the mess deck changed. The tension and irritableness vanished. Wild Angus began to collect the hymn-cards and, putting them under his arm as if they had been newspapers, he shouted " Extra! Extra! Read all about it! " and the rest began to laugh and skylark with each other as though they had just been told that they were all going home on leave.

The nerviness of the past week had been due not so much to fear as to the uncertainty. All those damned buzzes! They had raised hopes and lowered hopes until you felt yourself worn out. Now you knew. You knew the worst. There was nothing better to hope for and nothing worse to fear. You could set your mind, well, not exactly at rest, but at any rate on an even keel.

All of them now began various jobs that would need doing before they sailed. Some wrote letters—the mail would close for censorship at 1400—two o'clock—the next afternoon. Some began to dhoby, some went for a bath. Williams went to the Heads.

He was there when " action stations " sounded sharply on the bells. Short-long, short-long, short-long, they went, and immediately sea-booted feet began to pound along the washroom flat, past the Heads, and on to the Iron Deck. Williams was not last at Y gun. Calamity was even later. He had been standing naked in the washroom with a bucket of hot water pouring over his head when " action stations " sounded. Pat Maclure had been shaving. He raced to the rangefinder with half his face still covered with lather.

There were some hostile aircraft nosing about and Williams sat down on his little seat outside the shield with an H.E. shell in the tray waiting to be fused. Suddenly one of the for'ard guns fired and the echo of the crack rolled from one high rock to another until the whole fjord was filled with sound.

" That's the first time I've heard a ship's gun fired in anger. Why, bless me! I've been in action."

All this time, instructions were pouring through the earphones from the T.S. " Target in sight, right ahead, Blohm and Voss, independent firing," said Professor Cole, excitement in his voice. But the orders did not affect Y gun. As the target was right ahead, Y gun could not bear. Two more shots were fired by the for'ard gun, and then, after a slight lull, the Bosun's Mate piped " Secure " followed closely by " Hands to dinner."

" What the hell is a Blohm and Voss ? "

" A Blohm and Voss is an ill-omened bastard," said Jock. " It's one of Jerry's scouting planes. You can always tell it. It's got a twin fuselage. You'll see plenty more and they always mean trouble."

That evening the crew watched a paddling race between the whaler and a crew from another ship. Jimmie, in grey flannel trousers and a white sweater, stood in the stern of the whaler yelling encouragement to his crew. The Skipper, dressed in civvy tweeds, stood right aft with a pistol which he fired when the first crew came past the winning-post. The rest stood on the quarter deck, shouting encouragement and insults, which came back at them in echoes from the overhanging rocks.

Next morning the side party were over the side painting. They were within twelve hours of beginning what might be the most perilous adventure of their lives. Yet here they were, slabbing on paint, paint which they knew would have been knocked off by the sea within twenty-four hours. They did not mind. It was something to do.

They were given a make and mend that afternoon. There was a last rush to write letters before the mail closed, and then they fished, slept, read, or talked in the autumn sunshine on the upper deck.

Calamity Taylor did none of these things. Instead, he painted the funnels. He had been caught by the Buffer having a bath when both watches of the hands were mustered amidships and had been given five days' Number Eleven. That included work during non-duty hours.

166

Williams leaned over the side talking to Harrison, who had looked more depressed than ever when he came back from leave. They talked, of course, about the convoy. Harrison had been on one before, and Williams asked him about the state of the sea, the cold, the length of the trip, and what it was like to be in action.

" You don't notice much while the action's on, but you feel bad afterwards. At least, I did."

" You don't look so good now. Is there anything the matter ? "

Then the whole story came out. Harrison was engaged to a girl who, to say the least of it, was flighty. She wrote to him while he was at sea to say that she was going out with other men. Well, there was nothing much to that. But he knew his girl and was suspicious. When he got home on leave she had said that it was all very well for him to talk, but she betted he went out with dozens of girls. What was it they said about sailors—wives in every port ? Well, she didn't see why she shouldn't have men friends while he was away enjoying himself with other girls. He could do what he liked about it.

Harrison had thought of deserting. He felt that if he could manage to stay on the spot, he might be able to get his girl in hand. But his mother had stopped that. It was no good going to gaol. He'd be even less able to keep an eye on his girl there than if he'd been at sea. So he had come back, on time, but without heart.

They went below. There the messes were preparing for supper, still joking and laughing, but stopping suddenly in the middle of their laugh to catch every word of any pipe that the Bosun's Mate called. They cleared the supper things away, put on sea-boot stockings and sea-boots, pulled on a few jerseys, and sat waiting.

3

" *Close all X doors and scuttles.*"

At once Forster shouted, " Here we go! we're off! " and the seamen raised themselves off the lockers and began to shut portholes and pull down deadlights. The shafts of evening sunlight were switched off one by one as the deadlights fell. " I wonder when we'll next see sun coming through these ports," said Lovelace.

" *Special sea-duty men to your stations. Fore part for'ard, after part aft.*"

They all trooped from the gloomy mess deck into the evening light of the fjord. They took a quick look round their part of the ship to see that everything movable was tightly lashed and secured for sea. Then the quarter-deck men, having no anchor to weigh, just hung around. Williams stood by the guard-rail and looked over the side.

There was no sound in the fjord. The surface of the water was unrippled, there was no one moving on the moorland which ran from the water to meet the foot of the towering rock-side. The little white corrugated-iron farmhouses just opposite the *Marsden* seemed untenanted. The rocks on one side were already black with evening shadows, but the tops of the other side were turning red as the now invisible sun hit them at a steep angle.

In spite of all his efforts, Williams could not help being reminded of his own Yorkshire moors. He said to himself, " You're going to help honest Joe." But then his thoughts would be dragged back home. " I wish I was in the garden looking across at Standedge instead of at this bleeding fjord."

The faintest of movements at his feet recalled him to the *Marsden*.

" There we are, the first turn of the screw," said a voice beside him, and he turned to see little Rattler Morgan also staring at the rocks.

Rattler had been many years at sea. He had seen many actions. But Williams wondered if he, too, was a little nervous or depressed. Rattler's face was always white. You could not tell his feelings from that, but there seemed to be a wistful look in his brown eyes as he looked at the land for the last time.

By now, other destroyers which had moored deeper into the fjord were beginning to pass the *Marsden*, following each other silently in line ahead. The only noise came from the *Marsden's* own cable as the anchor weighed and from the gentle throbbing of her engines turning her screws. Now the *Marsden* herself was beginning to move. She swung round slowly and gently nosed herself into the line of destroyers, and, in it, steamed for the opening in the boom. She was last but one.

It was turning cold and the red on the rocks was changing into black. They looked once more at the tops and wondered what eyes were looking down on them, what fingers were already tapping out warnings to the enemy.

The destroyers passed, one by one, through the boom, and than fanned out facing the boom in single-line abreast as if to bow out the cruiser and the aircraft carrier. On the *Marsden* Ginger Howard and his mates were already closed up on the Oerlikons and one crew was standing by on the point-fives.

" *Second part of port watch to cruising stations* "—and Y gun's crew made their way to B gun.

Williams was now wearing one pair of long, thick, ordinary pants, one pair of long, extra thick, special-issue pants, one pair of long football stockings, one pair of bellbottom trousers, with one pair of sea-boot stockings and a pair of sea-boots over the top of them. On his upper half he was wearing a vest, a jersey, and a jumper, with two sweaters over them. Over all was his duffel coat. In addition he wore a balaclava and a pair of fur-lined gloves.

168

He went straight on lookout. It was growing dark and the glasses were no longer much help. He was just trying to re-focus them when a voice behind him said, " Do you see anything, lookout ? " He recognised the Skipper's quiet voice and at the same instant saw red flashes from the cruiser, which was dimly outlined some distance away.

" Yes, sir; the cruiser's firing star shells."

" No, they're not star shells. They're Oerlikon tracers. You want to watch out. This time to-morrow you may be seeing German tracers."

The second part of port watch turned in thankfully at midnight. They were very cold.

The ship was still in four watches the next morning, which meant that the second part of port watch would not be on duty again until the Afternoon. But, like everyone else, they had to lash up and stow their hammocks before " breakfast," and like everyone else except the men actually on watch they had to fall in amidships at 0800 and work part of ship.

Williams was detailed to sweep X-gun deck and it was from there that he got the first sight of the convoy, the first convoy he had ever seen.

The convoy had accumulated in all sorts of places. It had begun with ships either alone or in pairs setting out from all sorts of ports and meeting small escorts in prearranged places. Gradually the single ships, the pairs, and the escorts had joined together and sailed towards Iceland, where they had met the other ships, which the *Marsden* had seen accumulating there, and more escort. The cruiser, aircraft carrier, and accompanying destroyers, including the *Marsden*, were the last to join.

Williams leaned on his broom and stared. The merchant ships were in three long lines with the cruiser and the aircraft carrier in the centre. All round these three lines was the close escort of destroyers, arrow-shaped, in front of them, and spreading back round the sides was the outer screen of destroyers including the *Marsden*. At the rear of the convoy were two destroyers, and two trawlers for survivors, and the two submarines, pushing along on the surface.

The convoy was doing perhaps 10 knots compared with the *Marsden's* usual speed of about 22 knots. X and Y gunshields were barely rattling, and though there was plenty of throb about the ship, it seemed that the convoy as a whole was standing still. There were white clouds at either end of the convoy, but the centre of it, as seen from the *Marsden's* position on the left flank, was lit with sunshine. The sight of the merchantmen, smoke coming placidly from their funnels, reminded Williams and Dowson of the view of the Oldham mill chimneys as seen from the top of Austerlands. Bunched together, they also seemed a sitting target for any U-boat, but Wild Angus said that the position of

169

each ship was carefully worked out and carefully maintained to give a U-boat the smallest possible target.

From time to time the *Marsden*, like the other destroyers, put on a little speed and moved up the lines. Then she would turn again and move back to her original position. The sea was calm and the whole scene looked peaceful. The only exceptional reminder of war, to men accustomed to the sight of warships, was the presence of three aircraft which circled round the convoy on the horizon and well separated from one another. Two of these were British. Sub-Lieutenant Carr came on to the gun deck with his glasses and identified them as a Swordfish and a Catalina. The third was German. It was one of those Blohm and Voss's.

" That bloody thing or its mate will shadow us all the time. It keeps just out of range and sends messages back about our position. We shall catch up with something before long."

But they caught up with nothing that day. All that happened was that at 1230 they went into two watches. This meant that the whole of port watch, and not just a part, went on duty for the Afternoon Watch, while the starboard watch remained below with their heads down. This arrangement suited Williams well. For one thing, Y gun's crew was on the three-inch high-angle gun in day defence stations, only going to B gun for night defence, and the three-inch gun deck was the most comfortable position in the ship. It was amidships, where the motion of the ship, if any, was least marked. It was well sheltered and there was plenty of room to make oneself comfortable on lockers. For another thing, Williams, as sight-setter, had to keep his phones on all through the watch, which relieved him of the duty of climbing to the bridge to do a turn as lookout. So, as soon as he came on watch, he was able to settle down to read, with his phones over his ears.

He read continuously. It kept his mind away from home and away from the sea. During the next twelve days, during which they were at defence stations when they were not at action stations, he read almost every minute of daylight hours on watch. He read *The Little Nugget* by Wodehouse, *The Pandervils* by Gerald Bullett, *South Sea Tales* by Jack London, *Into the Land of Nod* by H. A. Vachell, and many more. The one snag was that he seemed continually to be running across such phrases as " The next two months passed swiftly " or " He spent the winter in Cannes. When spring came . . . "

" I wish to Christ these next two weeks could pass as quickly as that," he thought to himself.

The rest of the gun's crew also read—read anything they could find either in the ship's library or lying about on the mess deck— *The Moon is Down*, *Ariel* by Maurois, *Real Life Detective Stories*, *Lost on Venus* by Edgar Rice Burroughs, *Famous Crimes*, and *Mr. Fortune Speaking*. George Barber got hold of a paperbacked book called *Kiss the Blood on my Hands*, which, he said,

170

was " real literature—mooch better nor James 'Adley Chase."

Calamity split his reading between this and the Bible. He had become absorbed in the Book of Kings and complained contemptuously about the military tactics of Jehoshaphat. But Calamity was having troubles of his own. When the rest of the gun's crew went off watch and got their heads down during the two hours of the " First Dog," he had to go on with his painting. He still had two days of his " number eleven " to work off. He had barely finished his extra work before it was time for him to go on watch for the " Last Dog." What with lack of sleep, snatched meals, and extra work in the cold air, he soon became worn out and made a fool of himself on lookout. The Skipper came suddenly behind him and asked him if he could see the cruiser clearly.

Calamity said " No."

" Why not ? " asked the Skipper.

" Spray's got over my glasses, sir."

" Well, why don't you wipe your glasses ? "

" My handkerchief's right inside my duffel coat and I can't get at it easily."

He was given a sharp dressing-down by the Skipper, a dressing-down which was publicly repeated before the whole watch by the Jimmie next morning and harped on by the Buffer for some days. He was reminded at every turn by authority that he had endangered the safety of the ship by sheer laziness, but most of the crew sympathised with him and did their best to get him as much sleep as possible until his " number eleven " was finished.

Two watches made a curious difference to life on the mess deck. It divided each mess by watches. Since the whole of port watch was on duty while the whole of the starboard watch was below, and vice versa, a man saw little or nothing of friends in the other watch unless they happened to relieve him on his gun. Williams went for four days without seeing Duchess Dowson.

The two watches almost became hostile camps in each mess. They complained about the amount of food the other had eaten or the state in which the other had left the mess when it went on watch. The starboard watch would come below and drip that the port watch had eaten all the butter. The port watch would come below and drip that the starboard watch had left them with all the dishing up.

Occasionally, a man from the duty watch came from his gun to the Heads and looked into the mess deck. He then went back to his gun and reported that the other watch was woofing two loaves of bread and it was no wonder that there was never any left when they themselves got down to the mess deck. These hostilities were never very serious, but they were there, all the same. They were outlets for the nervous tension which was creeping once more over the crew.

171

During the day several ratings were given a strange job. At sea the Skipper used only his sea-going cabin immediately beneath the bridge. The ratings were to turn the day cabin into a temporary sick-bay. They moved the furniture, took up a thick carpet, and installed camp beds. When they had almost finished, the Engineer Officer put his head through the door, saw the preparations for receiving the wounded, said, "I call this rank defeatism", winked, and took his face out again.

But it was not easy to remain good-humoured. The cold, during the night watches, was bitter. Five men kept themselves from freezing by huddling together in one side of a gunshield, but they soon became stiff from cramp as well as cold, since their clothing left them no room to move. When there was a dummy run the gently heaving heap of humanity in the shield became a struggling mass frantically trying to free itself. When there was no dummy run, the hours dragged. It was only during the last half-hour that cheerfulness broke through the cold, and when, at five minutes to the hour, the pipe of " Starboard watch to defence stations" was reported, the gun's crews pulled themselves to their feet and began taking off a few layers of clothes in readiness for the rush to the mess deck below, the quick gulp of ki, the hammock, and oblivion.

It *was* oblivion for the most of the crew. Once or twice, as he pulled off his sea-boots and climbed otherwise fully clothed into his hammock, Williams wondered whether he would wake up again. He was as far for'ard as a man could get on the mess deck. If the ship struck a mine or was hit by a tin fish while he was in his hammock, he would have little chance of escape. Even if he were not killed by the explosion, he would have to get out of his hammock, and run the full length of the mess deck and along the washroom or canteen flat. By that time, as likely as not, he would have been drowned by the inrush of water. But he was always too tired to let this trouble him for long. It would flash through his mind and the next thing he would hear would be " A-L-L the port watch," followed so soon afterwards by " Port watch to defence stations."

This pipe woke port watch on the second morning at 0340. Their first thought was, " Damn that bloody pipe "; then, " Well, that's one day gone. Only sixteen more. Not much longer than a peacetime holiday, and God knows that used to go quick enough."

When they reached their defence stations, they heard that the aircraft carrier had signalled two hours before that she was having engine trouble and would have to stop. The *Marsden* and four other destroyers had been left circling round her while the remainder of the convoy went on their way. The carrier was still hove-to now.

172

"I hope to Christ we don't have to go on without her. Air attacks will be no joke with no planes of our own."

"Perhaps she'll have to go back to Iceland and we'll be sent back with her."

But the carrier reported that she could now go ahead at three knots and later that she could make full steam. They soon caught up the convoy.

At eight port watch had three-quarters of an hour for breakfast and for sponging their already black faces. Then they had to fall in to work part of ship. Apparently parts of the upper deck needed painting and tired hands were told to get busy with brushes and pots of paint.

Only one man did any serious work. The rest stood and gossiped until Jimmie came near. Then they dived for a brush. As it happened, the one man who *was* working had put his brush down a moment before. It was snatched by one of the loafers and the hard worker was left without a brush in his hand. Jimmie eyed him, but said nothing.

"Afternoon watchman"—that was the port watch—had only just been piped to dinner that morning when "action stations" sounded, long-short, long-short, for aircraft warning. There had been aircraft about all day. Two were Liberators, a third turned out to be a Sunderland. After she had been fired at by several ships in the convoy she hurriedly dropped flares for recognition signals. Another was the inevitable Blohm and Voss still circling round, well out of range of the guns. Neither the Liberators nor the Sunderland seemed to make any attempt to interfere with it, and it ignored them.

But the sounding of "aircraft action stations" showed that some other plane had come into view. Calamity ran on to the Iron Deck, struggling into his duffel coat as he ran, and when he was abreast the three-inch high-angle gun it fired at a very low angle indeed. The shell hit the water not many hundred yards away. The blast completely deafened him. It also surprised the Skipper, who had given no orders to open fire. Apparently Jimmie had raced on to the three-inch as soon as "action stations' sounded, shouting, "Why the hell don't you open fire? Can't you see the bastard? Go on, fire!" and the layer had pressed his pedal before he elevated the gun.

Luckily no one was hurt, least of all the unidentified plane, which sheered away from the convoy and was not seen again. But Calamity remained deaf.

Shortly afterwards the Bosun's Mate piped "Port watch to defence stations," which meant that the wretched port watch went without the greater part of their dinner and an indignant starboard watch was left with all the dishing up.

Port watch were not long undisturbed. After about twenty minutes the *Marsden* swung round and went slowly to the rear

173

of the convoy. There she turned and came behind a large, smart-looking tanker. She was going to top up her oil-tanks and the whole port watch were mustered on the fo'c'sle to pick up and secure the lines which the tanker would pass back to her on floats.

The sea was not rough, but the *Marsden* was pitching enough to send occasional showers of spray over the fo'c'sle, wetting the seamen and making the deck slippery. As there were more seamen there than was necessary for the job, and as all of them slipped on the wet deck, there was some confusion and much shouting from Jimmie.

" Come on," said Jimmie to a crowd who had dropped back for protection from the spray behind A gun. " Still afraid of a little salt water ? " and went himself to the stem of the ship.

The Buffer stood by with a grapnel and, as the floats from the tanker came near, he hurled his grapnel at them. The first time he missed. The second time the hook pierced the float and, amid shouts from Jimmie, the port watch tugged at the grapnel and brought the float inboard. The float was attached to a thick, light rope which floated on the surface. The rope was attached to a wire on the tanker. Port watch now pulled rope and wire across the intervening sea. When the end of the wire came inboard, it was attached to the capstan engine and hauled in. The far end of the wire, on the tanker, was attached to a pipe line.

These operations were watched critically by the Skipper of the tanker. He stood on a little bridge aft with a microphone in his hand and from time to time gave directions or advice in a pleasant conversational voice.

" I suggest you put that wire through the bull-ring," he said, as though he were sitting at home and advising the *Marsden*'s skipper to try the sherry instead of cocktails. " I think you'll find it easier to take this line first." His quiet, matter-of-fact voice contrasted sharply with the confusion on the fo'c'sle, where a good thirty men were hauling on ropes and wire, while struggling to keep themselves upright and dry. "What size nozzle have you? Two and a half inch or five inch ? You'll be using the five inch, I expect. It's quicker, of course."

By the time the operation was over, every seaman on the fo'c'sle felt that they had never done a worse job and wondered what the merchant seaman skipper on the tanker must think of the Royal Navy.

But Jimmie looked at his watch and said, " Lads, you've done that in record time. It's a bloody good job," and pointed to another destroyer which had begun to oil from a second tanker long before and was still at it.

" What the hell was all the shouting about, then ? " asked Pat Maclure as he went back to defence stations.

Even in the daytime it was bitterly cold on watch. Williams huddled himself on the three-inch locker underneath an extra coat and his blanket and read. The others also read, but from time to time they would get up to warm themselves and miniature fights broke out. George Barber was always setting on Calamity or Harry Rhoades and usually getting the worst of it. But it kept him warm. Poor Calamity was quite deaf and Barber would go to him and say in a normal voice, " Let me and thee sneak oop behind Rhoades and attack 'im. But the idea is, see, that once we've begun, me and Rhoades turns on thee."

Calamity only heard a few words, but got the idea that they were to attack Rhoades. He nodded his head and grinned. But of course the fight ended with Calamity on his back and the other two on top of him.

" You double-crossing bastard. You wait till I get up," he shouted 'to George, who looked surprised and injured.

" 'E says Ah double-crossed 'im. All Ah did wur to catch 'owld uv a leg. 'Ow wa Ah t' know whose leg it was ? "

All this helped to pass the time and kept their minds off anything else.

On the third morning, just after eleven, they were sitting as usual on the three-inch locker, reading, when there came two unusual sounds. First the vibration of the engines suddenly ceased, and second, almost simultaneously, there was the sound of heavy feet pounding along the deck. It was " action stations."

Y gun's crew leaned over the side of the gun platform waiting for the regular three-inch crew to relieve them. The first man up said, " Flicking sub.," and went to his position on the gun. By the time Williams got to his place on Y gun the *Marsden* was going full speed away from the convoy and the depth-charge crews were standing by. Almost immediately came the order, " Let go depth charges," and a barrel rolled from the trap into the sea, exploding with a flash that seemed to travel flat along the surface, a sharp crack, and the usual geyser shoot of black water and smoke. Seconds later, a black-faced man shot out of the hatchway to the stewards' flat immediately in front of the tiller flat. It was Pat. He had been down in the bilges fetching a new jar of rum for the morning's issue when the depth charge exploded. He said that the sides of the ship seemed to be caving in. He thought the *Marsden* had been hit. He waited on the upper deck until three more charges had been dropped and only went back to the bilges when the T.I., ordering " Set to safe." showed that the action was over.

No one seemed to know whether they had got the sub. or not.

4

On the fourth morning the port watch, not being on duty, had to work part of ship. Williams as usual found his way to X-gun deck, which not only gave a good view of the convoy, but was also conveniently out of the way. If he stood in front of the gun, he was shielded from the view of the bridge, the Buffer, or anyone else who might object to smoking.

It was a lovely crisp morning with bright sunshine. He leaned on his broom in the lea of the gun, smoked, and talked to George Barber. George, besides being intensely superstitious, was a great betting man. He had studied racing form so carefully since he was a schoolboy that, at the Sheffield iron foundry where he worked as a moulder, his workmates used to come to him for tips. With the bets he made for himself and the rake-off given him by his mates for successful tips he seemed to make more than he earned by his moulding.

George was in a betting mood that morning. He had made that Russian trip before and was prepared to bet Williams anything he liked that they would get heavy air attacks from the following day onwards.

" Ah knows Jerry's form. Jerry's reliable. Nivver lets thi' down. 'E allus cooms, same time, same place. We could 'ave set our watches by 'im in t' Med. when we were goin' to Malta. Ah'll bet thi' 'e crops oop to-morrer."

At that moment there was a heavy explosion far away at the rear of the convoy.

" Looks like he's cropped up to-day." Williams's stomach fell slowly into his sea-boots. He stared at a black cloud of smoke on the horizon. Obviously a ship had been torpedoed. They could not tell whether she was a merchant packet or an escort. But *some* ship had been hit. A red glow was showing through the black smoke. The ship was burning.

The Marsdens had known that there were submarines in that cold grey sea. Yet somehow this visible proof awoke fears that imagination had allowed to lie dormant. They thought of the men on that torpedoed ship, now possibly gasping in the ice-cold sea. They thought of themselves and the *Marsden* and fully realised, for the first time, that so long as they were on this trip, they might at almost any second hear a crash and die.

Williams and Barber stared. The flames on the torpedoed ship could now be plainly seen. The men who had survived the explosion were being given the choice of burning or freezing. A destroyer was dashing towards the burning ship to take off survivors, while three others raced round in circles, dropping depth charges. Would the rescuers be in time ?

Sub-Lieutenant Carr came on the gun deck and peered at the ship with his glasses. " It's a merchant packet all right." Then " By God, it's that Russian packet that was lying near us in the fjord. Do you remember ? The one that fired those Oerlikon tracers over our masts."

They remembered. They also remembered that the Russian ship had women on board. The flames seemed more terrible than ever.

176

Then there were more explosions.

" Depth charges ? "

" No. One of the destroyers is trying to sink the ship by gunfire."

A sudden shout from Barber. " Christ, there's anoother one. Look at ower there, not far from yon trawler. Look at 'er. By God, she's caught a packet. She's going down reet away," and there was another black cloud of smoke on the horizon at the rear of the convoy but well away from the first ship to be hit.

This second hit really shook Williams. While Barber was jumping up and down in nervous excitement, he stood quite still and said nothing. But he was afraid. A tight band seemed to clamp itself round his forehead, holding his whole face taut and strained. He could only stare at this new black cloud and watch one of the small trawlers racing through the water for survivors.

At last he said, " Haven't ' action stations ' gone ? "

" No," said Carr. " We can't do anything. Too far away. We'll get plenty of action stations in the next few days, don't you worry."

They had " action stations " within an hour. Port watch had given up any pretence of sweeping and had walked back into the mess deck for tea when the bells began to ring short-short, short-short, for submarines, and seconds later they were all clumping along the Iron Deck.

Every Oerlikon in the convoy had opened up. But they were not aiming in the air. They were blazing at something on the surface in the centre of the convoy and the red tracers were spitting into the water or flying dangerously near other ships. Then they saw it . . . the black conning-tower of a submarine slap in the middle of the convoy.

The U-boat commander had submerged a good way ahead of the convoy and gone down to a great depth where he hoped to be out of reach of Asdics. He had listened through instruments of his own until the convoy was overhead and then had slowly surfaced. He meant to come to periscope depth just after the rear of the convoy had passed overhead. Then he could let loose his tin fish and submerge again before the escorting destroyers could swing round and drop their depth charges.

But he had been unlucky. He had misjudged his time, surfaced in the middle of the convoy, and received a depth charge on his tail which had brought him right up. He was pumped full of holes by a hundred Oerlikon guns and splintered to atoms by another set of depth charges.

" That'll teach the bastards to come near this convoy," said Calamity. " But, flick me, they've got some guts to come *that* near."

There were no more explosions that day, and no more " action stations." They heard in the evening that most of the crew had

177

been saved from the first torpedoed ship. There had been several
women on board and one of them had given birth to a still-born
baby on the destroyer that rescued her.

" Talk about Jerries having sum goots," Barber yelled into
Calamity's ear, " but what about these 'ere Russian women ? Y'
don't get our tarts coomin' to sea and 'avin' babies."

" I should flicking well think not. Seems silly to me. She
must have known. Flick it. The voyage hasn't lasted nine
months."

There had been only ten survivors from the second ship, which
had sunk so quickly. All of them were in a bad way.

The Marsdens felt depressed, tired, and numb. The effect of
broken sleep was beginning to tell. The ease with which the
U-boats seemed to have sunk those two ships made them wonder
whether this carefully planned and heavily escorted convoy was
going to get to Murmansk with any merchantmen left at all.
True, only two had gone so far, a small fraction of the total which
remained. But there were days and days of attacks still to come.

They realised next day that the *Marsden's* ordeal had hardly
begun.

Chapter Eleven

Action: First Day

The next day was Saturday. The sky was white with snow-
clouds touched with only occasional patches of blue. The cold
on the gun during the Morning Watch had stung and it was not
much warmer sweeping the decks during the Forenoon.

But it was now 12.45 p.m. Y gun's crew had had their tots
and dinner and had settled down to read on the three-inch gun
platform. Their minds were almost entirely on their books, but
not quite. One small part listened for some change in the
sounds of the ship—speeding up the engines, clumping feet,
shouts, or any sudden turn of the rudder—which would mean
either that "action stations " had sounded or that action of some
sort was imminent.

The warming came from running feet, which made Y gun's
crew jump up. Almost immediately the first of the three-inch
crew arrived, closely followed by the Jimmie, who was in charge

of the gun during action. Williams was last to be relieved, but he pulled off his headphones and gathered his tin helmet and anti-flash gear in his hand, ready to rush for Y gun.

He arrived there breathless and found that some of the others were also showing slight signs of nerves. It was to be aircraft action this time—not just dropping a few charges on some sub.—and all of them felt that the real thing was beginning. One side of the gunshield was cluttered with cork lifebelts, and George Barber, in tones of irritation quite unlike his usual placid speech, was saying, " Clear all this flicking stoof art o' road, for flick's sake."

Williams pushed past him into the shield, climbed over the cork lifebelts, seized his phones, slapped them on his head, and shouted above the rattle of the gunshield, " Y gun well. Y gun closed up, cleared away." Then he climbed out of the shield again, pulled down his little seat, and sat on it. He pulled his balaclava over the headphones and his anti-flash helmet over his balaclava, pinned his mouthpiece through the helmet, and pulled on his long white anti-flash gloves. He fumbled for his fuse key, fixed it to the cap of the shell which Jackie Low had put on his tray, took it off again, saw that the fuse was set to long barrage of 0.42 or 4,200 feet, and then looked around him.

The first thing he saw was a cork lifebelt lying on the deck in front of him. He was already wearing his own rubber belt. But he had heard that they were often punctured by shrapnel, while the cork lifebelts were shrapnel proof. Looking at the lifebelt, he began to feel exposed. But the trouble was: to put the lifebelt on, he would have to take the earphones off and get the connecting wire outside the belt. But that would take two minutes and anything might have happened by then. He sat on his stool, gazing at the belt and hoping that none of the others would pick it up.

Then the Skipper's voice sounded. He was talking from the bridge through the loud-hailer. He said: Hullo, Marsdens. Signal received. A formation of enemy planes is approaching the convoy. It's about fifty miles away at the moment on the starboard beam. Keep your eyes open."

Fifty miles away! How fast did bombers go ? Wasn't it about 300 m.p.h. ? At that rate they would not be over the convoy for another ten minutes or so. Williams dived for the cork lifebelt, unpinned his mouthpiece, pulled off his helmet, balaclava, and earphones, and handed the phones to Barber. " Here, George, Put these on a moment while I fix this lifebelt."

" What didst Ah tell thee, Bob ? Jerry's oop to form." George took the earphones.

Williams found that his nervousness had gone. He fixed his cork lifebelt, took back the phones from George, and was soon ready for whatever might happen.

179

" Thank God we get some decent warning. I'd be in the hell of a mess if it was ' action stations ' one minute and ' action ' the next."

Fifty miles away! Perhaps they're not coming for us after all. Then he grinned. The convoy was in the middle of the Arctic Ocean, the only possible target within 300 miles. It wasn't like being in a land blitz in London, hearing the sirens go and saying, " Well, they may only be going for the Thames Estuary. Perhaps they'll leave Central London alone for a change." This formation of planes could only be making for the convoy. " Don't you start any damned buzzes, not even to yourself," said Williams to himself.

On the bridge there was a good deal of sound. The escort ships had an inter-communication system by which the Admiral commanding the escort could give his orders or information and by which one ship could talk to another. Pat Maclure in the rangefinder, Venables and Denton, the two action lookouts, and Buck and Richards, the two Bosun's Mates who acted as part lookout, part messengers during action, listened to every word. First it was the Admiral himself giving some personal instructions, and Pat Maclure recognised the voice of the gold-braided, tubby little man who had come aboard the *Marsden* to welcome the crew to his command.

" So the old trout *did* go to sea after all! " said Pat out loud. " Flick me. He *is* all for it."

Next came some orders for the *Marsden*. She was to close on the convoy and form part of the inner screen.

" Bloody hell! "

The outer screen was to fan out still farther.

" Lucky sods."

Then came some more news. " The formation of hostile aircraft is now about twenty-five miles away. There is a second formation of hostile aircraft about fifty miles away, both on the starboard beam."

" Is there now ? " said the Skipper, whistling through his teeth. He picked up his own loud-hailer and gave the news to the crew, adding, " You see those blue patches in the sky ? Well, keep a careful watch. Sooner or later the planes will drop out of one of those."

The rest of Y gun's crew were now out of the shield. Their gun was loaded with a long barrage shell and there was nothing more they could do for the time being except keep a lookout. But Williams, as usual, was tied by his phones. He sat on his fusing seat and from time to time put his key on the cap of the shell in front of him to reassure himself he could fit it easily into the groves.

There was no longer any obvious sign of tension among the gun's crew. The *Marsden* was on the port side, and her crew

180

could see the centre of the convoy steaming placidly along with the cruiser in the middle. The aircraft carrier had moved just outside the convoy, between it and the close escort, and had already turned her head to the wind, ready for her Sea Hurricanes to take off.

All at once there was a distant sound of guns and Y gun's crew came running from the guard-rails to their gun position. Then, down the phones, came the nasal voice of Professor Cole, more hurried than usual, but quite clear. "Aircraft approaching above the clouds on the starboard side. Set long barrage."

Y gun was already loaded with a long-barrage fused shell. The shell on the little tray in front of Williams was also fused to the long barrage. Williams merely placed his key in the grooves, in case a new fuse should be ordered, and waited.

Other guns in the convoy were now firing much nearer this time, and them a sharp order came through his phones: " Target in sight, Green five-o. Planes diving through the clouds. Long barrage, commence, commence, COMMENCE." Immediately, Barber and Wright focussed their sights on the target, Wright swinging the gun round slightly and carrying Williams and his fusing seat round too. Wright shouted " Trainer on," and just as the other four-point sevens and the three-inch fired, Barber pressed his pedal and Y gun fired too.

Williams did not notice the flash. He barely heard the crack because his ears were so heavily guarded. Further, a sharp order had just come through, " Fuse o-seven-two," which meant turning the fuse on the shell in front of him from 4,200 feet to 7,200. He leaned forward slightly to look at the little numbers on the fuse and then wrenched his key round. The key slipped and the fuse remained at o-four-two. He snapped the key back into the grooves, pressed on it heavily, and tried to turn it more slowly. Again the key slipped. The shell in front of him was one from the racks which lined the guard-rails near the gun. It was heavily greased for protection against the weather and the key would not hold against the grease.

Meanwhile the other guns on the ship were firing hard, but Y gun remained empty with Williams struggling with his key. Above the din Calamity bellowed, " For Christ's sake chuck the bastard away," and seizing the shell off the tray he dumped it behind the gun. Immediately Low put a new shell on the fusing tray and Williams fixed his key in the slot. Again the key slipped. The shell was another from the ready-use racks and it, too, was covered in grease.

" Jackie, stop putting down those ready-use bastards. Give 'im a brand-new one from the shell-room."

The supply party from the shell-room had long ago provided shining new shells. Low dumped one on the tray, Williams fused it immediately, Calamity snatched it, dumped it on his own tray, and rammed it home with a new charge. But the targets were no longer in sight.

There had been three planes. Two had sheered back into the clouds when the convoy's guns fired. The third pressed on and dropped one bomb right in the centre of the convoy. It raised a great shoot of water abaft the cruiser.

For about a minute there was a lull. Williams looked at the sky over the convoy and saw that it was splodged with puffs of black smoke where the H.E. shells had burst. He was still looking at the bursts, hanging there like little umbrellas, when he saw a number of planes come out of a cloud into one of the blue patches. At the same moment the loud-hailer from the bridge called, " There are nine planes above the clouds immediately over the convoy," and guns from other ships began to roar and chatter and the sky was seared with tracer bullets. The *Marsden's* guns opened fire. Y gun fired twice, then stopped. " Won't bear, flick it," said Calamity, meaning that the target was too far forward.

Williams stood up and went as near to the starboard side as his 10 feet of telephone cable would let him. There he could see nine planes, some of which had already dropped their bombs and were speeding back into the clouds amidst a shower of tracers and puffs of anti-aircraft shells. Others were just dropping bombs and huge splashes rose suddenly near the ships. But every bomb missed except one. That hit an ammunition ship some three hundred yards away from the *Marsden.*

They heard no explosion, just a flash of black, red, and orange, and a tall column of solid black smoke, going straight into the air for hundreds of feet. The smoke hung there, motionless; but there was no sign of the ammunition ship. The ships immediately behind it had been showered with debris, but that was the only trace that was left. At one second there had been a ship with a hundred men on board, living, breathing, and fighting. The next second there were a few pieces of twisted iron on the decks of ships round about, but nothing more.

Y gun's crew could only stare. Jock said " Jesus Christ," but the rest could say nothing. They were not frightened. They did not feel pity for the hundred men who had been blown to atoms in a second. They did not think of them. They just looked numbly at the convoy, half expecting to see the ships in front of the ammunition ship look over their shoulders, shudder, and scurry away. They were somehow surprised to see them unruffled and apparently motionless, like men sitting in armchairs and smoking pipes on a Sunday afternoon. The only sign of the disaster was that thick column of black smoke, hanging in the air.

They were brought back to their places by the loudspeaker. " Another large formation of enemy planes, thirty to forty of them, is coming up on the starboard bow. Expect an attack at any minute."

They all peered into the sky where the small patches of pale blue were slowly being mopped up by heavy snow-clouds. It seemed to be snowing thickly on the starboard horizon and a few flakes of snow were falling on the *Marsden's* decks.

Suddenly the planes came. They dived from the snow-clouds in four lines, one behind the other. There were nine Heinkel 111s in each line, carrying torpedoes and flying almost abreast. They swooped, noses down, almost to sea-level, and came roaring towards the long lines of ships.

Every gun in the convoy opened fire—every gun, that was, except Y gun, which was swung as far forward as she would go and still could not get a target. The crew could only watch.

The lines of planes came at the convoy, well below mast height, with red tracers ripping through the air at them and H.E. shells bursting only a few feet above the water around them. The cruiser, in the centre of the convoy, put on speed and, with her bow heaving as she passed one ship after another, and her forward guns blazing, went to meet the planes pressing towards the convoy in immaculate formation.

The formation was broken by the concentration of fire. The planes in the first line began to wave and lurch as though they were little models dangled from strings. They skidded out of line, they spread out, rolling from side to side, but they kept on and, just before they reached the first ships of the convoy, they loosed their torpedoes, which splashed into the water, cutting white furrows towards the ships at 40 knots.

But the aim was bad. No airman could have kept a cool head in that blazing sky. The tin fish cut harmlessly by the ships while the planes swayed, tattered and smoking, down the lines, struggling to regain height and the safety of the clouds. No sooner had the first line loosed its torpedoes and gone swaying past than the second line came in. Only it was no longer a line but nine independent aircraft, spread out, trying to keep clear of the fire and to get in a shot wherever they could. One plane, separated from the rest, came heading straight for the *Marsden*.

The Duchess on his point-fives and Ginger Howard on his Oerlikons were ready for it; but while they were concentrating on this plane, carefully holding their fire until it came within range, a second plane, which had already loosed its torpedo, swerved off from the convoy and turned to climb. It, too, was coming over the *Marsden*.

The Gunner " T.," the officer in charge of the torpedo tubes, was standing on the point-five platform. The torpedo tubes were useless in aircraft action, so the Gunner " T." supervised the point-fives. He suddenly saw the new plane soaring from sea and yelled to Duchess Dowson. Dowson looked up, swung his guns round, and pressed the trigger. Nothing happened.

" Why don't you fire at it ? It's in range."

" I'm trying to flicking fire, but the flicking gun's jammed." The Duchess seized the crowbar which he kept handy and struck the gun with it. Then he pressed the trigger again and a stream of bullets poured into the belly of the plane as it passed overhead.

Meanwhile the first plane was coming nose-down at the *Marsden*. Just as the German navigator was reaching for the lever to release his tin fish, Ginger Howard fired his Oerlikon and fired so accurately that his tracers tore into the nose of the plane. The plane jibbed like a frightened horse. Her nose went up as the pilot involuntarily pulled back his joy-stick to avoid the red-hot stream. As it jibbed, the navigator released his fish but, instead of gliding smoothly into the water, it fell flat on the surface like a diver taking a " belly-flop." It bounced glistening as it fell, splashed, bounced again, as it came down level with the *Marsden*, and sped off towards the horizon. The plane staggered off with Ginger's tracers still ripping into it.

By now the other two lines of planes had raced through the convoy, dropping their torpedoes. Not one torpedo found a mark, but not one plane was seen to fall in the sea, although many were hit.

There was now a lull. They could clearly hear the drone of planes, but not all the planes in the Arctic sky were German. The carrier had let go plenty of hers, and two of them were circling her continually as she weaved her way in and out of the lines of ships to avoid bombs and to bring the wind into the proper quarter when her planes were landing or taking off. The rest had flown out of sight to tackle the Heinkels either above the clouds or beyond the horizon before they reached the convoy.

The Marsdens thanked God for those planes, but would the pilots be able to see the enemy or to land on the carrier ? Snow was falling heavily. Both ends of the convoy were entirely hidden and only the centre alongside the *Marsden* was at all visible, its black smoke showing clearly against the snow.

Suddenly the loud-hailer sounded again. " Another formation of planes is coming up on the convoy from the port side. It looks like our session now, boys."

Good God! Of course. We're on the port side. All the attacks, so far, have been coming from starboard. We haven't seen anything yet.

Then the bombs began to fall.

" Here they come, sir," shouted one of the bridge lookouts. " One, two, three."

" One, two, three what ? " said the Skipper.

" Bombs, sir."

" Well, why didn't you say so ? "

The Skipper had his glasses in the air. Suddenly he dropped them and picked up his inter-communication microphone.

" Look out, *Faulkner* ! Look out, *Faulkner* ! Bombs falling towards your stern, *Faulkner*. Look out, *Faulkner*. Bombs coming towards your stern."

The *Faulkner*'s skipper had barely time to order " hard to port " before the bombs fell. Three of them in a row, just abaft her stern. Sprouts of water must have splashed her quarter deck.

Other bombs were falling in the middle of the convoy. Everywhere Oerlikons and point-fives were rapping out their rat-a-tat-tat, but the four-point sevens were silent. The snow-clouds were now so heavy that the layers and trainers could see no target. It was only when the planes came out of the clouds for a moment to drop their bombs that anyone could see them, and they were back again so quickly that only the short-range weapon-men had time to get their sights on them.

Three bombs found a mark, all of them on merchant packets, one of which began to blaze violently. One of the inner screen destroyers went alongside to take off survivors, while two other destroyers stood guard. Two other ships were damaged, but were neither set on fire nor stopped. They struggled on with the rest of the convoy.

Suddenly there was an extra loud burst of firing and Y gun's crew became tense and strained. A stick of bombs was falling straight for the aircraft carrier, and Calamity was shouting at the top of his voice, " O God, don't let them hit her. Don't let them hit. DON'T LET THEM HIT HER. My God, she's hit. No. BY CHRIST ! SHE'S NOT. The bastards have missed. The bastards have MISSED ! "

Three high spouts of water had shot up just astern of the carrier, but she went on weaving in and out unhurt and unruffled.

" Thank God for that ! "

Whenever there was a lull in the firing, planes could be clearly heard by anyone who had not got his ears stuffed with cottonwool and covered with a variety of clothes and earphones. But no more bombs fell.

Soon the loud-hailer called, " Planes on the starboard bow. They are friendly. They are Sea Hurricanes coming in to land on the carrier," and fighters came circling in, one after the other, to land on the carrier's flight deck. The guns had ceased firing.

After a few more minutes, four glorious words came over the loud-hailer. They were: " Port watch to tea." This meant that the action was over, that the German pilots, what was left of them, had gone home. It also meant that it must be late. Port watch had the Afternoon. If they were being piped to tea, it must be after four. It was 1630, and the starboard watch were now officially on duty.

As soon as the pipe to tea sounded, the guns' crews realised that they were cold and tired. Their joints seemed frozen, their nerves numb. They staggered into the mess deck.

There, sipping a cup of tea, tiredness gave way to a feeling of exhilaration. They really had been in action now; and it was not so bad. It was no worse than a London blitz. In fact it was better. At least you could see what was happening. And these near misses did not bring houses crashing over your head. Unless you got a direct hit you were pretty safe. It hadn't been any joke. But it hadn't been terrible.

" What's that Jimmie like in action, Angus ? "

" Not bad. Not bad at all. He's really quite human. Just a bit excitable. Sort of man who goes looking for trouble. Nice as pie he was to-day, offering cigarettes all round and cracking jokes. Kept on lending us his binoculars when the Jerries were out of range. ' Come and look at that bastard over there,' he said to me once. Oh yes, he's not bad at all."

Then " action stations " sounded again. As they ran along the Iron Deck there was a loud explosion, and, looking to the rear of the convoy, they saw flames bursting from a merchant-man.

Almost before they reached their stations the *Marsden* heeled over in a sharp turn which almost threw overboard one of the depth-charge party who was slashing at the ropes which held a depth charge in place. The *Marsden* raced to the rear of the convoy and dropped four charges in quick succession. Then there was a long lull while Y gun's crew got steadily colder, until at last the loud-hailer called " Port watch to defence stations," and the wretched port watch, which had been on watch during the Morning, worked part of ship during the Forenoon, been at action stations during the Afternoon and the greater part of the " First Dog," now had to take themselves back on watch for the " Last Dog."

They dripped and grumbled as they settled down, huddled together to keep out the cold. " To think that this is Saturday neet," said Barber. " They've just opened pubs. If Ah wur at 'ome, Ah'd be listening t'football results on t' wireless, sitting by t' fire in an armchair wi' my feet on t' mantelpiece. Ah'd be getting ready to go out for one at the local in anoother five minutes."

The others did not want to think of home or pubs or safe return. No good making yourself more miserable than they were. They looked forward only to their hammocks.

At eight o'clock they went below and had a scare. There was a strong smell of burning. Was the ship on fire ? The

Skipper also noticed the smell as he stood on the bridge and sent Buck down to investigate.

Two minutes later Buck was back, leering as usual. "It's all right, sir. It's just that we've got King Alfred aboard."

The P.O. cook had been baking bread and had left it in the oven while he went for his supper. The bread had burned.

Action : Second Day

After three hours' sleep, port watch was duty again at midnight for the Middle. Snow was falling heavily and the gun's crew huddled more tightly than ever into the shield. Four men were already wedged in with their extra coats and blankets when a fifth arrived. Of course there was no room, but he lay on his stomach and began to burrow. He surfaced near the front of the shield and went into a doze. By three o'clock the dawn was breaking and the snow had stopped. Suddenly there was the ominous clump of running feet, giving warning that " action stations " had sounded. The Asdics had pinged another sub.

The Skipper on the bridge called to a signalman. " Tell the *Faulkner* we've got a ping. And tell that thing there, too." pointing to one of the trawlers. " No, don't use that little trigger lamp. Use the ten-inch. Tell the whole world! "

At that instant a tin fish burst in the engine-room of a merchantman. The men in the engine-room were killed instantly, but the rest of the crew were taken off by one of the trawlers before the ship sank.

" Starboard watch to defence stations " did not go until 0430. Port watch had lost half an hour's sleep.

They were on watch again by eight with no more than a cup of tea inside them. There was no bread and the language used about the P.O. cook ought not to have surprised him. But he said that the seamen only had to go without the bread, while he had to go without it himself *and* spend his " spare time " baking more. Some people did not know when they were well off, he said.

Y gun's crew had to sweep and shovel snow from the gun and off the gun platform and lockers before they could sit down and make themselves comfortable. The sky was bright and clear and the air bit at any exposed piece of skin. They tried to read, but soon became so cold that they had to get up and stamp their feet every few minutes to keep a little blood circulating. This interrupted reading and thrust back the burden of imagination on to their minds. The sea looked cold and merciless, like the eyes of a snake. They stared at it, wondering whether the U-boat men were as cold beneath it as they were on the surface. They shivered and went back to their books.

Twelve o'clock was a long time in coming. But, at last, Wild Angus came on the platform to relieve Charlie Wright, who went to the mess deck. Charlie came back in two minutes, looking a new man, and George Barber went off. Two minutes later he, too, was back, and told Williams that this Arctic air was nearly as good as Blackpool. It made a man feel so well. Then Williams went to the mess deck. By now the sky was weighted with heavy snow-clouds until sky and sea seemed joined in one grey, sullen mass. Flakes of snow were frisking across the deck. When one hit Williams's exposed cheek it smarted. Williams shivered into the canteen flat.

Two minutes later he was out again. The snow was coming down heavily now. It seemed soft and smooth and warm, like velvet. Sea and sky seemed merged together to form a down quilt which wrapped itself round the three-inch platform and kept the gun's crew snug.

" George, you're certainly right about this air. It does a man good."

" Anyone else going for his tot ? " said Wild Angus.

*   *   *

When the starboard watch came, the snow was falling so heavily that the convoy was completely hidden from the *Marsden*. " I'm going to get my head down this afternoon," said Raikes. " We'll not have any trouble. Bombers couldn't find their way through this. Crash my flicking great swede, that's what I'll do, me lads."

That's what Williams intended to do, all afternoon. He was getting cold again as the tot wore off, and he was tired. Three hours in his hammock was something to look forward to. But first, dinner. Somebody had made a particularly good duff that morning. It was crisp and had jam on it. All the time he was eating his " pot-mess " or stew, Williams watched his piece of duff. He had just taken the first bite of this duff when " action stations " sounded. He raced for Y gun.

The loud-hailer announced that a dozen planes were approaching the convoy. Some of the ships were still hidden by a curtain of falling snow, but the sky had cleared over the *Marsden* and the carrier was weaving her way into the light wind. Several of her planes had already taken off and more were in position on the flight deck.

Suddenly guns opened up in the convoy and the loud-hailer called, " Fifteen torpedo-carrying planes are immediately over the convoy. We must expect an attack at any moment." Five seconds later the *Marsden's* for'ard guns had opened fire, closely followed by X and Y guns. Immediately after Y gun fired her second shot, glass and metal showered on the heads of Y gun's crew and tinkled on the deck or on the shield. But it was not a hit. The concussion of the guns firing together had smashed the fog lamp which was fixed to the lip of X-gun deck above them, and glass, bulbs, and fittings had crashed down.

Y gun fired four more rounds and then Charlie Wright called out, " Y gun won't bear." The targets were right ahead and Y gun could not get at them. The crew groaned. It was maddening to sit still and let planes send their torpedoes and bombs at you without hitting back. Christ, it was cold!

Barber jogged Williams's arm and pointed towards the sea, shouting something. Williams turned in time to see a spout of water leap from the sea, less than fifty feet away from the *Marsden*. " That was a near one." A second spout of water shot up, just the same distance away and in the same position.

Williams had heard no sound of bombs whistling down. He did not even hear explosions as the bombs hit the water. His ears were too thickly guarded. So he felt no fear. He might have been looking out of the window at home and found that it was raining.

The loud-hailer was on again: " Another formation of enemy planes is over the convoy. They must be high-level bombers. They've just dropped two close by. Watch out carefully."

More planes were taking off from the carrier and with each one the Marsdens felt more and more comfortable. By God, those Jerries weren't going to have it all their own way up there! They'd bloody well wish they had stayed at home as the Sea Hurricanes got in among them. " By God, thur's one o' t' bastards coming down now." Barber pointed to a white speck, high in the sky. It was a parachute with a black object dangling from it.

But the black object was not a German. It was the pilot of a Sea Hurricane.

The lookouts on the bridge had watched the Sea Hurricane coming back towards the carrier. There seemed to be some smoke trailing from it, but it might well be vapour in the freezing air. All at once, the plane turned over. Was it a victory roll ? Then the pilot baled out and his white parachute fluttered and filled in the breeze. The Sea Hurricane was on fire, and though the pilot could have landed on the carrier, he was afraid of setting it on fire too. So he had come as close as he dared and then baled out. His plane flew steadily for a few seconds, then went into a dive and, gathering speed all the way down, crashed into the sea some hundreds of yards in front of the *Marsden*.

They watched the falling pilot and the two Sea Hurricanes, which began to circle, lower and lower, round the falling figure to protect him from attack.

The parachute fell fast and the man attached to it was clearly visible. He seemed to be sitting back comfortably, looking at the sea below him, the sea which bit off limbs and stopped hearts. One of the trawlers had turned out of line, but seemed to be moving in a most leisurely way towards the falling man. He hit the sea while the trawler was still some way off and for a few seconds his parachute bobbed about on the surface.

He was picked up safely. His electrical suit had cushioned the icy shock.

The loud-hailer again: " A circular torpedo has been dropped. It travels two hours in a circle unless it hits something first. So watch out."

Two minutes later there was a second warning. " Floating mines are being dropped ahead of the convoy. All of you, keep your eyes skinned and report anything suspicious." The loud-hailer had hardly shut off before it opened up a third time: " A new, heavy wave of torpedo bombers is coming at the convoy." Almost immediately the new wave arrived.

Guns opened up in the distance, then near at hand. Suddenly Calamity yelled: " Jesus Christ, they've hit the carrier," and everyone on Y gun jumped round to look, a sudden leap of fear setting their hearts bounding. But the carrier had not been hit. A bomb had missed her stern by what seemed yards and the shower of black water and smoke had sprayed her decks. But now the water was settling again and the carrier was weaving on. Next minute there was another high spout of water immediately abaft the cruiser and other spouts in a long straight line between the merchantmen in the convoy. The water from these spouts had not settled before Y gun was firing again with the rest of the guns. A line of torpedo bombers was coming in, just as they had done the previous day, and the convoy and her escort was giving this line everything they had got.

The line swept on unevenly, each plane swaying from side to side, then trying to steady itself before loosing its tin fish. Again the air above the ships was criss-crossed with red-hot streaks, as tracers, fired from all angles, tore across friendly decks towards the oncoming enemy. One tracer went through the for'ard funnel of the *Marsden*. Another lot came near to hitting Y gun's crew.

Williams had just fused a shell and was waiting for Low to put the next one on his tray when he saw the sea immediately in front of him burst upwards in little spouts, just as if heavy hailstones were hitting the surface. The spouts were within a few feet of the *Marsden's* side and were coming from a merchant ship in the convoy whose gunner seemed determined to fire and hit something, even if it was a friend. If he had raised his sights by a fraction, the gunner must have peppered anyone who happened to be on the *Marsden's* quarter deck.

Williams merely glanced at the spouts and turned again to fuse the next shell. He was astounded to feel so calm. Or was it that he was just so tired that his nerves could react no longer ? He turned the key, fused the shell, and saw it snatched by Calamity and rammed into the breech. A second later the gun fired. Two seconds later there was an almighty explosion.

The wave of torpedo-carrying bombers had swept down the line of ships, staggering and jibbing as they ran into the fire. One of the planes suddenly lurched, flames spurting out of it, and dived towards the sea, but it never got there. Instead, it crashed on to the deck of a tanker and its torpedo exploded with the impact. There was a flash, then a thick column of smoke rising straight in the air for hundreds of feet until it met a wind current which flattened the top.

One man, a Lascar, was picked up. He had seen the plane dive and had jumped overboard in the split second before the crash. No one else and nothing else could be found.

While the smoke was still hanging in the air, Barber shouted, " Thur's a torpedo còming behind us. It's coming straight for us. Thur, Bob, look thur. Just behind us."

Williams was wearing a great many clothes. He was tangled in his telephone wires. He could not be bothered to get off his seat and look round. A torpedo was coming straight for them, was it ? How odd! Then Barber gave another shout. " The bastard's passed in our wake," he yelled. Passed in our wake, has it ? How *very* odd, thought Williams. How very odd indeed. " I must be going nuts," he said to himself. " I ought to be frightened, but I just can't be bothered." He puffed at a cigarette, waiting for Calamity to snatch the shell from the tray.

But the shell stayed on the tray and Williams began to think of that piece of duff he had left hurriedly on the mess-room table. He felt very hungry.

He sat on, smoking, thinking of his duff and stamping his feet to keep warm. After a few minutes Wild Angus came round with two buckets filled with tea. They had been used for washing clothes and bodies. Men had been sick in them. But who cared ? They dug in gratefully. Ten minutes later the loud-speaker called " Port watch to tea." It was 1550 and in ten minutes the port watch would be on duty.

Williams took off his earphones, closed the ports in the gun-shield, and trotted to the mess deck. He went straight to the mess table and there saw an empty plate, but no duff. One of the men from the T.S. had come into the mess deck ten minutes earler and, seeing the duff, had swiped it, thinking, he said, that nobody wanted it.

" Nobody wanted it ? " said Williams in exasperation. " I've been looking forward to that all afternoon." The missing duff filled his mind, now it could not fill his stomach. It scarcely seemed to matter that they had all just come through a heavy air attack, that another ship had gone to pieces in a flash. The missing duff was all that he could grasp. It nattered at his mind for hours.

They had only been on watch for fifteen minutes after tea

when all hands were piped on deck to help in taking two casualties off a merchant ship. Williams left his defence station on B gun and went to the Iron Deck with Jock and Calamity. There, for the first time in four days, the three of them saw the Duchess. He looked very different. He was filthy, hands black, face unshaven, hair tousled and matted. But his eyes were bright and, though he looked tired, his face was lively.

" Why, Duchess, I do believe you're all for it! ' Picture of a really keen sailor, bronzed and fit, waiting for a chance to get a crack at the Hun.' "

Dowson grinned sheepishly. " I was flicking scared, but it was all right once we got the point-fives going. Shook 'em up a bit, that did."

" Point-fives! You might as well have chucked potatoes at 'em."

Calamity had stood by, not hearing more than one word in ten of the conversation. Now he broke in with " I say, Duchess, you're filthy, old man, just filthy. Letting the whole side down, you cad."

" I suppose you think you're Snowwhite."

It was quite true. They were all as dirty as the Duchess, dirt ingrained into their hands and soot in their hair and on their faces. They must have been getting steadily dirtier during the last few days, but, because they were always together, they had not noticed it. It was seeing the Duchess, a comparative stranger, very far from his usual self that made them conscious of their own dirt.

Just then the First Lieutenant came along the quarter deck. " Taylor, go forward and fetch a stretcher from the sick-bay."

Calamity could not hear a word. He just stood, taking no notice of the First Lieutenant until the Duchess nudged him. Then he looked aft just as the First Lieutenant bawled out the order a second time at the top of his voice. Still Calamity did not hear. But he could tell from the workings of Jimmie's face that he was expected to do something. He jumped, turned, and ran quickly for'ard without having the remotest idea of what he was supposed to do. Williams ran after him and, together, they brought the stretcher from the sick-bay.

When the *Marsden* had come alongside the merchant ship, she was greeted with grins, shouts, and rude signs from some twenty Lascars who had climbed on deck to watch. After two successive days of air attack in which they had been the main target, they could still grin.

The wounded men were swung across the narrow gap of sea in stretcher jackets and carried to the Skipper's cabin, where the Quack did what he could.

Both the men were soldiers—merchant ship's gunners—and had been hit by Oerlikon shells fired by another ship in the convoy when the torpedo planes were flying mast high down the lines. One man had been hit in both hands—so badly that the doctor had to take the hands off at the wrist. The second man had been shot in the stomach, and for him the doctor could do nothing except bandage him and give him dope. An operation was essential, and the only ships in the convoy that had an operating theatre were the cruiser and the aircraft carrier.

The *Marsden* went to the cruiser. It was evening and the sea was less calm than recently. On the Iron Deck, the crew looked at the black shape alongside and at the seaway rushing between. The cruiser was rolling slightly. If she lurched any more unsteadily she might well bump the *Marsden*, and it was clear who would come worst out of a bumping match.

The two wounded were brought on stretchers from the Skipper's cabin. They had been well doped—mercifully, because the ladder from the Skipper's cabin was narrow and steep and the men who hauled and pushed the stretcher were unskilled. Moreover, despite the evening air, the men's feet were stockingless and only partially covered by blankets.

Both looked lifeless. Their faces had no colour and their bodies no strength. The man who had lost his hands kept whispering urgently, " My wallet. My black wallet. In the cabin." Williams went to the cabin, asked the doctor for the wallet, and pushed it gently beneath the blankets of the handless man. The other man was begging for water, but, since his stomach was in ribbons, the doctor said that he must not drink; but Calamity fetched a glass of water and a clean handkerchief, wet the handkerchief and kept rubbing it over the man's lips until it was time to swing him over to the cruiser.

The cruiser lowered a rectangular tray on a crane. The first man was placed in his stretcher on the tray, then the crane lifted the tray from the deck and swung it gently over the seaway to the deck of the cruiser. The second man was taken across in the same way and the two ships parted. Within ten minutes a surgeon had begun to operate, while the ship lurched and heaved and the convoy steamed on towards Russia.

The sight of these two wounded men, with the colour drained from their faces and blood oozing through their bandages, oppressed everyone. Neither man had been more then nineteen, yet one of them, almost for certain, was coming to the end of his life already, far from home, in cold wastes of sea.

When the First Dog watch was over, Port watch crawled to the mess deck feeling worn out, and the mess deck made them feel worse. They noticed, now, that it was covered in soot and dirt, either carried in by the blast of the guns or else shaken from the deckhead by concussion. Several of the electric-light bulbs had been smashed and the pieces were lying on the deck. The remaining bulbs gave no more than quarter light, dirty and forbidding.

Williams sat on a bench and looked blankly in front of him, reminding himself that they still had another two days, at least, of air attack to look forward to on the outward trip, not counting anything that submarines might do and without thinking of the trip back. As he sat, trying to fight off his gloom, Jack Price flopped beside him.

" What's the matter, Bob ? "

" I'm tired, Jack. I'd like to sleep for a week."

" Chroist, sleep for a week? Oi could sleep for a bleeding year."

Above their heads the Skipper was just completing his forty-eighth sleepless hour on the bridge.

Action : Third Day

No one in port watch had more then three hours' sleep that night. They had the First Watch from eight until midnight and were on again for the Morning from four until eight. They came in for breakfast, cold, tired, and hungry, to find that the bread had run out again and that there were only two cups left in the mess. Most of them drank from an empty fruit tin, and, with that as breakfast, mustered on the Iron Deck at 0900.

There was some real work to be done, this time. The decks were covered in snow, which had to be swept overboard, and then there was the debris from the previous days—glass from the fog lamp, empty cartridge cases from the point-fives, soot, and strips of paint which had peeled or chipped off various parts of the ship. It took them till dinner-time to make the mess deck and the upper deck reasonably tidy.

Dinner had been brought forward half an hour, which meant that the port watch, which would be on duty during the Afternoon, began to eat at 1130 and relieved the starboard watch at noon instead of at 1230. This was to fit the Luftwaffe's time-table. On each of the two previous days, one or other of the two watches had its dinner interrupted by the arrival of the Luftwaffe at 1245 and then had had to go back on watch, after the attack, without having time to make a proper tea. Since, as George Barber had said, you could rely on Jerry's form, the timetable was altered.

" Shifting the watches about ? " said Jock. " Nelson would turn in his grave."

To-day everyone had had his dinner, and the dirty dishes were cleaned and cleared away by 1230. At 1255, ten minutes late, " action stations " sounded. A large formation of enemy planes was approaching the convoy.

There was no snow falling and the snow-clouds themselves

were less dense. Overhead, there were a few patches of green sky and where, presumably, the sun was, was bright yellow.

It was a good day for high-level bombing. The bombers could shelter in the clouds, come out to drop their bombs quickly before the anti-aircraft guns could get their range, and nip back to safety, but for the first time many of the merchant ships put up balloons, which hung below the clouds and might give a nasty shock to any airman who did his nipping in and out in the wrong place. The balloons were smaller than those used on land and, of course, they moved. They looked comic and childish. For some minutes, nothing much happened. The Skipper called the ship's company on the loud-hailer, warned them that the " large formation " was now only ten miles distant, and told them to keep an especially good watch on the green patches of the sky. " The planes will probably dive through one of those. In the meantime, I've got the summary of the one o'clock news for you. You might like to hear it." And while the whole convoy waited for certain attack, the Skipper began to read news about the fighting in Russia and Egypt.

He had been reading for about a minute when he suddenly stopped. " There they are now! Here, Yeoman, you finish this," and while the Yeoman of Signals read the remainder of the bulletin, the Skipper made his preparations to meet the attack.

There was a burst of firing, a whole series of spouts as bombs crashed into the sea, and then a lull—for the guns' crews. Most of the planes were keeping out of sight. You could hear their engines above the clouds, but it was only once in a while that the gunners had a chance to get their sights on a target and then, as often as not, they could not fire because Sea Hurricanes were in the air and after the same target. After a few minutes' lull there was a burst of fire from the ships away on the starboard side, then silence, broken when Harry Rhoades suddenly shouted, " Look, lads, there's a couple of Sea Hurricanes after a Jerry. By Christ, they're shifting! And so's he."

The gun's crew, with no firing to be done, jumped out of the shield and rushed to the side to watch the chase while Williams, like a goat on a chain, got as far as his telephone wire would let him. The Sea Hurricanes were streaking after a Ju.88 which at the moment was crossing over the convoy and trying to make enough height to win the safety of the clouds.

" Bet they get 'im before 'e's out of sight," shouted George Barber, dancing about like an elephant.

" Go on, you bastards, fly, can't you ? Bring the bastard down," shouted Jock.

They all forgot themselves, their gun, and their ship in the excitement of watching the chase. They were disgusted when the planes went out of sight before the kill.

Thereafter there was a long lull. The Skipper said on the loud-hailer: " By the way, you'll be glad to hear that one of those two gunners we took off yesterday is out of danger, but I'm afraid the other is very ill." Later he reported that two German submarines had surfaced some five miles ahead of the convoy to pick up survivors of a crashed bomber. Two destroyers had been detached from the convoy to race ahead and investigate, but the rest of them stayed where they were.

They had nothing to do. In the T.S., Professor Cole and his mates began to learn shorthand to pass the time. The Professor had bought Pitman's shorthand book. He knew nothing about it, but was ready to teach it to the others. The guns' crews talked, and listened to the planes which were still clearly audible.

" What the hell do these boys think they're doing ? " asked Jock as he looked at the sky and saw nothing.

Two minutes later bombs were falling all over the place. Some fell two miles ahead of the convoy, some seemed to drop right on the horizon to starboard. A few brought up high spouts of water in the convoy itself. But not one hit a ship and not one scored even a near miss.

Then there was silence for a little, without even the droning overhead. But after twenty minutes it began again. Another formation had arrived and was going through the same routine as its predecessor. It showed itself beneath the clouds on the starboard side of the convoy, received a terrific burst of flak and turned back into cloud cover. There it stayed, zooming about and waiting for a break through which to drop its bombs. But the breaks in the clouds were getting fewer.

Once something *did* drop through the clouds. It was a parachute, without anything attached to it.

" Well, Ah wonder now," said Jock. " Is that a secret weapon, or is it sheer forgetfulness ? "

But for a long time that was all that came down.

At last the Skipper spoke. " The planes are still overhead. They're waiting for a chance to bomb. But they've a long journey home. They'll have to go off soon to get their tea."

Ten minutes later they *did* go off, dropping their bombs indiscriminately in the sea as they went, with Hurricanes after them as hard as they could go.

It was not until the starboard watch was piped to tea at 1550, however, that they realised that no gun on the *Marsden* had fired a single round during the action. They felt more tired than ever. It seemed that doing nothing in action was more of a strain than firing the whole afternoon.

Port watch had the Middle. That is, after three hours' sleep they had to get up at midnight and keep watch until four. The cold was more stinging than ever. The crowded state of the gunshield made sleep of any sort impossible and did not even give warmth. After an hour, Williams could stand it no longer. He asked Jock for permission to make ki for the gun's crew.

The galley was beautifully warm, but, even so, Williams was surprised to find Harrison standing there by himself. He presumed he was off watch and could have been in his hammock. He was obviously very tired. Yet there he was, standing motionless and vacant, looking at the galley fire.

" Hallo. What's up ? Can't you sleep ? "

" No, I'm too tired."

" Well, why not get your head down in your hammock ? It'll rest you a bit."

" Bob, I've lost my nerve. The moment I get in my hammock I begin thinking about subs. and mines and how we'd be trapped if anything hit us. I want to keep near the open air."

" You poor sod! Look, why don't you put a duffel on the deck and lie down here ? You'll be near the open air and you'll be warm. Here, have a cup of ki and lie down."

It was only later that he remembered Harrison was in port watch and should have been on the point-fives.

By two o'clock it was getting light and Y gun's crew switched their station from B gun to the three-inch. A quarter of an hour later, pounding feet along the deck showed that " action stations " had sounded. The *Marsden* quickly heeled over in a sharp turn and her engines speeded up.

" What the hell's the matter now ? " asked Calamity when he saw the rest of the gun's crew jump to their feet.

It was a sub., well and truly pinged by Leading Seaman Jeffries.

Jeffries was getting a strong echo when he warned the bridge, but it became obvious almost at once that the sub. knew she was being chased and was taking evasive action. She twisted and turned well beneath the surface, but Jeffries could follow her movements through his instruments. As the sub. turned, the *Marsden* turned, manoeuvring to get herself into the right postition for dropping her charges. At last, the Skipper dropped the charges, four of them, one after another.

When the last charge had gone, the Skipper hove-to. He felt certain that he had got a sub. at last and was determined to get evidence. The Admiralty were sceptical unless you had evidence.

After the last charge Jeffries had got no further ping. That might mean that the sub. had escaped. It might mean that she had been blown to pieces. The *Marsden* looked for the pieces. Scrambling-nets were put over the side and several men climbed down almost to the level of the sea. The rest of the crew on watch lined guard-rails and stared. There was a large patch of oil, which bubbled from below and spread slowly over the surface. That might not mean much. U-boat commanders had been known to force oil to the surface just to fool their attackers. But there were other things on the surface, and the Skipper, leaning over the side of the bridge, shouted directions to the men on the scrambling-nets.

" Get that bit of wood. And that one. Reach for it. Reach for it. That's right. Now bring it up here. Look out, there's another piece. Bring that up. And what's that thing there ? A glove ? Is there a hand in it ? Pity! The Admiralty would have liked a hand. Still, bring it out. What's that piece of paper ? Fish 'em all out and let's have a look at 'em."

The catch was carried to the bridge. The pieces of wood, said the experts, were part of the inside lining of a sub.'s conning tower. The glove had a German tag in the lining. The piece of paper turned out to be a small paper packet with German written on it.

The crew were glad when the engines started again. It seemed certain that they had got the sub. this time. But if, by any chance, they had missed her and she was still lurking below, the *Marsden* would make a sitting target. The cold, green water looked less inviting than ever.

As they began to pass the first ships of the convoy, the Jimmie held up pieces of wreckage and shouted the news to the merchantmen.

They grinned and cheered and waved their hands.

Breakfast that morning was worse than ever. There was, again, no bread and several new epithets for the P.O. cook were thought up and used freely. Starboard watch were working part of ship during the Forenoon, but by ten o'clock every one of them had sidled into the mess deck and climbed into his hammock. They were woken at 1130 by the pipe of afternoon watchmen to dinner. Most of them ate their dinner with their fingers because there were only five knives and two forks.

All of them—port and starboard watch alike—were in a dreadful state. They were not allowed to undress, so that a real wash was impossible. They could wash their hands and faces, but these were soon dirty again, and anyhow, when they came off watch they were usually too tired to bother about anything except food, a warm drink, and sleep. Invariably as zero hour approached, a sense of foreboding pervaded the whole ship, adding to the strain of the dirtiness and exhaustion. They all longed to climb into their hammocks and sleep for a week, then get up and loll in hot baths; but the mere thought of such impossibilities was enough to drive them crazy.

While all of them were worn out, some were much worse than

198

others. Harrison was becoming lifeless. When you spoke to him he seemed to have barely strength enough to reply. His face was set in heavy blankness. Duchess Dowson had said that Harrison was all right in action. But as soon as the action was over and his imagination began working again, he relapsed into gloom and from gloom into washed-out apathy.

Nevison seemed to be going the same way. He looked really shaken. His round face had become flabby, there were black rings around his eyes, he scarcely said a word, he jumped and quivered whenever the guns fired. Raikes kept an eye on him and tried to banter him into some of his old liveliness. But it was not much use.

Meanwhile the port watch was eating dinner with one ear listening for the ominous ringing which would send them scurrying into the cold air outside. The starboard watch were on their guns, in magazines, in shell-rooms, or sitting on cabinets of flats, waiting for the same sound. Redfern on the three-inch platform tried to read, but as the minutes crept on it became harder and harder to concentrate. He was always cocking an ear to catch the sound of heavy boots or hear any change in the rhythm of the engines.

But the first warning of the coming action came from the carrier. " Hurricanes are taking off. Looks like zero hour." said Raikes, looking over the edge of the gun platform, and two minutes later clumping feet showed that " action station " had sounded.

Williams had half hoped that there would be no attack that afternoon. They were known, now, to be out of range of torpedo-carrying aircraft and the weather looked too bad for bombers. Snow was not falling at the moment, but it had never been far away during the past three days and heavy clouds hung over the convoy now.

Still, there he was again, sitting on his stool with a shell in front of him and talking down the phones to Professor Cole, who wanted to know what was happening. " Damn-all at the moment, Professor, but it won't be long now."

He was right. Almost as he spoke, a stick of bombs came out of the clouds and fell in the sea before a single gun from the convoy had opened fire. Immediately the guns put up a barrage, more to keep the planes in the clouds than with much hope of hitting anything. Y gun had sent out seven rounds of long barrage and the other guns had just reached double figures when, from the clouds, a bomber suddenly came diving down.

The lookout spotted it. " Bomber diving, Red three-five, angle of sight two-five." But the bomber was not diving deliberately. It was crashing into the sea. One of the guns had had a lucky hit. The plane fell in front of the *Marsden* and the for'ard guns' crews stopped firing to watch it drop. The Skipper called to them: " Any of you claim that ? "

" Yes, sir, we do," shouted A gun's crew.

" Yes, sir, we do," shouted B gun's crew.

" That's ours," shouted the Oerlikons.

" We got that one," said Pat Maclure, putting his black face out of the rangefinder.

" Well, go and pick it up. Don't leave your litter all over the place."

Ten minutes later another plane came down. No one on the *Marsden* saw it fall. All they *did* see was some object floating towards them which Newton on A gun first took to be a sub. Without waiting for orders, he had his gun trained on it and was ready to fire when a Hurricane, diving low, swooped over it. In the nick of time Newton pressed his safety latch over and saved the Hurricane from a shower of high explosive.

That was all the excitement. Again a few bombs dropped near the horizon, but again no ship in the convoy was hit. Just after 1500 the Skipper called: " Well, it looks as though the boys have gone home for an early tea. Port watch to defence stations," and, with immense relief, the starboard watch went back to the mess deck for a quick sleep while the port watch passed the remainder of the Afternoon on the upper deck.

And that was all the air attack they had for the remainder of the voyage.

* * *

They were due to return with the home-bound convoy. The thought of turning back into the danger area and running through another four days like the last four was enough to keep their spirits down. Yet the thought of going home made their weariness more bearable. When zero hour in the afternoon came and went without the ominous ringing of the alarm bells, the tension which all of them had felt during the past week began to diminish, and then, without warning, the loud-hailer called: " First part of port watch to cruising stations, remainder secure and fall out."

At first they could not believe it. Then came overwhelming relief. For the moment they were safe. The *Marsden* would never go into four watches and cruising stations if there was the slightest danger, but now, at two o'clock in the afternoon, they could climb into their hammocks. It did not matter that it was snowing hard. Let it snow. It did not matter that the wind was blowing and the ship beginning to pitch and roll. Let it blow. Let it pitch and roll. The next three hours would be hours of deep sleep, even for the Skipper, who had now left the bridge for the first time in ninety-four hours.

When, at six, the second part of port came up for the Last Dog, they found that the *Marsden*, other destroyers and two submarines had broken away to join the home-bound convoy.

The one great difference this made to life on the *Marsden* was the speeding of the engines. The ship had been compelled to crawl at anything from twelve to nine knots for more than a week. Without vibration and without much movement, life in the ship had seemed to be dying slowly. But now things were stirring. They were making a steady eighteen knots with the two submarines speeding behind them on the surface like two silent dogs. Every man on the ship, even Harrison and Nevison, felt themselves quicken to the speed of the engines.

They went back into two watches at nightfall. But they had all had a little extra rest; and though the cold was more chilling than ever, the guns' crews began to sing once more, which was something they had not done for days.

Early next morning they found the new convoy and began the first day's journey home. The new convoy was much smaller than the old, but it was faster, and though the *Marsden* had to cut her speed when she reached it, she *did* seem to be moving faster than on the outward journey.

But the return journey started badly. Towards three o'clock there was an explosion at the rear of the convoy and near-by destroyers turned to circle a ship which had been hit by a torpedo. Three of the destroyers dropped depth charges. A fourth went alongside to take survivors.

Port watch, doing a Middle, could see everything in the Arctic daylight. Within a few minutes the stern of the torpedoed ship settled into the water, but her stem remained visible for more than half an hour. It was still showing when the starboard watch came on deck for the Morning.

" Was that another merchant packet they got ? "

" No; it was one of the escort. Just finished four months in Archangel. Coming home for leave."

" Poor little basstud! " said Price. " Jerry couldn't pick on a big 'un, could 'e ? 'Ad to pick on a carrot size, and then you bet 'e wirelesses 'ome that 'e's got a cruiser. Poor little basstud! "

Late that evening the *Marsden* and another destroyer were to leave the convoy temporarily and make for the South Cape, there to pick up a tanker which had been supplying oil to the convoy on the outward journey. This was good news. It would take the *Marsden* from the danger zone for at least twenty-four hours and allow her to move fast. Even if they were moving fast out of their way and would get home no sooner, it was something to feel the ship moving.

The *Marsden* was beginning to move rather too much. A stern sea had sprung up, washing waves over the quarter deck and rapidly turning the mess deck into shambles. Kettles and fannies clashed together as they swung from the deckhead,

201

anything left on the mess tables or insecure on the mess deck itself was swished from one side to the other.

" This life's only fit for animals," said Calamity.

" Not it," said Price. " Even the cat's chokka."

They peeled off from the convoy at 1630 that afternoon, taking another destroyer with them. As soon as he saw this second ship Williams said to Pat, " Why, bless me, if that isn't the *Marsden*. Whatever bloody ship are *we* on ? "

" That's our sister-ship, man. The *Meltham*. Both made by the same firm and spend most of their time in the same dock. They're identical. I bet the *Meltham* has got a leaky steam-pipe in *her* mess deck."

The *Marsden* led most of the night, but when the port watch came to defence stations at four the next morning the ships had changed positions. The *Meltham* was 300 yards in front with the *Marsden* in her wake; and, yes, by God, land on two sides of them, clearly visible. They were steaming up a long fjord into a red morning sky. The water in front of them was churned white and creamy, with occasional glints of blue, as the *Meltham* tore through it. The rocks, rising steeply on either side, were sharp, steep, and black.

As the morning light strengthened, the rocks lost some of their blackness but none of their menace. They were almost entirely covered with steely ice, with brown tufts of brittle, life-less grass showing through. Grass and ice looked forbidding, dirty, and cold; yet the seamen crew stared at them as though they had been the Old Kent Road or the Yorkshire moors. In spite of the bitter cold, they felt warmed and rested by the sight of land and the sudden freedom from fear that land brought.

They found the oiler at the far end of the fjord and tied up to her for a refill. " Well, boys, we're as far North as we can go without being explorers," said Jimmie.

Almost before the hawsers were made fast, Pat had climbed on to the oiler and gone foraging, while the rest of the crew gave the mess a quick clean and had breakfast. Then there was a rush for the washroom. Men who had not taken their clothes off for eleven days seized buckets or bowls and crammed them-selves into the tiny washroom to scrape and soak the first layers of dirt.

Williams could not get near, so went on deck. He was startled by the stillness. Apart from that search for the remains of the U-boat, the ship had not been motionless since they left Iceland. He had become so used to vibration that he missed it when it was not there. Then he heard a dog bark.

It really *was* a dog . . . with a little red coat on, barking at the ship's cat, which was making her first appearance on the upper deck since the *Marsden* had left Iceland. The dog had come from the oiler and was pleased to have a new walk which actually included cats.

At ten they mustered amidships and were told they would be sailing again late that afternoon. They spent nearly an hour clearing the snow and ice from the decks and chipping ice from the shells in the ready-use racks on deck. Then Williams went back into the mess deck which now was lit, not by a few dingy electric bulbs, but by daylight flooding through the open ports. He stripped off all his clothes, borrowed a bucket, filled it at the galley, and wedged his way into the still crowded and steam-filled washroom.

A quarter of an hour later he was pulling clean thick under-wear over his now shining body. In another five minutes he was standing in Paradise.

In his right hand he held two oranges, foraged by Pat from the oiler. In his breast pocket were two bars of chocolate, also from the oiler. In his left hand was his tot. He stood in front of the electric stove in One Mess, looked first at his right hand then at his left, thought of the chocolate in his pocket, the three clear hours that afternoon for sleeping, and that they were going home. Whatever happens after this, he thought, I wouldn't change places this moment with anyone in the world.

Everyone was talking at once and talking of home. " What day of the week is it ? Saturday ? I'd be going off to a football match any time now."

" Bet we'll get some leave for this when we get back."

" I'll bet there'll be some mail for us when we get back. Let's see, my Judy writes once every three days. I haven't heard from her for, what is it ? Three weeks now and there's about another week to go. That will make it nine letters at least from her alone."

They ate a big dinner, mostly with their fingers, and slept until 1530.

Then they sailed—the *Marsden* leading, then the tanker, and the *Meltham* last in line. Snow fell as they sailed down the fjord, and the wind blew it into little drifts or froze it to the decks. Once more the guns' crews huddled in their shields, trying to keep the circulation going. Once more they came down from watch into a mess which was gloomy and dingy.

Williams finished the Middle with his fingers so numb that he could not hold a cup of ki; and the ki was so hot that it scalded his half-frozen lips when he tried to sip it. He thawed himself in front of the stove, drank his ki at last, and climbed into his hammock. Late that afternoon they would rejoin the convoy, and in about a week at the latest they should be home. Would they get leave ? They wouldn't need another boiler-clean just yet and you didn't get leave just for helping to do a good job. Still, there was a chance, a chance of getting back to a house that did not rock, a house in which you could stretch, a house in which there was a bath. O God, for a real bath!

He fell asleep.

He dreamed that he was sitting in a boiling hot bath at home and that his small nephews were scrubbing his back with a wire scraper. "Don't drop that over the side, James, or I'll take you aft with your cap off."

"I haven't got a fiicking cap to go aft with off."

"Don't scrape the paint off my back with the scrubber, Gerald, or you'll paint it on again in the Dogs."

"Don't be so silly. We haven't a dog."

The telephone downstairs began to ring.

"James, go and answer that phone. I can't get out of this bath."

"Like flick, I will. Carrot fashion. Answer it yourself."

"Gerald, you go."

"No."

"Well, tell your Judy to go."

"No, answer it yourself."

And Williams, sitting upright in his hammock, heard "action stations" sounding on the alarm.

Chapter Twelve

THE bells jerked thirty-eight weary seamen of port watch from their sleep. It was 6.15 a.m.

Five seconds later, thirty-seven of the thirty-eight had jerked themselves from their hammocks and begun to stuff their feet into the first sea-boots they could find. In another fifteen seconds they were merging into one wordless, jostling, hard-breathing throng which pushed and plunged along the narrow, ill-lit flats to daylight and the Iron Deck.

Within sixty seconds, action stations were manned; sixty seconds more and most of the *Marsden's* guns were ready to fire. Only then had the crews time to look round, to notice the beating of their hearts and to ask each other, "What the hell is happening *now*?"

Williams had realised almost at once that this alarm was different from anything he had heard in the past ten days.

Usually the alarm bells electrified his body without touching his brain, so that he would find himself delivered at his own gun by a series of automatic movements which he neither initiated nor controlled. But this time, while he was still forcing his sea-boot-stockinged feet into his sea-boots, his brain had begun to work. That bell was sounding an unusual note. For the first time it was sounding staccato shorts.

That meant surface action; but what surface action meant, God alone knew.

So, as he joined the jostling throng, he was more conscious than usual—conscious of tripping over a box of onions in the gangway, conscious, when he inadvertently straightened his back, that he had cracked his head against a hammock and that the hammock was hard because there was a body still in it.

He shook the hammock and shouted, " Action stations," and the face of Harrison peered over the top, a sleepless face, white and strained.

" Action stations be flicked," said Harrison and relapsed into his hammock.

Williams left it at that and raced along the quarter deck to Y gun. The other six members of Y gun's crew were already there, each going quickly through his familiar routine to clear the gun for action.

Jock Forrest, with that flaming red oilskin of his unbuttoned and flapping in the wind, was shouting " S.A.P., man," to Jackie Low, who from force of habit had brought an anti-aircraft shell from the ready-use racks.

" S.A.P. I've heard that often enough in drills. And now we're really going to use it. Hell! "

Back went Low. He kicked and pulled at a pointed S.A.P. shell in the racks to free it from ice, and then, cradling its 57 pounds' weight like a baby in his arms, he ran back to the gun. The baby was roughly seized by Calamity, who banged it on the tray. " Where's that bastard charge ? "

The charge was still in the deck locker, the door of which appeared to be frozen stiff. Anyway, Harry Rhoades could not open it and came running to Jock empty-handed, with his face nearly as red as his hair. Jock and the impatient Calamity went to the locker at the rush and, with the help of some foul language from Calamity, a stream of advice and directions from Harry, and a couple of swift kicks on the handle by Jock, the door swung on its hinges.

Calamity snatched one of the polished brass cylinders, tore back to the gun with it, and dumped it on the tray. Jock pulled out two more, handing one to Harry and carrying the other himself, and laid them by the gun within easy reach.

Williams, meanwhile, was trying to get into the gunshield; but George Barber was crouched in front adjusting his training receiver and Williams had to wait outside. But he grabbed his earphones from their hook, put them on his head, and made contact with the T.S. with the formula he had used hundreds of times before.

"Y gun, T.S."

Back came the voice of Professor Cole: "T.S., Y gun."

"Y gun well."

"Tell 'em we're closed up, cleared away," shouted Jock, loud enough to carry through the rattle of the gunshield and pierce the layers of clothing round Williams ears.

"Y gun closed up, cleared away, bore clear."

He was still outside the shield, and while Charlie Wright swung the gun round, first to one side and then to the other to make sure that it was not frozen, Williams had to walk round with it, talking down his mouthpiece, to avoid being pushed over the breech.

"Like one of those B.B.C. running commentators," he said to himself. Then aloud to Barber: "Hurry up, George; I want to get in."

"'Ang on a minute. Ah can't get this bloody receiver fixed wi' these bloody gloves on.",

George pulled off his anti-flash gloves, and a few seconds later he had moved back to his seat and allowed Williams to squeeze past him to the front of the shield. Williams immedaately moved the pointer on his own range dial to 1,000 yards while orders streamed through his earphones. "All positions, line up. . . . Positions for check receivers . . . check receivers." The vibration in the gunshield was now so great that Williams could barely hear what Cole said. But he knew the orders by heart from long practice and only needed to catch one word to know what the rest were.

"Have they said anything about loading yet ? " shouted Jock. "Tell 'em we've got S.A.P. and a full charge on the tray."

Before Williams could say a word the order came from the T.S.: "All guns with S.A.P. and full charge load, load, load, LOAD."

"All guns with S.A.P. and full charge, load load, LOAD."

Jock swung open the breech, Calamity swung his laden tray on its hinges into position and, putting his gloved right hand at the base of the charge, rammed both charge and shell along the tray into the breech, pulling his hand back sharply as the breech closed automatically behind the charge. Then he pulled back the tray to its original position, Jackie Low banged down a fresh shell and Rhoades a fresh charge.

"Tell 'em we're loaded."

"Y gun loaded with S.A.P. and full charge."

Then they all waited.

* * *

The after supply party had organised itself into chains. One of these stretched from the magazine under the wardroom, up the hatchway to the wardroom flat, and there split in two, one part sending charges to Y gun and the other pushing them up through another hatch to X gun. The second chain began at the shell-room beneath the officers' cabins, split in two when it reached the top of the hatchway in the wardroom flat, and supplied X and Y guns with shells.

At this moment the lights in the shell-room were shining brilliantly, reflecting themselves in the polished wood of the shell-racks and the deck. They also shone on two figures.

Sinbad was already scurrying like an excited but friendly rat to the farthest rack, there to get the first batch of S.A.P. shells for which the guns were calling. He came back with a shell in his arms, handed it to his companion, and panted: " There you are, Shortarse. Push that up."

Shortarse bent his knees. By this manoeuvre he was able to bring his head from the officers' cabin flat into the shell-room below. Then, lowering his hands slightly to the level of Sinbad's chest, he took the shell and swung it in one motion into the hands of the first member of the supply chain above, while Sinbad scurried back for a refill.

" Don't bring too many, Sinbad. We'll only have to put them all back."

When, between them, they had sent up a dozen shells and gathered another dozen within easy reach, Shortarse brought his head through the hatchway and stretched his six feet four and a half inches of body along the shell-room deck. Sinbad called " What's happening ? " to the supply chain, and getting the answer that no one knew yet, he said, " I hope to Christ it's not the *Scharnhörst*. Hey, Shortarse, do you think it's the *Tirpitz* ? "

" Yes, Sinbad, I know it's the *Tirpitz*. And the *Scharnhörst*. One of the stokers told me." Shortarse closed his eyes.

So Sinbad flopped on the deck, pulled out a copy of *No Orchids for Miss Blandish*, and began to read.

" Coo!" he said a moment later, " this tart didn't 'arf learn a thing or two before they'd finished with 'er."

* * *

Just as Sinbad opened Miss Blandish, Jimmie leaned over the side of the three-inch gun platform, put his glasses to his eyes, and stared.

Two minutes before he had been on the bridge, in charge of the ship, when one of the lookouts had reported what he thought was smoke on the horizon on the starboard beam. Jimmie had swung his glasses immediately. Yes, it did look like smoke. But it might just as easily be cloud. These damned snow-clouds were hanging about everywhere. You couldn't tell which was cloud and which was sea, sometimes. But that didn't look like either. It looked like smoke. What the hell could it be ?

He had been expecting to see smoke that day—but not to starboard and not for a good ten hours yet. The *Marsden* and the *Meltham* were steaming a course and speed which should bring them back astern of the convoy late that afternoon. Had the convoy reduced speed ? Had there been another attack ? Had some ships become separated from the main body ? If so, what the hell were they doing to starboard ? They ought to be right ahead.

He jumped across the bridge, pressed the plunger which set the alarm bells ringing, and shouted to a signalman, " Tell *Meltham* that there's something like smoke on the horizon, Green four-five, range about fifteen miles."

As the bells began to ring, he seized a voice-pipe to the Captain's sea-going cabin immediately below the bridge. " First Lieutenant, sir. There's smoke on the horizon, Green four-five. I've sounded action stations."

" Very good. I'll be up."

Fifteen seconds later he was. The Jimmie handed over the ship to him, slid down ladders, cannoned into several seamen who were straggling to their action stations, and finally reached the three-inch platform.

The platform was still disorderly. During daylight, one complete crew was always on watch at this gun. When " action stations " sounded, X gun's crew was on watch there, and instead of rushing immediately to their own gun, they had to wait until the regular three-inch crew relieved them.

Jimmie arrived to find the change-over still proceeding. Some of X gun's crew were pushing their way down the ladder from the platform, some of the regular three-inch crew were still trying to push their way up. Jimmie brushed two of these aside, took the short ladder in one stride, and cannoned into the X gun sightsetter, who, with ear-phones still attached to his head, was standing at the top of the ladder looking for his relief.

The impact carried the sightsetter across the platform and sat him down on the locker at the far end. Jimmie stopped his own headlong rush, saw the sightsetter on the lockers, and shouted, " What the hell are you lolling about down there for ? Don't you know that action stations have gone ? Get off to your gun."

He then cannoned into Wild Angus, the captain of the gun, who was about to ram a projectile into the breech. " What fuse have you got on that ? "

" O-four-two, sir."

" Well, get an O-eight-o. You're bloody stupid."

" And you're flicking solid."

" Are you swearing at me ? I'll get you ninety days for that."

" Oh no, you won't ! We're in action and I'm allowed to swear at the flicking admiral now."

" Load the gun," said Jimmie, stepping to the starboard side of the platform and putting up his glasses.

A moment later he turned back to Wild Angus and said in the friendliest of tones, " Hey, Angus. Come and look through these glasses. What do you make of that ? "

" Well, sir," said Angus with equal friendliness, " it looks a bit like smoke. Or is it just cloud ? "

*　　　*　　　*

It was not cloud. It *was* smoke. And the first man to see it for certain was not the First Lieutenant, not even the Skipper or the lookouts on the bridge, but the Duchess, who, coming from Oldham, could recognise smoke when he saw it. He had been on watch since 0400 when he had relieved Harrison on the point-five gun platform. He had spent the time either huddled in the little canvas shelter on the platform or walking moodily up and down to keep himself warm. His gun was set to fire and had been kept so for days and nights in the freezing cold with the help of a crowbar, lifted from the engine-room, and a blow-lamp he had brought from home.

When " action stations " sounded, he went to his gun and looked it over thoroughly, wondering where Harrison, who in acton was his communication number with the bridge, had got to.

Harrison was still in his hammock, staring at the deckhead.

The Duchess came from behind his gun and looked over the side of the platform at the cold, grey sea. " I'd rather have the Med.," he said to himself. " Come to that, I'd rather have the Manchester Ship Canal," and suddenly a longing for home came on him so strongly that he could almost hear the clatter of cotton-spinning mules and smell the smoke of the mills. The smoke . . . the smoke . . . " Why, flick me, there *is* some smoke. And not from any ruddy mill chimney either. Harrison, tell the bridge there's smoke, Green four-five. HARRISON. Oh, hell! "

Dowson saw the phones lying on the locker, took one step towards them, changed his mind, turned round, and bawled up to the flag deck. There, Ginger Howard was just beginning to strap himself to his Oerlikon gun. He disentangled himself and put his head over the side of the deck.

" Ginger, tell the bridge there's smoke on the starboard side. Green four-five," bawled Dowson, but, as he did so, one of the starboard lookouts himself called, " Bearing Green four-five, the object on the horizon is definitely smoke, sir."

The Skipper stopped speaking down the engine-room voice-pipe, swung his glasses to Green four-five, said " Very good " in a casual voice to the lookout, told the Yeoman of Signals to warn the *Meltham*, and went back to the engine-room phone.

"Look here, Chief. It *is* smoke. I don't know whose. But with this tanker on our hands, we don't want to be spotted if we can help it, so, for God's sake, don't let *us* make any smoke. And you'd better be ready for some speed. Get Number One boiler flashed up. What can we do on the two ? H'm."

He left the voice-pipe and called to the director tower behind him. "You've seen that smoke, Burton ? "

Lieutenant Burton *had* seen the smoke. He had been woken in his bunk by the alarm bell and had walked deliberately and purposefully to the bridge and thence to the director tower just as, in peacetime, he had set off to collect the rent from some recalcitrant tenant on the housing estate he managed. He had squeezed himself into the narrow tower alongside the Buffer and Rattler Morgan and had phoned the T.S. to order S.A.P. on the guns.

He was about to warn Pat Maclure in the rangefinder above his head to get his sights on Green four-five when he heard Dowson's shout. He dropped the voice-pipe to the rangefinder and turned again to the T.S.

"Smoke on the horizon, bearing Green four-five." He paused a moment to look round at the Buffer and Rattler Morgan. When he saw that both men had their eyes to their telescopes and were turning their handles to lay and train their sights, he turned back to the T.S. mouthpiece. "All guns follow director."

* * *

It was now 6.20 a.m.

Back on Y gun, Williams received the order from the T.S. to follow director. He formally repeated it to Barber and Charlie Wright, though he knew that both were already obeying it. Charlie Wright had had his eye on his receiver almost from the moment he reached the gunshield. Barber had had to set his to zero and come out of the shield to let Williams in. He had then picked up a cork lifebelt from the deck of the shield, put it on, and sat down on his seat. But from then on, his eyes, too, had been continually on his receiver.

As soon as the pointers moved, both Barber and Charlie swung their handles to keep the gun in line with the director. So did layers and trainers on X and B guns.

But the trainer and layer of A gun did not. The first member of A gun's crew to reach the fo'c'sle at a lumbering trot was Newton, captain of the gun. He took two steps along the deck and sat down on his bottom with a thud which shook the ship as much as it shook him. He levered himself up with the help of a deck locker and gingerly walked the rest of the way, for the deck was covered with two inches of snow and under the snow was a layer of ice.

Newton's first job on reaching the gun was to untie and remove the breech-bag which protected the breech from the weather. But the breech-bag ropes were frozen stiff. He cut them away with his knife after nearly a minute's hacking. The breech-bag itself was like wood. Newton and Jack Price, his rammer, pushed and tugged at the bag for a quarter of a minute without moving it. Suddenly the bag came off with a rush and Price, who was tugging at the end, sat down on the deck with the bag on top of him.

Nothing about him moved except his mouth. " That basstud bag. That flicking basstud bag. Oi've never seen such a flicking basstud ship as this. Even when the basstud engines go, the flicking basstud steering busts. And if the flicking steering's all roight, the flicking basstud bleeding runt of a gun is frozen stiff, Oi bet the bleeding Jerries 'ave proper de-icing gear on their guns. Their guns don't bloody well freeze, not bloody likely. But we 'ave to do without, just because the Government or the flicking firm that built this basstud ship wanted to cut the cost and save more money for their basstud selves. Oi dunno," he said, changing his tone suddenly from anger to weary resignation and picking himself up.

Newton left Price exploding on the deck. He seized the lever to swing open the breech. The lever would not move. He tugged at it. The trainer got his hands on it and both tugged. Still it did not move. They all got out their knives and dug and chipped at the ice round the breech, then tugged at the lever again. It was no use.

" Sightsetter, are your phones working? Well, tell the T.S. that we're frozen up and can't open the breech. Tell them to send the G.I. up here."

* * *

Professor Cole, sitting at the phones in the T.S., received the message from A gun. He turned to the G.I. at his side and said, " A gun is frozen. They want you up there, Chief."

The G.I. looked at Cole impatiently. His small figure seemed more than ever pent up with scarcely controllable exasperation. His skin was drawn tightly round his forehead and cheek-bones, so that the outline of his skull showed plainly. His pale, expressionless eyes stared steadily at Cole from his tense, white face.

" Flick!" he said.

He picked up a voice-pipe, called Lieutenant Burton in the director, said, " A gun is frozen, sir. They can't open the breech. I'm going up there now," and pattered from the cabinet, his big ears standing out of his head like the wings of a bat. Professor Cole turned to his mouthpiece, called A gun and said, " The screaming skull is on his way up now."

Harry Robertson, the B-gun sightsetter, was listening on his phones and heard the messages passing between A gun and the T.S. " A gun's frozen up," he said to the rest of his crew.

Frank Hales, the captain of B gun, left the shield and moved to the side of the gun deck. Looking over, he saw the G.I. pattering past, straining to keep control both of his feet and his feelings. Hales went forward to look over the front of his own deck on to the gun below. He saw the G.I. patter to the breech, snatch at the lever, wrench it, look quickly at the mechanism, say something to the A-gun sightsetter, and patter away again, quivering. Hales came back to his gun and asked Harry Robertson what was happening.

" The G.I.'s just sent for the Ordnance Artificer."

Hales pulled a face, adjusted his Sherlock Holmes deerstalker's hat, and took his long, lean, slightly stooping figure back to the guard-rail to look across the sea.

A moment later he heard the crunch of feet in the snow on the fo'c'sle below him, and saw the R.N.V.R. Lieutenant Seeley come stumbling breathlessly to the foot of B-gun deck ladder and begin to climb.

" What does this little fuss-pot want now ? " thought Hales, but he said, " You know there's trouble on A gun, sir ? They're frozen up."

Lieutenant Seeley paused half-way up the ladder and blinked at Hales. " Oh, are they ? I see. Thank you." He slid to the bottom of the ladder again. A moment later he, too, was wrenching at the lever. After some seconds he gave it up with a " Yes, I see. Frozen up," and hurried to the bridge to tell the Captain.

The time was now 6.25 a.m.

Lieutenant Seeley had just climbed to the bridge when one of the starboard lookouts, called, " Green four-five. An object. I think it's a mast, sir."

Skipper, Navigator, and Yeoman of Signals swung their glasses, and after a few seconds the Skipper gave the formal " Very good " to the lookout, quickly followed by " By God there they are . . . three of them. Do you see them, Pilot ? Can you, Yeoman ? Starboard lookout, don't take your glasses off those masts. Report anything more of them you see. Burton," he called into a voice-pipe, " have you got those masts ? "

* * *

Lieutenant Burton *had* got those masts. He was already telling Pat Maclure in the rangefinder to get a range; and Pat Maclure was swearing.

Pat had only been eleven minutes in the rangefinder. His balaclava covered nearly all his black, unshaven face and the

212

hood of his duffel coat covered his balaclava so that all that could be seen was his nose, and the whites of his eyes staring from the blackness like two pale lights at a pithead. On his hands he had three pairs of gloves, two woollen and one fur-lined. On his legs he had oilskin trousers over his bellbottoms, two pair of thick long pants, a pair of seaboot-stockings, a pair of socks, and his sea-boots. Over all, besides his duffel coat, he had three long sweaters and a watch-coat.

Yet he felt he was freezing, not very slowly, to death; and now he had got to get a range, which meant taking off at least two pairs of gloves to adjust and focus the instrument before him.

The trainer swung the rangefinder slightly to starboard, and soon Pat had caught two images of the centre mast in his sights. Quickly turning knobs in front of him until the two images merged into one, he shouted "Cut," the trainer pressed a pedal, and the figure 23,300 yards stamped itself on a clock in the T.S. and the director.

Lieutenant Burton reported to the Skipper. "Well," said the Skipper. "Now we wait and see."

He turned his head and became aware of two men standing behind him, obviously wanting to speak. The first was his servant, who was holding a cup and saucer. "Yes, Denney, what is it?"

"You rang, sir. I've brought you your morning coffee."

"I didn't ring, you fathead. That was action stations. Still, I'll have the coffee."

The second man was Lieutenant Seeley. "Excuse me, sir, but A gun is frozen up. We're doing all we can to get it right. All we can. Yes, I think we'll get it right. Yes."

The Skipper looked through him and then at him. "Is the G.I. on the gun?"

"Yes, sir."

"And the O.A.?"

"Yes, sir."

"Very good." The Skipper lifted his glasses again to Green four-five. Then he picked up the loud-hailer, and called the ship's company.

"Hallo, Marsden's. There are three unidentified surface craft thirteen miles away to starboard. You can see their masts now coming over the horizon. They may be ours. But I don't think so. I should say they are fast destroyers. If they are German, we'll have a job on our hands—two against three.

"They'll certainly have spotted us by now, so the *Meltham* and ourselves will turn in to meet them. I'm telling the tanker to keep on her course at maximum speed and catch up with the convoy as soon as she can. Don't forget that it's our job, to keep these boys, if they're German, away from the tanker at all costs and to smash them if we can."

213

He then told the Yeoman to flash two signals, one to the tanker, the other to the *Meltham*, sent a bosun's mate to the wireless cabinet with a warning for the convoy, said " Starboard twenty " down the voice-pipe to the wheel-house, and, when the ship had heeled over, steadied her on her course with a call of " Midships " and rang " Full steam ahead " on the engine-room telegraph, all without turning a hair.

The time was now 6.30 a.m.

* * *

It was daylight—had been for hours—but a daylight grey with snow-clouds which hung in the windless sky. Except for the men wrestling with A gun and the stokers forcing more and more steam from the boilers, the *Marsden's* crew could now do nothing except wait and watch.

The masts, whether British or German, were still some 21,500 yards away. The *Marsden's* heaviest guns, the four point-sevens, had an extreme range of only 16,000 yards. So, even with the *Marsden* and the *Meltham* going head on, and full speed, towards the unknown ships, it would be five or six minutes before any British gun could fire.

The *Marsden* plunged her stem into the sea, then heaved it up sending ice-cold spray over the men who still worked desperately to free A gun. Her stern rose and fell, quivering gently as the screws churned deep in the water, shaking violently whenever the pitch of the ship brought the screws near the surface. Y gunshield rattled like a tinker's cart rumbling over granite setts, so that Williams had great difficulty in making himself heard when repeating the warning from T.S.: " Target in sight, bearing Green one-o."

Not that *that* mattered .

Now that the ship had swung round to face the target, Y gun was temporarily out of action. When Charlie Wright had trained her as far for'ard as she could go, she was still 30 degrees off the target. It was the old story. Charlie merely repeated his usual formula: " Y gun won't bear," and got off his seat to join the rest of the gun's crew who were standing on the starboard side of the gun staring silently ahead.

Jock Forrest had buttoned his red oilskin by now and put his duffel coat over it. His anti-flash helmet covered most of his face, but his brown eyes were left unprotected and unhindered. He stood still by the guard-rail, looking steadily at Green one-o.

Beside him, and a good head taller, for all his slightly bent shoulders, stood Calamity, fidgeting with his rammer's glove. His helmet was pulled down low on his head, so that his face, now almost white with nerves, was fully visible. His mouth was slightly open and his gaze, though also fixed on Green one-o, was not intent.

" This flicking waiting is getting me down," he said.

214

Harry Rhoades, either unconsciously or to keep himself steady, was humming his invariable " *I don't want to set the world on fi-er,*" and Jackie Low, for perhaps the fiftieth time in three months, cut in with " It's all right, Harry. You'll never set nothing on fire. Not with that voice, you won't," at which Harry, as usual, smiled and went on humming. Jackie held out a bag of liquorice allsorts, and as he did so, Williams noticed that his face was bare.

" Jackie, where's your anti-flash helmet ? "

" Dunno. Can't find the bastard. Some bastard's pinched it. Probably you. 'Ave a liquorice allsorts ? "

Charlie Wright joined Barber, who was standing a little in front of the others and giving an excited running commentary. " Thur they are . . . you can see them quite plain. Three of 'em. Look, that one's opened fire. No it 'asn't. It's joost smoke. You can see t' funnels quite plain now. The middle one's got two. That one on t' reet's got two . . . no, yon's a mast . . . it's only one funnel . . . but t' one on t' left *'as* got two. We must be nearly in t' range. . . . Ah'm not a bit nervous . . . art thee ? "

Charlie pulled at his sharp-pointed beard, looked at Barber, looked at the three ships ahead, and looked back at Barber, " Yes. I'm nervous. Bloody nervous. Flicking bastard nervous."

Williams remained in the gunshield, staring at the sea and wishing to Christ he was home.

In the shell-room, Sinbad and Shortarse were asking for news. Sinbad had put Miss Blandish away as soon as he heard the distant tones of the loud-hailer and even Shortarse had gathered himself together and stuck his head through the hatchway into the cabin flat. Neither could distinguish the Skipper's words.

" He said something about Jerries, didn't he ? Ask 'em what he said, Shortarse."

Sinbad's comment when the news at last reached him was a long drawn " Oo-oo-oo." Shortarse lowered his head through the hatchway, sat down, and said nothing. But his eyes, for once, were wide open.

On the three-inch platform, Jimmie, with his cap on the back of his head and a cigarette stuck in his mouth, held his glasses to his eyes with both hands, except when he took one away to suck a great gulp of smoke.

" I'll bet those are Jerries," he said quietly to Wild Angus, and a picture flashed into his mind of the last time he had been in a surface action with his old ship. That scrap had ended, for him, with four hours in the sea.

" Gosh! I've been in the oggin once. I don't want to go in again. Not in this temperature, anyhow."

Wild Angus was also thinking of the temperature. He had heard that when a man fell into the sea in this part of the world, he was lucky—or unlucky—if he lasted ten seconds. Most men were killed outright by the icy shock. He shuddered. "Looks like we'll have plenty of time to think about the oggin to-day, sir. A high-angle gun's not much use against surface craft."

"I'd use a pea-shooter on the bastards if I couldn't find anything better."

On the point-five platform the Duchess was still looking at the sea and at the distant shapes which were gradually emerging from it. His figure was now erect and alert, his face had lost its tired look and, for the moment, he was not thinking of home or telling himself what an ass he had been ever to join the Service. He was thinking, instead, that his point-fives, with an effective range of just over 1,000 yards, would be about as much use in a surface action as the Jimmie's pea-shooter; and if he had got to be in a scrap at all, he wanted to be right in it.

"Flick me! They've opened fire," and, far away on the horizon, there was an orange flash and a belch of smoke.

"Where the bloody hell is Harrison?"

Harrison by now had climbed listlessly out of his hammock and was standing by the side of it.

"Have you got a cigarette, chum?" he called to one of the for'ard supply party who were at the far end of the mess deck, ready to hoist ammunition to A and B guns above.

The supply man pulled out a packet and threw it across the five yards which separated him from Harrison. Harrison stooped to pick it up, and as he straightened his back again he felt a sharp pain in his head and heard a crash behind him.

Not knowing what he did, he began to walk. He walked steadily aft along the mess deck, heard one of the supply party call "Are you all right?", walked through the door into the canteen flat, saw the lights coming from the open door of the T.S., and sagged to the deck.

The first shell fired by the leading enemy destroyer had hit the *Marsden*, piercing the wafer-like starboard plates, flashing across the mess deck and thence through more wafer-like plates into the sea beyond. It had not exploded, but splinters from the plates had spurted about the for'ard end of the mess deck. One had cut the steam-pipe leading from the boilers to the capstan engine. Another had cut the ropes on which Harrison's hammock swung from the deckhead. A third had lodged in Harrison's brain.

The time was now 6.34 a.m.

* * *

That opening shot was a shock to the Skipper, though he did not show it. From the moment he had come on the bridge he had felt sure in his own mind that the smoke on the horizon was coming from German ships. He had made certain of it a

216

minute ago when the *Marsden* had flashed a recognition signal and received no reply.

But he was not expecting the enemy to open fire so soon.

The rangefinder had just given him a range of 18,600 yards, well outside the extreme limit of the *Marsden's* guns, and now the largest of the oncoming enemy ships had fired her first salvo and had hit. Obviously, she was one of those new German destroyers which were more like light cruisers with more and heavier guns than those carried by the *Marsden* and the *Meltham.*

" Hell's bells, that's going to put up the odds."

His glasses were on the enemy ships, and he saw that the two smaller destroyers seemed to be pulling ahead of the larger one, which had altered course to widen the angle.

" So that's their litttle game, is it ? Now that she's got our range, the large one is going to hang back and pot at us while the two small ones come into range.

" If I zig-zag, I may put her aim off, but I shan't be able to take a crack at her for some minutes more. If I go straight ahead, she'll certainly hit us again; but provided she doesn't cripple us, we should be hitting that outside small basket inside two minutes. I'll keep straight on."

He picked up the mouthpiece of the inter-communication system. " *Marsden* calling, *Marsden* calling. Maintain course and speed and engage the left-flank enemy ship as soon as you can. We'll go for the one on the right flank. Over to you, over."

Back came the *Meltham*: " Message understood, *Marsden*. Good luck to you."

The Skipper then called Burton. " We'll tackle that right-flank destroyer. How are the guns ? "

" A gun is still frozen, sir, and Y gun won't bear. Both B and X guns are ready to fire."

" Oh, hell! I'd forgotten Y gun. Still, I can't change course yet to bring her on. We'll have to do without her. What's the position on A gun ? "

The position on A gun was about the same. The breech lever was still immovable, the O.A. was still working on it and Lieutenant Seeley was still staring at it intently in a knowing way and telling the crew that " We'll free it any moment now. Yes."

The waiting crew were nearly as frozen as their gun and were crowded together for warmth under cover of the over-lapping B-gun deck. They had felt the shock when the shell had hit the for'ard mess deck below them, but no splinters had come their way.

" That's roight," Price said. " Let 'em blaze away at us. Go on, you basstuds, blaze away until you're ruddy well black in the face. We won't 'arm you. We're on a flicking pleasure cruise with guns that aren't meant to foire. Oi dunno."

The enemy were still out of range, would remain out of range for another one and half minutes at this rate. But the Skipper knew better than Price what it was like to wait, doing nothing under fire. Away to starboard he saw again the orange flash as the large German destroyer fired her second salvo.

"Open fire," he called down the voice-pipe to the director and immediately the director-layer pulled his trigger.

One gun fired.

There was a flash from the muzzle of X gun and a 57-pound projectile whirled through the air to drop in line with, but well short of, the right-hand small destroyer. As soon as the recoil was over, Raikes, the captain of the gun, swung open the breech, letting out simultaneously a cloud of black, choking smoke and an empty brass cylinder which shot back into the netting at the rear of the gun and thence fell to the deck.

Before the ejected cylinder had stopped rolling, Redfern had snapped his loaded tray into position and forced a new pro-jectile and charge up the breech; and while Nevison and Booth-royd were putting down a third projectile and charge on the tray, Raikes had closed his interceptor, connecting his gun to the director, and setting his gun-ready lamp burning there.

A and Y guns were not intended to fire. But B gun was. Yet when Burton pulled his master trigger, B gun remained silent.

"Flicking misfire," said Hales, changing over a switch according to the gunnery drill books and keeping his gun-ready lamp burning in the director.

Burton pulled his trigger a second time. Again there was a flash from X gun and a shell whirled through the air to fall short of the target. Again, on B gun, there was silence.

"Another flicking misfire. Press your pedal, gunlayer."

The gunlayer pressed his firing pedal. There was a click and nothing more. The striker was going forward, but it was not igniting the charge.

At that moment there was a distant boom, a shrill whining through the air, and then four splashes, the nearest one not ten yards from the side of the ship and level with B gun. Spray from the splash hit Hales.

"What the hell was that?" said Carter, the B gunlayer, beginning to climb out of the shield.

"Only some shell splashes."

"How far away?"

"Oh, the nearest one was a good seventy yards away and well aft. Must have given the boys on Y gun a fright."

"Oh, them!" said Carter contemptuously, climbing back on to his seat.

"Sightsetter, tell the T.S. that we've misfired three times. Tell them to send the G.I. up here."

The G.I. was on B-gun deck in less than half a minute, more

white-faced than ever. He was followed by Lieutenant Seeley. Hales and the G.I. ignored the officer and went into a huddle by the breech.

" Have you tried a new charge ? " asked the G.I.

" No. I switched my circuit and then I tried gunlayer's firing. I think the striker's bust."

" Try a new charge."

" Why not have a look at the striker ? It may be frozen."

" Ditch the flicking charge."

So Hales swung the breech open, Lovelace, the rammer, seized the bright, fully charged cylinder, dragged it from the breech, and hurled it into the sea. Then, running back, he took the waiting shell off the tray, snapped the tray over, and rammed a new charge into the breech.

Hales set his gun-ready lamp burning again, and when, a moment later, the director-layer pulled his trigger, there came a roar and a flash from X gun; but from B gun, silence.

" Ditch that flicking charge and try another," said the G.I., almost beside himself with fury.

Again the quick opening of the breech, the rush to the side, and a shining cylinder plopping into the sea; again the gun-ready lamp burning, the flash and the roar from X gun, and from B gun, silence.

" Gunlayer's," said the G.I. sharply.

At that Carter pressed his pedal. A click . . . then silence.

" G.I., I really think you should have a look at the striker. Yes, I really do. It might be frozen. Yes. Or it might be broken. Yes."

The G.I., mastering his feelings, was turning towards Seeley when a voice made him look up. He saw the Skipper's head and shoulders leaning over the bridge.

" For God's sake get that gun going, G.I."

Before he could reply, the G.I. felt a stab in the middle of his back, and wheeling round, sank to the deck in a heap. Hales, clutching at his own back, slumped on top of him, and Lieutenant Seeley, blood spurting from his forehead, fell forward across the pair of them.

On the bridge the Skipper stepped back with one hand to his head and the other groping feebly in search of support. The hand found the binnacle but could not grasp it and the Skipper sank to the deck.

" Tell the First Lieutenant to take over," he said a few seconds later.

A shell, coming from almost dead ahead, had pierced the top of the gunshield, sending splinters in all directions. One of these had hit the Skipper between the eyes, another had caught Hales at the bottom of his spine, a third had gone through Lieutenant Seeley's cheek and, forcing its way upward, had stopped in his brain. The shell itself did not explode on the shield but cut through it, went staight through the G.I., through the splinter plates which surrounded the gun deck and into the sea.

The time was now 6.40 a.m.

* * *

Before Jimmie could reach the bridge, the Skipper was dead. His body was carried by Buck and Richards, the two Bosun's Mates on the bridge, and the two starboard lookouts, to his seagoing cabin, and Jimmie took command of the ship.

He stood for the first time on his own bridge in a ship which had been hit twice already, which already had two guns out of action, which had just lost her regular and experienced Captain, and which was now only 11,600 yards from a superior enemy force. If he had had a moment to think, he might have screamed.

But he had no time. Anyway, he was red with anger. Over and over again as he ran from the three-inch to the bridge, he had repeated, half out loud, "The bastards . . . the bastards," and when he saw the Skipper's body slumped on the bridge he had almost cried with rage. For a moment he felt like racing his ship forward on her course and trying to ram.

But then his mind cooled and cleared.

First, he glanced over his shoulder and saw that the tanker, keeping steadily on her original course, was far away to port, pushing her engines for all they were worth to get out of the way and join the convoy.

Next he called the director for reports on the guns and heard that X and Y guns were still intact but that Y gun would not bear. Then he looked at the enemy.

The enemy ships were steaming in inverted V formation, the two smaller ships forming the feet, 3,000 yards apart, and the large ship lying some 2,000 yards behind to form the head. The *Marsden* and *Meltham* were in line abreast, about 1,000 yards apart and outflanked by the two smaller enemy ships. So far, the *Meltham* had concentrated on the left-flank ship and had scored two hits. *Marsden's* one gun had been firing at the right-flank ship without hitting once.

The large German destroyer had been left to choose her target, unhindered, and, at first, fired at the *Marsden*. But when she saw that only one gun was replying, she switched to the *Meltham*, which zig-zagged violently, both to escape the enemy fire and to bring as many of her guns as possible to bear on her two targets.

Jimmie saw that unless he could bring help, the *Meltham* would be overwhelmed by the fire of the big destroyer and her left-flank escort. But unless he first accounted for the enemy on the right flank, he would never be able to give help to anyone Not in this world. " I must get that bloody gun to bear right

220

away," he said to himself, and called "Port ten" down to the wheel house. When he had widened the angle between the *Marsden* and the enemy ship, he steadied on the new course.

The alteration of course put the director off its target and set Rattler Morgan furiously turning his handles to bring his sights into line again. Every move of his handle moved the pointers in the training receivers in X and Y guns and set the trainers there swinging their guns round.

In a few seconds Y gun was on the target for the first time. Charlie Wright called out " Y gun bearing," Jock closed his interceptor, and when the director-layer pulled the master trigger, two shells shot away from the *Marsden* towards their mark.

Both landed. The crack from Y gun had burst through the coverings round William's ears and deafened him. He had shut his eyes to avoid the flash, but was not able to shut his nose to avoid the smoke and fumes which accompanied it.

He turned for air towards the open port at the front of the shield, saw, through it, the stem of the enemy destroyer pointing towards the *Marsden* at an angle of about 40 degrees, and then saw a burst of smoke spurt up from near her bridge and another spurt of water just in front of her bows.

" We've hit her. Boys, we've hit her. Smack on the bloody bridge."

As he shouted, the reloaded guns fired again and caught Williams unawares. His hands jumped off the range handles, something thumped his ear-drums, and his eyes and face seemed caught in a flaming whip.

Then the flame cleared and from behind the gun came an exultant shout: " We've got 'em again. Hey, the bastards are on fire. Christ! What a bloody good shot! " Jackie Low was dancing with excitement.

" For flick's sake, give us another shell, Jackie," shouted Calamity.

" Jackie, you watch that tray. Flick Jerry! " shouted Jock Forrest, for Jackie, jumping up and down to get a better view, had forgotten that the tray was empty and that he was still cradling a shell in his arms.

He turned quickly, dumped the shell on the tray, and the gun fired again. The flash, whipping back through the gunshield, caught Jackie full in the eyes and blinded him. It cut through his balaclava and scorched his skin, unprotected by any anti-flash helmet. He staggered back and tried to pull off his bala-clava. But his hands were shaking so violently that he could do no more than clutch at it.

One of the supply party ran to him, took him by the shoulders, forced him into the wardroom flat, and there pulled off his bala-clava for him. Jackie's face was black with soot and dust, his mouth was drooping wide open, and his eyes were vacant. He could not speak. One of his hands gestured feebly and meaning-lessly in front of him.

The supply number half-dragged, half-led him down to the temporary sick-bay in the Skipper's main cabin, laid him on a camp-bed, and ran back on deck. There, Harry Rhoades was trying to do Jackie's job as well as his own, shovelling shells and charges on to the tray so that the impatient Calamity was never kept waiting. But it was too much for one man and Jock shouted across the gun. " Tell the T.S. to send the shell number from A gun. Tell 'em Jackie's hurt."

But as Williams put his lips to the mouthpiece, there was a crash overhead and the phones went dead.

* * *

Two shells from a salvo had hit the *Marsden* simultaneously. One had struck for'ard some feet above the waterline, flashed across the torpedo-men's mess deck, and landed in the main switchboard, immediately putting out the lights and cutting the director circuit. Emergency lights began to burn dimly in various parts of the ship, but the director remained cut off from the T.S. and the T.S. remained cut off from the guns.

The other shell had struck the breech of X gun and exploded. Five of the crew were killed.

Raikes's head, with its usual grin still showing, flew off his shoulders into the sea. Parts of Chris Boothroyd were spattered over the deck. " Our Albert " Forster slumped over his layer's handles with the back of his head blown off. On top of him fell the sightsetter, with his phones still attached to his head, but his head detached from his shoulders. The trainer was pierced through the belly by his own training handles and jammed against the side of the shield. He lived through fifteen seconds of writhing agony and then fell limp.

The two who escaped were Nevison and Redfern.

Nevison had lost his nerve after the first few rounds. He had run back to the lockers, put his head in his hands, and refused to get up. Every time the gun fired, his whole body shuddered and his mouth let out a gasping groan as though he was gripped with spasms of pain.

Seeing this, Redfern had taken to rushing over to the hatch-way, grasping the shells from the supply party below and dumping them in the tray himself. After ramming the charge and shell home this last time, he had run and bent down to gather the new shell from the supply chain.

He had just straightened himself again when a whistling in front of him made him look up. He saw a shell, saw it in the air, coming straight for his gun. He screamed " Look out," slumped on the deck with his shell beneath him, and a second later there was flame all round him.

When he looked up again, there was no tray to his gun, no

222

breech to ram the shells up, no top to the gunshield, and only the remains of a crew. He ran towards the gun and saw the trainer gasping and retching in the half-upright position to which his warning had roused him. He put his hands through splinter holes in the shield and tried to free the body by tugging the side away. But he could not move it, and suddenly he was sick.

Then he turned, ran past Nevison down the ladder to the quarter deck, and looked for Sub-Lieutenant Carr.

Carr had been on X gun from the beginning of the action until about a minute ago, when he had gone down to Y gun to see that all was well there. Redfern found him acting as shell-supply number in place of Jackie Low.

"Mr. Carr, we've been hit. The crew's been wiped out, sir."

Carr glanced up, recognised the voice rather than the blackened face inside its blackened helmet, and realised that the shower of metal which had sprayed Y gun thirty seconds before had been the result of a direct hit on the gun above. He took Redfern's arm.

"Here, you take my place on the gun. Shell supply. I'll go and see."

He ran as fast as his clothes would let him, feeling for his morphia syringe as he ran. But when he reached X gun he saw there was no need for his syringe. Three bodies round the gun were certainly dead. "Our Albert" Foster was certainly unconscious, with blood still dripping from the head, but Carr thought there was a sign of life in the pulse.

He decided to go for'ard for the Doctor, and as he turned from the gun, he saw Nevison still huddled by the lockers. He went to him.

"Are you hurt?"

Nevison looked up slowly, shook his head, then began to notice a strange silence about the gun deck. He did not know that a shell had exploded eight feet away. He had taken the explosion and flash for just another round going off and had kept his head tightly in his hands. The few splinters which had not gone into and through the gunshield had shot over his head.

"What's the matter, Nevison? Were you hit anywhere?"

Again Nevison shook his head and this time rose slowly to his feet. But Y gun fired again; his whole body shuddered and he dropped back into a crouch, resting his elbows on his knees and his head in his hands.

"Come on, Nevison, you'd better get down to the sick-bay for a bit," and, taking his arm, Carr pushed him in the direction of the temporary sick-bay in the Skipper's cabin, then turned for'ard and ran for the Doctor.

Nevison stumbled aft towards Y gun, but as he reached the entrance to the wardroom flat, Y gun fired again and he dropped with a moan on to his haunches and stayed there, not daring to lift his hands from his ears. Every time the gun fired he moaned and shook, until at last Calamity noticed him and yelled out, " For flick's sake, get him away. He's giving me the jitters." One of the supply party dragged him to the Skipper's cabin.

*   *   *

Sub-Lieutenant Carr reached the main sick-bay on the fo'c'sle. The Doctor was not there. He had gone down to B gun and found the gun's crew pulling at the bodies of Hales, the G.I., and Lieutenant Seeley.

The crew had not, at first, realised that their gun had been hit. The shell-supply number had not even heard the crash, although he was standing only four feet from the gun; and when he saw the G.I. reel and fall, he thought at first the man had fainted.

" I've been expecting him to do that for months."

Then the other two had piled on top of the G.I.

" Flick me! They must have been hit. Just like the movies!" The supply number stood still.

No one else on the gun moved. Their minds could not grasp that three men had been killed before their eyes. They stood or sat—and looked.

The first man to stir himself was the sightsetter, Harry Robertson. He had felt the thud on the gunshield, felt the whole shield jump and quiver, but did not realise that anything unusual had happened until he looked at the sleeve of his duffel coat and saw that it was slashed.

" I've picked up the wrong duffel coat again," he said, and then noticed that the shoulder was gashed as well. From his shoulder his eyes travelled over the gun to where the three bodies had piled up. He stood on tiptoe, then climbed on the elevation receiver. There he stayed, looking. Slowly his eyes thawed and life came back to his brain.

" Oh, my God, move them, somebody."

The sound of his voice stirred the rest of his crew. Carter eased himself slowly off his gunlayer's seat and waddled to the other side of the gun, followed by the remainder of his crew. Still no one wanted to touch the bodies.

" Someone better go for the Quack," and Lovelace turned without a word and clambered down the ladder.

But the Doctor was already on the bridge and Lovelace went back without him to the gun. The others had just begun to lift the body of Lieutenant Seeley from the heap when the Doctor himself came up the ladder and took charge. There was nothing much he could do here. The three bodies were dead.

" Boys, we'll have to put them over the side. Will you all give me a hand, please ? "

Carter slowly bent to lift the shoulders of Lieutenant Seeley, another man lifted the legs.

" Will you go down the ladder and take the body as we lower

224

it ? " the Doctor said to Robertson and Lovelace. Then, in silence, the body was taken to the head of the ladder and there Carter took the weight, eased the legs into position over the ladder, and gently lowered while Robertson and Lovelace stretched their arms to catch the dangling feet, then the knees, then the waist.

When the body had been lowered, Carter fetched two heavy shackles and a piece of rope from the B-gun cabouche and came down to the body, which the others had now lifted to the guard-rail. He tied the shackles to the rope and the rope to Lieutenant Seeley's body.

" Up and over," said the Doctor. The men lifted and pushed, there was a spash, bubbles rose and went rapidly astern.

" Poor little bastard," said Carter, and climbed back to B-gun deck for the body of his best friend.

As he reached the top of the port-side ladder, he saw the head of Sub-Lieutenant Carr emerging up the starboard ladder in search of the Doctor. Close behind came the massive form of Lieutenant Burton.

The time was now 6.55 a.m.

* * *

When Williams realised that Y-gun phones were dead, he was speechless. To himself he thought: " There they go again. These damned earphones are good lads in harbour. At sea they're as poor as spit . . . poorer, in fact. Christ Almighty!"

He did not realise that the phones had gone dead because every circuit in the ship had been cut.

But Lieutenant Burton realised it. He felt the shock in the director as the shell pierced the side and crashed into the main switchboard. More, he saw his gun-ready lamps go out. He turned at once to the Buffer. " I'm afraid the director's out. We'll have to go into gunlayers' firing." He opened the door and stepped on to the bridge to report to Jimmie.

" Hell," said Jimmie. " Bosun's Mate." A second's pause. " BOSUN'S MATE."

" Here, sir," said a gentle voice immediately behind him.

Jimmie turned his head and saw a pleasant-faced boy of nineteen behind him. " Richards, go aft and tell Mr. Carr that he'll have to fire Y gun in local control. The director's out. Then come back here as quick as you can. Burton, you'd better go to A and B guns and see if you can get either of them going. And see what they're doing with the holes in the side."

" Aye, aye, sir," said Burton, and was striding away when a shout from the Yeoman of Signals stopped him.

" There's Mr. Carr coming to the fo'c'sle now, sir. I think he's going to B gun. Yes, he is, sir."

" What the devil is he doing there ? Burton, tell Carr to get

225

back aft. And tell him the director's not working in case Richards has missed him."

Burton went to B gun, where he found the Doctor preparing to go aft with Carr. He gave Carr Jimmie's message, winked at him, then looked at the mess at his feet. " Come on," he said to the rest of the gun's crew, " I'll give you a hand with this."

Then he saw the gun. " I say, Carter, this doesn't look too badly damaged. What was wrong before ? "

" Hales thought it was the striker, sir."

" Well, let's clear up the mess and then you keep the rest of the crew here for the time being. They're all right, are they ? Nobody else hurt ? Good. As soon as you can, have that striker out and look at it. I'll send the O.A. up here." He looked down and saw the body of Hales. " And I'll send Newton up from A gun to take over captain."

He caught hold of Hales's shoulders, manoeuvred the body to the ladder, and lowered it. Then he clambered down the ladder himself and strode to A gun.

The O.A. and Newton were still hard at work on A gun, unscrewing, turning, pulling, and hammering. The crew were still huddled, freezing cold, behind the gun, stamping their feet, ducking their heads whenever they heard the whine of a shell, peering from time to time across the sea at the enemy ships.

" How's it going ? "

" Not so good, sir," said the O.A., pausing for a moment and blowing on his numbed hands. " In fact, I don't think we can get it going. Not this morning, at any rate."

" Well, leave it, O.A. B gun has been hit, but it's not badly damaged. Go up there and see what you can do. Oh, and Newton, I want you to take over B gun. Hales has been hit. The rest of you come with me. I've got a job for you."

He walked sure-footed on the icy deck, down the ladder to the Iron Deck and into the washroom flat leading to the fore mess deck. The flat was dark. It was full of steam.

Burton led A gun's crew along it, spluttering and coughing and groping. After the icy cold of the fo'c'sle the flat was warm, but the contrast between the fresh clean air and the choking steam was too much for their lungs. Price stumbled three yards along the flat, then stopped to cough violently. The man behind him bumped into him, and Price, struggling to swear, nearly choked himself with gulps of steam.

He stumbled forward again, bent almost double, and tripped full length over a pair of legs. The owner of the legs said nothing. He was Harrison. He was dead. Price got as far as " What the flicking hell . . ." when he was stopped short by another fit of coughing. He stumbled and lurched into the mess deck.

The steam was now coming in hot waves, followed immediately by icy gusts of air, then more steam, damp and stifling.

226

Price drew back. " What the 'ell's 'appened ? Chroist, it's worse nor King's Cross. Oi'm getting out. Rather be basstud froze than flicking boiled."

Then an icy gust cleared the air for a few seconds and Price was able to pick out the emergency light which hung from the deckhand. In those few seconds he saw shapes leaning over the hatchway which led to the for'ard shell-room and magazine, saw that water was slopping inches deep at his feet, saw hammocks, blankets, and books lumped together in sodden heaps on the deck, and saw daylight through the ship's side.

" Chroist! They've left a basstud porthole open."

But it was not an open porthole. It was the hole through which the first shell to hit the ship had sped into the sea. Lieutenant Burton had seen the hole, too, just as he was tying a handkerchief over his mouth and nose in the hope of keeping out the steam. Without thinking, and before he had tied the hand-kerchief securely, he called out, " Who's in charge here ? " took in a gulp of steam, and choked. By the time he had recovered, a white-handkerchiefed face was peering at him through the fog and saying, in a muffled voice, " Leading Seaman Jeffries here, sir." Burton took one hand off his handkerchief and pointed to the hole.

" Christ!" said Jeffries, and stumbled across to it.

He found that the hammock he had stuffed into the hole some minutes before had been dislodged. He groped on the deck, found the hammock soaking wet, and began to force it back into the hole. Burton, handkerchief now secure, came to help him, and between them they stuffed it in, leaving part of it sticking out to sea and the other part drooping inboard towards the deck like a flabby sausage.

" How about the other hole ? "

Jeffries led the way to the starboard side and showed him another hammock securely in place.

" What's all this steam ? " said Burton, after looking at the hammock, then realised as he spoke that there was a steady hissing above his head.

Looking up, he saw where the splinter had cut the steam-pipe to the capstan engine. Boiling water had poured out when the splinter had first struck, but now it was only steam.

" I've sent for a stoker to switch the steam off, but no one's come up yet, sir."

" Send again; and we'd better get everyone out of here until the air clears."

Burton and the members of A gun's crew joined Jeffries and his three supply men on the Iron Deck. There, huddled for warmth by the galley, and smoking hard, was another group of about twelve men, including the remainder of the for'ard supply party and several others who, Burton suspected, had no business in that part of ship.

" I'm going to form you into a chain to take charges and shells aft to Y gun as soon as we get the mess deck clear of steam. You had better come over to the port side. It's a bit too hot here."

Literally, it was bitterly cold, both on the port and on the starboard sides, but Burton was not talking about the weather. The starboard side was exposed to the enemy, as a shell, hitting the sea not twenty yards away, reminded everybody.

The group stirred itself rather listlessly and trooped to the port side. Then Burton thought of something. " Will one of you go up to the rangefinder, please, and tell the men there to come down. They'll be freezing to death. Price, you go."

" There 'e goes. Picks on me, 'e does. Whoi couldn't 'e 'ave sent someone else ? Nah! It 'as to be me," said Price as he climbed one ladder after another to the rangefinder and warned Pat Maclure and his two companions that: " Burton says you're no flicking use up there and you're to come down."

Pat Maclure could scarcely move, because there was so little room in the rangefinder, and because he had no feeling in his legs and only numbing pain in his hands. Slowly and gingerly he drew off his top pair of gloves by putting the fingers in his mouth, shutting his teeth, and pulling; then he managed to slide a hand into his pocket. When he pulled his hand out again a medicine bottle came with it. Pat put the cork between his teeth, drew it out, and handed it to Price.

" Here you are, man, sippers."

Price took the bottle, sucked some of the contents into his mouth, rolled it round his tongue for a moment, then swallowed it.

The rolling *Marsden* became a gently swinging hammock, the heavy snow-clouds turned themselves into soft eiderdowns, the ice round his spine melted, and a gentle glow ran down his diaphragm and, reaching his stomach, fanned out like an opening flower.

" Thank Chroist for that!"

" Don't thank Christ; thank me, man," and Pat had a swig.

In a second the rangefinder had vanished from his mind. In its place was a log fire, blazing in a hearth, the sound of chickens and ducks quacking outside, and the sight of windows glazed with snow but tight shut to keep out the wind.

" All right, Jack, tell Burton we're on our way."

The time was now 7.16 a.m.

*   *   *

When Pat reached the Iron Deck he found the group, now twenty-five strong, still huddled together in or just outside the washroom flat. Most of them were smoking restlessly, but one or two more were stretched face downwards on the deck, only

228

looking from under their duffel hoods to ask, "Is that ours?" when the crack of a gun or the whistle of a shell forced the battle into their ears.

"What the hell's up with them?" asked Pat.

He could not understand why anyone should feel gloomy on such a lovely morning. Then he remembered that the morning was piercing cold.

"What's happening?" he said to Price.

"Old Burton's going to form us into a basstud supply chain to take stuff to Y gun. They're just waiting till the steam clears off the mess deck. That flicking basstud pipe has been leaking again and they've only just excavated a stoker to switch the flicking steam off."

Two minutes later a supply chain had been organised and charges and shells had begun to pass from hand to hand along the line. This flow soon affected the after supply party. Pat, the last man in the chain from the mess deck, kept running to the gun, dumping his shell or charge near the tray and running off for another. In a short while the accumulation of charges and shells round the gun interfered with the crew and Jock shouted:

"Pat, whur the hell is this stuff coming from?"

Pat came close to him and tried to whisper. But the periodic crack of the gun and the rumbling of the shield carried his whisper away. So he shouted, "Burton's getting all the stuff out of the for'ard magazines. I think he thinks there's a danger of flooding. Or maybe he's trying to keep the boys' mind off the fight. There's a lot up that end with nothing to do."

Jock nodded and told his own supply party to send no more for a time. When this order reached Sinbad and Shortarse in the after shell-room, both asked breathlessly, "What's happened now? Has Y gun been hit?"

They had been having a nerve-racking time. They could see nothing of the action, but could feel a great deal and hear almost all. They heard the splashes of shells in the sea and the sharp crack of the guns, they felt the concussion when the *Marsden* was hit, but had no way of telling quickly where or how serious the damage was.

At the first hit they had begun to imagine the ship sinking with them bottled deep down in her without a chance of escape. For a few seconds they had stared at the open hatchway, expecting at any moment to see the cascade of water which would be the end of both of them.

But then the warm lights from the cabin flat, the sound of voices from the supply party, and the occasional sight of a face reassured them and kept them at their job.

Then there had come that terrific crash above their heads and a staggering blackness as the lights went out.

"That's done it, Sinbad."

229

But Sinbad did not hear. He was half-way up the ladder to the cabin flat. He paused with his head out of the hatchway and shouted, " What's happened ? Are we sinking ? Where did that one hit ? "

Getting no answer, he tumbled out of the hatchway and groped his way to the ladder leading from the cabin flat. He stumbled past two figures in the dark, and was stopped by a third who was astride the ladder.

" Lemme get by."

" It's all right, Sinbad. There's no danger. They've hit us again, but they say there's not much damage."

Sinbad recognised the voice of Arthur Denney, the Skipper's servant, and was calm at once.

" I just wanted to know. It's flicking awful down here in the dark, not knowing."

" I bet it is. I'll try to get you a light. And I'll let you know what's going on."

So Sinbad went down the hatchway again and found Shortarse struggling with the emergency light which swung from the deckhead.

" The vibration's smashed this flicking bulb. What's happening up top, Sinbad ? "

Sinbad went along the dark recesses of the shell-room, no longer scurrying, but feeling his way to the rack he wanted. Then he came stumbling back with shells which Shortarse stacked near the hatchway.

At last a streak of light appeared. Arthur Denney had found a torch which he flashed into the shell-room. " Here, Shortarse, you'd better fix this on the hatchway so you can see what you're doing. Have you anything to fix it with ? "

Shortarse felt in his pockets and found his knife lanyard. He tied an unseamanlike knot round the torch with the lanyard and fixed it to the hatchway support.

" By the way," said Denney, " you know the Skipper's gone, I suppose ? "

" Gone ? Gone where ? Oh, I see, killed ? Just now ? My God, is the Jimmie running the ship ? Hey, let me out of here! "

" Pipe down, Sinbad, or I'll very probably slash you," said Shortarse. He was just about to ask for more news of the Skipper and the progress of the battle, when from above came a sudden exultant shout like the sound of a football crowd when the home team scores.

" What's happened ? What the hell's happened ? Something good's happened. We must have hit one of the bastards good and proper," shouted Sinbad.

One of the bastards *had* been hit—hit " good and proper ".

*   *   *

A minute before, Jimmie had seen the enemy change course.

230

She was no longer steaming directly towards the *Marsden*, but had swung on to a parallel course which would bring her abreast and about 3,000 yards distant within the next minute.

" By God, I'm going to fish her," said Jimmie.

Because the circuits were cut, he could not fire the torpedo tubes from the bridge, nor communicate directly with the torpedomen amidships. So he sent Buck with a message.

" Tell the T.I. to stand by tubes."

The T.I. began to insert the impulse charges into his torpedoes and prepare them for firing, and the Gunner (T.) came on the bridge to adjust the B sight, which would give him the range and angle at which the torpedoes should be fired.

" Are you ready, Guns? " said Jimmie. " We'll have to fire by signal from the bridge. Here, Richards, tell the T.I. that he's to fire when he sees this yellow flag drop like this," and he gave a demonstration. " Find out whether he's ready and report back here at the rush."

The Gunner (T.) finished his calculations on B sight and Jimmie handed the yellow flag to Buck, who was back from the tubes. " Stand by the starboard after the lookout, where you can see the T.I., and when you get the order ' Fire A ', drop the flag. Do you understand ? "

Buck went to his place and waited while the Gunner (T.) stared at his B sight and Jimmie stared at the rapidly approaching enemy destroyer. " Come on, Guns; we ought to fire now. What are you waiting for ? "

But the Gunner (T.) said nothing, merely staring at his sight. All of a sudden he shouted " Fire A ", Buck dropped his flag, the T.I. pulled a lever, and, with a quick " phut " of compressed air, a torpedo slipped from the first tube, splashed into the water, and began cutting towards the enemy ship.

" Fire B," shouted the Gunner (T.). Buck dropped his flag a second time and away went the second tin fish.

At once the enemy destroyer began to alter course, and as she did so, the Gunner (T.) made some quick adjustments on his sight. " For Christ's sake let the others go," shouted the Jimmie. " We mustn't miss her. We'll be finished if we do."

The Gunner (T.) went on with his calculations until he was exactly ready. Then he shouted " Fire X " and, a few moments later, " Fire Y ", then he left his sight and, with Jimmie, the Yeoman of Signals, and the Navigator, he looked over the side and watched.

The first two fish had missed. The enemy destroyer had swerved and they had passed in front of her. She was beginning another swerve when there was a burst of black smoke by her quarter deck, followed immediately by a brilliant flash and volumes of smoke.

" My God, we've hit her! Well done, Guns! My God,

what a shot! " yelled the Jimmie, catching hold of the Gunner (T.)'s right hand.

" WE'VE hit 'em. Take that, you bastards. Oh boy, what a hit!" yelled the supply party on the Iron Deck.

" We've hit the bastards! Christ, *have* we hit them! " shouted Williams on Y gun, looking through the open part of his shield.

Everyone on the ship, whether they had seen the flash or not, clutched at his neighbour. Those who could, jumped up and down on the deck, dancing with each other in relief and thankfulness.

The third tin fish had hit the enemy below the wardroom and exploded her magazine. One second the enemy ship was there; the next second she was not. That was all there was to it.

The *Marsden's* ship's company were beside themselves.

The time was now 7.35 a.m.

* * *

Their jubilation was short-lived.

As soon as she saw her left-flank escort disappear in the burst of flame and smoke, the large enemy destroyer switched her target from the *Meltham* to the *Marsden*. Her first salvo was short, and Sinbad and Shortarse heard the splashes as the shells dropped into the sea. Three shells from the second salvo went whistling over, making the improvised supply party duck their heads. The fourth shell hit the starboard side, smashed its way through No. 2 boiler-room, and exploded in No. 3.

No one in No. 3 boiler-room survived. Three men were killed instantly by flying splinters.

No one in No. 2 boiler-room was killed. But in its flight the shell had cut the main steam-pipe, showering water and steam on the five men working near. The emergency lighting had been smashed, but not even the most brilliant lights would have helped the men.

They clutched at the ladder-rails and at each other with swollen, pulpy hands and could hold to nothing. But pain and terror drove them upward until the first man reached the platform and the iron door at the ladder head.

The door was shut and swollen hands could not press the handle down to open it. In another minute they would have died if the door had not been opened from the outside.

The Chief Stoker had been in No. 1 boiler-room, flashing it up for extra speed. When the shell exploded in No. 3, he was knocked over. The next thing he knew, he was in the piercing cold on the Iron Deck and with him were the two stokers who, seconds before, had been working with him below.

It took him some seconds to get back his wits. Then he ran to the hatchway leading to the iron door of No. 2 boiler-room. Panting with exertion and shock, he dropped through it, and looked through the narrow circle of glass in the iron

232

door. He could see nothing. He forced back against the handle and pushed. The door opened an inch. He put his head through the hatchway and told one of the No. 1 boiler-room stokers to come down with him.

They both tied handkerchiefs round their faces and threw their weights against the door. It opened enough for the Chief to jam his foot in as steam came pouring out. He got his shoulder in, then his whole, wide body, finally forcing himself through to the inside.

The weight of the still struggling mass forced the door shut behind him. With all his strength he tugged first one heaving body and then another from the door, piling them on the platform at the ladder head. Then, as the stoker on the outside forced the door open again, the Chief caught the first body he could feel and threw it through the door. The stoker outside lifted the body through the hatchway, where Maclure, waiting above, pulled it on deck. Two other still semi-conscious stokers were pulled out this way, two more stumbled out on their own. Then the Chief and his No. 1 stoker themselves climbed out, gasping.

In the clear light of the deck the Chief looked at the five men he had rescued.

" For Christ's sake, get 'em to the sick-bay," he said, turning his face away.

* * *

The nerves of Sinbad and Shortarse in the shell-room had by now become accustomed to the sound of shells splashing in the sea and to the occasional shaking of the ship. They stood or sat in the semi-darkness of the shell-room, sending up S.A.P. from time to time whenever the extemporised supply from the for'ard magazine was inadequate.

Every few minutes they asked for news and had danced together in unequal waltz when they heard of the destruction of the enemy destroyer. The dance had come to an abrupt end when Sinbad had knocked his head against a shell-rack. He was still rubbing his head and cursing Shortarse when he heard something that made him quiver like a jelly.

The ship shuddered in a way she had shuddered several times before that morning, and " Another hit " said Shortarse when suddenly the vibration of the screws ceased. So did the rattling of the broken emergency lamp above their heads. There came a low, moaning sound, gradually becoming fainter, like an engine running down. . . . Like an Engine Running Down. . . . LIKE AN ENGINE RUNNING DOWN.

" Christ, the flicking engines have stopped," said Sinbad. " THE FLICKING ENGINES HAVE STOPPED." He rushed for the ladder. He got to it second and received a kick in the face from Shortarse's heel. He stopped, leaned back from the ladder until the way was clear, then bundled himself to the top.

On the quarter deck he joined Shortarse and the whole of the after supply party, who were strung out in a hesitant line looking for'ard. When the crash had come and the vibration in the gunshield had suddenly stopped, one or two of Y gun's crew had left the gun and run a few paces towards the sound of the crash. A shout from Jock brought them back to their job; but every time one of them had a moment to spare from helping to fire the gun, he would turn to the group and shout, " What the hell has happened ? Where did it hit ? What's the matter with the engines ? "

Then another yell from Jock stirred the after supply party. The for'ard source of shells and charges dried up suddenly. One of the improvised party had come running to Jock with a charge in his arms, shouted, " We've been hit in the boiler-room. The stokers are in a hell of a mess," dropped his charge and ran back. Since then, nothing more had come and Y gun was empty.

Jock's shout startled Sinbad and Shortarse out of their strained concentration on the Iron Deck and sent them back almost automatically to the shell-room. In a few moments the after supply party was functioning again. " Christ, we're done for now," they said to each other, but the shells and charges came up and Y gun reopened fire.

The time was now 7.45 a.m.

*   *   *

Y gun's crew were lucky. During the next twenty minutes they had something to do. Harry Rhoades had his charges and Redfern his shells to dump on the tray. Calamity had his tray to swing over and shells to ram home. Charlie Wright, eyes to his telescope, kept the gun pointing towards the large enemy destroyer which had now become the *Marsden's* target, and Barber, calling out " Oop two 'undred " or " Down one 'undred " from time to time so that Williams could set his dials to the continually changing range, kept the enemy firmly in his sights. Whenever Jock called " Ready ", down went Barber's pedal and the gun fired.

The Engineer Officer was also busy. He had shot out of the engine-room and raced for'ard along the Iron Deck. There he found the Chief Stoker gaspingly ordering the improvised supply party to get his men to the sick-bay.

" For God's sake, let's get Number One going," said the Engineer. He turned to the two stokers who were standing near him. " Come on, lads. We must get down to Number One."

But the two stokers did not move.

" Come on, boys. I know how you feel. I'm scared myself.

234

But we've got to get that bloody boiler going. Otherwise we can all say ' good-bye '. Come on, lads."

Then Pat Maclure: "For Christ's sake, men, get down. We're flicked if you don't."

One of the stokers turned on him. " It's all right you talking like that. *You* stay on the flicking deck. If we get a fish in us, it's not you who's trapped below. Go and flick yourself."

" All right. It's not my job down there. I'll only be in the way. And I'm as flicking scared as you are. But if you'll get down there, I'll come with you. *And* hold your flicking hand."

He walked to the hatchway and lowered himself. When only his black face was showing, he called " Come on, men," and dropped like Satan into Hell.

The Engineer followed him; and the Chief Stoker, with a final " Come on, lads, I know how you feel," and each arm round a shoulder, guided the two stokers to the hatchway, saw them go down, and followed himself.

Thereafter, apart from Y gun's crew and the after supply party, they were the only men on the ship with any work to occupy their minds through the long, agonising wait.

Jack Price could not bear it in the sick-bay, where he had led the stokers. He came to the Iron Deck to join the rest of the improvised supply party. He wanted to be with people whose faces, though strained, could still jerk out a smile and who had lips to speak with. He felt in his duffel coat, pulled out a cigarette packet, and found it empty.

" Chroist! Oi dunno. Oi can't even smoke now. For flick's sake, gimme a fag, mate ? "

" Sorry, Jack; this one's my last. Have a draw ? "

Lieutenant Burton had been into No. 1 boiler-room to see how the Chief was getting on and was now on his way back to the bridge.

" Have one of mine," he said to Price, holding out a cigarette-case. " Go on. Help yourself." Then he turned to the others. " Is anybody else out of cigarettes ? Price, go aft and find the canteen manager or his assistant. Tell one of them to open the canteen for a few minutes to sell the boys some cigarettes. And let everyone know. Get someone to take what they want to Y gun and the after supply party."

" Aye, aye, sir."

Price came back with Ray Forbes, who opened the canteen and handed out packets of Woodbines and Players.

" Give us twenty packets of something for Y gun. Oi'll dish 'em out to the supply party as well. Pay you later."

" All right," said Ray, giving credit for the first time in his life.

As soon as they had got their cigarettes, the seamen moved back to the Iron Deck. It was bitterly cold there, but at least they could see what was happening and would not be trapped below decks if the ship went down.

The first news that greeted them when they regained the open air was a shout of " The *Meltham* is making smoke. She's been hit. No, she hasn't. She's laying a smoke-screen round us." And sure enough, there she was, altering course to starboard and steering, with smoke pouring from her funnels and from the smoke-floats on her quarter deck, across the *Marsden's* bows.

" Thank God for that! " said one of the group, and suddenly he was down on his knees, repeating over and over again,

" O God, let this be over soon! Let it be over SOON! "

But these prayers were not answered.

Seeing the *Marsden* stop, the large enemy destroyer flashed a signal to her remaining escort and both ships now concentrated their fire on her. Worse, the larger ship swung to starboard and began to close in just as the *Meltham* let out her first belches of smoke. The smoke-screen had come between the small enemy destroyer and the *Marsden* when the large escort destroyer swung still farther to starboard and fired one torpedo, quickly followed by another.

The *Marsden* was a sitting target. She was almost broadside to the enemy's tubes, and she was stopped. Jimmie saw the torpedoes leave the enemy's tubes, saw the white bubbling streaks making straight for his ship, jerked out "Here they come, boys," and stood there, looking, his whole body erect and stiff, as though hypnotised by a snake about to strike.

The group on the Iron Deck saw those white streaks too, and knew what they meant. None of them could uproot himself to run to the other side of the deck. One man lifted his arm and pointed, with his mouth opening and shutting without saying anything. A few stepped back from the guard-rails, clutched whatever they could find, and shut their eyes. But most stood where they were, Jack Price among them.

Jack's eyes were fixed. His teeth were dug into his lower lip. His fists were clenched. " Oi want to live. Oi don't want to be killed in a basstud war," and then, without warning, his whole body relaxed.

" Oi dunno. Oi dunno. May as well go now as to-morrer."

At this moment the first of the two torpedoes should have struck the ship. It was aimed truly amidships, but it passed directly underneath were Jack Price stood and carried on harmlessly for another two miles. The second torpedo came at the stern and passed under the screws. The German torpedo men had misjudged the *Marsden's* draught and had set their fish at too low a depth.

For ten seconds not one man who had been watching the white streaks speeding towards them at thirty knots could realise that the tin fish had missed. They stayed where they were.

Then Jimmie suddenly unfroze, rushed to the port side of the bridge, looked over, and there, sure enough, were the white streaks darting away towards the horizon. He shouted, picked his tin helmet from his head and threw it into the air, whence it plopped into the sea.

" There, you didn't get me after all. Take my tin hat instead."

" Whatever's the matter ? " said Lieutenant Burton.

Then he, too, saw the furrows.

" Well, bless me! " He wiped his forehead; and the smoke-screen laid by the *Meltham* hid the large enemy destroyer from view.

The time was now 7.53 a.m.

* * *

When the thick black smoke poured between them and their target, Y gun's crew stopped firing almost for the first time since the action began; and as their minds relaxed, their bodies became aware of heavy weariness weighing on them. Williams noticed the soreness of his ears where the earphones had pressed against them. Barber and Charlie Wright felt the stiffness in their backs, the tiredness of their arms, and the strain on their eyes. Jock's legs were aching. Calamity Taylor saw that the knuckle on one of his hands was bleeding where he had caught it against the tray. Harry Rhoades and Tony Redfern sat down on the deck, where they at once became aware of the cold and moved into the shelter of the wardroom flat.

All noticed for the first time the stillness of the ship, an ominous stillness, a stillness which might be broken at any moment by the whistle of a shell and the crash of an explosion. But all the sounds they heard at first were the slightly muffled cracks of guns as the two enemy ships fired at the *Meltham* and she replied. Then these stopped as the *Meltham* swung to complete the circle of smoke round the *Marsden* and put herself out of the enemy's view.

The silence lasted two minutes. By that time the *Meltham* had completed her circle and come back into view of the smaller enemy destroyer. Each immediately opened fire on the other, and the sound of their guns, muffled though it was, jerked Rhoades and Redfern to their feet and pulled taut the nerves of every man on the ship.

Then came something which made both nerves and bodies jump. There was a loud crack as of several guns going off together, not ahead where the *Meltham* and her immediate enemy were blazing at each other, but amidships from the starboard side. Seconds later there was a familiar whistle, then three bursts in the air above their heads and, almost immediately, a shower of shrapnel tinkling on the deck or raising little splashes in the sea.

237

The large enemy destroyer was firing anti-aircraft shells over the smoke-screen, and her aim was good.

The men grouped along the Iron Deck ran for cover. Some rushed from the starboard to the port side, some turned into the canteen flat and stood there pulling at their cigarettes. But the darkness and the feeling of being enclosed was soon too much for them, and, risking the shrapnel, they came out to the others on the Iron Deck, where at least they could see what was going on.

" I wish those bloody stokers would get a move on," said Harry Robertson, who had now been sent down from B gun with the rest of his crew. They had tried to change the striker, but the striker appeared to be frozen in. " Why the hell don't they keep their boilers going properly, then we wouldn't be stuck like this in the middle of the flicking oggin. God, let's get moving, let's get moving," and then he thought, supposing we get hit in No. 1 boiler now, we'd never get away.

He fought to shut this thought from his mind. Never get away. Never see home again. Never get back to his job, never get to the bottom of fellmongering. Never get away. Never see anything more except icy sea.

Then the unexplainable relaxation which had come over Jack Price swept over Harry. He saw there was nothing he could do. He could worry and strain himself until he was silly, but that would not get No. 1 boiler working any sooner nor put the Jerries off their aim. A sigh, almost of relief, came out of him and he stopped struggling in his mind for life.

" Well, this looks like the end, lads," he said, as another shower of shrapnel crashed and clattered around them. " Cheerio, lads. Let's hope we take some more of the bastards with us when we go."

He did not even duck the shrapnel, but leaned back against the funnel for warmth, and smoked, almost at ease.

But it was not the end.

Jimmie had been striding up and down the bridge, peering into the smoke, now on this side, now on that, and every once in a while he seized a voice-pipe and shouted down to the boiler-room, " Have you got that boiler going yet ? How long are you going to be ? For Christ's sake, hurry."

These messages had been received by Pat Maclure, who had stationed himself by a voice-pipe and so made sure that the men who were working on the boilers would not be interrupted.

When Jimmie shouted his first message, Pat called to the Chief Stoker, " Jimmie's asking how long you will be."

" A good fifteen minutes yet."

Thereafter, Pat had not troubled the Chief, but had answered Jimmie himself, more and more tartly each time. Jimmie was about to bustle the boiler-room again when he saw something

238

that made him yell. "Bosun's Mate. BOSUN'S MATE. Tell Y gun to open up with everything they've got on Red three-five. That bastard is coming through the smoke-screen." And sure enough, coming through the black smoke, was the large enemy destroyer.

Jock Forrest had seen it as soon as Jimmie. So had Barber. "Look thur. Thur. Red three-five. THUR. Clear as anything. Range o-one-five."

Williams turned his handles and shouted "Sights set."

"Are you on, Charlie ? "

"Wait a minute." Then, "Trainer on! "

"Ready! "

Barber pressed his pedal and a shell flew out of the gun. It landed smack on the enemy ship, hitting her just above the waterline.

"You've got her, George. Slap in the bloody mess deck," shouted Williams with his head half out of the open port. "Bloody good shot." He turned back to his dials.

"I've dropped her a hundred, George."

Barber nodded, and when Charlie called out "I'm on," he pressed the pedal again and another shell flew out and caught the enemy amidships. She had turned her head, intending to go back into the smoke, and the second shot caught her while she was broadside on. It burst on the deck, sending up smoke which was quickly followed by flame.

"We've got her on her three-inch gun platform. If she's got a three-inch gun platform."

"If she 'ad a three-inch gun platform, she 'asn't got one now." George fired again, this time at the stern of the ship as she swung back into the smoke. But as he fired, he saw the flash of the enemy's after gun and, seconds later, felt the *Marsden* shake as a shell exploded in her side.

The shell had hit for'ard on the port side, bursting into the washroom and exploding there. The washroom was wrecked. The out-board side was burst wide open to the sea, the sliding door in the washroom flat was ripped out of its sockets and slammed against the opposite side of the flat. The partition between the washroom and the Heads was splintered and bits of metal, ricochetting along the flat, killed two men standing there. Another piece, flying on to the Iron Deck, hit Harry Robertson in the back of the neck. Still another went through his chest and tumbled him against the after-funnel.

Jack Price ran to him and tried to lift him. But Harry cried out that his neck was hurting, that he could hardly breathe, and begged not to be moved.

"Loi there, then, Harry. Oi'll fetch the Quack. You'll be all right."

"No, I won't. I'm going to die."

239

Jack patted his shoulder. "Don't talk troipe. Oi'll 'ave the Quack 'ere in no toime and we'll get you to bed in the Skipper's cabin."

But when he came back with the Doctor, Harry was dead.

Lieutenant Burton came round to the washroom as soon as he heard the crash. He looked through the gaping doorway and saw the damage. Collecting as many men as he could find, he led them to the mess deck and made them bring hammocks to the washroom flat.

He sent several men to the timber rack for planks, oars, or any other wood they could find. Then he climbed into the remains of the washroom, fixed oars and planks in a criss-cross pattern over the hole, and began to pile the hammocks against the criss-cross.

After ten minutes of hard work the daylight was blocked out. The party were wedging the last of the hammocks into position when they heard a sound that made their hearts leap—and not, this time, with fear.

At first the sound was barely noticeable, just a tremor along the deck, barely marked enough to cause even a jingle in Y gun-shield. But every second the sound grew louder, the tremor turned to a shaking and the jingling into a rattle.

The stokers had finished their job in No. 1 boiler-room and the screws were turning again.

As life came back to their ship, hope and strength came back to the crew. They did not laugh or cheer, but strained looks smoothed themselves off faces. Men smiled at each other, said "Thank God for that," and began to look for jobs.

They ran more shells and charges away to Y gun, which was standing ready to flash out again at the first sign of a break in the smoke-screen. When they found that the after supply party was providing everything the gun needed for the time being, they pulled up the ammunition from the for'ard magazine and shell-room and stored it along the canteen flat and even in the Heads. They helped to clear the mess on X gun and put the bodies over the side; and all the while the *Marsden* felt her way forward through the sea and then began to press more boldly towards the slowly thinning smoke that hedged her in.

The time was now 8.10 a.m.

*   *   *

For the moment, Y gun was not firing and her crew had time to think. Williams looked through his port at the sea and at the thinning smoke, wondering what they would find on the other side. He listened to the crack of guns, to the high explosives bursting over their heads, and to the tinkle of shrapnel as it fell on the gunshield or the deck, and he, too, felt resignation stealing over him.

"Oh well, I should like to see Mother and Father again," and

240

his mind went off to thoughts of Eternity. What a thing Eternity must be! Ever and ever, without end. The mind could hardly grasp it, any more than it could grasp the universe, infinity, or the ether. Just try to imagine something going on for ever and ever, never coming to an end, but going on and on and on! For a split second his mind held this unimaginable everlastingness, then recoiled from it in terror more penetrating than anything he had felt during the action. He turned his eyes and mind back to the smoke-screen in gratitude.

Jimmie had decided to swing round in a ninety degree turn. He could hear guns booming ahead where the *Meltham* was struggling to beat off the attacks of two enemies. He believed he could pierce the smoke and come out on her port side, away from the larger enemy ship, and turn his one remaining gun on the smaller ship in the hope of sinking her. Then it would be two to one against the larger.

So he brought the stem round, judged the position of the *Meltham* from the gunfire, and plunged into the smoke. Out on the far side, he found he was 1,000 yards astern of the *Meltham* who was 4,000 yards from the smaller enemy ship.

The *Meltham* had taken a hammering. Her two for'ard guns were still firing, but the after guns were silent. She was badly holed amidships. But she seemed to have given back more than she had received, for the enemy was firing with only one gun and was either stopped or going ahead dead slow.

Jimmie called the engine-room for more speed, but the *Marsden* could do no better than sixteen knots on her one boiler and it was time before he could order " Starboard ten " to bring her level with the *Meltham* and outside the enemy.

Just as he had given the order, the larger enemy came in view. She, too, had slowed. That hole near her waterline was probably giving her trouble. And one of her for'ard guns was certainly out of action. Jimmie could see its twisted muzzle through his glasses.

The second of her for'ard guns was out, too. The gunshield was certainly riddled with splinters. He could see the holes quite plainly. She was coming at right angles to her escort and was almost broadside; and before the Jimmie could send the Bosun's Mate with his order, Y gun had opened fire.

The first shot was short by 400 yards at 5,000 yards range. The second was barely short at all—spray from the splash must have soaked anyone on their iron deck.

The third burst on the deck near the wardroom flat, and Jimmie strained at his glasses, wildly hoping that, somehow, the after magazine had been pierced and that the enemy would vanish in a cloud of smoke as her escort had done forty-five minutes before.

But the smoke of the shell explosion cleared and the ship kept on her course, unruffled. Worse, the two after guns now fired, and, seconds later, Jimmie saw an explosion in the *Meltham's* side and then, second by second, saw the white wake behind her narrow and shorten until it vanished entirely.

" My God, *she's* copped it in the boilers now. Chief, *Chief*, make as much bloody smoke as you can. Yes, you bet that's a change. We're going to lay a smoke-screen round the *Meltham*. She's stopped."

Jimmie altered course, then picked up the loud-hailer and called the crew. " Boys, the *Meltham* has been hit. She's got one in the boiler—just as we had—and will be stopped for a quarter of an hour. We're going to screen her. Remember she saved us; so we'll keep those bastards off her now."

He put down the loud-hailer and then realised that it did not work. The circuits were cut. He had been talking to himself. He reddened, caught Buck's twinkling eye, and laughed. " Go aft, Bosum's Mate, and tell Sub-Lieutenant Carr to get those smoke-floats going."

But Sub-Lieutenant Carr had not waited for the order. As soon as he saw the *Meltham* stop and the *Marsden* begin to make smoke, he knew what was happening. He ran in front of Y gun and, like a schoolboy letting off fireworks, set going the smoke-floats on the quarter deck.

With Y gun cracking out shells in a steady stream at the larger enemy and hitting with four consecutive shots, *Marsden* surged forward until the *Meltham's* flank was screened with smoke. Turning to starboard, she swung across her bows while Y gun switched her target from the larger to the smaller ship. After a minute's steaming, she turned again to starboard to complete the circle of smoke round her sister-ship.

The larger enemy was now out of sight behind the smoke and her smaller escort would shortly be hidden too. Y gun kept blazing at a widening range until, just as they turned again in the last lap of the circle and so hid both targets, Williams, through his open port, saw a shell burst on the fo'c'sle of the smaller target and send up a tall umbrella of smoke, followed by a series of bright flashes.

" We've got her. I think we've got her in the magazine. Oh hell! Hell! Hell's bloody bells! The bloody thing's hidden behind the smoke now. I can't see what happened. Hell! "

The *Marsden's* shell *had* crashed through the deck of the German fo'c'sle and exploded in her for'ard magazine and the explosion of the shell *had* exploded her charges in the magazine. The explosion of the charges had blown off the bows of the ship. The bows sank at once, leaving the remaining two-thirds precariously afloat and taking water rapidly.

The time was now 8.25 a.m.

*   *   *

The *Marsden* completed the circle of smoke round the *Meltham*, and then, instead of turning to make a second circle, which would have brought her head-on to the enemy, she altered course slightly to port and steamed away.

Though this widened the range, it made sure that when she had cleared the smoke and got the enemy in view again, Y gun would be able to bear. She steamed on with every man on deck standing tiptoe to catch the first sight of the enemy and to see what that last explosion had meant. But no ships came into view.

Instead, the crew saw a narrow circle of black smoke and shouted to each other, " One of the bastards is on fire. God, what a hell of a smoke!"

Then they realised that whatever might be happening beyond it, the smoke they could see was a screen and not a fire.

" You'd better drop something into the smoke, George," shouted Jock, and Barber, looking through his sights, called " O-five-o, Bob." Williams turned his range dial to 5,000 yards and the gun fired.

Sub-Lieutenant Carr watched the fall of the shot through his glasses, thought he saw it clear the smoke and fall beyond.

" Bring her down a bit."

" Down two hundred."

Again the gun fired, and this time the shell seemed to drop right in the near wall of smoke.

" Up one hundred."

The next shell, instead of being lost without trace in the smoke, sent up a flash where it had fallen.

" I think you've got something there." Carr was right. In more ways than one. For after the first flash there was a second —deep red through the smoke—followed by that ominous whistling, then a spurt of water not ten feet from the *Marsden*, dead in line with Y gun.

Williams heard the spattering of metal against the shield. He felt something burning his shoulder. He saw Barber put his hand quickly to his left thigh, heard Calamity shout, " Oh, flick me, something's bit me," and saw him cup his left wrist in his right hand, drawing his breath in sharply as he did so.

But he neither saw nor heard Jock Forrest slump on the deck with one hand to his head. The first he knew of *that* was several rounds later, when he saw Newton from A gun run to the shield and stand in Jock's place.

" What's happened ? Why's Newton here ? Has Jock been hit ? "

" It's all reet. Jock's got one in t' head. They've got 'im stretched out in t' wardroom flat, and whenever one o' supply party trips over 'is feet 'e cusses like mad. 'E's all reet, tha knows."

243

Sure enough, whenever there was a lull in the firing, Williams could hear a plaintive voice from the wardroom flat. " Look out for me bloody feet, ye flickers. Are ye all blind, ye bastards? Go on. Fetch a mallet off Y gun and hit me ruddy corns with it. Dig in, ye clumsy great bastards. Don't mind me. Ah'm only wounded."

Williams smiled at Barber and both went on with their job, The time was now 8.35 a.m.

* * *

Marsden turned directly towards the ring of smoke from which that last shell had come five minutes before.

And then she was enveloped in smoke. The smoke was still thickish. It was a dirty yellow. It tasted of oil. It was a mass of black smuts, which got into the Duchess's eyes and nose.

" Market Street, Manchester. On a November night. In the flicking blackout." He strained his eyes for whatever lay ahead.

Throughout the ship, for 100 long seconds, men stood like the Duchess, staring before them, coughing and spluttering in the smoke, gripping whatever was nearest to them, some muttering, some holding back their fears behind tight lips, some just standing, their minds blank and numb.

Now the smoke was thinning. Involuntarily each man craned his neck. Some who wanted to shut their eyes found them held open. Some who wanted to run for the cover of the canteen flat felt themselves held where they were, staring ahead, their eyes smarting and streaming from the smoke.

The smoke cleared. The crew brushed hands quickly over streaming eyes, leaned forward still farther and saw—nothing. There was nothing in the circle of smoke.

Behind them was the smoke they had just come through. Ahead of them there was more smoke. But between there was nothing, nothing except cold, grey sea.

One enemy had sunk. The other had turned for home.

Then the Yeoman called, " The *Meltham* is flashing, sir," and there, out of the smoke-screen, and steaming slowly towards them, was their sister-ship, her signal light twinkling impatiently. " Steaming on one boiler. Can make fifteen knots. Propose rejoin convoy. How are you ? " wrote the Yeoman on his signal pad and handed it to Jimmie.

Jimmie suddenly remembered that the Skipper of the *Meltham*, a Lieutenant-Commander, was the senior officer and that he should have reported his own Skipper's death and asked for orders.

" Make this signal, Yeoman. Regret Captain killed in action. Can make about eighteen knots. One gun still firing. Suggest retain contact with enemy."

The shutters on the *Marsden's* signal light opened and shut in a steady clatter and then were silent. Back came the answering flashes. " Think we should rejoin tanker and convoy. Propose leading at fifteen knots. Will you follow ? " The lights stopped for a moment, then began again. " By the way, thanks for the screen."

Jimmie read the message and suddenly smiled. " You're welcome," he flashed, and swung the ship's head for home.

The time was 9.6 a.m.

Epilogue

AT 9.10 Buck piped " Port watch to defence stations."

But Y gun's crew did not go immediately to the three-inch platform. As soon as they stopped firing and relaxed, they felt pain in various parts of their bodies. Calamity's left wrist ached, Williams's left shoulder burned; and when Barber eased himself from his layer's seat and tried to stand, his leg gave way and he fell on the deck. Rhoades and Redfern guided him to the Skipper's cabin, followed by Calamity and Williams.

As the warmth below came through their frozen skin, the pain became sharper, but they forgot it when they saw a man stretched on a bed with a red oilskin over him and his forehead bound in bandages.

" Jock! "

They went over.

" How are you, Jock ? "

But Jock made no sound or movement. His eyes were shut. and his mouth open. He was not breathing.

" Died ten minutes ago," said the sick-berth attendant. " What's wrong with you chaps ? "

He had to say it again. The five men stared at Jock and said nothing, trying to realise that he was dead. Then Calamity, in a slow, weary voice, said, " He can't walk. Got something in his leg," and pointed to Barber.

" Anyone else hurt ? "

Calamity held out his wrist and Williams pointed to his shoulder.

The shoulder was only grazed. Calamity's wrist was also grazed, but the S.B.A. thought there might be a bone broken. Barber had a piece of metal in his thigh. When Williams and Calamity had been bandaged, they were allowed to go, but Barber was kept in the sick-bay. He was put on a bed next door to Jackie Low, who was staring vacantly at the deckhead and seemed to recognise nobody. Nevison was close by, sitting on the deck, shivering no longer, but looking white and shaken.

" How are you feeling now, Nev ? " asked Calamity gently. " Bloody awful, wasn't it ? Still, it is all over now."

Calamity and Williams went to the three-inch, where they

found Newton on watch by himself. " Go on for'ard, boys, and get yourself some tea and something to eat before you come on watch. I'll hang on here. I've had my tea."

" Jock's dead."

The two of them went slowly for'ard to the canteen flat. They waited their turn for a cup and dipped it into one of the fannies of tea, took a slice of bread and butter, and began to eat. Charlie Wright came by with a tin of corned beef in his hand, followed by Rhoades, who had a chunk of bread.

" We're taking these on to the gun for all of us."

" Charlie, Jock's dead."

" I know. Harry's told me." He went out.

Calamity and Williams followed him when they had finished their tea.

The starboard watch had got the mess deck into some sort of order by dinner-time. The two holes in the side were firmly stopped with hammocks, the water had been mopped up, the smashed crockery thrown over the side. The galley was untouched, and when the port watch came off duty they found a hot dinner and a double tot of rum for each man. They ate almost in silence, with fingers now stained with blood as well as grime. Then they looked to see if their hammocks were still slung or whether they had been thrust through the holes in the mess deck or piled against the timber supports in the wrecked washroom.

Calamity and Williams both found their hammocks intact, but Calamity's wrist was now so painful that he could not use it to pull himself up into his hammock. He lay on the lockers and Williams covered him with a duffel coat.

At tea-time the buzz was that the *Tirpitz* had come out, with a cruiser and two destroyers. She must be after them, and not a man on the *Marsden*, except possibly Jimmie, felt he had any fight left in him. The port watch was just preparing for the First Dog when " action stations " sounded the surface-action warning. It seemed like a death-knell. The men went to their guns or other stations, but they hardly knew what they were doing.

Y gun's crew was greatly changed. There was Newton instead of Jock, and the A gunlayer in place of Barber, and Price in place of Calamity, whose wrist prevented him from getting a grip on his tray. Redfern, being in the starboard watch, was replaced by A-gun shell-supply number. They went through their motions to clear away the gun and waited for orders.

These came quickly from Sub-Lieutenant Carr, who said that five blobs of smoke were to be seen on the horizon dead ahead. None knew what they were, yet. If they were enemy ships, Y gun would have to do the fighting. It was still the only gun on the *Marsden* that could fire.

They waited in icy foreboding. Carr went up to X-gun platform and looked through his glasses. He came back a minute later to say that there were five ships coming towards them, one of them biggish like a cruiser, the others probably destroyers, but he had hardly made this report when there was a sound of running feet, a series of shouts followed by bursts of cheering, and Buck came on to the quarter deck shouting that the *Meltham* had flashed the oncoming ships. They were British destroyers, which had turned back from the convoy, when the *Marsden* had wirelessed that she and the *Meltham* were engaging three German destroyers.

Y gun's crew shouted themselves hoarse, shook each other's hands, smiled, and repeated " Thank God " over and over again.

The five destroyers made a screen round the two damaged ships. One remained at the head of the line with the *Marsden* and the *Meltham* behind her, while the remainder ranged themselves on each flank.

Just before dusk the *Meltham* dropped back abreast of the *Marsden* and the two ships quietly slipped their dead into the sea. The Skipper's body was wrapped in a Union Jack, but a second Union Jack could not be found. So Jock was wrapped tightly into his red oilskin.

The seamen stood on the quarter deck, bareheaded, in silence, while the *Marsden*'s engines ran down and the screws ceased to turn. Then Jimmie said, " God, we beg You to receive into Your keeping the bodies of two seamen, one our Captain, both our shipmates. We beg that they may have peace and that we may be worthy of them."

The two bodies were slipped into the water, the *Marsden*'s screws began to turn again, and eight hours later the seven ships rejoined the convoy.

They went alongside the cruiser and transferred the scalded stokers and Barber to her sick-bay. They oiled from a tanker, and for two days stayed with the convoy, dropping depth charges from time to time and, despite their injuries, acting as part of the escort.

At the end of the second day, when they were three days from home, they received a signal to proceed independently at their best speed, and, accompanied by another destroyer, they went off at fifteen knots.

With the speeding up of the engines, the approach of home, and, as they moved south, the decreasing cold, life in the *Marsden* quickened. The strain of the horrors they had been through and of the possible dangers they still faced lay heavily on their minds, just as the loss of shipmates burdened their hearts, but at least they felt able to talk again, instead of sitting in stunned silence.

Calamity began it. As the port watch were eating supper

that night he said to Williams, " Well, Bob, I know now what was meant by the valley of the shadow of death. I feel as though I was still in it. Poor old Jock! "

" What 'ad got into 'Arrison ? " asked Price. " 'E wasn't the sort of chap to lose 'is nerve. But 'e was walking around loike two pennorth of deadly noightshade for more than a week before 'e was killed. 'E was never roight after coming off leave. What was up ? "

" It was his girl."

" Chroist, some of these tarts want a kick in the slacks."

" I was scared when I thought of my Judy," said Harry Rhoades. " I kept on saying ' I'm not doing to die until I've seen her again.' But it didn't do any good. I was scared just the same."

" Oi bet there wasn't a man on the ship 'oo wasn't scared. Some just showed it more than others. Poor old Nev! 'Ow is 'e, do you think ? Might 'ave kept 'im in the sick-bay a bit longer. 'E looks pretty shaky to me. And Jackie, too."

" Jackie's all right again now, aren't you, Jackie ? Swigging your liquorice allsorts as though nothing had happened."

" I know I'll never go near a gun again without my anti-flash gear," said Jackie. " I wonder where it is. Somebody must have swiped it."

Jackie could see again, but was still shaky.

" Don't look at me, mate," said Sinbad. " We don't need no anti-flash gear in the shell-room, thank God. Even the lamps wouldn't flash. I hate the dark."

" Sinbad, you were grand," said Shortarse. " I never once had to wait for a shell. Or at least, only once," and they suddenly grinned at each other when they remembered how they had shot up the ladder and on to the deck when the *Marsden* was hit in the boiler-room.

" What was Carr loike ? Looks as though 'e'd be all roight in a foight."

" And that Jimmie was all right. I thought he'd be prancing around yelling. But he was as cool as could be. I wasn't very much surprised, was I ? "

" 'Is being on the bridge scared me more than the engines running down, mate. But he did all right. I didn't get much of a surprise, either, did I ? "

There was hardly any swearing, not because of the swear-box —what had happened to that, by the way ? It was just that none of them thought of swearing. Every word was kindly, in tone as well as meaning. They had often shouted at each other, even when they meant no offence; but now they showed their friendliness. Nevison with his nerves, Jackie with the remains of his shock, and Calamity with his injured wrist were all treated with a kindness and consideration not previously seen on the mess deck. Everyone felt that they had been together through something terrible. The nearness of death had welded them in fellowship. They were shipmates. They were a ship's company. The *Marsden* was no longer merely a ship. She was a community.

They came in early in the morning before dawn had reddened the islands. They passed long lines of silent ships and gazed thankfully at familiar landmarks just discernible in the starlight. They went straight to an oiler, and almost before they had tied up to it Jimmie ordered " Away motor-boat," and Charlie Wright was packed off to the depot ship for the mail.

He came back just as the *Marsden* was ready to leave the oiler. He had brought seventy-eight bags with him.

Three hands went down to the ship's office with Charlie and Lieutenant Burton to sort the letters by messes, while the remainder of the seamen worked in the mess deck, scrubbing it clean at four o'clock in the morning, or stood by on deck, first to cast off from the oiler, and then to moor to the buoy.

From time to time one of them would climb down into the office and come back with reports about the mail. It was that large, it had overflowed from the office into the office flat. They were carrying it to the messes—seventeen journeys so far. It was overflowing on the mess deck. The tables were full and piles were mounting on lockers and on the deck itself.

" You've got the General Post Office, Bob. Oi should say there's a 'undred letters in your poil."

" How many have you got, Jack ? "

" Just a postcard, without a stamp on it."

As soon as they had tied to the buoy, there was a rush.

" That's your pile, Bob."

" Here, Harry, your Judy doesn't know there's a paper shortage."

" Hi, Duchess, you've got some of mine in that lot."

They picked up handfuls of letters and sat down wherever they could to read. Soon, only a few piles remained untouched. On the top of one pile was a letter addressed in spidery handwriting to A. L. Forrest, Leading Seaman. Another pile was Harrison's. Was there one from that girl ? A third pile was " Our Albert's." The Duchess quietly took them all back to the ship's office.

After the first quick tearing open of envelopes, there was the usual silence for a few minutes. Then each one began to make comments on his own letters, pass on pieces of news, make jokes, and add up the number of pages he had received. By the time the reading had finished, they were all full of thoughts of home and, what was more, had begun to realise that home was no longer far away. They were safe. They need worry no more. There would be no more subs., no more planes, no more surface craft, no more "action stations," for the time being. They could relax at last.

They were almost hysterical. The load of fear, which, whether they had been conscious of it or not, had always been there, lifted and left them light-headed. They laughed at any joke, they sang and skylarked. Then they had breakfast.

At 0900 they mustered. Jimmie said, "I'm not going to work you this afternoon. But you can see for yourselves there's a good deal of mess that wants clearing up. So we'll get down to it this Forenoon. At eleven the Admiral is coming on board to speak to us. You can muster in overalls. I'm going to find out about repairs. I think we'll have to have a bit of patching here, but I shall do my damnedest to get the bulk of the work done down south, so that we can get some leave."

At 1100 the Admiral came aboard. He was the same Admiral who had welcomed them before. He was the same Admiral who had directed the escort on this last Russian convoy. His cruiser had left the convoy when it reached safe waters and had arrived ahead of the *Marsden* and *Meltham*. He looked, as he had done before, spotlessly clean, fresh-faced and chirpy. But the crew's feeling towards him was different. They knew him now as an Admiral who really did want to go to sea. He was an Admiral who only a few hours ago had come back from sea. They listened to him.

First, he read two telegrams from the First Lord of the Admiralty, one congratulating the convoy on its successful run, the other congratulating the *Marsden* and *Meltham*. Then he said: "*I* congratulate you, too. And I think that I can give you something better than congratulations. I think that I can guarantee you some real leave. However, you'll know for certain about that in a few days. In the meantime, I expect you'll want to get some sleep. I think we can take it," he said, turning to Jimmie, "that the main brace has been spliced."

That afternoon a draft chit arrived from barracks for all C.W.s on board. They were to return, as soon as their reliefs arrived, to appear before the Admiralty Selection Board and, if passed, to begin their officers' training course. The reliefs were expected next day.

Their first thought was thankfulness. In all their experiences on the ship, at the back of their minds there had always been the knowledge that their present time at sea would end after about four months. That had been a comfort. Now they were back from Russia they felt they never wanted to see the sea again. They only wanted to go home. But then they thought of the ship. They had a right on that mess deck. They were not strangers. No one would say "Christ, who the hell is that?" when they walked in. But as soon as they left, they would be

251

outside its community. They would be leaving men with whom they had shared danger and discomfort.

No doubt if Jimmie had said, " You can stay if you like," they would have said, " Not bloody likely. We want to go home." But the thought of leaving their messmates *did* make going home seem less attractive.

No seaman can say more than that.

" So you're leaving us ? " said the Duchess. " You lucky bastard."

" Yes, I suppose so," said Williams. " And yet, I don't know. It *does* get a hold on you. Look at yourself. You've never stopped dripping about the Navy since you joined. Yet you've got a stripe on your arm and you'll sign on for another twelve when your time is up."

" That's because I'm solid. You ought to know better. Have a cigarette." He flashed an open packet under Williams's nose and stowed it away.

" Thanks, I will." Williams grabbed the packet out of the Duchess's breast pocket. " You won't lose flick all by that."

" No, and the gain will be in proportion. I know. I hope to Christ you're not an officer on my ship."

" I hope to Christ I am. First thing I'll do will be to make you paint the side with a gale blowing."

" I wish I was a W.C.," said Calamity. " If I came back on this ship as an officer, the first thing I'd do would be to get the Iron-deck party shovelling muck on to the Iron Deck, leave it there and get their flicking great swedes down. Do you think I'd make a good officer, Bob ? Talking posh and eating oranges ? Really, the state of this ship is filthy. Absolutely filthy, it *actually* is. It's simply atrocious."

" What the hell's atrocious ? "

" I don't know, but Jimmie used it at me once and I could tell it wasn't a compliment. Second sight. That's me."

Next morning they had a short voluntary service on the quarter deck in memory of their shipmates who had been killed in the action. Everyone attended, unrecognisably clean in their Number Ones.

They stood, bareheaded, among their friends, listening to the Navy prayer.

When the service was over, Jimmie spoke. " Lads, you've had a lot of praise. I'm not going to praise you. You did your job, did it well, and that's all there is to it. In three days you'll have to put up with the loss of another night's sleep. They are going to patch us up here and then let us go to Newcastle for proper repars. Then you'll get your leave—and it won't be only seventy-two hours this time. Turn for'ard, dismiss."

Three hours later, Williams, Redfern, and the other C.W.s were in the motor-boat chugging across the anchorage to the depot ship, where they would board the ferry. They looked back at the battered *Marsden*. It was amazing how attractive she seemed, the farther they got away from her. She glinted, blue and white, in the October sunshine, looking like a ghost ship. Already her realities were fading.

" I wish we had been able to say good-bye properly to the lads," said Redfern. " Typical Navy. They get us ready with our bags packed two hours too early. Then they heave us on board and away in half a minute. I never saw Calamity at all."

" I did. Gave me a couple of bars of nutty to take to my niece. Jackie Low gave me a bag of liquorice allsorts. And Pat gave me sippers."

" Do you know, I feel ashamed of leaving them—not that wild horses could drag me from my leave. But you know what I mean."

" Yes. When they've finished their leave, they'll have to go back again to Russian convoys and that leaky mess deck."

They came alongside the depot ship and, with the motor-boat tossing and heaving at the foot of the gangway, they had, somehow, to transfer themselves, their kitbags, suitcases, and hammocks from the motor-boat to the ladder without getting wet. It took all their concentration, and when at last they climbed the ladder and reached the deck, they realised that they had not said good-bye to the Duchess, who was coxswain of the motor-boat that day. They leaned over the rail, but the motor-boat had already pushed off and was turning in a wide circle on her way back to the *Marsden*.

The Duchess was standing upright with hands on the tiller, looking ahead. They gazed after him, longing to wave the good-bye they had forgotten to say, and just as the motor-boat rounded the stern of the depot ship, the Duchess took his eyes for a second from his course, turned, saw waving arms, and waved a long straight arm in reply.

Then he went out of sight, and they turned inboard from the rail.

O Eternal Lord God, who alone spreadest out the heavens, and rulest the raging of the sea; who hast compassed the waters with bounds until day and night come to an end; Be pleased to receive into thy Almighty and most gracious protection the persons of us thy servants, and the Fleet in which we serve. Preserve us from the dangers of the sea, and from the violence of the enemy; that we may be a safeguard unto our most gracious Sovereign Lady, Queen Elizabeth, and her Dominions and a security for such as pass on the seas upon their lawful occasions; that the inhabitants of our Island may in peace and quietness serve thee our God; and that we may return in safety to enjoy the blessings of the land, with the fruits of our labours, and with a thankful remembrance of they mercies to praise and glorify thy holy Name, through Jesus Christ our Lord. Amen.

WAR—NOW AVAILABLE IN GRANADA PAPERBACKS

Alexander Baron
From the City, From the Plough   85p ☐

J M Bauer
As Far As My Feet Will Carry Me   £1.25 ☐

Ian Mackersey
Into the Silk   95p ☐

Tim O'Brien
Going After Cacciato   £1.25 ☐
If I Die in a Combat Zone   £1.25 ☐

James Webb
Fields of Fire   £1.95 ☐

Laddie Lucar
Flying Colours   £1.95 ☐

Leonce Peillard
Sink the Tirpitz!   £1.95 ☐

All these books are available at your local bookshop or newsagent, and can be ordered direct from the publisher.

To order direct from the publisher just tick the titles you want and fill in the form below:

Name _____

Address _____

_____

Send to:
Granada Cash Sales
PO Box 11, Falmouth, Cornwall TR10 9EN

Please enclose remittance to the value of the cover price plus:

UK 45p for the first book, 20p for the second book plus 14p per copy for each additional book ordered to a maximum charge of £1.63.

BFPO and Eire 45p for the first book, 20p for the second book plus 14p per copy for the next 7 books, thereafter 8p per book.

Overseas 75p for the first book and 21p for each additional book.

Granada Publishing reserve the right to show new retail prices on covers, which may differ from those previously advertised in the text or elsewhere.